W9-DAX-640

JERUSALEM VIGIL

**Center Point
Large Print**

**This Large Print Book carries the
Seal of Approval of N.A.V.H.**

ॐ श्री गणेशाय नमः

*J*ERUSALEM VIGIL

BODIE AND BROCK THOENE

CENTER POINT PUBLISHING
THORNDIKE, MAINE

To Rachel, Jake, and Luke
with love and *shalom!*

This Center Point Large Print edition
is published in the year 2001 by arrangement with
Viking Penguin, a member of Penguin Putnam Inc.

The text of this Large Print edition is unabridged.
In other aspects, this book may vary from the original
edition. Printed in Thailand. Set in 16-point Plantin type by
Bill Coskrey.

ISBN 1-58547-132-1

Library of Congress Cataloging-in-Publication Data

Thoene, Brock, 1952-
    Jerusalem vigil / Brock & Bodie Thoene.
        p. cm.
    ISBN 1-58547-132-1 (lib. bdg. : alk. paper)
    1. Israel-Arab War, 1948-1949--Fiction. 2. Jews--Palestine--Fiction. 3. Large type books. I.
Thoene, Bodie, 1951- II. Title.

PS3570.H46 J49 2001
813'.54--dc21

2001028486

But when the hour of night arrived, as the Lord had said to Jeremiah, they went up together onto the walls of the city, Jeremiah and Baruch. And behold there was a sound of trumpets, and angels came out of heaven holding torches in their hands, and they stood on the walls of the city. And when Jeremiah and Baruch saw them, they wept, saying, "Now we know that the word is true." . . . And Jeremiah spoke, saying, "Please Lord, let me speak before you." And the Lord said, "Speak my chosen one, Jeremiah." And Jeremiah said, "Behold, Lord, we know that you are delivering the city into the hands of its enemies, and they will carry the people off to Babylon. What do you want me to do with the holy vessels of the Temple service?" And the Lord said to him, "Take them and deliver them to the earth, saying, 'Hear earth, the voice of him who created you . . . Guard the vessels of the service unto the coming of the Beloved One.' "

Jeremiah and Baruch went into the sanctuary and, gathering up the vessels . . . they delivered them to the earth just as the Lord had instructed them. And immediately the earth swallowed them up.

And when as morning, behold the host of Chaldeans surrounded the city . . . But Jeremiah, taking the keys of the Temple went outside of the city and, facing the sun, he tossed them, saying, "I say to you, sun, take the keys of the Temple of God and keep them until the day in which the Lord will question you about them. Because we were not found worthy of keeping them."

4 Baruch 3:1–11, 18–19; 4:1–5

■ ■ ■ ■ CHAPTER 1 ■ ■ ■ ■

The green 1937 Dodge sedan raced through the silent streets of Tel Aviv toward an obscure dirt airstrip where a Piper Cub aircraft warmed its engine. Thirty-two-year-old Moshe Sachar and his twenty-two-year-old wife, the beautiful blue-eyed, dark-haired Rachel, tuned the radio of the automobile to listen, with all the Middle East, to the explosive event about to take place barely a mile away.

It was after noon on May 14, 1948. The citizens of Tel Aviv gathered on Rothschild Boulevard, in the heart of the city, outside a small stone museum where artifacts spanning three thousand years of Jewish history were collected. Among the most recently added treasures was the two-thousand-year-old Isaiah scroll that had surfaced in Jerusalem on November 29, 1947—the very day the United Nations voted for the establishment of a Jewish homeland in Palestine.

For Moshe and Rachel Sachar, the timing of the scroll's discovery and the contents of the book itself carried eternal significance. The ancient prophecy was about to come true.

Out of blood and fire Judea will fall. Out of blood and fire it will be reborn. . . . The birth of Israel was poised to become a reality.

Six tortured months had passed since the U.N. declaration to end the British Mandate in Palestine and divide the territory into two nations: one Arab, the other Jewish. Hundreds of Jews and Arabs had already died in battles that raged throughout the region. Jerusalem, slated to become an international city, had been under siege by the Muslim forces of the Grand Mufti of Jerusalem, Muhammed Said Haj Amin el-Husseini, for months.

With the massacre in the Muslim village of Deir Yassin by Jewish terrorists, Arab civilians took flight from Jerusalem; entire neighborhoods emptied. The void was filled by a flood of Jihad Moquades from all over the Arab world. They were the Holy Strugglers of the Grand Mufti's Irregular Army.

Fury and brutality against the Jewish population escalated. In Jerusalem on April 13, a convoy of seventy-five Jewish doctors, nurses, and medical staff had been massacred on the way to Hadassah Hospital. Rachel Sachar was among the few survivors.

As the roads out of Palestine glutted with refugees, cries to drive the Jews into the sea rang in Arab capitals from Iraq to Egypt. Seventy-five million Muslims united in Holy War against the half-million Jews in Eretz-Israel.

And the battle between the age-old brothers Isaac and Ishmael was only beginning.

On this humid May morning, the frantic call had come to Tel Aviv from Jerusalem Haganah Headquarters: "The British troops are pulling out a day early! The road to Tel Aviv from Jerusalem is open for the English to withdraw! Send a convoy of men and ammunition at once!"

Everyone was caught unprepared for this news. A break in the storm! Moshe, who had secretly been a Haganah officer for years, was ordered to attempt infiltration into the Jewish Quarter of the Old City of Jerusalem. A twenty-minute flight from Tel Aviv might get him there in time. Rachel was to remain behind in Tel Aviv to work with the

Jewish Agency for the new state as immigrants flooded her ports. Arrivals would be recruited straight off the boats to form the reserve army for Israel's defense. There was no other way.

This afternoon Rachel would say good-bye to Moshe, perhaps forever. Her five-month-old adopted baby would be taken to the Jewish Agency infant center, an air-raid shelter where children of Agency workers were cared for. Then Rachel would go to the waterfront to welcome the survivors to their new homeland . . . and the new war.

The Dodge turned off the main road onto a dusty lane through an orange grove.

The sharp sound of a gavel rapping on a table echoed across the airwaves.

"Turn it up," Moshe said, his deep brown eyes intent as they sped away from the city center.

"David Ben-Gurion." Rachel whispered the name of the leader of Zionism into her daughter's ear, as though he were a prophet crying from the past. "Listen, Tikvah. For the first time in two thousand years . . ."

There followed a reverent silence. The baby turned her face toward Rachel's breast.

Then Ben-Gurion's clear voice began without introduction:

In the land of Israel the Jewish people came into being. In this land was shaped their spiritual, religious, and national character. Here they lived in sovereign independence. Here they created a culture of national and universal import and gave to the world the eternal

8

book of books.

Moshe and Rachel exchanged a glance of knowing. There was much more meaning behind the words.

As a professor at Hebrew University, Moshe had been part of tracking down the whereabouts of the Isaiah scroll and reclaiming it, as well as helping organize the defenses of the Yishuv, the Jewish population in British-controlled Palestine. There were more treasures to save than this one scroll. The urgent request for Moshe Sachar's help had come from Shlomo Lebowitz, Rachel's grandfather, a respected rabbi trapped behind the walls of besieged Jerusalem.

Ben-Gurion continued:

Exiled from the land of Israel, the Jewish people remained faithful to it in all the countries of their dispersion, never ceasing to pray and hope for their return and restoration of their national freedom. Impelled by this historic association, Jews strove throughout the centuries to go back to the land of their fathers and regain their statehood.

Overcome with emotion, Moshe pulled the Dodge to the side of the road and idled its motor. Resting his forehead against the steering wheel, he reached out to grasp Rachel's hand.

"It is . . . ," he whispered, *"happening,* Rachel. It is not a dream."

In recent decades they returned. They reclaimed the wilderness, revived their language, built cities, and vil-

lages. By virtue of the natural and historic right *of the Jewish people and of the resolution of the General Assembly of the United Nations, we hereby proclaim the establishment of the Jewish State in Palestine, to be called Israel.*

"The prophecy . . . Isaiah 43. We are alive . . . we are alive to see it," Rachel said, tears streaming down her cheeks. She glanced at the scar on her left forearm where she had burned off a Nazi tattoo with the blade of a red-hot knife. "We have lived," she murmured again, thinking of those who had not, and of the baby in her womb, who would be born into the new state.

We offer peace and amity to all the neighboring states and peoples. Our call goes out to Jewish people all over the world to stand by us in the great struggle for the fulfillment of the dream of generations: the redemption of Israel! With trust in the Almighty we set our hand to this declaration in the city of Tel Aviv on the fifth day of Iyar, 5708, the fourteenth day of May, 1948.

■　　■　　■　　■

There would never be a time to celebrate the new nation of Israel for the young kibbutzniks at Kfar Etzion. Today was the end of the world for them.

"Run! Make for the grove!"

The wildflowers he trampled underfoot were blood-red anemones, but Daniel Caan took no notice. Dragging his sister, Suzannah, by the arm, Daniel led their flight away from the horror, the butchery, taking place in Kfar Etzion. Behind them Arab machine guns, like a continuous roll of drums, only partially masked the screams of fifty Jewish settlers being slaughtered in the square of the kibbutz.

Daniel had seen Ahkmed al-Malik, the Arab commander, give the order to fire after the surrender. There was no mistake; it was a massacre, and they could not expect mercy if they were recaptured.

His friends, boys and girls who had come with him to Palestine, lay torn to shreds by the murderers' weapons. Those who had been family to him and his sister after their own family had disappeared into the abyss of Nazi Germany were gone forever. There was no turning back for Daniel or Suzannah. Escape or die: those were the only options.

Ducking around a boulder, Daniel and his sister surprised an Arab soldier wielding a knife. The man was bent over the body of a dead kibbutznik. By his curly hair, it could have been Daniel's friend Asher . . . only there was no way to tell since the Arab had cut off the victim's ears, nose, and lips, and gouged out his eyes.

Suzannah screamed, and the alerted Jihad Moquade whirled around, sweeping the knife in a vicious circle.

There was no time to change direction; any delay and fifty more Arabs chasing them from the kibbutz would be on them. Dropping his grip on Suzannah's wrist, Daniel jumped inside the Arab's guard. He rammed his forearm into his opponent's throat, then allowed the momentum to carry into knocking the man down and falling on top of him. "Run!" he yelled again to his sister. "Hide! I'll come for you."

With no chance to see if she obeyed, Daniel wrestled for possession of the knife. At sixteen, Daniel was not much taller than his fourteen-year-old sister, but he was desperate, and that desperation gave him frenzied strength. Twisting the coughing Arab's grip back on itself, Daniel jammed his knee into his adversary's side. When the man's eyes widened, and he struggled for breath, Daniel put all his weight into forcing the blade downward, plunging it into the hollow of his rival's throat.

He jumped up at once. The sounds of pursuit were close, just over the rise they had crossed in their flight. Suzannah was nowhere to be seen. Daniel prayed she was already in the Lover's Glade, burrowed deep into the brush.

Vaulting the low rock wall that marked the kibbutz boundary, Daniel dashed downhill toward the only refuge he could conjure. Nine miles from Jerusalem and any rescuers, surrounded by thousands of murderous Arab Irregulars, Daniel knew their only hope was staying free until nightfall and then slipping away over the barren hills. It was a slim hope, indeed.

"Suzannah," he whispered hoarsely when he reached the trickle of water and the first line of locust trees. A rattle of stones from the hill told him that those hunting them were near. His heart pounding, he thought of Asher and the others. To be captured meant that he, too, would be slain and mutilated, his ears dried and hung from an Arab watch chain.

Daniel sprinted past three trees, ducking his head to pass close to their trunks, then jerked sideways toward a pile of dead branches. There was only one chance. Behind the fallen limbs was a boulder and behind the boulder was a hollow, no bigger than a coffin, but covered from above and on three sides. Daniel had been there with Moniek; Moniek, whom he had last seen lying dead of a mortar attack in the cellar of the abandoned German monastery that was Kfar Etzion's headquarters. At least Moniek had died before they could rape her as they had raped the other women in the kibbutz. *Merciful! Merciful death! Be merciful, God!* The memory of their cries for help renewed his terror. *Oh, God! Why had they done such things to the girls? Why? Oh, God! Where is Suzannah? Don't let them find Suzannah!*

Suzannah was not in the cave. Daniel cursed himself for never showing his sister the secret trysting spot. He had been trying to protect her. Innocent, beautiful Suzannah. Fourteen was too young to see what she had seen! *Oh, God! Don't let them . . .*

Worming his way backward into the shelter, Daniel flung the brush and leaves across his trail, scooting as far behind the rock as he could. When he stopped to listen, all he could hear was his own tortured breathing.

Then: someone was coming. Daniel understood the Arabic perfectly.

"I saw them clearly, Captain al-Malik," whined a voice eager to curry favor. "Indeed, truly there were two, a man and a woman."

The commander snarled, "Good, Hassan. But it would have been better if you and your men had tended to business instead of looting. This pursuit would not then be necessary."

"Of course, of course," Hassan el-Hassan agreed. "But we will find them, treacherous Jews, and they shall die by my own hand. Here, look. I have gathered four watches from the dead Jews. Take this. It is the best. German made."

Al-Malik grunted. The Arab captain paused, evidently taking his piece of Jewish loot, then his feet crunched upon the gravel as he walked nearer to Daniel's hiding place.

Daniel's breathing roared like the snorting of a bull in his own ears. *Oh, God! Dear God! Will he hear? He will hear. He comes so near to me. He must hear my breathing! I will die. He will cut my face off like Asher! Don't let them find Suzannah! Don't let them make her watch what they do to me! Oh, God!*

The strong smell of Turkish tobacco drifted past.

"A fine smoke, Hassan," called al-Malik. "Did you find any more cigarettes on the Jews? I would rather have cigarettes than this watch."

"No more. This one fellow offered them to me if I would not shoot his brother."

Daniel squeezed his eyes shut. *Oh, God! He's talking about Arthur and Sammy!*

"He begged me, 'Don't kill my brother! Kill me instead.' " Hassan laughed. "Then I took his cigarettes and shot them both. I cut off their right ears. You see? Both right ears. Alike, eh? Easy to see they were brothers."

Daniel dug his hands into the earth. He suppressed the groan of agony that welled up in his chest. *Sammy! Arthur! Dead!* These two brothers had crossed the borders of the broken European nations in the same truck with Daniel and Suzannah. Thirty cartons of cigarettes per Jew: that was the cost of their lives and transportation to Palestine. Now they were nothing, their lives of no more account than the ashes falling from the burning tobacco.

There was a scream, a girl's scream, and the pounding of running feet.

It sounded like Suzannah's scream. *Don't let it be her. Let me be wrong.*

Bootsteps moved away from Daniel's hiding place. Suzannah's voice. There was no mistaking it.

Biting his lip to keep from shouting, *Leave her alone,* he listened as an argument broke out. One Arab voice shouted that he should have her first because he had found her; but the one called Hassan asserted that the right was his.

"She is mine," al-Malik announced.

Maybe they won't kill her. Maybe she will be alive, after.

Daniel could not move. There were at least three of them. They had machine guns, knives. Asher's mangled features came to him. If he ran out, surely he and Suzannah would both be killed. *Don't move,* he told himself.

Burying his head in his arms, Daniel pounded his fist against the rock until blood trickled downward.

After a long time, there was a burst of gunfire, and then everything was still. Blackness closed over Daniel's vision as, mercifully, he lost consciousness.

■　　■　　■　　■

The hour had arrived for the exiled Jews of the Diaspora to call Israel their nation. The conclusion of two thousand years of foreign rule over Jerusalem and Palestine was at hand, thirty years of British occupation in Palestine finished.

Destined to be a footnote in the long and tumultuous history of the Holy Land, the soldiers of the British empire joined the ancient warriors of Babylon, Persia, and Greece, the legions of Rome, the Arabs, Crusaders, and Turks. Like the conquerors who had come and gone before them, they were also leaving.

The fate of the infant State of Israel and its key city, Jerusalem, would once again be decided by war between Jews and neighboring nations.

In the Jewish Quarter of the Old City, where a remnant of Jews had lived continuously since the days of King David, a population of rabbis, old men, women, and children was defended by fewer than two hundred members of the Haganah. Synagogues, Torah schools, soup kitchens, and homes had been transformed into outposts where a ragged band of fighting Jewish volunteers hoped to hold back the tide of Muslim rage that threatened to destroy their way of life forever.

Among the rabbis were some who regretted the departure of the English. The foreign presence alone, they believed, had preserved the Quarter from destruction. But most residents of the Jewish Quarter, while they feared the result of the coming battle, embraced the departure of the latest conquerors.

The sad skirl of the bagpipes reverberated through the labyrinth of Jerusalem's Old City streets. Above that echoed the haunting call of the shofar. Again and again the mournful ram's-horn trumpet resounded until all eyes lifted to the sky, expecting the arrival of an angelic host to rescue the beleaguered remnant of the Jewish race.

No heavenly beings descended, however.

On the steps of the Great Hurva Synagogue, Rabbi Shlomo Lebowitz and his ten-year-old grandson, Yacov

Lubetkin, waited with a delegation of rabbis as the men of the Suffolk Regiment began their last march through Jerusalem. Over the domed rooftops Haganah officers led their men to the forward positions being evacuated by the British.

As the pipers played, Yacov stood at attention and saluted the pitiful army of his infant nation, Israel. Then, touching his eyepatch—a legacy of Muslim terrorism—he saluted the tattered remnants of the Jewish flag that waved atop the dome of the synagogue.

Along the Street of the Jews, past the Yeshiva schools and the sacred halls of learning, the regiment passed. Tottering, bearded rabbis, watching the soldiers go, kissed the fringes of their talliths, then covered their heads with the garment that had been the sign of their faithfulness for thousands of years.

Rabbi Lebowitz leaned close to his grandson's ear and spoke. "In this hour the longing of every Jewish heart is met. You, my boy, must remember what you see. You must never forget that you have lived to witness the fulfillment of the Lord's promise to his chosen." He recited the words of Jeremiah 30:3 so Yacov would hear them and remember:

> *This is what the LORD, the God of Israel, says:*
> *"Write in a book all I have spoken to you. The*
> *days are coming," declares the LORD, "when I*
> *will bring My people Israel and Judah back*
> *from captivity and restore them to the land I*
> *gave their forefathers to possess."*

Yacov, breathless, looked up at the sky and said, "I will

not forget, Grandfather." Together they recited the words of the Shema with the rabbis: "Hear, O Israel, the Lord our God is One Lord. . . ." As the British soldiers turned the corner, the boy exclaimed, "They are coming, Grandfather! Coming to us!"

The troops of the Suffolk Regiment marched to the steps of the Hurva. The command was given to halt, and the pipes fell silent. Somewhere in the distance a note from the shofar lingered on the air.

Rifles unslung, soldiers stood blinking in the sunlight as the aged scholars looked back at them.

The colonel saluted smartly, then extended his empty hand to the side in a gesture that called his captain to the fore. The captain placed a short, rusty iron bar into the colonel's outstretched palm and stepped back.

Yacov's eyes widened as the British officer ascended the steps and stopped directly in front of Rabbi Lebowitz. With a curt nod the colonel offered the bar to the old man. The boy drew his breath in sharply. His grandfather clutched the key to one of the seven gates of the Old City of Jerusalem. It was the key to Zion Gate!

The officer spoke with emotion as tears brimmed in the rabbi's eyes. Grandfather grasped the key tightly and bowed his head in thanks.

The officer spoke in a quiet voice. "From the year A.D. 70 until this moment a key to the gates of Jerusalem has never been in Jewish hands. This is the first time in nineteen centuries that your people have been so privileged."

Grandfather intoned, "Blessed art thou, O Lord, who has granted us life and sustenance and permitted us to reach this day." Addressing the colonel, he said with dignity, "I accept this key in the name of my people."

The Englishman inclined his head, turned, and barked an order to his regiment. At that command the British troops marched quick-step from the battleground of the Old City of Jerusalem for the last time.

Behind them, remaining on the cobbles of the courtyard, were six bandoleers of precious bullets and ten members of the Haganah, who had entered the beleaguered zone dressed as soldiers of the Suffolk Regiment.

These ten men, to the rear of the column, peeled off in ones and twos. As they melted into the shadows of doorways and the shelter of bunkers, they reclaimed all but one of the cartridge belts.

Yacov reached out to touch the key. Then, as the ominous rattle of Sten-gun fire sounded beyond the walls of the compound, he dashed out to retrieve the last belt of ammunition.

"Hurry, boy!" Grandfather called to him.

The bandoleer burdening his frail shoulders, the child bustled to where a Haganah fighter crouched, scanning the rooftops for Arab snipers. The soldier glanced at the boy.

"Good work," a familiar voice commended Yacov.

Yacov gazed with astonishment into the face of his bearded brother-in-law, Moshe Sachar. *"Oy!* You! You are here!"

"Where else should I be? Who knows the Old City better than I do?"

Yacov turned to grin back at his grandfather, who had taken shelter behind the sandbags of the Hurva portal. "Grandfather! It's Moshe!"

From his hiding place the rabbi shouted, "And where

else should he be? *Nu!* Praise be to the Almighty!" His remarks were punctuated by the distant explosion of a mortar shell. He held up the key, waving it broadly for Yacov and Moshe to see.

"He has it." Moshe slipped the ammunition around his neck. "We'll need that key to open Zion Gate when men from the New City can be spared to reinforce us here in the Quarter."

"Where is my sister?" Yacov asked.

"Rachel is well. And baby Tikvah with her. With Ben-Gurion."

"Ben-Gurion." The name of the new leader of Israel was some comfort to Yacov in spite of his awareness that even now the Arabs massed on the other side of the Old City barriers to attack.

Moshe checked his Sten gun. His sun-bronzed features tensed as his dark eyes roved the rooftops for his compatriots.

"That's fine. Fine," Moshe replied absently.

From across the courtyard Grandfather commanded, "Moshe! Moshe! Grandson-in-law! *Meshuggener!* Come!"

Despite the peremptory message, it was clear to Yacov that Moshe felt compelled to move among his troops with encouragement and the plan for resistance. In the time Moshe had been away from the Old City, dissension had increased between factions within the religious community and members of the military. And Moshe Sachar, as a secular scholar who had grown up within the confines of this peculiar world, was the only one who could effectively bridge the gap.

"He will want to hear about Rachel and the baby.

20

And, of course, the rabbis will need to hear good news about how we will get food and such since we are cut off." Yacov prodded his brother-in-law to first consult the spiritual leaders of the district. "Some are afraid of what will happen now that the English are gone. And . . ." Yacov hesitated. "There is something else he needs to show you. He said you'd come back . . . that the Almighty told him in a dream you'd come back and you were the one."

"The one." Moshe half-smiled and sighed.

"He is not exactly *meshuggener*, but he dreams. You know. He dreams of this and that, and this time you were that."

"The tunnels, is it?"

"He won't show me." Yacov tapped his temple. "So, he's an old man, *nu?* Something about the tunnels. A secret, he says. A very old secret. No one knows about it anymore but him. I am too young. . . ."

Moshe glanced anxiously at his watch. "The ammunition." Then, "The tunnels?"

Moshe Sachar had himself supervised the digging of subterranean passageways beneath the Jewish Quarter. With the Hurva Synagogue at the hub, tunnels from one basement to another reached out to the far corners of the district's boundaries. Safe from the Arab snipers who looked down into the Quarter from the minarets, citizens and Haganah men alike could travel beneath the neighborhood. The passageways had been pushed out as far as the rim of the Armenian Quarter, where defenders occupied the Armenian bakery.

"You should ask him," Yacov said solemnly. If Grand-

21

father knew more about these vital links, Moshe needed the information. "Dov and six others are in the machine-gun nest on the roof of the synagogue. They have three Sten guns and four bullets between them. You came just in time. They can use the bullets, *nu?*"

Moshe nodded and placed his hand on the boy's shoulder. Shadows lengthened on the stones of the court-yard as the two dashed back into the shelter of the Hurva to be gathered into the rabbi's embrace.

■　■　■　■

The high interior dome of the Hurva was hung with rickety scaffolding on which young Haganah defenders lay with aged single-shot Martini rifles. These they aimed through the windows down into the Arab Quarter of the Old City.

The real defense of the synagogue would come from the men with Sten guns out on the roof. Wordlessly Moshe Sachar sent Yacov clambering to the top of the edifice with one bandoleer of ammunition for Dov Avram, Ehud Schiff, and the others who protected the building against attack. Every cartridge was precious. The others would be divided among the Haganah defenders, giving each man three additional bullets.

"Moshe!" cried the old rabbi, kissing him on each cheek. "I knew you would come back! And my Rachel? She is well? And the baby?"

Moshe patted the pocket of his tunic and withdrew an envelope. "She sent you and Yacov this letter, with her love."

Rabbi Lebowitz held the message to his heart. "Then

she is well?"

"Healthy. Praying for us here to stand."

"And may the Almighty hear her prayers. It doesn't look so good, you know."

Of all men in Jerusalem Moshe knew the desperate position of the Jewish Quarter. He gently clasped the rabbi's arm. "The colonel gave you the key to Zion Gate."

"A blessing it is. A sign."

For months Zion Gate had been locked by the British, preventing supplies from passing into the Jewish zone. This was indeed a blessing. "Shaltiel promised to send more defenders to us if we could get the gate open. We'll need the key."

"Of course. Of course." Rabbi Lebowitz shoved the bar into Moshe's hand, and Moshe hung it around his neck on its leather cord. "Take it already. I have had my moment of glory, *nu?*"

"And the tunnels? Yacov said something about the tunnels."

Putting a finger to his lips, Yacov's grandfather scratched his grizzled beard, glanced furtively over his shoulder, and drew Moshe into an antechamber, closing the heavy door behind him.

His demeanor became suddenly grave. "I will not live."

"Don't talk of such things."

"So you think this old man will live forever?"

"You'll live to see the great-grandchild Rachel now carries."

At this news the rabbi brightened. But his smile vanished with the staccato popping of a Sten gun. "It is enough I know my Rachel carries your child. You are a good man, Moshe Sachar. *Nu?* An honest Jew and an upright scholar, even if you are not a rabbi. There are things here I must show you. Secrets I cannot take to my grave. But not now. Not at such an hour of glory. I must read Rachel's letter. You must see to your men. Already the Muslims howl at the gates of our little world."

▪ ▪ ▪ ▪ CHAPTER 2 ▪ ▪ ▪ ▪

Less than three hundred yards north of the Old City wall, on Saladin Road, was an Arab coffeehouse. The salon, which dealt in boiling hot, syrupy brew and sticky pastries, was scarcely wider than its entry. More like a corridor than a shop, the room served a single file of customers whose robes brushed both the side wall and the glass-fronted counter when they turned around.

At the rear of the room a curtain separated a tiny kitchen from the shop; beyond this a second drape screened a flight of steps that led downward into a cellar. It was up these stairs that Kasim Dajani was struggling, toting a wooden crate stocked with the tools of his trade.

The slender and easily blocked passageway was precisely what made the coffeehouse desirable for the operations Dajani carried on there. During the period when British soldiers might burst into Arab businesses to search for terrorists, it was impossible for the English troops to push past the customers and reach the bottom of the stairs before Dajani and his supplies had vanished into connecting underground passageways.

Kasim Dajani was a dynamiter, an explosives expert, so good at rigging car bombs and booby traps that he was part of an elite group of the Mufti's terrorists known as the *Tadmir*. He had learned his trade from Fredrich Gerhardt, former SS commando and, until his recent death, the head of the Tadmir. It was Gerhardt who noticed the peculiar talents of Dajani, praising him and bringing him to the personal attention of Haj Amin el-Husseini.

But now the British were gone and soon, Dajani prayed, the Jews would be gone as well. It was immaterial to him whether they left by bus, ship, or coffin, whole or in pieces, alive or dead, but leave they should, assisted by Dajani's destructive creations.

In the meantime, however, the departure of the English simplified Dajani's work. "Out! Out!" he shouted at two wrinkled Bedouin men who had barely tasted the first sips of their afternoon coffee. "The shop is closed!" And he proceeded to shove a tray of sesame-seed sweets out of the way. He set his crate down in the space created and gingerly, lovingly, began removing and sorting handfuls of detonators and coils of fuse.

Dajani was assisted by three helpers, including a pair of orphan boys, brothers. Their names were simply Daoud and Gawan; they had no other.

The other assistant was the shop's proprietor, Haroun Najid, whose name curled in Arabic script over the entry. Najid was swart and hairy, and he sweated profusely. He was also terrified of Dajani.

Dajani's fingers danced over the components of death and mutilation with the deft touch of a concert pianist. "Now is our time," he said. "We will carry out twenty-five, perhaps fifty actions every day until the Jews are bled to death." His eyes flashed with hatred. "Gerhardt will be avenged," he vowed. "And for his part in our hero's death, we will take particular pleasure in finding the Jew, Moshe Sachar. We shall scatter his bones to the four winds of heaven."

Kasim Dajani insisted that Najid tug the roller blinds down over the coffeehouse window. "But exalted captain," the baker puffed obsequiously, "the Britishers are gone, you see. There is no need for secrecy anymore."

Usually Dajani railed at the stupidity of his accomplices, but this time he was in an expansive mood. "The visit to the souks of Damascus was especially profitable," he said, indicating the wealth of explosives spread out on the glass above the trays of baklava. "The generosity of the Mufti complements his ingenuity. Listen." Dajani's nimble fingers made a birdlike fluttering gesture, signaling Daoud, Gawan, and Najid to draw closer and pay attention. "The Mufti, who will soon be His Highness, the king of Jerusalem, convinced certain infidel benefactors that he is most anxious to prevent war. They contributed large sums of American dollars and British pounds, all in the name of peace!" As Dajani chuckled at the success enjoyed by Haj Amin at the expense of the decadent Westerners, the terrorist's colleagues responded with laughter, though none of them exactly understood. "Fifteen thousand pounds I had in my hand, brothers. A king's ransom for lovely dynamite and prima-cord."

"But why must we close the shades?" Najid persisted. "Do we not wish to announce this good news?"

"Idiot!" Dajani erupted. "We wish to share the news, yes, but not the supplies! Do you think we want every beggar and cutpurse, every captain of five ruffians attracted by the power we wield here, to claim to be a loyal soldier of the Mufti? *I* will say who will deploy these riches and no one else. Now go, Haroun. Go to Captain al-Malik and receive from him a target. Tell him I will soon have twelve large mines ready. Daoud and Gawan will remain as my helpers."

Najid's anxious face relaxed when he understood he would not have to assemble any of the bombs. "At once," he agreed, rattling the frame of the door as he shot through it before Dajani could change his mind.

"Daoud," the dynamiter ordered, examining a detonator and length of fuse, "fetch a half-dozen milk cans from the cellar."

■　■　■　■

It was hot. The flies were buzzing. Dajani lay down on a cot in the back room of the pastry shop and ordered the two orphan boys out of his sight. Gawan and Daoud, bowing, backed from the room. Once out of Dajani's reach, they grinned at one another and took flight.

Delicious freedom!

They raced through the streets toward the long, vaulted bazaar in the heart of the Old City. No matter the war raged. The triple aisles of the souk teemed with activity. There were, after all, thirty thousand Arabs within the confines of the walls. Killing Jews took enormous energy; feeding the soldiers of the Holy War had become a thriving business. Foodstuffs poured into the Arab-held sections of the Old City through Damascus Gate.

Along the Street of Bad Cookery the stalls of butchers

displayed live chickens waiting to be purchased, murdered, plucked, and dismembered. Sheep heads, arranged on a bloody shelf, stared out at their own carcasses hanging from hooks in the ceilings. With weapons slung over their shoulders, strutting members of renegade Arab bands examined the bounty and gloated that on the other side of a wall their Jewish enemies were starving.

Daoud and Gawan reduced their pace through the bazaar to a walk. Meandering through the stalls of vegetable merchants and sellers of pita bread, they covertly stuffed their pockets. Then they ambled toward their usual hiding place, the deserted wreckage of an old hotel where other urchins also took shelter. There they settled down to eat.

Sunlight streamed through the holes in the roof, illuminating the home of the homeless.

Gawan looked up and smiled. "I hate Dajani."

Daoud, through a mouthful of pita, responded, "He is our sponsor, thank Allah. At least we are not as we used to be."

"What? Here we are back to where we used to live, eating stolen bread. What has changed except he beats us and makes us do whatever he wishes?"

"He is a patriot. A great killer of our enemies, the Jews."

"I did not mind the Jews so much. It was good in the old days when we used to light the rabbi's lamps on Sabbath. He paid us well and was kind. Kinder than Dajani."

Daoud gave his brother a shove. "Shut up. If someone heard you, they would think you liked the Jews."

"But I do. I did . . . before. . . ."

28

"It is not the will of Allah that you like anyone you are not supposed to like. The Jews are . . ."

"Never mind. The old Jew was much nicer than Dajani. I hate him the most. No matter that he is a patriot. He beats me and shouts at me. And he stinks worse than a goat."

"To be a good destroyer of Jews a man must have passion, they say."

"Or be crazy."

"That, too."

"Well, I hope Dajani sleeps a long time." Gawan sighed with contentment. "It is a good thing to pretend there is no war."

"War is a holy thing. Dajani says we will have lavish reward for killing Jews. A life in Paradise and seventy beautiful virgins."

Gawan made a face. "I would rather have all the lamb shashlik I could eat."

■   ■   ■   ■

The basement of the Hurva Synagogue was bustling with two dozen women from the Old City Jewish Quarter. Moshe came down the steep steps to view the long rows of tables and tin bowls waiting to be filled for the children who ate two meager meals a day there.

"*Shabbat shalom,* Moshe Sachar." Hannah Cohen, her face damp with perspiration and her eyes watering, left off chopping onions and shuffled to embrace him as he entered the kitchen. She served as head cook and ramrod of the charity.

The communal soup kitchen called *Tipat Chalev,*

29

meaning "Drop of Milk," had seen better days. Laundry tubs, converted to soup kettles, steamed over kerosene stoves.

"You are well?" he asked.

"Every day I get a little older. On one hand this is better than the alternative. On the other hand . . ." She waved her hand in the air as if he would understand. "So we have a state, *nu?*" she said with a smile. "How does it feel after so long?"

"Good. Overwhelming. You are . . . persevering here."

"So what did you bring in with you? Supplies? Food?"

"Bullets."

"So we're serving bullets to the children now? Five hundred I'm feeding here, in case you have forgotten." She put her hands on her hips and glared at him. "And a thousand others in the Quarter besides the *Kinder.* Everybody has a mouth. Everybody has a stomach. I have some pounds to lose. But not the babies."

"The State of Israel is a few hours old. Give it a day," he said, trying to humor her, but realizing the situation was desperate.

"Me? I would rather have milk for the Drop of Milk so the children could go to sleep without crying."

Moshe assured his old friend, "Commander Shaltiel in the New City is making plans to break through to us here. To resupply the Old City defenders."

"Is it defenders I am worried about? The children are hungry. What we have left is onions, onions—*gevalt!* for soup! A little this, a little that. For the *seiglings* we have powdered milk left for one cup tomorrow. Even water is so precious that we wash three times, then scrub the floors with it."

"Be patient. The big push will come soon. I promise."

"When? And don't tell me sooner or later. Later is now. True? Of course true."

"Yes," he agreed. "I need to know exactly what we have as far as food supplies."

She sniffed her fingers with disdain. "Onions. Enough for thin soup for, say, five days. So, the children are gleaning weeds, *nu?* Dandelions growing in the cracks of the cobbles. They say there are some who have hoarded food supplies, but I don't know where."

"The British have left behind a cache of tinned rations. I'm guessing it's enough food for three days for one hundred soldiers."

Hannah's eyes sparkled. "Three days? Three days? What we can do with rations enough to last one hundred Englishmen three days! *Gevalt!* My mother, may she rest in peace, would be spinning if her daughter, Hannah Cohen, couldn't make a feast to feed a thousand and last a week!"

▪ ▪ ▪ ▪ CHAPTER 3 ▪ ▪ ▪ ▪

A coil of school buses, their original yellow paint visible only on the roofs that protruded above the armor-sheathed sides and mud-spattered fenders, snaked away from Tel Aviv harbor. "Look, Lori!" Alfie Halder announced. "Here we are. The Promised Land!" Sweeping his hand over the scene, Alfie offered it to his companion as if he were Moses presenting the first sight of Canaan to travel-weary Israelites. From the rail of the steamship *Joshua Reynolds,* Alfie continued describing the scene, a nearby cargo ship, the outline of the city, and the rest of the waterfront. He also paid tribute to the dappled green and brown of the shoreline and to the obscure outline of the Judean hills that reared up their shoulders in the east.

At six feet, four inches, Alfie towered over the golden-haired young woman who stood near him at the starboard side. "Is you not happy to be here?" he queried.

"Sure," Lori said doubtfully. "The sooner we get off this tub, the better."

Lori Kalner's twenty-six-year-old husband, Jacob, duffel bags thrown over each shoulder, emerged from the bowels of the ship. "There you are, Jacob," Alfie said. "I thought you was lost."

Grinning widely, Jacob dumped their meager belongings in a heap and clapped Alfie on the back. "Not a chance. It took me nine years to get back to this view, dirty buses and all. I wouldn't miss it for the world."

Before the conflagration of the Second World War engulfed Europe, Jacob and Alfie, whom the Germans called *Dummkopf,* had escaped from Nazi Germany and fled to the British Mandate of Palestine. But once there, the young men were interned as enemy aliens. They were eventually deported to Cyprus, and it had taken years for Jacob and his wife to be reunited. Even then, Palestine was not open to them. Jacob, Lori, and Alfie were listed as "undesirables with known illegal Zionist affiliations."

Eventually, in late January 1948, they succeeded in convincing an underground cell of the Haganah, operating out of Marseilles, France, to let them join another attempt to run the British blockade. The *Joshua Reynolds* had smuggled human cargo since the Nazi surrender: Czech Jews who fought a guerrilla war against Hitler's thugs; Polish Jews who served in the Red Army, then returned home to find Warsaw as anti-Semitic as the Nazis; German Jews reprieved from the gas chambers. All hoped for a secure life on a kibbutz or in Jerusalem; none had been welcomed by the British authorities.

One day's sail from the Palestine coast the ship received a wireless message: *No need to run the blockade by night. Statehood is ours!* The *Reynolds* was one of the first vessels of the Aliyah Bet, the "second immigration," to moor up and discharge her weary passengers legally. The buses were waiting to carry them to their new lives.

■ ■ ■ ■

Major Luke Thomas ran his fingers through his red hair and then thoughtfully twisted one end of a neatly trimmed handlebar mustache. Displayed beneath his gaze was a map of Jerusalem, with blue pins representing Israeli forces and red ones denoting Haj Amin's men.

To understand the battle lines swirling around the Holy City, it was necessary to grasp the geography of the place. The Old City walls enclosed a square mile controlled by the Arabs. The Jewish Quarter existed as an off-center bubble at the southern edge of the Muslim territory. A tiny area, no more than four hundred yards on a side, the Jewish district was sandwiched between the Temple Mount and the Armenian Quarter.

While terrorists like Kasim Dajani and Arab Irregulars

like Ahkmed al-Malik attacked the Jewish enclave, the Mufti's troops were themselves besieged from the western approaches to Old Jerusalem's ramparts.

Thomas, a good friend of Moshe Sachar's and lately retired from His Britannic Majesty's forces in Palestine, was currently under the command of the highest-ranking Haganah officer in Jerusalem, David Shaltiel. While waiting for Shaltiel to speak, Major Thomas studied the military situation as presented by the commander.

Shaltiel, veteran of both the French Foreign Legion and the Nazi concentration camp of Dachau, at last pointed again to a map of the Old City spread on the battered, green-painted wooden table. "To preserve the Jewish Quarter," he said, "we must break through at least one avenue and set up a permanent line of communication and supply. What I propose is a three-pronged assault."

The other commanders and their aides leaned forward expectantly. Shaltiel's headquarters contained representatives of all the independent Jewish commands. Some of them abhorred each other almost as fervently as they did the Arab Irregulars. Scanning the room, Thomas noted how the Palmach troops deliberately slouched in their chairs to avoid any appearance of military discipline while the Haganah men sat rigidly upright. The Irgunists, because their organization had been part of the massacre of Arab civilians at Deir Yassin, sat in a tight knot, as if sensing the lingering condemnation emanating from the rest.

Around the corners of the room were the others: Youth Brigade kibbutzniks, tanned bronze and wearing shorts, jostled members of the Home Guard, white-haired and armed with canes.

Major Thomas was aware that as much as they mistrusted each other, they shared a common skepticism of him, an Englishman and a Christian.

"The Palmach will attack from the south," Shaltiel was saying. "First Mount Zion, then Zion Gate."

Little mixing of battalions was planned. Palmachniks would only submit to being led by Palmach commanders, Irgun by Irgunists, and so on.

"Irgun to attack from the Hospice of Notre Dame north of the Old City wall and secure the passage of New Gate."

The Irgun officer, a savage-looking, one-eyed Russian Jew, squinted his remaining eye. "Of course you will assign the armored vehicles to us. We will need them at the gate and to guard our flank on Suleiman Road."

"No," Shaltiel said flatly. "Our armored force will be used by the Haganah attack. The north and south assaults are diversionary. The shortest route to the Jewish Quarter is straight through Jaffa Gate and along the Street of the Chain. That is where the armor will be used."

"So," the Irgun leader shouted, "he means it is for the glory of the Haganah that he has kept the main attack for himself!"

Gritting his teeth, Shaltiel said, "Operation Pitchfork must be successful if the Old City is to be saved, and its success depends on each of the three elements doing its job."

"Ha!" bellowed the Irgunist. "Then why not put our entire force into an attack at the northeast corner of the Old City? This not only will liberate the Jewish Quarter but will defend the entire city from counterattack."

"I did not call this meeting to ask for your opinions," Shaltiel corrected, "but to give you your orders."

"An assault on Jaffa Gate is suicidal anyway," protested the Palmach commander, Nachasch. "The Arab gunners on David's Tower will never let you get close enough to storm the portal . . . not even if the Irgun can draw some Arabs away for a few minutes."

"I'll give you a few minutes, you toy soldier," the Russian retorted.

"It seems to me . . . ," Major Thomas remarked loudly in Arabic.

The room grew instantly hushed at the wholly unexpected language. "It seems to me," he repeated in Hebrew, "that you are quarreling like Bedouin tribesmen. Who will get what share of glory! Are your heads full of sand? If the Jewish Quarter and Moshe Sachar's defenders are not relieved within two days, the Mufti's men will overrun them. Only Commander Shaltiel has a plan that can be launched immediately. Commander, my men are ready. When do we go?"

"Sunday night," Shaltiel replied, "if the rest can prepare."

The Irgunist glared across the length of the table at the Palmachnik. "We'll be ready while the boy scouts are lacing their boots," he said.

After the meeting, Major Thomas approached Shaltiel privately. "I fancy you know what I'm going to say," he suggested.

"You are not as ready as you pretended?" Shaltiel said wryly.

"Spot on. We are at less than half strength. I cannot

launch an assault on such a fortified position with the numbers I now have. And we must first carry out a reconnaissance of the Arab defense at Jaffa Gate."

"You'll be getting reinforcements tomorrow."

"But will they be trained? Will they be equipped?"

"You'll get what I have to send," Shaltiel concluded.

"And weapons? Ammunition?"

Shaltiel clapped Luke Thomas on the shoulder. "There are ten thousand rifles in Jewish hands in the entire Yishuv," he said. "Less than a thousand mortars. Not one tank, not one cannon, unless you count those left from the last century."

"But what about new shipments?"

An underground Jewish organization known as *Rekhesh* had worked secretly for years to purchase and stockpile arms. Some of these had been smuggled into Palestine under British noses in crates labeled FARM MACHINERY. But rather than risk discovery and seizure by the British, the Rekheshniks had delayed shipping the bulk of the weapons until the Mandate was close to expiration. In doing so they had walked too fine a line.

"The *Borea* got to Tel Aviv yesterday. Four million bullets, machine guns, field artillery, and shells."

"But that's tremendous news!"

Shaltiel shook his head. "A British cutter forced her to sail to Haifa and did not release her till after midnight. She is being unloaded in Tel Aviv now, but who knows if we can keep the road open long enough to bring up the equipment? It will aid the rest of Israel, but as for Jerusalem . . ." Commander Shaltiel shrugged.

"And for now?" Luke Thomas asked.

"As always," Shaltiel said, "I'll send what I can. You will have to make it work."

■　■　■　■

The air of the docks in Tel Aviv smelled of onions, creosote, and rotting seaweed. Stevedores were busy unloading a battered cargo ship laden with enormous wooden crates stenciled in English with the words FARM MACHINERY and TRACTOR PARTS.

Jacob Kalner's eyes narrowed as he observed the bustling activity on the quay. "Farm machinery," he said to Alfie with satisfaction. "Captain Leonard told me what's in the crates. War-surplus artillery from America. And under the onions? Czech-made rifles. A million rounds of ammunition for defense against the Arabs. It's the roads, though. Everything depends on getting the stuff into the hands of the Haganah."

At the head of the gangplank of the *Joshua Reynolds,* Lori seized Jacob's arm. "Promise me!" she said urgently as they moved forward in the long line. "Promise me we won't be separated again! Not after all the years . . . after all the days of not knowing if you were alive."

Jacob rubbed his hand across his mouth as they descended to the dock. "You know in Marseilles," he temporized, groping for the words, "the Haganah told us there would be fighting."

"Fighting, yes!" Lori replied fiercely. "I said I would come to this godforsaken place with you. And I came because you are the only family left to me. I will fight beside you, but not be parted from you. Never again."

"All right," Jacob snapped without meeting her eyes. Other passengers were watching them, listening to the sharp edge of her words. "We are scheduled for a kibbutz in the north anyway," he said, uttering the only thing he could call to mind to finish the discussion.

A long, black automobile motored into the center of the throng of refugees, and from it emerged a stub of a man with a bald dome surrounded by untamed tufts of curly white hair. Murmurs of amazement swept through the crowd. Whether the wondering phrases were in Yiddish or French, English or Dutch, the name *Ben-Gurion* was on every lip.

The face of David Ben-Gurion, formerly the head of the Jewish Agency and now the first prime minister of the State of Israel, was known to the refugees. A Polish Jew who had begun life as David Green, this *son of a lion cub,* as his adopted Hebrew name proclaimed, was their papa.

"Look," a woman behind Jacob Kalner gushed in Yiddish. "Such a welcome they have for us! The president himself has come to greet us!"

"Prime minister, Mama," her nervous thread of a husband corrected.

Despite the admiring words called out toward him, Ben-Gurion's face was serious, even darkly so. The Arab war against the Jews had begun immediately and in earnest.

Pushing through the stream of refugees, Leonard, the Haganah officer who had accompanied the *Reynolds* from Marseilles, bustled down the walkway and saluted the man he called "Boss." From under his arm he produced a notebook and opened it to a three-page typed list of names. At the top, in block capitals, was printed PASSENGER MANIFEST.

The line of arrivals continued to move slowly forward, though no one had boarded any buses as yet. Jacob was close enough to overhear part of the conversation between Ben-Gurion and the officer.

"How many between sixteen and sixty?" Ben-Gurion asked. Then, "I know they aren't trained. Would I be here myself if we could spare the time for training?" Finally, "The pass to Jerusalem is open. We may not have another chance. Jerusalem. Tonight. All of them."

Jacob saw the Haganah officer swallow the words of protest he had been trying to offer. The man stepped back, saluted crisply, and mounted an empty cable spool as a rostrum. "Attention! Attention!" he called. "Everyone stand still and keep quiet." It took several minutes to translate this instruction into the required languages. "You will be boarding buses for the trip to the barracks, after which processing will begin and supper will be served."

A cheer from the crowd interrupted his speech. Weeks of being seasick, intensified by confinement belowdecks in cramped, often reeking conditions, had robbed many of the immigrants of their appetites. Now, mere steps on dry land in fresh air had miraculously restored their hunger. "Except," the officer continued, "we have an urgent need in Jerusalem. Able-bodied men between ages sixteen and sixty will leave at once for the Holy City."

"What?" the woman behind Jacob demanded loudly. "What did he say, Aaron?"

Lori glared a cold warning at Jacob. "I would never have left London . . ."

Just then, a dark-haired beauty with cobalt-blue eyes

emerged from Ben-Gurion's car to stand beside a gray-haired, barrel-figured matron. Each spoke briefly to the prime minister, who then got back in the car and was driven from the docks.

"Rachel Sachar and Rose Smith will help direct the women refugees," the Haganah officer announced, pointing toward the two as if grateful for the chance to divert the crowd's ire from himself. "Right-hand row of buses are for men sixteen to sixty. Everyone else, to the left."

"I have to go," Jacob said, gently disengaging Lori's grasp and leading her into a narrow canyon of shipping crates and out of the view of the crowd.

"If you leave this time, Jacob, you won't find me when you come back." She yanked her arm free. Her blue eyes flashed. Jacob knew she was thinking of the eight painful years they'd spent apart.

"You don't mean that."

A flock of seagulls screamed and wheeled in the sky above them.

"I mean it. I won't be deserted again. You're Jewish. I'm . . . what is it your people call me? *Goy? Shiksa?* This isn't my battle."

"I took an oath before God that if I ever got back here . . ."

"But what did you promise *me*, Jacob? What?"

Jacob had found his faith in years of suffering with only half-witted Alfie as company in the displaced-persons camps, while she, exiled daughter of a German pastor executed by the Nazis, had spent the war in England and lost everything, even her ability to believe. What difference did

41

Jacob's certainty of divine purpose make to Lori? It only widened the gulf between them.

"I promised I will always love you." He stooped to kiss her, but she shoved him away.

"Go then. But don't look over your shoulder because I won't be behind you. I'll never say good-bye to you again, Jacob. There have been too many good-byes in my life. I don't know who you are anymore. I don't know who I'm supposed to be. I don't care! If you hadn't come back . . ."

She did not say it, but both knew what she meant. If he had died in Warsaw, she might have married someone else. Had a child or two by now. Opened a linen shop in Primrose Hill Village. Forgotten the pain of loneliness by loving an ordinary man and living out an ordinary life.

"I'm sorry," he said simply. "I love you."

She turned her back on him and did not watch him leave.

■   ■   ■   ■

There were two obvious absences among the crowd of mostly French and Italian newcomers gathered before Rachel: the elderly and children between the ages of three and twelve. Babies and toddlers by the score squirmed in the arms of weary mothers, but where were the school-age children?

Rachel knew the answer, but her mind rebelled at the awful reality that they had not come to Eretz-Israel because they had not survived. Over the last decade an entire generation of Jewish children had been decimated again and again. Only one in ten had outlasted the Holocaust. These little ones on the waterfront of Tel Aviv had been born since the end of the war.

She could not bring herself to look at them. She remembered, too well, the faces who were not there. Her brothers, her mother and father . . .

She forced herself to smile and focused her eyes on the packing crates at the back of the crowd. *It will not always be like this,* she wanted to shout. *The loss will not always be so fresh. You will not always look around you and wonder where they have gone, why they are not with you, why they do not come when your heart calls their names.*

She knew that time in the new country would encourage healing. But for now, their husbands had gone to fight, their hopes of an ordinary life had been smashed by the certainty of war, and there was nothing to say that could console them. *By tomorrow there will be more wounds to deal with.*

Rachel first spotted the young woman with short blond hair and eyes reddened from weeping as she emerged from between two stacks of wooden crates. She stood out amid the swarthy, Mediterranean-looking crowd. In her mid-twenties, tall, slender, and sunburned, she wore men's apparel in spite of the heat. *Not religious. That is apparent by her clothing: baggy blue wool trousers; a man's white shirt, open at the neck and sleeves rolled up as if she is ready to work; blue cable-knit sweater tied at her waist. Swiss? Dutch, perhaps?*

She stood aloof, as Rachel had once done. Somehow she did not belong. She looked away as if she did not notice when a child waved to her over its mother's shoulder. It was plain in the way she crossed her arms and raised her chin to glare defiantly after the departing transports that someone she loved had gone to Jerusalem. Anger and bitterness hardened her pretty features.

Rachel could not explain why she was drawn to her of all the women and children who stood waiting to be told where their life would take them. They were caught in a current they could not fight against. But this woman seemed the most isolated, the most vulnerable. Perhaps Rachel saw herself as she had stood among the dispossessed only six months earlier. *Before Moshe. Before Leah and the baby. Before I knew I was not alone. . . .*

■   ■   ■   ■

Moshe Sachar continued making his rounds of the Old City. His next destination was the hospital of Misgav Ladakh, located between the dome of Nissan Bek Synagogue and the Porat Yoseph Yeshiva School. *Misgav Ladakh* meant "Refuge for the Downtrodden." It received title and reputation from the Rothschild family of Jewish philanthropists, who donated the money to build and staff the charity ward in 1854.

The entry to the hospital, normally a flight of steps open to the air and sun, had become a constricted archway of sandbags and boards. Once a day the Arabs dropped mortar shells on the hospital.

A pretty, plump, dark-haired woman with anxious eyes accosted him as soon as he entered. "Are you a physician?" she asked. "Am I glad to see you! Doctor, we need help over here."

Interrupting the appeal, Moshe explained his duties and

then asked about the situation with the medical personnel.

"There are two nurses," Esther Rheinhart explained, "and no doctor. I brought in my husband, Manny, a week ago. Shrapnel. His neck. A scratch only, I told him, the big *seigling*. A nurse and me, we sewed it up. Not too bad. Then she said, 'Can you stay and help?' 'Of course,' I said. 'I learn quick.' We got some morphine, some medicine, some blood plasma, what's to learn? But since then? *Oy gevalt!* Bullet holes! Operations! What if the bullet is in deep, too deep to dig it out? And what if, God forbid, someone gets the infection or needs amputation? Five serious cases right now. We saw six people die who didn't need to. We can't even bury them. They're stacked out back in a shed. We have only two nurses and four volunteers, and we need more help in here, yes? Yes?"

Moshe backed out hurriedly, promising to do what he could, as soon as he could.

■　　■　　■　　■

The high command of the Mufti's forces in Jerusalem was centered in the mimosa-shaded halls of the Rawdah School. Classroom of Arab patriots and planning chamber for riots and insurrections against the British, the institution doubled as headquarters and munitions depot. Just below the northwest corner of the Temple Mount, the location had been King Herod's Jerusalem palace two millennia earlier.

Captain Ahkmed al-Malik, recently arrived from his conquest of Kfar Etzion, railed at Khaled Husseini, cousin of the Mufti and technically the overall commander of

Arab forces in Jerusalem. "I know you have mortars and machine guns," al-Malik raged. "Give me what I require, and I will drive out the rabbis and old women in one day. You have heard what happened after I took charge of the kibbutz operation." Behind al-Malik six pairs of men wrestled with obviously weighty crates. These wooden boxes, which were stacked in a corner of the room, were each labeled in English: GRENADES, TYPE 2 FRAGMENTA-TION, QUANTITY ONE GROSS.

"I do not doubt your zeal," Husseini said, "but I cannot spare any munitions. The Jews will be attacking our western defenses at any moment, and I must not divert any weapons to kill rabbis and old women." The bench on which Husseini sat was littered with Sten-gun clips. When Husseini pushed himself back from the table, the incline of the bench caused machine-gun bullets to drip onto the stone floor. The edge of the bench over which the cartridges fell was carved with a verse from Muslim scripture: HE WHO REJECTS THE GOD OF ABRAHAM IS A FOOL.

"Can you not see you are playing into the hands of the Jews?" al-Malik stormed. "Reduce the Jewish Quarter to rubble at once instead of wasting time. The loss of the Jewish district will demoralize all their forces throughout Palestine."

"Ah," Husseini corrected, "but there, you see, you do not have my plan in mind."

"Do you have one?" al-Malik sneered.

Khaled Husseini chose to ignore the remark. "Since the Haganah have committed themselves to rescuing the Quarter, we are keeping their forces engaged here."

"And they ours," al-Malik muttered. Then, louder, "Is it

46

not important to complete the conquest of Jerusalem before the Arab Legion of King Abdullah arrives?"

Husseini waved dismissively. "You, Captain, will blunt the Haganah assaults and cause them to exhaust their ammunition; then we will counterattack and drive them off the land altogether. The sea will run with their blood, but all in good time . . . all in good time." The gesticulating hand waggled just below a framed, hand-lettered verse from the Koran: *Pay back a transgressor only to the limit of the transgression, for Allah rewards the merciful.*

■ ■ ■ ■ CHAPTER 4 ■ ■ ■ ■

S ix hundred women and children watched as the convoy of buses carrying sons, husbands, and fathers rumbled away from the docks of Tel Aviv. A boy riding on his mother's shoulders waved in farewell. As dust and exhaust obscured the square, a baby in her grandmother's arms wailed a protest.

No one spoke except with their eyes. Not one voice argued the injustice of this moment or recited the litany of farewells that had been played out between Jewish husbands and wives, brothers and sisters, over the years. They had set their hearts upon Israel as the land where they would never have to say good-bye again. But at the first trumpet call their dreams had dissolved.

Lori adjusted the scarf over her blond hair. The sun brutal against her back, she worried about the children who were being made to wait in the heat. Above all, she was furious that Jacob had gone without her. *As though a place means more than our life together.*

Could the battle for Jerusalem be any more devastating than what Lori had survived during the Blitz in London? Forty thousand civilians had died, and Lori had survived it all without Jacob.

As the late-afternoon shadows lengthened, another column of trucks and buses slid into the square.

At the front of the milling crowd, two women climbed to the top of an enormous wooden crate. One was Rachel Sachar. The other was a sunburned, bulky-framed woman with a bullfrog mouth and an American accent. She announced cheerfully through a bullhorn, first in English and then in French, "Dear ladies, I am Madame Rose. *Oui?* I will not keep you long, as I know well what it is to travel with little ones. I myself began with a flock in Paris, flew away with them during the Nazi occupation, and, like you, set my heart upon Israel! Mothers and children! Family groups! Please form a queue at the rear of the lorries for transportation to temporary quarters. The English have kindly left their barracks behind for you to occupy. They built fine kitchens for their soldiers, these English. And they've left crates and crates and crates of rations and tins of milk for the babies."

As an audible sigh of relief arose from the crowd, Madame Rose stepped down and Rachel Sachar, tall, slim, and beautiful, took the bullhorn. Children, big-eyed, ill-clothed and half-starved, looked like hungry baby birds waiting in their mothers' shadows. Rachel did not look at them, nor at any other faces. Instead, she focused her gaze on a point at the back of the crowd as if she preferred not to see the suffering in each face. Lori resented this woman's smile, her too-calm demeanor.

In Polish, Dutch, German, and Yiddish, Rachel instructed: "Welcome to Israel! My name is Rachel Sachar, and I will do my best to help you with any questions." Her voice was cheerful, like a Guide Friday beginning a tour of Westminster Abbey. It grated on Lori. "I know you have come a long way. But with God's help you have arrived in a new home. Now your nation needs your help. You have offered your husbands, brothers, and sons, you say. What more does Israel need? We have learned courage through travail and again must have hearts like lions!"

She focused on no one. Could she not bear the expressions of grief on the faces of her audience? "Those of you who are without children, if you have any special skills, we are looking for women ambulance drivers or those who can handle a large truck over difficult terrain. We know many of you did the work of men during the war. You are prepared, well trained. If you speak several languages and could serve as an interpreter for our soldiers, please step forward. Nurses are urgently needed at the front. If, with God's help, you are willing and able to place yourself in harm's way once again, register with me. Three buses at the rear of the convoy have been provided for your transportation."

Lori had already begun to elbow her way through the crowd before Rachel Sachar finished her speech.

■　■　■　■

Sixty-four young women from among the passengers of the *Joshua Reynolds* gathered at the buses to the rear of the convoy. Lori recognized a score of them from the voyage from Marseilles.

Thirty minutes had passed since the transports carrying Jacob and every other able-bodied male immigrant had rumbled away from the waterfront. Already Lori regretted her harsh words, her refusal to tell him how she really felt. If the circumstances of her life had taught her anything, it was that life was too uncertain to ever walk away in anger from someone she loved.

I need to see him again. Just long enough to say I didn't mean it. To wish him well. Tell him love isn't enough anymore. I need a life. Peace. Say good-bye. It can't work here. It'll never work between us. Then I'll go back to London. Start clean.

Rachel Sachar and two stern-faced young Haganah officers handed out pencils and short information forms.

The space for special skills was listed above the place for the name.

SKILLS: Served 3 yrs. London Volunteer Fire Brigade. During Blitz was trained for treatment of trauma injury. Ambulance duty. Fire fighting. Assisted in defusing unexploded bombs on three occasions.

NAME: Lori Kalner   AGE: 27   GENDER: Female

HEALTH: Excellent

HEIGHT: 5'7"   WEIGHT: 125 lbs.

CITIZENSHIP: Resident alien/ political refugee/ Great Britain

COUNTRY OF ORIGIN: Germany till 1939/ escaped to England prior to war.

LANGUAGES SPOKEN FLUENTLY: English, German,

French
MARITAL STATUS: **Married**   DEPENDENTS: None

Impatient to be gone, she returned her paper to one of
the Haganah officers, who raised an eyebrow as he
scanned the sheet.

"Where's your husband?"

"On the road to Jerusalem."

"Planning on joining him at the King David Hotel for
tea?"

"I was putting out Nazi incendiaries in London while he
was interned by the English on Cyprus."

He half-smiled at the irony of her reply. "Those English
have a strange way of saying thank you, eh? Sounds like
you should have been on the first bus to the front. What did
you enjoy the least about living in London during the
Blitz?"

"Digging dead children out of the rubble while their
mothers waited. That was the hardest. If the whole family
went together . . . that wasn't as bad, somehow. But the
babies . . ." She knew from his expression that he did not
doubt she had served on the Fire Brigade.

Testing her further, he inquired, " 'Assisted in
defusing . . .' What does 'assisted' mean?"

She answered honestly. "I knelt to the right of bomb
specialist Bobby Gilmore, handed him his tools, and
prayed we would live to be very old."

At this he grinned. "Sounds useful. Could you do it
again?"

"Pray or hand Bobby his tools?"

"Both."

"Bobby is dead. In a million pieces. Not on my shift, but I guess that makes me a failure in the prayer department."

He shrugged, taken aback by the matter-of-fact nature of her reply. "What sort of bombs?"

"Two five-hundred-pounders. One doodlebug."

"The V-1? Impressive. The Arabs won't be sending any of those our way, but you're hired. Gutsy lady. Climb aboard. Your story is worth a free ride to Jerusalem."

■　■　■　■

Lori joined the queue of female recruits shuffling onto bus number 2.

Above the babble of voices she heard the familiar drone of British Spitfire fighter aircraft approaching from the south. Anxious faces turned skyward. Conversations dropped off.

"Fighters!" exclaimed a bespectacled young woman fearfully.

Lori said calmly, "It's all right. They're ours. British Spitfires. Approaching fast." She had heard these same engines ten thousand times above London. On how many occasions had she stood on Primrose Hill and watched the dogfights overhead as Royal Air Force pilots battled Nazi Luftwaffe aces to the death?

Rachel Sachar glanced at Lori in alarm. "British planes?"

Lori raised her arm to point over the rooftops of the Tel Aviv waterfront as two fighters came in low. The target-shaped roundels, which served as identifying marks for

British aircraft, were clearly visible on wing and fuselage. On the undercarriage of each was what Lori recognized as a single one-hundred-pound bomb.

"Spitfire!" the man with the clipboard shouted in terror. "Take cover! Take cover!"

At this alarm a collective wail rose up from the women in the open plaza. Panic ensued as mothers flung themselves to the ground, covering their children.

Lori extended her hands at the incomprehensible scene. Only she and a handful of others remained standing. "But they're ours," she said, then her words were lost beneath the buzz of the engines and the screams of the crowd.

Rachel Sachar bolted to her, yanking her down. "Egyptians! Egypt . . ." The machine guns of the intruders exploded, cutting a bloody swath through the women and children. Lori was splattered with the brains of a woman who only moments before had been talking about her brother. Bullets ricocheted off the armor of the bus and fragmented, wounding several others.

"But . . . but they're ours," Lori repeated over and over. "Spitfires."

Her mantra of disbelief did not dispel the reality of death and horror unfolding before her. The burst did not last more than seconds, yet the screams of the wounded and the bereft overflowed the square. Lori raised her head and saw the carnage in the plaza. The color red surrounded her: blood on the dead; blood on the living. Dozens of dead lay torn apart among the terrified survivors. Children lay beneath slaughtered mothers. Mothers cradled their lifeless young.

The fighters pulled up suddenly and banked in a wide

turn over the harbor. Was it over?

"They're coming back!" someone shouted.

A man's voice commanded: "Onto the bus! On the bus! Get on!"

Lori remembered the damage caused by even one bomb. She knew the marauders were not finished. They had one goal: to flatten the harbor of Tel Aviv. Springing to her feet, she charged toward the shelter of the bus. The driver ground the gears and revved the motor. Others pushed and shoved behind her and before her, carrying her up the steps.

Running up the aisle toward the back of the vehicle, Lori remembered the burned-out hulks of London buses. Had she climbed into her coffin?

Outside, the ominous thrumming of approaching Spits matched the renewed cries of the helpless victims.

The back emergency door was open. Women clambered up and in, piling on top of one another. No protection there. Lori saw the first bomb detach lazily from the undercarriage, like a satchel falling out of the sky. It wobbled a bit, then glided through the roof of the bus station. Lori dropped to the floor, shoving her head beneath a seat.

There was a fraction of a second before the walls of the building bulged outward, then a long moment before it collapsed. That same instant the concussion slammed against the side of the vehicle, rocking it up on two wheels, holding it aloft, then dropping it back again.

Then there was silence. The blast had deafened her. Merciful, it was, shutting out the screams. Daylight dimmed, as if a great fog had closed over the sun.

Dust, Lori thought. *Always the dust, blocking the sky,*

covering the slaughtered, choking the living . . .

There was a lurch of forward motion as the driver managed to slam the vehicle into gear and make a run for the safety of a side street.

■　■　■　■

Moshe was in a storeroom below Hurva Synagogue with Dov Avram, a leader of the Old City defenders. Together they reviewed the ammunition and military equipment of the Jewish Quarter.

"Even with what came in today," Dov said, "we have less than one hundred rounds of rifle bullets for each man."

"What about machine guns?" Moshe asked.

"Two . . . only two," Dov said, pushing up his glasses. "Both light, air-cooled types. We have a Czech fifty-caliber, but it broke, and no one here knows how to fix it."

"I'll see to it later," Moshe suggested, then asked, "Grenades?" His head down, poring over figures on paper and a map showing the outlines of the Jewish district, Moshe did not see the advancing interruption that stopped Dov's mouth. When Dov failed to answer his question, Moshe repeated, "Grenades?"

Dov, facing the entry, instead remarked, "Rabbi Akiva is here, Moshe."

The bearded, portly figure framed in the doorway wore a homburg. His expensive suit coat, buttoned high on his chest, revealed a brocade waistcoat. Akiva, the mayor of the Old City Jews, was the single most important political figure in the Quarter. Dov had married his only child, Yehudit, but without his permission, and Akiva had not spoken with her since. A firm opponent of statehood, Akiva had desperately wanted the British to stay. He did not approve of the Haganah, Ben-Gurion, the new nation, and, most of all, he did not approve of Moshe Sachar.

"Sachar," he said without other greeting. "You have come back. I hoped we were rid of your troublesome presence permanently."

"Yes, Rabbi," Moshe acknowledged, trying to stay civil. "Or no, if you prefer. But since the British are gone, and we have to work together . . ."

"We will never work together, you meddling apostate," Akiva huffed, inflating both his chest and his words. "It is you who will get us killed. We lived in peace with our Arab neighbors before and would still be at peace if it were not for you *apikorsim.*"

Among certain ultra-Orthodox Jewish sects, Israel could never be reborn before Messiah came. Any attempt to set up a Jewish state by human means was heresy of the worst sort and certain, according to Akiva and his like, to bring divine retribution down on the Jews.

Picking his words carefully, Moshe said, "The British have withdrawn their troops. Like it or not, we must defend ourselves. Surely you would not sacrifice the women and children of this Quarter."

Akiva's piggy eyes bulged. "It is you who sacrifice them! Get your soldiers together and go, then the rest of us will negotiate with the Arabs to keep the peace."

"I cannot do that, Rabbi," Moshe said. "And you would not survive long if we did."

"Bah!" Akiva exclaimed, turning his back to Moshe and leaving with a flurry of steps.

"Rabbi," Dov said, calling after the man, "your daughter asks about you. She prays for you."

Akiva stopped midstride and, without looking around, uttered distinctly, "I . . . have . . . no . . . daughter." With that he resumed his haughty exit, scowling at adults and children alike. Behind his back Leo and Mendel, the stocky Krepske brothers, made glowering faces, stuck out their bellies, and marched along, arms swinging, in mocking imitation.

Dov grimaced. "So, Moshe, would you care to trade in-laws?"

■   ■   ■   ■

Two enemy planes. Two bombs.

And so the War of Independence began.

The dead on the Tel Aviv waterfront were counted: twenty children under the age of three, twenty-six adults. There were sixty wounded. Nurses, needed desperately in Jerusalem, were instead rushed to overcrowded clinics around Tel Aviv.

And Rachel Sachar found herself on an armored bus traveling up the pass of Bab el Wad.

She knew Jerusalem well. She would help fill the gap in manpower there. Tikvah was as safe in the Agency air-raid shelter as any child in Israel was anywhere. This much, at least, was a comfort to Rachel. She had toyed with the idea of taking the baby with her to meet the ship. Thank God she had not done so.

The vehicle was three quarters occupied. The passengers were silent, stunned by what they had just witnessed, lost in their own thoughts, or asleep. The bus joined a larger convoy on the outskirts of Tel Aviv. Rachel sat behind the driver, a forty-year-old American Jew named Golden, who hailed from Chicago.

In the gathering gloom, the towering edifice that marked the beginning of the gauntlet was visible against the pastel sky. Clouds of dust and the rumble of two hundred trucks echoed like thunder against the canyon of Bab el Wad. There was a delay as fifty British troop lorries were met coming down the road from Jerusalem.

"That's the last of them guys," the driver sneered as they passed. "They're out of Jerusalem. And good riddance."

"We are late." Rachel tried not to worry, though she was told that the intent was to reach Jerusalem while the British convoys were still on the road. The presence of British troops, even in the midst of withdrawal from Jerusalem, would prevent Arab attacks.

"I drove a bus in Chicago," he said, glancing at Rachel in the mirror. Rachel saw his concerned eyes and knew he was trying to make conversation, keep it light. "I ain't afraid of gangsters. Not even the Mufti's thugs, see?"

Rachel could not reply. Her mind returned to the carnage on the Tel Aviv docks, then to the men on the road up ahead who had left their wives and children behind. They would not know what had transpired until they reached Jerusalem, and perhaps not even then. How many would fight and die, holding the belief that their families were alive and safe?

Golden spoke again. "They were after the shipment of weapons, see? Not the people. Wasn't like the Nazis, was it? Killin' Jews on purpose. They didn't want to kill people, y'know? We just happened to be there, see? Those planes was . . . it was the ammunition and stuff. Good thing they missed, or there'd have been nothin' left of any of us." His pained eyes flickered to her face in the mirror, then back at the road. "We gotta find the good in this, don't we?"

Rachel nodded but could find no good in it. She looked down at her hands, wishing he would be quiet, wishing people did not always feel compelled to put the best face on something tragic beyond comprehension. *The children! The children!*

"Nothin' I could do," he said in a low voice. Suddenly Rachel knew he was not speaking to her but to himself. "I saw them comin' when everyone else did. Saw that bomb kinda floatin' in. Looked at them kids over there . . . then they were gone. I had to get the rest of us out of there, see?"

She was so tired. Rising, she put a hand briefly on his arm. His shoulders sagged at her touch, and tears coursed down the lines of his rough-hewn face. "Yes. Thank God they did not hit the ammunition," she said. Then she walked down the aisle to the seat where Lori Kalner slept.

■ ■ ■ ■ CHAPTER 5 ■ ■ ■ ■

It was past sundown before Daniel awakened to the sound of footsteps in the wadi. The sickening memory of where he was and why came crashing in on his mind. *Suzannah. Asher. Everybody dead but me!* The searcher approached nearer and nearer to his hiding place. Daniel could hear his labored breathing. *There is only one.*

Maybe I can take him. Escape before he calls the others!

A yard from the cave the man halted, stood for a long moment, and then called to someone on the ridge. "There is no one here, Your Honor. No one at all. Perhaps he was wounded. I will seek him out and finish him if he is here. I will have his shoes for my trouble."

Daniel drew in his breath sharply. He knew the voice. It was the blind beggar! The one who camped in the wadi sometimes and came to the gates of Kfar Etzion for an occasional handout of food or a bit of clothing. *Blind! Not blind, but a spy! Ungrateful old stray! We should have shot you instead of feeding you!*

"Oh, yes! Yes, Your Honor! Never mind. I shall tend to it."

There was a tense silence. The old man's breath wheezed. He did not move away, but after a time he stooped, as if to search for tracks in the sand. Was he armed?

Daniel grasped a stone and prepared to crush the beggar's skull before he could raise the alarm.

The man cleared his throat. The brush in front of the cave rustled.

Beads of sweat trickled down from Daniel's forehead, stinging his eyes.

The beggar spoke again, this time addressing the mouth of the cave in a whisper. "I know you are in there, boy."

Daniel held his breath, willing his heart to be quiet.

The voice was full of pity. "They are everywhere. Your companions are all dead. All. Do not come out until you hear the trill of the nightbird three times."

I could kill him and run! How many secrets did he tell

the Arabs? There is a chance if I run. The thief! The liar! He'll tell them. Collect a reward.

"I will bury your sister, boy. Her suffering is over."

How does he know she is my sister?

"You must not look back. Head north to Jerusalem. Fear not! The God of your fathers goes with you!"

From the ridge came the demanding inquiry of Hassan el-Hassan. "Have you found anything, old man?"

"No, Your Honor!" The beggar whined his reply. "I am pissing, sir." Then, speaking to the hiding place again, he warned, "Follow the wadi over the hills to Jerusalem. Tell them what you have seen. This same fate awaits the Jews in Jerusalem if they surrender to the Jihad Moquades of the Mufti. They are everywhere along the road from Hebron."

■　■　■　■

Muhammed Said Haj Amin el-Husseini, Grand Mufti of Jerusalem, progenitor of countless riots and self-proclaimed champion of the rights of Palestinian Arabs, glared at his companion with undisguised irritation. *"Holding* Musrara? An Arab neighborhood? It is not my will that we *hold* anything," he scolded. "It was my express directive that our forces *seize* Jerusalem's strongpoints as soon as the British withdrew." Blue eyes blazing, the Mufti rounded on his aide, Ahmed Shukairy. "Was I not clear in this?"

"Indeed, Haj," Shukairy replied. "But the English moved their soldiers a day sooner than expected. And then the Zionists . . ."

"Allah, give me patience," Haj Amin prayed to the crystal chandelier of his hotel suite in Damascus. "I am surrounded by incompetence. All right, tell me the news." As soon as he gave this order, the Mufti swirled his robe around his small, thin form and darted with a flurry of delicate steps toward the adjoining salon.

Shukairy, who knew his chief's habits well, was prepared for the transition and hurried alongside. "We have completed the conquest of the Jewish settlement of Kfar Etzion," the aide offered, hoping to improve the Mufti's mood with a bit of positive news. "The revenge for our people killed at Deir Yassin is complete. One hundred fifty Jews are no more."

"A small kibbutz nine miles south of Jerusalem." Haj Amin snorted, oblivious to the catalog of the slaughtered. That fifty of the casualties had surrendered before being massacred was of no consequence either. "More news?"

Hastily shuffling a stack of cables, Shukairy read, "Our troops have captured the Hospice of Notre Dame de France."

Straightening the folds of the bulletproof vest personally given him by the Führer, Adolf Hitler, Haj Amin observed, "The most strategic location on the northwest of the Old City. It is well. More? What of the Allenby barracks?"

"We had them in our possession," Shukairy noted, "but were driven out by an artillery barrage."

The Mufti rounded savagely on his assistant. "Cable my cousin and Captain al-Malik: The barracks will be retaken without delay and all objectives seized as fast as possible in order to keep pace with the other successful assaults. Also, put that statement out on the radio. Say again that our goal is the elimination of the Jewish state, a conclusion expected at any moment."

"To frighten the Zionists into surrendering?" Shukairy guessed.

"To keep King Abdullah from interfering," Haj Amin exploded. "There must be no question of our immediate and total success in the Holy City. Abdullah may be king of Jordan, but Jerusalem is mine! Go!"

■　■　■　■

In his hilltop palace overlooking Amman, Jordan, King Abdullah squinted down at his chessboard and announced with a soft note of satisfaction, "Check and mate."

His prime minister, Tewfic Abou Hoda, who had seen the inevitable approaching for the past three moves, tipped over his king in concession. "Congratulations, Your Majesty," he said.

Abdullah sighed. "Would that the affairs of the world could be settled as pleasantly, eh, Sir John?"

The wishful remark was addressed to the other occupant of the room, the commander of Abdullah's Arab Legion, known to his troops as Glubb Pasha. The Englishman was seated on a low cushion on the floor. Though Abdullah was no stickler for ceremony, Glubb's British sense of propriety made him keep his head lower than the king's—a feat not easily accomplished with the diminutive monarch. "Indeed, Your Majesty. You tried to be reasonable and conciliatory and did your best to prevent this war from starting."

The three men sitting on the spot where Abdullah had once lived in a tent knew what was meant. The king, alone among Arab rulers, was not opposed to a Jewish state in Palestine. He had even met secretly with Golda Meir of the Jewish Agency in the hope of averting war, urging the Zionist leaders to postpone the call for statehood. Abdullah made no secret of the fact that he despised the dissolute King Farouk of Egypt and Farouk's protégé, the ambitious Grand Mufti, Haj Amin el-Husseini.

Abdullah was not without ambition himself. The Hashemite family had lost much of its former glory to the Saudis, and Abdullah longed to be recognized as a leader in the Arab world. When the United Nations voted to partition Palestine into Jewish and Arab states, the king's desire was to annex the Arab portion to his own principality of Transjordan. More to the point, Abdullah had the forces to make good his claim: the ten-thousand-man Legion was the best equipped and best trained of all the Arab armies, it was based closest to the heart of Palestine, and it possessed a striking force of armored cars, troop carriers, and twenty-five-pound field artillery pieces that stretched several miles in length.

Those forces had been unleashed. The Arab Legion was already across the Jordan River to both the north and south of Jerusalem.

"Tell me again how you read the British reaction to our thrust into Palestine," the king asked Glubb Pasha.

"The British government much prefers you to the Mufti, sire. They have not forgotten how cozy he was with the Führer. They will not protest against any conquest . . . even to Tel Aviv and the seacoast, provided . . ."

"Provided we stay out of Jerusalem," Abdullah concluded, stroking his mustache and short, pointed beard. The agreement that supplied Transjordan with British advisors and British weaponry hinged on one significant proviso: the Holy City, sacred to three faiths, was, by U.N. resolution, to remain an international city, not part of a Jewish nation or any Arab state. Glubb Pasha's reassurance on this point allowed the withdrawing British to deliver ammunition secretly to the Legion—millions of rifle rounds and thousands of artillery shells—instead of dumping it into the sea.

"We will abide by our promise," Abdullah said. "The Holy City should remain a place of peace."

■　■　■　■

Shhh-kuh . . . shhh-kuh. . . . For thirty minutes Daniel lay weeping quietly as he listened to the rhythmic scraping of the beggar's spade against the sand of the wadi. *Shhh-kuh . . . shhh-kuh . . . shhh-kuh . . .*

The grave was not very deep or wide. It took less time to dig than it would take Daniel to turn the soil in one row of a tiny garden plot.

Such a common sound: the sound of a spade cutting the earth, preparing the ground for planting, for new life. It was May. Time for sowing. Daniel had grown to love the tilling of the soil. There was something about the daily monotony of work in the kibbutz fields that had begun to heal the wounds of loss. He had believed!

The shovel fell silent. Daniel heard the old man drag the body to the grave, heard the thump as she was rolled into it, then the splash of gravel falling over her like petrified rain. Daniel bit his hand to keep from crying out. He tried to pray, but there were no prayers large enough to contain his grief. *Hear, O Israel.*

He composed a jumbled eulogy.

We commit to God ... to the earth of Zion ... Suzannah Caan. A pretty girl. Fourteen years old last week. Daughter of Joseph and Isabelle Caan, who died with everyone else in the family in Treblinka. Dust to ashes ... all ashes. Mama. Papa. Four brothers. Two sisters. My family. My family! Survived by ... there is only one who survived ... brother ... me ... coward ... hiding in a cave while she was raped.

Oh, God! Why ... why didn't I die? Why didn't I fight for her? Oh, God! There is none left but me.

Here lies Suzannah. She liked to sing. Her hands were like Mama's hands. I liked to look at them sometimes and think of Mama. Her hair was brown. Eyes brown. Like Papa. Mama's chin, though. She smiled a lot. She was smart and ... everyone liked her ... the other kids liked her ... they are dead too ... except me. We sang together. Will I ever sing again?

What was it? The words ... and their swords shall be beaten into plowshares!

When? When? Oh, God! What harvest can come from such a planting as this? Suzannah. You were all I had left. Papa said I should take care of you. Live! he commanded! Live for us who die too young! Suzannah! Die too young? You never had a chance to live! Suzannah! Papa did not mean you should die and I should be left alone to live!

Swords ... plowshares. Shovels. Pruning hooks.

Mama said that in Eretz-Israel we could till the land and have plenty to eat. You would never be hungry again, Mama said. Take her home to Zion, she commanded. Suzannah is your baby sister, she said . . . in Zion . . . plant cabbages and live! They will not kill Jews in Zion, she said . . . it is our home forever. Nowhere else in the world, you see? Oh, God! Are You mocking us? Why do they kill us here? You promised. Is this a kind of terrible joke? Did You see what they did to her? Where were You, God? Suzannah! They did not tell us when we came that we would one day plant one another in the sand.

Abruptly the sounds of the burial ceased. Daniel lay blinking into the darkness. Had this thing happened? Could it be real? Or was he locked in an endless nightmare? No, no. It could not be real. He would awaken. Such a thing could not have happened.

The nightbird sang from the brush. The instructions of the old man returned vividly to his mind. *I am already awake! Jerusalem!*

The bird trilled for the third time as Daniel emerged from his hiding place in the wadi. A dry, warm wind stirred the sage, sending the sharp scent of high-desert pollen through the air. Daniel made no effort to conceal himself. He looked up at the stars in amazement. So many. So bright. Still there? Why had they not fallen? How could they shine as if it were last night when everyone was still alive?

Jerusalem!

Suzannah's grave was there, steps to his right. He wanted to fall on it and call the Jihad Moquades to come kill him, too. *Mama! I'm sorry. So sorry. They kill Jews here, too. I don't know why they killed her. I didn't take good enough care of her! Papa! Must I live now for her as well? For all of you? Oh, God!*

He turned his back on it and stumbled up the wadi toward the north.

■　■　■　■

"King David to Gideon," the radio in the cubbyhole off the Hurva soup kitchen blared. "Come in, Gideon, acknowledge, over."

Keying the microphone of the wireless, Dov's wife, Yehudit Avram, said, "Gideon here. Go ahead, King David."

Prior to Moshe's arrival with the radio, the only communication between the Old City and the rest of Jewish Jerusalem was the telephone in Rabbi Akiva's house. Since the mayor denied the use of his phone to his political opponents, it was of no use to Moshe and the Haganah.

"Is Moshe Sachar available? Over."

Moshe was located and brought to the radio. When he identified himself, he discovered the other speaker was his close friend Major Luke Thomas. "What is the situation there?" Thomas asked.

Quickly Moshe outlined the status of the Quarter.

Luke Thomas accepted the report, then queried, "Can you speak privately, Moshe? Over."

Looking around, Moshe noted the women cutting up onions for soup, the boys laboriously cranking the handles of grain mills, and the phalanx of dishwashers. All had stopped everything they were doing at the first crackle of static from the radio and were eyeing the speaker expectantly. "Afraid you don't understand the situation here, over," Moshe said, "but go ahead."

"Bad news, I'm afraid. Kfar Etzion has fallen to the Irregulars."

Every face in the room grew solemn. Everyone knew of the kibbutz south of Jerusalem. "How many dead?" Moshe asked. He and the rest stared at the radio. Only hissing came from it. "How many . . ."

"All of them," Luke Thomas's voice said. The words crackled, but the poor reception did not disguise the emotion behind the message. "We think . . . no survivors. A massacre, carried out by Ahkmed al-Malik. Prepare yourselves for the worst, and . . . prepare yourselves for the worst."

"Got it," Moshe said grimly. "No surrender. Over and out."

■   ■   ■   ■

When Lori finally awakened, it was dark. Rachel Sachar sat beside her.

Lori's thoughts were a jumble of images. *Air-raid sirens blaring across London. People running for shelter in the Camden Town tube station. Rubble-filled streets and smoldering ruins. The cries of the trapped and dying beneath the wreckage! God! Help me! God! God!*

"Are you all right?" Rachel asked.

Lori jerked away from her and sat up, rubbing her eyes as if to brush away the memories. "Tel Aviv," she said flatly, remembering. "How many?"

"One hundred and six casualties."

Rachel did not break down the dead and wounded, the number of children and the number of adults. Lori did not want to know. They had been on the ship with her, all of them. Every day she had overheard their giddy conversations, had watched the children as their mothers told them stories about the Promised Land. Prophets and kings. Milk and honey. Bread and eggs. Strudel and blintzes. As if Father Christmas would be at the dock to greet them. *The hope they had for this day! Now this!*

"I fell asleep," Lori said.

"It is good you can sleep."

"A trick I learned during the Blitz. Sleep when you can, where you can." Then in amazement she whispered, "Spitfires."

"The Egyptian air force flies war-surplus British planes. Our people are bringing more German ME-109s here. Flying from Czechoslovakia. Any day. Any day they are coming. Then what happened in Tel Aviv cannot . . ."

"I'll remember that." Then she recalled Rachel's shoving her to the ground. "Thanks for knocking me down before anything else did."

"I tried to stay in Tel Aviv. I have a baby girl there. They said . . . with so many hurt . . . every able-bodied person is needed in Jerusalem." Rachel was rambling, as though the attack had left her unable to focus.

"I have to find my husband when we get there," Lori said. "I have to tell him . . . something." She pictured him laying his head in her lap, smiling up at her. Suddenly she knew she needed and wanted him in her life. *I love you, Jacob! I've always loved you!*

"Your husband was recruited for Jerusalem?"

"Recruited? I would have called it shanghaied. Kidnapped."

"My husband also is in Jerusalem. In the Old City. With my grandfather and brother. My grandfather is a rabbi there and . . ."

For Lori, the strain of the past eight hours exploded. "A baby in Tel Aviv. A grandfather and a brother. You know where your husband is. Most of the rest of us, you know . . . I would have stayed in London for the rest of my life if my husband had not wanted to come here. The bombing is finished there, and I lived through it. He's a Zionist, and I'm . . . nothing. England would have given me citizenship. I earned it. But Jacob . . . Eight years of marriage, and we've had three months together. A few hours of heavy breathing beneath the tarp of a lifeboat on a ship of fools before you people recruited him. I'm not here because I want to be. I told him. Told him if he left me now . . . So if you don't mind . . ."

Rachel observed her for a moment. "It has been hard for you."

Lori looked away angrily and muttered, "Bloody right, honey . . . thanks to the German Luftwaffe. Not one bomb fell in Jerusalem during the entire war, I hear. A couple of Arab riots. But now it's caught up with you."

At this, sadness crossed Rachel's face, and she stared openly at Lori.

"What are you looking at?" Lori demanded.

"You speak English quite well."

"Bloody well, thanks. Learned that on the Fire Brigade too." She began to mimic the Cockney accent of her

71

coworkers. "Cor blimey, luv! Fetch us a stretcher, dearie! This 'un's dead and the toff's bloody leg is blown off!"

Lori smiled bitterly. "How's that?"

"We have all seen too much."

"There's more to be seen."

"It will not last forever."

Lori cursed under her breath. "It never ends."

Rachel replied, "You will find peace one day."

"Not bloody likely," Lori emphasized, enjoying shocking this too-kosher sabra, who had probably never set foot out of a synagogue's shadow until now.

Rachel raised an eyebrow, studying Lori like a schoolmaster measuring an obnoxious child. "You will feel at home, at least. Our soldiers swear in seven or eight languages."

"English is fine with me."

"You can instruct them."

"Right."

The bus roared impatiently as it crawled forward on the rutted road. A British armored car, marked with a hastily painted Star of David, moved alongside, slowed, then shot ahead into the darkness. The whine of gears accompanied the steep climb of the highway.

"Where are we?" Lori asked after a time.

"The pass of Bab el Wad. Tonight our men hold Latrun overlooking the gorge. Tomorrow . . ."

"Tomorrow what?"

"This is our only supply route from the west into Jerusalem. Without this road Jewish Jerusalem will be cut off."

"What about the east?"

"East of Jerusalem is the Jordan River. Across the

72

Jordan are ten thousand Jordanian troops equipped with English arms and led by an Englishman, Sir John Glubb. In Jerusalem are the troops of the Mufti. All of them want to take back a piece of Jerusalem stone as a souvenir. So says Ben-Gurion."

"North?"

"Syria. Iraq. Others."

"South?"

"Egypt. They've hired fighter pilots from the German Luftwaffe and a few English pilots from the RAF. Flying British Spitfires."

"Tell me this: is anyone fighting for this place actually from here?"

"Some," Rachel answered. "But everyone would like to be. Except you, of course."

■   ■   ■   ■

His feet stumbling on the loose stones of the dry creek bed, Daniel paused once more to listen. He heard no voices and no sounds of pursuit, but the night pulsed with an arrhythmic thumping—*crump . . . barooom*—like distant thunder resonating over the Judean hills.

It was not thunder, Daniel knew, but shellfire; mortars and artillery pieces of the Arabs spattering jagged shards of metal on more Jewish settlers.

The vibrations drew him onward.

Staggering in and out of wadis that promised north and then promptly turned west, following the barest traces of goat trails that maddeningly disappeared into impenetrable thorns, Daniel kept on course toward Jerusalem by the crash of the guns.

Kfar Etzion was called the rampart of Jerusalem, outpost of the Holy City, first line of defense of Yerushalayim. Well, the first wall was breached, the outer defense shattered. The Haganah troops needed to be told that the rampart was down and that no mercy existed for the defeated. This was no ball game in which the vanquished were congratulated on their losing effort. Surrender meant destruction. Did anyone else in Israel understand? They must!

It was this vague but keenly felt sense of purpose that drove Daniel on through the dismal night. That the Arab weapons were between him and Jerusalem seemed no irony. He marched to the sound of the cannonfire to deliver one message: No surrender!

A rock turned under his foot, spilling his ankle sideways with a wrench and dumping Daniel over the lip of a drop into an unseen crevice. Branches tore at his face as he fell, and he landed on a boulder that bruised his side and stole his breath.

The clatter of his fall coincided with other noises: the flap of sandals on uneven shale and the rustle of leather cartridge belts against coarse robes. Jihad Moquades.

The group of Arabs following an intersecting watercourse had no fear of discovery or ambush. They owned the desert and ruled the night. Let pitiful Jews huddle in armed camps. They, the valiant Irregular forces of the Grand Mufti of Jerusalem, would soon root them out and destroy them.

"Hurry!" an eager young voice urged. "Captain al-Malik wants us on the Mount of Olives before daybreak."

Daniel pressed his elbow into his injured side, as if

74

keeping the pain constant would somehow stop him from crying out.

Another Arab retorted derisively, "It is all well for the great captain! He rides in a motor vehicle on the Hebron highway while we must skulk through the canyons. We will get there soon enough, never fear."

"We should not have stopped to take the curtains from the Jewish synagogue," the younger voice complained again.

The debate and the slapping sandals passed Daniel's hiding place without a pause.

"Curtains!" the older retorted. "I have a fine silver candlestick for my day's service. How else are we to be paid?"

The words grew less and less distinct as the file of Arabs rounded a curve of the hillside.

"At least we should not have taken the spoil home to our village before setting out again," the anxious soldier protested.

"There will be plenty of Jews to kill," Daniel heard, the faint words blown back like a two-thousand-year-old echo.

Crump . . . barooom. The shelling continued. It was a good sign, Daniel knew. When the guns ceased firing, it could only mean the Jews had been overwhelmed and the Arabs were victorious.

Reaching upward, Daniel grasped the spiny base of a seven-branched sage. The spicy smell and the thorns combined to rouse him and help him overcome the pain in his ribs.

Crump . . . baroom.

On toward Jerusalem once more.

■ ■ ■ ■ CHAPTER 6 ■ ■ ■ ■

T he sky above the Jewish district was frosted with stars. The night seemed unnaturally peaceful. It was the first Sabbath of the revived nation of Israel. A night to remember.

Dov Avram said quietly, "They will attack tonight because it is *Shabbes.* They will not think we will defend ourselves, *nu?*"

A handful of defenders manned the sandbag barricade that marked the boundary between the Jewish Quarter and the Armenian Quarter. Among them was a young woman.

Yehudit Avram had promised to take up arms when the English were gone, so Dov trained her with the other Hasidic recruits gleaned from the Torah schools of the district. For weeks they practiced loading and shooting without bullets. Targets nailed to the wall of the basement of Nissan Bek Synagogue were named Mufti Haj Amin and King Farouk. Until tonight Yehudit, like the majority of the other Old City volunteers, never possessed a real cartridge, but she was ready. Moshe Sachar had returned with ammunition, hope, and promises of deliverance from the outside. The Haganah High Command would not have sent him had they not intended to break through, would they?

While new resolve emboldened every heart, however, Kfar Etzion was on every mind.

Dov and Ehud Schiff, a Romanian Jew who had hazarded his life and freedom again and again to shepherd illegal immigrants, including Rachel Sachar, to Eretz-Israel on his fishing boat, stared out into the dusky, crooked street as if it were the floodgate of a dam about to open. Nervous fingers poised on triggers as they waited for the inevitable.

"Make every bullet count," Dov whispered, remembering Warsaw, when his comrades had hurled rocks and homemade gasoline bombs at Nazi panzers. Dov comforted himself that the enemy beyond the Jewish barricades was not as formidable as the Nazis had been. Calling the action against the Warsaw ghetto *Einkesselung,* "encirclement," the Germans had created what the Jews called *kesl,* a cauldron of fire and smoke that consumed partisan forces. Even so it had taken a month for the ghetto to fall.

Tonight, across the barriers that ringed the Jewish Quarter, Dov knew the leaders of the forces they opposed had been trained in terrorism by the Nazis during the war. As for the rabble who followed them, they were the spiritual brothers of those Germans who pledged to annihilate the Jews forever from the face of the earth.

As David Ben-Gurion had proclaimed the State of Israel, the Muslim troops in the British Mandate donned their shrouds and made a pledge to Allah and his prophet that they would give their lives to defeat Israel. To die while killing Jews conferred eternal blessings and matchless honor upon the souls of the faithful. The war against the Jews was a holy war—a *jihad*—which could not end until the last Jewish baby had its brains dashed out against the Wailing Wall. *Insh' Allah!*

■ ■ ■ ■

The long convoy moved toward Jerusalem yard by yard.

Peering through the slit windows of the armor sheathing, Lori could vaguely make out the charred hulks of Jewish vehicles that had not survived the gauntlet. The walls of the gorge rose up in a V from the constricted road. There could be no return to the coast. The Haganah retained a tenuous grip on the post of Kastel, at the top of the mountain that guarded the highway. It had already changed hands from Arab to Jew and back again numerous times. Each time the Zionists managed to hold out long enough to gain a bit of relief for the besieged Jewish sector of Jerusalem.

Tonight the rumble of trucks jarred rocks loose to tumble down the ravines and strike the sides of the vehicles with reports like explosions. With every blow, Lori jerked upright, thinking they were under attack.

There was no sleeping through the long night. She was aware the thunder of the convoy could be heard for miles. While Jewish defenders found hope in the sound, the Jihad Moquades plotted their destruction.

Folding her arms across her chest, Lori studied the shadowed forms of her fellow passengers. Each woman carried a story of terror and loss. Had they survived so much and come so far only to die in a ditch at the side of this road? Ten years and a war had taught her that such a thing was indeed possible. Happily-ever-after was the exception, not the rule. Again and again she had seen family, friends, and strangers come to similar ends. While fleeing Germany, a desperate woman had flung her baby into Alfie Halder's arms. And Alfie, true to his caring nature, had brought Lori the child, giving up his place on the boat to save the infant. So she had rescued the newborn

78

from the Nazis, only to lose him to a German bomb in England. She had ceased believing in a God who took a personal interest in her or heard her prayers.

As the hours passed she remembered the white Georgian house across from Regent's Park in London where she had lived with her mother, Helen Ibsen, and the baby, named Alfie after his gentle-spirited benefactor. When she left it to go to the market in Primrose Hill Village, their home had been filled with life and beauty. Returning thirty minutes later, she found a heap of smoldering ruins in its place. A stick of German bombs aimed at Regent's canal had hit first the church, then a string of townhouses along the road. The third bomb made a direct hit on her family's building. Into the night Lori had wept, prayed, and waited, hoping somehow they had survived. They found the body of her mother first. The lifeless form of baby Alfie was removed from the wreckage six hours later.

If I had been with them . . . to die with them. To die believing life was going to be good again someday! To believe God was there.

Like the house on Prince Albert Road, Lori's life was gutted. Bitterness flooded into the space where hope once thrived. The innocent belief that God was merciful or interested in the fate of good people died in Lori that day.

And was not six million dead in the camps further proof? How many prayers had been raised to the unfeeling skies? How many mothers had carried their babies to meet death?

Lori was certain each woman on this journey had suffered enough for a hundred lifetimes and yet they had come here, once again hoping. Lori had come simply because Jacob was all she had left of her life—the war had taken everything else. When she found him again, Jacob had optimism enough for both of them. She remembered their conversation . . .

"Come with me to Palestine."

"London is my home."

"We will build a new life."

"How long will it last?"

"We will be happy. . . ."

"Until something happens. And it will happen, you know."

"We will have children. . . ."

"Love a child again? When I could lose him? How can I?"

The clank of rocks against the roof of the bus startled Lori from her reverie. The bus moaned, jolted forward, and stopped. The driver, his features indistinctly seen by the faint glow from the instrument panel, peered forward through his slit window. "Why are we stopping here?" he muttered. "This is not a safe place."

By crouching and squinting, Lori could see out the side. The shine from a half-moon revealed a wide gravel shoulder and then a rim that fell away steeply into a canyon. She easily agreed this was not a safe place.

From overhead came the clank of metal on metal and then a rattle as something spun off the roof of the bus. The noise was not even as frightening as the rattling rocks and yet Rachel Sachar bolted awake and grabbed Lori's arm. "Down!" she shouted. "Everyone get on the floor! Grenade!"

An instant later there was an earsplitting roar from just

outside, and a flash of flame illuminated the interior of the transport even through the slits. The bus rocked up and down on its axles from the concussion.

A piece of shrapnel whirred through a gap in the armor and spiked itself into the metal beside the window where Lori's head had been seconds before.

The passengers screamed. Women who had reacted too late to the warning to reach the floor were thrown over seatbacks or on top of one another. Rachel and Lori were intertwined in a tangle of arms and legs.

A second explosion succeeded the first, farther back in the convoy. Then a hail of rifle fire increased the din as shots pinged off the plating. "Drive!" Rachel shouted to Golden. "Move us before they close in!"

The driver did not speak. When he tugged on the gearshift lever, the transmission ground but did not engage.

"Move us out of here!"

A supply truck in front of them took a direct hit from a grenade, lifting partway off the ground and bursting into flames. The driver bailed out one side and the guards the other, only to be cut down by gunfire.

"Go around!" Rachel ordered. "Drive around it!"

With a final crash, the protesting gears meshed, and the bus lumbered forward past a rocky pinnacle. The passengers cheered.

"Keep down," Lori heard herself say in an unnaturally calm voice. "Stay low! This isn't over yet."

More bullets rang against the armor, and then the sound changed as a Jihad Moquade above them fired down into the unarmored roof.

A woman in the seat in front of Lori struggled upright. "My glasses," she said. "I've lost my . . ."

There was the sound of a hammer blow overhead accompanied by the screech of metal as a bullet ripped through the roof. The woman searching for her spectacles threw up her arms and said, "Ohhh," then folded over.

Lori yanked a babbling, panic-stricken passenger out of the way to reach the wounded woman. "Hold on," she encouraged. "I'll help you. Just hold . . ."

The flames from the transport truck flared up, brightening the interior of the coach again. The woman beside Lori was dead. The bullet had struck her between collarbone and shoulder and traveled straight down. On the floor by her right shoe were her spectacles.

From the hillside above the gorge came renewed gunfire, this time the short buzz-saw bursts of Sten guns. The bus continued rumbling forward, around one curve, another, and a third. Then it idled to a halt again.

The passengers wailed, "Why are we stopping? Is it another attack?" Several of them curled under the seats, sobbing.

"It's Haganah!" Golden called with relief.

"You'll be all right now!" was shouted in Hebrew from outside. "Our patrol caught the Moquades and drove them off. Is there any ammunition on this convoy?"

"Six or seven back in the line."

The Jewish soldier thumped his thanks on the side of the bus and ran away.

"Why don't they do a better job guarding the road?" Lori stormed. "They must be more prepared for the next line of buses!"

"With the Syrian army comin'?" the driver said, clashing the gears again. "By tomorrow they may all be prisoners . . . or dead."

■　　■　　■　　■

Rabbi Akiva sat at his walnut desk and contemplated the black telephone that occupied the center of the ink-stained blotter. The arch of its handle resembled a camel's back, a thought that had recurred to Akiva so many times that thinking of it again irritated him. Even though he was certain he was alone—his aged crone of a housekeeper had gone to bed in the basement hours earlier—Akiva was reluctant to pick up the receiver.

He knew what he was going to do, had no doubt he was correct, and yet he hesitated. The step he was about to take was irrevocable.

He picked up the phone.

As the other party's phone rang, Akiva drummed his pudgy fingers on the desktop. Finally: "Yes, what is it?" said a voice Akiva recognized as Taj Khalidi, a prominent member of the Muslim Arab community in Jerusalem, a merchant and a politician, not a warrior.

"*Salaam,*" Akiva said, using the Arabic word for "peace." "I must speak with you. You know I have done my best to keep the peace and to resist the fanatics. We have always remained friends, you and I."

Without any trace of emotion Khalidi said, "And now?"

"That Haganah leader . . . the one the British removed from the Old City . . . he is back."

"Sachar?"

Akiva nodded gravely at the telephone. "The same. He is rallying the Quarter. Even a few of my own people are swayed by his words. And he brought more men, bullets, and a wireless. I need help in dealing with him."

There was a long silence on the line, then Akiva heard, "We will get back to you. Always remember, we are men of *shalom,* you and I. We are bound to do what we can."

Hurriedly Akiva added, "There is one more thing. The Quarter is swirling with stories about Kfar Etzion. Do you know anything about it?"

This time there was no hesitation before the reply. "Of course. The kibbutz you name fell in a matter of minutes, showing the futility of resistance."

"They say . . . a massacre?"

"Lies!" Khalidi's voice exploded. "Zionist propaganda! Seeing that they were surrounded, and having been abandoned by the treacherous Haganah, the farmers surrendered peaceably and were given safe passage to Jordan . . . after their wounded were tended, of course."

Akiva nodded at the phone again. "I knew that was the way of it," he said, his relief pathetically obvious. "It is another trick to stir up the people."

Oozing sympathy for the beleaguered mayor, Khalidi said, "I will see what can be done to help you, my friend. But it is late. Remember: peace at any cost. We will speak again soon."

■　■　■　■

Taj Khalidi put down the receiver. Picking up a glass of coffee from a silver tray, he placed a sugar cube between his teeth and sucked the thick brew through it. Khalidi spent a moment composing his next message to the Arab command at the Rawdah School. He would report that the Jewish Quarter had received a last reinforcement of men and ammunition but apparently no more machine guns or mortars or food.

It sounded as if the Quarter was wavering on the edge of capitulation. Curse the luck that returned that Sachar fellow and his encouragement. It would help matters if he were dealt with promptly.

■　■　■　■

Dov Avram and Ehud Schiff had done well commanding and holding the Jewish Quarter of the Old City in the last weeks of the Mandate, Moshe thought. He made his way from barricade to lookout along the perimeter of the Quarter. The most impressive Haganah lookout was at the top of the spire of the Armenian Church of St. Jacques.

As civilians and clerics had fled from the Christian and Armenian neighborhoods within the walls, Dov had organized the Jewish advance house by house, structure by structure, until the defensive borders had been pushed as far as the massive twelfth-century, Crusader-built church on the verge of the Armenian Quarter west of the Jewish district. Its tower overlooked the streets beyond, as well as Zion Gate. Possession of this bastion was a miracle of good fortune.

To the Armenians, who claimed to have first entered Jerusalem with the Roman conquerors in A.D. 70, the structure was the center of their worship. It was the traditional site for the beheading of the apostle St. James the Greater in A.D. 44. The head of the martyr was said to be entombed there, along with the body of St. James the Lesser.

The two priests who remained behind to tend the flames of the lamps viewed the Haganah defenders with a smoldering resentment. But for Moshe, tonight, the edifice built to honor the martyrs was the fortress that might save the Jewish Quarter from martyrdom.

The sign above the door, COUVENT ARMENIEN JACQUES, was already punctuated with bullet holes.

Moshe entered the dimly lit interior of the cathedral, mindful of the eyes of painted saints and martyrs following his progress. Twenty-four defenders manned the fortress. Some were sleeping, while the others stood watch.

The church was built in the shape of a cross. Its interior was ornate, rich with blue and green glazed tiles, mother-of-pearl inlaid doors, and thick Persian carpets. The air resonated with the scent of centuries of incense and smoke from oil lamps. Within the compound were a school, a seminary, and a library containing four thousand priceless manuscripts. Though the Armenian Patriarch had left the Old City, his cries of protest against the defensive use of the enclave were reported in newspapers as powerful as *The London Times.*

Moshe encouraged the sentries, then climbed the cramped spiral steps of the tower that opened at the top with a vista of Jerusalem beyond the Old City wall.

Two Hasidim, bearded and solemn in their black coats and broad hats, manned the station. One carried an Enfield rifle, the other a Sten gun. The ramparts of Zion Gate were plainly visible to the south. Beyond that, outside the walls,

Moshe could see the dome of the Church of the Dormition on Mount Zion. *If our fellows could capture Mount Zion,* he thought, pondering the impossible, *we would have the Arabs at Zion Gate between a hammer and an anvil!*

"Shabbat shalom," Moshe said.

"It is peaceful," said one, his features indistinguishable. "Nothing happening. Nothing at all tonight. I thought they would come."

The other agreed. "I wish it was day. I am seeing things. A cat. A dog. My bones are jumping out of my skin with every shadow."

"Will they come tonight, Reb Moshe?"

Moshe scanned the silhouettes of the Old City buildings. "They will come when they are ready. And when they think we are not, eh?"

"I am ready. I could not sleep even if Hannah Cohen appeared in a vision with hot milk and a featherbed."

"And I. If we see anything we will shoot. Everyone will know, eh?"

Moshe did not tell them that when the Arabs attacked, there would be no mistake about what it was.

■　■　■　■

His home being within the sights of Arab snipers on the Western Wall, Rabbi Lebowitz had moved to a tiny basement room opposite the Hurva with Yacov and Shaul, the dog. The boy lay sleeping on an iron cot at the foot of the old man's bed. The dog, a tailless, shaggy, mottled thing of gray, black, and tan, had been brother and sister to Yacov for the past three years. A blessing, this mongrel was.

Tonight the stub of a candle guttered on the table where Grandfather placed Rachel's unopened letter. From the early days when Rachel and Yacov's mother had written from Warsaw, the rabbi had learned to savor the anticipation of words upon paper. There were times in the beginning, before the troubles, when he had let a letter from Warsaw wait for days before he opened it. Always there were pictures. Always news of the boys in Torah school. Rachel learning to read Hebrew. The birth of Yacov. Happy news. On and on.

And then it was not happy news any longer.

This white, crisp envelope from his granddaughter was sure to contain good news. Grandfather already knew about the coming baby. This was very good. He would savor it awhile longer before opening the letter and reading the news as though for the first time. *Marzipan for his soul. Blintzes for the heart.* How he cherished the letters.

This would be, he was certain, the last letter he would ever receive. Something about the last of anything. Should he not wait awhile to read?

Yacov sniffed and rolled over. "So, you have not opened it yet?"

"I thought I would wait for you to wake up."

"So open it already. Read," the boy urged in a sleepy voice.

Grandfather tugged his eyebrow and fumbled with the envelope as the boy stared at him. Using a butter knife as a letter opener, he slit the seam carefully. A photograph fell out. *Rachel. Baby Tikvah. Moshe.*

"Like your mother, she writes," Grandfather mumbled to Yacov as he held the image up to the candle. "A picture.

Better almost than words, *nu?*"

The boy studied the old man. "Grandfather," Yacov said at last, "do you think we will ever see Rachel again?"

The question, serious and sincere, startled the rabbi. "Such a question," he replied, frowning.

"I was dreaming . . . Mama . . . they were hurting her again. . . ."

Yacov had dreamed many times since he had come to live in the Old City. Terrible visions of fire and blood. But Yacov had been so young. He could not possibly remember. It was only that the boy had seen the smiling faces of his vanished family in the old photographs and he loved them and longed for them. He knew—everyone knew—what their end had been.

"Just a dream," the old man soothed.

"They . . . are like the Nazis. They want us dead, too."

"Just a dream."

"No. I heard them tonight. *Alihu Itbach al Yahud.* Slaughter the Jews. They shout it in Arabic, not German."

This fact the rabbi could not argue. "It is the same in any language."

"But why? Aren't we like everybody else? When I fall upon the cobbles I bleed like a Muslim boy. I have hands to play like a Christian child. A voice to speak. A belly that is hungry. A heart that beats and loves and hurts some-times. Are we not the same?"

"We are the people of the Covenant. A promise made by the Lord is a promise that is eternal. We Jews were chosen to belong to the eternal God, and so His great enemy, the fallen angel Lucifer, is our enemy."

"But always it is ordinary people who hurt us, *nu?*"

89

"The devil has made an army on earth by deceiving mortal men. Those who would make the Almighty a liar must first make God's promise a lie. But the prophecies are ever true. What is written in the Book is what comes to pass. To make God a liar means destroying the people of His promise. The enemies of the Lord of Hosts may kill some of us or even most of us, but never, never, will all of us be killed. A remnant of Israel will survive to welcome Messiah when He comes home to Jerusalem to rule the earth in righteousness. As long as there is an Israel, it is Satan who is proved the liar. The Word of the Almighty has declared it! *Omaine!*" He sighed. "Do you understand, boy?"

"Sometimes. Sometimes I understand. Sometimes I hate them as much as they hate me."

"Remember, *nu?* God is love. Those who hurt and destroy others by word or deed are children of the Evil One. Satan is called the Father of Lies. Pity them, Yacov, for what they have done to our people. They have jabbed their finger in the apple of God's eye. His memory is long." With that, the rabbi opened his Bible to Jeremiah 31 and began to read:

"The time is coming," declares the LORD, "when I will make a new covenant with the house of Israel . . . I will put My law in their minds and write it on their hearts. I will be their God, and they will be My people . . . Only if these decrees vanish from My sight . . . will the descendants of Israel ever cease to be a nation before Me."

Yacov smiled faintly and lay back on the groaning cot. He tugged the ear of his dog. "When will Messiah come,

Grandfather? How long?"

"Today we have a state, *nu?* After two thousand years of wandering we are home again. And so, though I will not see Messiah this side of the grave, I believe you will, Yacov. He will come soon to Zion. The prophets have foretold that in the last days there will be tribulation for mankind, and then will come Messiah, the King, and the Day of Judgment. It is written that first there will be a land of Israel. And the children of Israel will return to the homeland. One hundred years ago my grandfather would not have believed that it could be true. But here we are. Today that much is fulfilled. The rest may follow in your lifetime."

But now, this is what the LORD says—
He who created you, O Jacob,
He who formed you, O Israel:
"Fear not, for I have redeemed you;
I have summoned you by name; you are Mine.
When you pass through the waters, I will be with you;
and when you pass through the rivers,
they will not sweep over you.
When you walk through the fire, you will not be burned . . .
Do not be afraid, for I am with you;
I will bring your children from the east
and gather you from the west.
I will say to the north, 'Give them up!'
and to the south, 'Do not hold them back.'
Bring My sons from afar
and My daughters from the ends
of the earth."

Prophecy concerning the
return of exiles to the restored
land of Israel, from
Isaiah 43

■ ■ ■ ■ CHAPTER 7 ■ ■ ■ ■

The bus carrying Jacob and Alfie through the night labored up the winding highway. Jacob knew the road connecting the Holy City to the sea was the lifeline of Jerusalem, a throat the enemies of Eretz-Israel were anxious to strangle. Punctuating the route were the hollow remains of trucks firebombed by the Arabs and the scavenged frames of lorries overturned in ditches, mute testimony that the journey was not always uneventful. Still, it was hard to connect these metal cadavers with the loss of human life.

The driver almost perched on the steering wheel as he peered through the slit in the armored windscreen. He betrayed constant agitation, starting at every unexpected bump in the road. Yet, despite his example, the mood of the immigrants was upbeat. Their dockside fears retreated with each passing, undisturbed mile. As displaced persons Jacob and the rest had been moved countless times in scores of buses. This was merely one more such journey, except better because it was a homecoming. Perhaps there was a war somewhere up ahead, but it was not possible for that thought to suppress their delight at being in Israel. At last the long, sometimes aimless-feeling quest was nearly complete.

To Alfie, dozing at his side in the front row of seats, Jacob said, "We're almost there! Jerusalem. Seeing the Holy City is like seeing the face of God."

"We're going to see the face of God?" Alfie asked sleepily. "When?"

"Soon. Around one of these next few bends we'll see it."

The bus creaked over a string of potholes placed to keep the transport bucking like a fractious horse. The driver, fighting the chattering steering wheel, swung wide on the curve to the left, then swooped the vehicle away from the edge of the cliff and back toward the center of the roadway.

Jacob, staring out the forward-looking slit for his first glimpse of Jerusalem, spotted the figure in the roadway before the driver. "Stop!" he yelled. A boy, arms upraised and waving, was directly in the path of the bus.

"A trap!" the operator shouted, pushing the accelerator to the floor.

Jacob lunged for the wheel, jerking it to the side so that the left front tire bounced over a rut and the fender scraped a rocky ledge. When the transport bounded up and down, the engine stalled.

Alfie, awakened fully by the clamor, studied the crumpled form of the boy who had thrown himself away from the careening trajectory of the bus. "He was on the ground," he said. "But now he's getting up again."

"Please!" a weary voice demanded. "I must get to Jerusalem. I have news from Kfar Etzion."

The dim light was enough to show Jacob the slight build of Daniel Caan. His face was bruised and streaked with blood, and he winced with every breath. "I knew you were a Jewish convoy because people on the last bus that passed were singing," he said. "But they would not stop. Take me to Haganah Headquarters at once."

■　■　■　■

Lori tucked the eyeglasses into the pocket of the dead woman, as if it mattered.

The body was wrapped in a canvas tarp and carried

back to a cargo truck. Blood dripped through the wood-plank floor of the vehicle, staining the road to Jerusalem. Tense hours passed until buses and transport trucks once again slowed and came to a halt.

"What is this about?" called a rough-looking woman with a French accent. "Give us guns back here. I am getting nervous."

Lori, her clothes scarlet with blood, felt sick to her stomach.

"We're two miles from Jerusalem," Golden assured his passengers as the column crept forward again. "This much of the road is ours. Take a look!" He gestured through the grime on his constricted view.

In groups of six, the women crowded forward to see the Holy City for the first time. There was laughter and weeping for the joy of it. They had lived to see Jerusalem when many of their number had perished before their eyes.

"Do you want to go forward?" Rachel asked Lori when their turn came.

Perversely, Lori shrugged. Turning her head away, she peeked out the window as the country opened up, revealing the rugged landscape surrounding Jerusalem. Beneath the pastel sky of predawn, wildflowers splashed the hillsides with blue and red and yellow. Involuntarily her mind flashed on the words of Luke 12:27, her father's favorite verse: *Consider how the lilies grow. They do not labor or spin. Yet I tell you, not even Solomon in all his splendor was dressed like one of these.*

The sayings of Jesus had helped Pastor Karl Ibsen when life had become unbearable in Germany. But sacred words had not saved him, Lori thought. *All this . . . Israel . . . it would have meant something to him.*

With an unexpected bend in the road, her perspective shifted toward the east. At that instant the top of the sun exploded into the sky above Jerusalem, reflecting off the golden Dome of the Rock. The crenellated wall of Suleiman encircled a forest of minarets, church towers, and synagogues. The Citadel's stone towers glowed pink in the light of the first full day in the life of the nation of Israel.

Beautiful! It was, Lori thought, every picture she had ever seen as a child. Looking at such a view, she remembered her mother's reading to her the story of Jesus in Luke 13, weeping before he entered the great city just before his death.

O Jerusalem, Jerusalem, you who kill the prophets and stone those sent to you, how often I have longed to gather your children together, as a hen gathers her chicks under her wings, but you were not willing!

She thought of her mother, of the dead passenger, of a thousand others she had pulled from the destruction of London. Inexplicably her throat constricted with emotion. Her eyes brimmed.

"It is breathtaking," Rachel said. "Is it not?" She smiled. "I weep too, when I see it in such a light."

Lori wiped her eyes irritably with the back of her hand and explained away her tears. "I was thinking of my mother. And my father. They always wanted to come here."

"And my mother and father dreamed of living here.

96

Mama tried for visas before the war. But in Warsaw everyone wanted out."

Lori frowned and looked curiously at Rachel. "But I thought you said your grandfather . . . lived in the Old City?"

"And my baby brother, Yacov. He was smuggled into Palestine by the woman who was with me yesterday afternoon, Madame Rose. She sailed with children from France on the brave ships of Dunkirk, to London, then was given my brother to carry. She brought him on to Palestine. A lovely lady, Madame Rose. She helps take care of the immigrants. A Christian lady. Like your husband she was interned by the British in prison on Cyprus for a time. But you see, some made it here during the war. Some after. I arrived six months ago."

"Where were you during the war?"

"I . . . remained . . . in Poland."

Images of living skeletons behind barbed wire and the open door of an oven revealing a grinning skull came to Lori's mind. She was ashamed. "I was rude yesterday."

Rachel arched an eyebrow. "Yes. You were. But we have more to worry about than that, eh?" There was forgiveness in her voice, a determination to be a friend. "We have miracles to pray for, and we must give our prayers hands and feet to do what God requires to create a miracle."

Lori rubbed her hands wearily over her face. No use arguing the credibility of miracles with a Jewess who had survived the war in Poland. "What sort of miracle did you have in mind?"

"Israel is one day old today. Survival is a good start.

Israel is a miracle. What nation in history has been born again after being scattered to the four winds for two thousand years? It was written that it would be so in the latter days of this world. The prophets foretold that a remnant of Israel would return to the land and that the generation who sees this gathering of the remnant will see the Messiah come."

"You believe this?"

"Thus far it is true."

"And if Israel does not survive? If it dies on the road to freedom like that poor woman . . . like too many others . . . ?"

"Then it will not be time for the Messiah to come to us here in Israel, eh? And I will live and die and meet Him somewhere else. There was an old rabbi. Very old. When we were waiting for the trains . . ." Rachel paused, aware she had said more than she intended.

"Go on," Lori encouraged.

"There were about five thousand of us. And we *knew* we were going . . . where none of us wanted to go. He stood up on a bench and held his hand thus." She pantomimed a glass being lifted. " 'Jews,' he said, 'why are you sad? Today we are going to see Messiah! If I had wine, I would drink a toast! *L'Chaim!*' " Her eyes held the cherished vision of the fearless rabbi. "They are with Messiah in heaven. I am called to live awhile, *nu?* So I fight for Jerusalem. I would like it if my children could grow up safe in Israel."

"Many survivors immigrated to America. No war in America. No Muslims fighting a holy war against Jews. I have cousins in America," Lori said, thinking of the bloodstains on the floorboards, the body growing cold in the back of a truck.

"There is no place left on earth where I may be who I am, touch the Western Wall, remember I am born a daughter of Zion, walk where the prophets walked. Where Yeshua walked. Even though it may be Via Dolorosa, *nu?*"

Via Dolorosa. The street where Jesus carried His cross. In the morning light Lori glimpsed the scar on Rachel Sachar's left forearm. What did it mean? *Warsaw. Yes. What camp? Her mother...father, a rabbi.* This young woman already knew what it was to walk the Way of Sorrows.

Rachel continued, her clear cobalt eyes thoughtful, "I have a baby girl in Tel Aviv. The child of my dearest friend, Leah. She and her husband died in Jerusalem. And my husband and I will have another baby in the winter. So, you see, we have no option but to survive." She patted her stomach. "Maybe there will be peace before I have the baby."

That was doubtful, Lori thought as she glanced away at Jerusalem. A plume of smoke billowed up from the one-mile-square confines of the Old City. "No option," she repeated wearily. "I can understand that."

■　■　■　■

Daoud and Gawan gathered round with other boys from the Arab Quarter as a hero of the Jihad and avenger of Deir Yassin displayed the tray.

"Ears! The ears of Jews!" Hassan el-Hassan cried.

Approval trilled among the adolescent crowd.

Daoud said to Gawan, "Who has ever seen such a thing?"

Gawan, wide-eyed, half-sick, said, "It is like the day Houdi impaled the litter of puppies on a stick."

Daoud looked startled. He had not liked seeing the dead puppies skewered by the bully Houdi. In fact, they had fought over it. Although Daoud had received a black eye for his trouble, it had not brought the animals back from the dead. What was the use of arguing? Puppies or Jews. What was done was done.

Daoud asked, "Were they alive when you cut them off?"

Hassan puffed himself up proudly like a lizard claiming a rock for his own. "Some were. They struggled terribly, these Jews. But *Insh' Allah,* I was more powerful than they. You see how many I have collected? Thirty-seven."

"Did you kill them with your own hand?" Daoud asked.

"Of course," Hassan answered.

Another older boy said, "What was your greatest victory?"

"Ah!" Hassan was pleased by the interest. "It was upon the soil of Kfar Etzion! Two brothers, back to back. They had machine guns. They saw me approach and fired, but the bullets did not touch me. Forward I went, up the hill. Allah and his Prophet guarded me. Forward, on and on . . ." And the tale continued, up to the final battle to the death and the slicing off of the infidels' ears.

Gawan, who had seen many Jihad Moquades die of late, did not believe Hassan waded through bullets to fetch Jewish ears. He screwed up his face at Daoud when the soldier finished and invited the boys to touch the ears of their enemies.

"I do not want to," Gawan whispered.

"You must," Daoud urged. "The others will think you are a coward."

Gawan hung back, afraid to touch the cursed things and yet more afraid of being labeled a coward among his comrades.

Daoud strode to the front and put out his hand. Hassan placed one ear on his palm. "This is the ear of the elder brother," said Hassan, placing another in the boy's hand. "There, you see? You can tell I do not lie. Brothers, eh? They are almost identical."

Daoud swallowed hard. He turned to Gawan, involuntarily looking at his brother's ears. Gawan's face was pained, green. He extended his hand to take the things, but Daoud did not give them to him.

Daoud turned back to Hassan. "What will you do with them?" He replaced them on the tray.

The Jihad Moquade asked, "Do? Do? I will keep them on a spike beside my narghilla, and when I sit with my comrades to smoke, we will see them and remember how we destroyed the Jews in Kfar Etzion. Of course, by then I will have many more. By then we also will have destroyed all inside the Jewish Quarter."

The two brothers strode away from the gathering, their heads bent close together. "You see," Gawan said, "it is like the puppies."

"Yes," Daoud agreed, wiping his hand on his trousers.

"I do not like this man even more than Dajani."

"No," Daoud said. "You have to be crazy to serve Allah and the Prophet, they say. This fellow serves

Mohammed well."

■   ■   ■   ■

Looking out a window on the top floor of the King David Hotel, Luke Thomas gestured toward the tower of the Church of St. Jacques within the Old City. "Madness!" he exclaimed to David Shaltiel. "It is utter madness to give up that tower. It is our only post inside the walls that has any height to it. Surrounded by minarets and huddled below the Temple Mount, the Old City defenders are ducks in a barrel, except for that belfry."

"Calm yourself, Major," Shaltiel responded. "This isn't my idea."

"No, but you must make them see differently. That tower is midway between Zion and Jaffa Gates and gives us line-of-sight firing into both."

Shaltiel said sternly, "We *have* to withdraw from there. No more using the church as a military position."

Luke Thomas marshaled his arguments carefully. "When we were fighting our way across Germany with First Army, do you know what part of the villages were always damaged first?" Answering his own query, Thomas continued, "The church steeples. The Nazis used them as machine-gun nests, sniper posts, forward artillery observers. We had to knock them out first, or they would use them to hurt us. We knew it, and they knew it."

"Doesn't matter. This is a direct order from Ben-Gurion to me, and from me to you, and from you to Moshe Sachar."

"And when the Mufti's thugs take it over and shoot into the back of the Hurva Synagogue, what then?"

"Won't happen," Shaltiel said. "The patriarch has given his assurance that the church grounds will remain strictly neutral. No advantage to either side."

■　■　■　■

The radio in Tipat Chalev rattled to life. Ruth Kleingelt, spelling Yehudit at the post, sent one of the kitchen helpers to locate Moshe.

"Moshe," Luke Thomas said, "brace yourself. You have to withdraw your people from the tower of St. Jacques, over."

"What's the joke?" His mind whirling with the implications, Moshe lost his command of radio jargon.

"No joke," Thomas said. "Shaltiel's direct order. It seems that the Armenian Patriarch has complained to the U.N. about the sanctity of the church being violated."

"So?" Moshe said scornfully. "What did the U.N. ever do for us?"

"True, but the Patriarch also got the ear of President Truman. Truman leaned on Ben-Gurion, and there it is. It seems the Holy City is to remain sacred, even in a war."

"Anybody tell the Arabs to stop shelling synagogues?" Moshe muttered. "Do they know it will make opening Zion Gate that much harder?"

"Affirmative," Thomas replied. "Move everyone back to Ararat Road. That is the new defensive perimeter."

■　■　■　■

The face of God!

Alfie Halder studied Daniel Caan's features.

Unmoving in the chair in the lobby of the King David Hotel. Waiting to be seen by someone—anyone—so he could warn them! Blood-streaked face. Matted hair. Torn clothing. Cut hands. Eyes staring straight ahead at pigeonhole mailboxes behind the check-in counter as if a terrible motion picture were playing there and he could see it.

Alfie had seen such expressions before. *Suffering! The eyes of Christ on the burning crucifix when the Nazis took it out of the chapel in the Brandenburg hospital. And then again in the eyes of the patients waiting to die and be burned. It was the beginning of sorrows. 1938. Berlin. The beginning of burning books and burning Christs and burning Jews.*

Standing in the queue leading to the latrine, Alfie did not look away from the young man.

Jacob said in a low voice, "Stop staring, Alfie. He's been to hell, that's plain enough."

The face of God. Suffering. Been to hell. Alfie had first seen such expressions in the eyes of a paralyzed boy in the hospital in Berlin. His name was Werner. Werner could not move anything except his eyes. His eyes were like those of the weary youth sitting there now . . . *lonely. Filled with sorrow.* Alfie had carried Werner to and from the ward. He had fed him when the Nazi orderlies said he should be left to starve. And then when the orderlies began to take the boys away one by one and never bring them back, Werner had been taken and Alfie had escaped. They would have killed Alfie because he was stupid, but he hid in a tomb behind the church and they did not find him. Alfie never forgot the look in Werner's eyes. *Suffering! The face of God!*

"Where are we going?" Alfie asked Jacob. He did not want to leave the ragged young man with the paralyzed soul who grieved alone in his chair beneath the crystal chandelier. He wanted to pick Daniel up and carry him into the garden if there was a garden. He wanted to show his soul that there was sunlight and flowers were blooming somewhere. Just as he used to show Werner in the hospital and the other boys before they were killed.

"We are going to get uniforms," Jacob explained distractedly as the line inched forward. "We are citizens of Israel. We'll get guns, too."

"Guns?"

Jacob cocked an eyebrow at Alfie. "When they ask you what you did in the war, tell them you are strong. Tell them you helped with transporting things, see? Say you can help pack things like ammunition and radios."

"I would like a radio," Alfie agreed.

"Tell them you can carry anything."

"What about him?" Alfie glanced back at Daniel Caan. "What will they do with him?"

"He'll tell them what happened. Then they'll let him sleep. He's been to hell," Jacob repeated.

"Then he'll need to sleep," Alfie responded. Hell was a horrible place. Alfie had been there in Germany, and he knew.

Three officers strode from the corridor. "There he is." One of them pointed to Daniel Caan. Alfie saw Daniel look up sharply. The muscle in his cheek twitched. He would have to repeat to them what happened. They would ask him everything, and he would have to speak aloud of the things that had led him to this place.

A tall man with a handlebar mustache spoke kindly in an English accent. "Daniel Caan?"

"Yes."

He answered to his name as if it were unfamiliar to him. Going to hell changed people, Alfie knew. When they came back, sometimes they were strangers to themselves.

"You escaped Kfar Etzion."

"Yes." *Shame!*

"Commander Shaltiel would like a word with you. Then you can get cleaned up. Eat. Rest."

"I want to fight."

"Yes. Of course."

"Some of the same ones . . . they're in the Old City by now. I heard them talking."

"Will you come this way, please?"

■　■　■　■

His cheeks gravel-scraped and sunburned and his clothing in shreds from hiding in thornbrush, Daniel Caan was hustled across the expansive marble lobby of the King David Hotel and into David Shaltiel's office. The sergeant who delivered him saluted and said, "Here he is, sir. Survivor and lone escapee from Kfar Etzion."

Daniel cringed at the name of the settlement, as the images of the horrors he witnessed threatened to overwhelm him.

"Sit down, lad," Major Luke Thomas said kindly, drawing up a chair. "Water?"

His hands brushing his cracked and blackened lips, Daniel nodded and sat down. "You need to know what happened," he said.

"Take your time," Shaltiel suggested. "About fifty of our people, kibbutzniks and Haganah, have gone into captivity in Amman, Jordan. The Red Cross is seeing to them there. But thus far you are the only one to elude the Arabs and come back to report."

Gratefully accepting a drink of water, Daniel took a long swallow before replying. When he spoke, his words were bitter far beyond what seemed reasonable for a sixteen-year-old: "There won't be any others. The Arabs killed them all." The hand holding the glass shook, and water sloshed out onto the carpet. "Rocky Hill . . . that's our last outpost before the monastery . . . held them till dark. Our men were out of ammo anyway, and they tried to slip back into the kibbutz at night. Some made it. My friend Asher . . ." Daniel stopped. "They didn't just kill him . . . they . . . his face, it . . ."

"What happened the next morning?" Luke Thomas asked, urging Daniel past the memory of the mutilation.

The boy continued. "They shelled us that night, but they didn't attack at dawn, like we expected. We thought maybe there was time, maybe armor would break through from Jerusalem, rescue us. Then about eleven we heard it, the engines. Their armor, rolling down from Lone Tree and Rocky Hill . . . everywhere. And Arabs all around us, coming over the hills. A thousand, two thousand, I don't know."

Daniel's shoulders quivered, and his eyes saw nothing inside the hotel room. "We'd mined the road, but the mortar shells must have cut the wires. Anyway, nothing worked, nothing stopped them. They were inside the fences. A few of us got back to the monastery walls. Their captain, al-Malik, said, 'Jews. Why die when the battle is lost? Surrender and save your lives' . . . save your lives," Daniel repeated faintly. Then his fingers constricted around the chair's arms, and his jaw clenched till a harsh croaking came from his mouth. "No one must ever surrender to them!" he said fiercely. "Never! They machine-gunned some in a ditch and laughed when others pleaded for their lives. My own . . ." His words halted, then he said again, "No one must ever surrender to them. It is better to die taking a few of them with you."

■ ■ ■ ■ CHAPTER 8 ■ ■ ■ ■

T he troop of men into which Alfie and Jacob were mustered gathered in a Quonset hut not far from the Montefiore windmill. The company was commanded by an American named Barney Isaacson. His Brooklyn accent so mangled his English commands that Jacob had difficulty understanding him, and Alfie, whose English was limited at best, kept asking, "What did he say, Jacob?"

The sergeants and corporals of the outfit were mainly kibbutz-born sabras who spoke Hebrew. Fortunately, the bespectacled clerk of the recently constituted Haganah Rifle Brigade, pudgy Sergeant Pincus Chopinski, known as "Pinky," made up for all deficiencies. Because of his fluency in English, French, Yiddish, Hebrew, and his native Polish, he was much in demand.

Captain Isaacson kept threatening to shoot everyone for not moving quickly enough, when he was not muttering about shooting himself and ending his misery. "All right, settle down!" he bellowed, as if volume alone overcame language barriers. "Let's see what we got here."

The officer eyed Alfie's faintly cheerful expression suspiciously. "Is he off in the head? His ladder don't go all the way up?"

"He's fine, sir," Jacob defended stoutly. "He's a good soldier. He's with me."

"So?" Isaacson scowled, studying Jacob Kalner's twice-broken nose and wrestler's build. "Izat s'posed to tell me somethin'?"

"We were trained by the Hayedid, sir, in Warsaw. Captain Samuel Orde."

Isaacson nodded his approval. "I know the name. So does anyone else who ever studied the Haganah manual of military operations. It was written by Orde, God rest his soul."

For all his bullying ways, Isaacson could also be a man of decision. Thrusting out his hand toward Chopinski, he demanded, "Red stripe." When the sergeant produced a swatch of crimson cloth, Isaacson handed it to Jacob. "Here," he ordered. "Sew this on your left shoulder."

"What is it?" Jacob asked.

"You're a corporal of First Squad," Isaacson said. "Spare Parts Platoon. That means you guys go where you're needed and do what you're told, get it?"

Also in the Spare Parts Platoon were an Italian Jew named Mangus Bertolli and Sal Greenberg, a loudmouthed American who had defeated the Nazis single-handedly. Another recruit off the *Joshua Reynolds* was Chaim Alper, who had, like Jacob, spent most of the war in D.P. camps. An outspoken socialist, he claimed to have no religion. The next was a thin, pale, Polish Hasidic Jew named Hymie Slanik, who wore earlocks and had a number tattooed on his forearm. He said little, and what he did say was in Polish.

They were as diverse of shape and size as they were of speech. They had the fledgling nation of Israel in common and not much else.

Alfie raised his hand like a schoolboy. "I will like to carry the radio," he said in broken English.

"Right. Brigade pack mule. You'll carry plenty."

Alfie beamed.

There was a commotion at the rear of the room and not enough military discipline in the rawest Haganah soldiers to prevent heads from swiveling to see what it was.

Daniel Caan, his face scrubbed free of grime, making his sunken eyes, scrapes, and bruises more apparent, entered. He looked even younger than his sixteen years.

Interested comments in seven different languages swept the room. Everyone recognized the sole survivor of Kfar Etzion, and each had a tale of Arab atrocity to connect with the lone witness.

Then Isaacson was speaking again. "This mornin' Israel is . . . somethin' like a naked lady on Brighton Beach with nothin' but a pocket handkerchief to cover up with. So you guys added to the fabric make the kerchief bigger. A little here. A little there. Pretty soon we've got the hot spots covered. Get it? We plan to secure the Old City before the Arab Legion gets here." Stepping back and raising his voice so all two hundred men could hear, he announced, "Raise your hands and repeat after me . . ." And when they complied and took the pledge, he announced, "You are now part of the Army of Israel."

There was no response apart from the shuffling of feet.

"We got one day to learn you enough Hebrew so's you don't shoot each other. But our first job, see, is to get some nuns out of the way of the war. Let's get movin'."

■   ■   ■   ■

Ibrahim Saleh had walked all the way from his native Ethiopia. He had come to Jerusalem, he said in broken English, to fight for the Holy City. "Please," he said politely, "I wish to join the war. Thank you so much."

Saleh was seven feet tall. When he appeared in front of the dumbfounded Haganah recruiter, the officer's response was to reject the giant outright. "In the infantry he'd get his head shot off," the sergeant mused, "and he won't fit inside any of our armored cars. Better he goes back to Ethiopia."

Then Ben-Gurion's directive that no potential recruit should be turned away was circularized, and Ibrahim was duly sworn in as a member of the Jewish Defense Forces. The captain who did the swearing-in had to crane his neck to see if Ibrahim was saluting or not, but Barney Isaacson, to whom the towering black man was assigned, did far more swearing.

"What am I supposed to do with him?" Isaacson demanded after his stock of expletives had been exhausted. "I never seen no one that tall. Can't I chop him in half and make two midget troopers out of him?"

"That's up to you," the Haganah recruiter said cheerfully. "Don't you have other recruits used as supply carriers?"

"Oh, yeah," Isaacson muttered. "Thanks for reminding me."

"Please, sir," Ibrahim asked, "may I get uniform?"

"Yeah, yeah," Isaacson growled, then, glancing downward, he sputtered, "Just shoot me! What are those, flippers?"

"Please?"

"Your paws," Isaacson said, pointing at Ibrahim's bare, size-fifteen feet. "We ain't got any boots that size."

"No matter," the Ethiopian said with a lopsided grin. "I walk good without. From Addis Ababa."

Ibrahim was assigned duty as a porter, carrying duffel bags loaded with forty pounds of ammunition and supplies each up to the Haganah positions.

Also in the line of grunting workers were those too feeble to run with a rifle, those too blind to aim one, and Alfie.

■　　■　　■　　■

As Daoud stole a fistful of dates from a wicker basket, Gawan approached the opposite stall, slipped his hand between two haggling Holy Strugglers, and filched two limes.

During afternoon prayer, as the merchants bowed to Mecca, the brothers gleaned their suppers from the stalls of the souks with a skill rivaling that of the most accomplished thieves in Jerusalem. Along with stolen pita bread and a single kebab of roasted lamb, they carried a jug of tea. To top it off, Gawan had the good fortune to find a partially smoked cigarette protected by the cobbles of the lane. A treasure! A feast!

They settled down in the courtyard of a demolished hotel.

Gawan said, "Dajani is a fool."

"Yes," Daoud agreed. "He will get us killed, I think."

"Then our souls will fly to Paradise, and there we will be attended by . . . seventy cooks who will make us all the lamb *shashlik* we can eat."

"And Najid the baker? The baker will be there. Baking baklava. And strudel like the Jewish woman used to give us when we hauled away her rubbish and cleaned her courtyard garden. Remember the strudel?"

The strudel was something to dream about. Daoud nodded. "She probably cannot bake strudel anymore. They say the Jews are starving. Dajani says it is the will of Allah that the Jews starve inside their Quarter so that when we break through they will not be able to resist when we kill them."

Gawan sighed with disgust. "I tire of Dajani. He would not talk about killing them if he had ever eaten the old lady's strudel."

"Yes, I think he would. I think Dajani would sit in her kitchen, watch her bake it, steal the recipe, and then kill her."

Gawan munched his pita bread thoughtfully. "I think he will get *us* killed and never care that we are dead."

"Yes," Daoud said.

"Maybe we should leave. I do not like this war.

Everyone is crazy here these days. Everyone talks, talks, talks about killing the Jews. It is a dull time to live here. I would like to go to the sea. Jaffa, maybe. The begging would be good in Jaffa."

"Then he would find us and kill us as well. Besides, the Jews have taken Jaffa. Did you not hear?"

"All the better. Then we would not have to listen to this boasting about how many Jews would die tomorrow. *Insh' Allah!*"

Daoud sniffed and wiped his nose on the sleeve of his ragged tunic. "I see what you mean. I wonder what the Jews talk about nowadays?"

"Probably about how much they miss eating strudel."

■　　■　　■　　■

Major Luke Thomas spotted Rachel Sachar out of the corner of his eye as he emerged from the hotel with David Shaltiel. Clipboard in hand, she was conversing with a group of four middle-aged women about to climb into the back of an ambulance that would take them to a makeshift medical clinic to work.

Her long black hair was wet and braided, her trim figure defined even in the men's khaki uniform she wore.

"Stunner," Shaltiel remarked, following Luke's gaze.

"Moshe Sachar's wife," the major said, tugging his mustache in surprise.

"That's her, is it? Heard she was a looker but . . . lucky man. Something to come home to, eh?"

"What's she doing here? Moshe told me . . . I thought she was in Tel Aviv working with the Jewish Agency.

The D.P.s."

"A convoy of women recruits made it in from Tel Aviv an hour ago," Shaltiel explained. "Likely she came in with them." He glanced at his watch. "Listen, I'm late for the meeting with Nachasch. Mount Zion. I'll be back at two." A minute later he roared off in an armored car down Rehov Hamelech David toward the Palmach stronghold.

Thomas hailed Rachel as her charges left in the ambulance. Glancing up through thick lashes, her eyes sparkled. White, even teeth flashed a grin. "*Shalom,* Luke!" she cried, genuinely glad to see him.

He embraced her. "Moshe told me you stayed behind in Tel Aviv. On the Jewish Agency staff. What was it? Assigning arrivals . . . women recruits to the duty roster?"

Rachel explained the circumstances of her unexpected journey to Jerusalem: the bombing, the convoy, her feeling this might be the last opportunity for anyone to travel the road to Jerusalem for a long time to come.

"But you saw Moshe yesterday?" she asked eagerly. "He was well?"

"Airsick. You know he doesn't take to these little Piper Cubs. I personally welcomed him off the plane. Helped him stay on his feet until his stomach settled. Then bribed the sergeant to get him and a handful of others into the British ranks and into the Old City again. Not nearly enough."

"You have heard from him since?"

"Yes. He packed a wireless into the Quarter with him. It'll make a vast improvement in coordinating the attack from this side when the time comes."

"How is it there?" she asked, turning to face the Old

City walls as if she could somehow catch a glimpse of Moshe.

"I won't sugarcoat it, Rachel. The situation in the Jewish Quarter is not good. Ammunition. Manpower. Food supplies. Opposition from Akiva's band. Moshe says if the Quarter falls to the Mufti's Irregulars, the cost would be horrific in human loss. He estimates fifteen hundred civilians. Less than two hundred defenders. As far as the looting and vandalism, the Jihad Moquades could destroy two thousand years of history in an hour." He grimaced, thinking of what the same Muslim forces had done in Kfar Etzion. "So far the assaults from the Mufti's men have been manageable. But since the Suffolk Regiment is on its way home to England, we cannot expect that to last long. Outside the walls of the Old City we are doing everything we can do to break through. New Gate. Jaffa Gate. Zion Gate. The plan is under way."

"Break through," she repeated, then said, "I must be with you when you do. My place is with my husband."

"It will be dangerous. The attack is going to be . . ."

"More dangerous for me than everyone else? The Old City is my home. Grandfather and Yacov. Moshe. You will need medics. You cannot leave me out of this when everyone I love is there, *nu?* I have a right."

"Yes," he said reluctantly, "I suppose if anyone has a right, you do. I'll see what can be done. Medic. But I make no promises, Rachel."

A messenger charged out the portal, calling for Major Luke Thomas. "Sir! There's a transmission from the chaps you sent to the convent! Spare Parts squad? There is a problem. You are wanted urgently!"

·   ·   ·   ·

The two-way radio crackled. Luke Thomas leaned against the doorjamb as a self-conscious voice sputtered over the receiver.

"Come in. This is Jacob Kalner . . . Spare Parts . . . we are at . . . uh . . . the convent." An awkward pause followed as the voice questioned, "What's it called, Chaim?"

Dimly in the background came the reply: "Soeurs Réparatrices."

Jacob continued, "Right. I can't get my tongue around that. The French nunnery. Over."

Relieved at the progress of the squad, Thomas stepped forward and took the microphone. "Spare Parts, this is King David at Notre Dame. Have you secured Soeurs Réparatrices? Over."

"That's what I'm saying," came the exasperated reply. "The Arabs bolted before we got here. But the nuns won't move an inch. They are inside. We are outside. She . . . the Mother . . . says we'll have to shoot them before they'll break their vows. Over."

Thomas frowned and glanced at Barney Isaacson, who said, "We gotta get 'em out of there or no way can we attack New Gate. How many nuns?"

Thomas repeated the question. "How many sisters? Over."

"Thirty. The Mother Superior all by herself makes an army. Over."

Thomas asked, "Any casualties?"

"Only the nuns' cherry trees. And the Mother Superior won't give us the time of day. They're ready to die here. Never mind which side kills them. She says they are neutral. As if anyone is neutral. Says we are not to even *look* at the sisters. Won't talk to anyone unless we get a female over here. They're going to get it in the cross fire once this is under way. Send bullets and women, or we'll lose the war. Over."

Isaacson shrugged and addressed Thomas. "Bullets we can manage. We'll need to reinforce the convent for the attack. Fifty men ought to do it. But what women? Who speaks French? Can we oblige?"

Thomas said, "Rachel Sachar."

"Go get her."

■　■　■　■

"Rachel!" Luke Thomas said, hurrying over to her. There was such urgency in his voice that she was momentarily afraid, frightened for Moshe.

Spotting the flare of terror in her eyes, Thomas hastened to reassure her. "I think I know how we can get you into the Old City, if you are willing to risk it."

"Tell me!" she said.

"The Roman Catholic archbishop is going to take the nuns of Soeurs Réparatrices into the patriarchate office in the Christian Quarter. We will also send along a doctor and you as a nurse."

Her mind racing, Rachel added, "I have a friend, a Gentile, who speaks French and is knowledgeable about wounds. Will they take two nurses?"

"Of course," Thomas said. "Grab your things."

■　■　■　■

One bucket of water for bathing in the women employees' communal lavatory and locker room at the King David Hotel. The fragment of a bar of soap. Clean khaki trousers, shirt, socks, and men's combat boots on her feet, compliments of the British army.

Lori felt like a new woman.

Each member of the Jewish women's brigade was given a mug of coffee, a slice of bread, and a precious orange to gulp down before they were briefed and given assignments.

Rachel Sachar found Lori on a wide stone banister outside the entrance of the hotel. Rachel passed her a slip of paper. The word MEDIC was stamped across it.

It was what Lori expected.

"They have made us a team, you and I," said Rachel. "You are an experienced medic. Me, I know the city. You will need to know the city also. They are mimeographing maps. But there is a better way to learn. Come, I will show you where we are going. We must hurry. Our transport is leaving in thirty minutes."

She led Lori across the street to the enormous YMCA building, which, like the King David Hotel opposite, was firmly in the hands of the Haganah and bustling with military activity.

The tower of the YMCA, built on the crest of a hill overlooking the Old City, was visible from almost anywhere in Jerusalem. In the middle of the tower was the carving of a six-winged seraph, created from Isaiah's vision of the angels in attendance at God's throne. The Scripture from Isaiah, chapter six, was carved into the facade, an ominous warning in the face of the destruction now falling upon the city.

Rachel explained, "The tower was the first thing I saw when I came here. My grandfather told me that if I ever got lost, this hill and the tower of the YMCA was my beacon."

To the east the Valley of Hinnom separated the hill from Mount Zion and the Old City. Smoke spiraled up from an explosion in the Old City and drifted over the valley.

Entering the massive bronze doors, they made their way through the crush of soldiers and messengers in the front lobby to the elevator.

Rachel explained in Hebrew to the attendant, "A medic. She is new to the city and must learn which roads are open."

A slow ride up took them to a short, corkscrew-stepped passage to the top. Three Palmach soldiers stood watch at arched windows guarded by chiseled saints. A Davidka mortar and a radio were protected by sandbags.

Rachel spoke again in Hebrew, which Lori did not understand. The men laughed, bowed, and stepped aside, affording Lori and Rachel a view between Sts. John and James the Elder to the Old City in the east.

"My family is there, within the wall," Rachel said wistfully. "I will be with them when the Haganah breaks through. But you see . . ." She pointed toward Mount Zion and the Church of the Dormition. "The Arabs hold Mount Zion. This blocks our entry through Zion Gate."

Lori suspected that perhaps there was another reason

Rachel had been eager to ascend the tower. Lori said quietly, "It looks so peaceful from here. Hard to believe . . ." The distant concussion of a shell exploding in the east cut her short.

Rachel smiled sadly. She stared anxiously at the horizon, then began again. "On the left are the clock tower of St. Savior and the belfry of the Church of the Redeemer. The Jihad Moquades hold those positions. The Jewish Quarter is in the center of the Old City, between The Dome of the Rock in the back and the Armenian Quarter. Our defenders hold the Church of St. Jacques in the Armenian Quarter. See there? See the belfry? Moshe told me before he left that this outpost is a true blessing. It lets our men see Jaffa Gate and Zion Gate." With a broad sweep of her hand she continued. "There is the minaret in The Citadel. David's Tower, it is called. It guards Jaffa Gate. The Arabs hold that position. Your husband is in a French convent opposite New Gate. Which is one gate farther on the wall."

"You found him?"

"I asked a friend of Moshe's. I tried to get you placed in your husband's unit, but it seems they are part of a mobile force, filling in where they are needed. Currently they are at a convent across from New Gate. A Corporal Jacob Kalner sent a wireless message."

"Corporal!"

"Things happen fast in Israel. They are in need of assistance."

"A medic?"

"A woman who speaks French. And a Gentile. There are thirty nuns who must be evacuated. The sisters will not leave the convent in the company of men. I am going there myself to convince them of the danger. I thought you would want to come, too."

■ ■ ■ ■

Moshe, Ehud, Dov, and Rabbi Vultch leaned over four sides of a map of the Old City. Ehud, whose view was upside down, crowded against Dov so he could see better. Moshe had told them about the order to give up the tower of the Armenian church. Ehud bellowed and shouted; Dov and Rabbi Vultch merely looked worried.

"There is nothing to be done except comply," Moshe concluded when Ehud subsided into growling. "We need the men and money that come from America, and we do not need President Truman making things tougher."

"So? We don't make things tough enough for ourselves?" Rabbi Vultch said. "*Meshuggener.* True? Of course, true. Now what?"

Moshe showed them on the map where the curve of Ararat Road provided a buffer for the buildings of the Jewish Quarter. "But we cannot expect it to hold forever," he said. "Perhaps it can hold long enough for Luke Thomas to break through, but we cannot rely on that. Instead, we dig trenches and raise barricades on Ararat Road."

"Under the Arab guns on the south wall?" Dov asked.

"We have to evacuate the church tower," Moshe said. "But the timetable is up to me. We will not give up that spot until the ditches are complete. It will provide covering fire to protect the workers till then."

"Good," Ehud said with approval. "And I know how we can get all the sandbags we need."

■　■　■　■

Fifteen boys of the Chaim Torah School were assembled in Hurva Synagogue. They stood in a double row of knobby knees and matted earlocks. At the end of the first row, sitting as much at attention as any of the boys, was Yacov's dog, shaggy, skinny Shaul. Ehud Schiff, his hands clasped behind his back, paced before them as a captain paces the deck of his ship. The big man was a magnet for the children of the quarter.

Captain of a crew of landlocked midgets was the description he used for himself. The truth was, Ehud Schiff could organize the boys to accomplish as much as grown men.

Yacov, taking the leadership conferred upon him by his exalted position as Moshe Sachar's brother-in-law, straightened his eye patch and spoke for the group. "We are prepared to fight," he said earnestly. "Already every boy over the age of thirteen is carrying an English gun; why not the rest of us?"

"We are all in this fight," Ehud offered, "but not in the same way."

Spindly, red-haired Joseph Rabinowitz, his changing voice screeching like a badly bowed violin, protested, "Please, no more washing dishes in Tipat Chalev!"

"And no more chopping onions if Hannah Cohen is watching," added stocky Leo Krepske in the front row. "It's always 'Make it finer, make it finer.' What a *farshtinkener* business! *Oy gevalt,* onions, onions, coming out my ears, yet."

His swarthy brother, Mendel, slapped the back of Leo's head. "*Luftmensh!* As if you ever washed your ears anyway!"

"*Litvak!*" Leo whirled around. He grasped his brother's earlocks and was dragging the head they were attached to toward the floor when Ehud intervened.

"Enough," he said quickly. "I have other duties in mind."

"What?" fifteen voices asked breathlessly.

"It is most important, but dangerous. Commander Moshe says all of you over age ten will be assigned rooftops to patrol. You must carry back messages from the soldiers on guard there to central command. That is the only way we have of being warned of Arab attacks so we can send reinforcements where needed."

"This is good," Leo Krepske noted. "We can slip over the roofs and down alleys quicker than . . . than . . ."

"Than you did when you stole candy from Reuven Bennick's store?" Joseph offered.

That was the signal for the Krepske brothers to pounce on Rabinowitz. In the excitement Leo landed a punch on Mendel's chin, and Mendel yowled, "*Momzer,* watch what you're doing."

"Enough!" Ehud shouted. "Or back to Hannah Cohen you go!"

"What about those of us who are ten?" Yacov inquired, stretching up on his toes as if he could add years as well as height. He kept his fingers crossed behind his back.

Ehud said sternly, "This has been given much thought

124

also. We must dig trenches at either end of the Street of the Jews. And build two strong barricades along Ararat Road." He muttered under his breath, "This by order of the *meshuggener* American president." Then, continuing, "The dirt and stones must then be bagged to build up the ramparts, *nu?* Sacks, pouches, satchels, anything that can be formed into sandbags you should get. Then these must be filled and piled where needed. This is something you can do? Every sandbag placed may mean a life saved from an Arab bullet."

Yacov raised his chin in a soldierly pose. "So? We will dig. We will fill. We will start at once."

■ ■ ■ ■ CHAPTER 9 ■ ■ ■ ■

Crammed into the back of a commandeered British military ambulance was food for two days, paltry medical supplies, and a thousand rounds of ammunition to be divided among the fighters at the Hospice of Notre Dame.

Rachel Sachar and Lori Kalner shared the space with three middle-aged civilian medical volunteers and Dr. Hiram Baruch, a Czech physician who had survived the death camps.

It was thought that Baruch had the best chance of convincing the Mother Superior that the members of the convent should retreat to the neutral ground of the Latin Patriarchate situated in the Christian Quarter of the Old City. It was hoped that when the sisters left their convent—passed through New Gate under the watchful eye of the Arab Irregulars—Rachel and Lori would be with them, dressed as nuns, and that Dr. Baruch would be wearing the clerical garb of a Roman Catholic priest. From there, the three could somehow make their way to the Jewish Quarter.

Dr. Baruch was thirty-four years old, a graduate of the medical school at the University of Prague. The child of Jewish converts to Catholicism, he had been baptized in Prague's great cathedral. He had one year of internship at Sacred Heart Hospital in the Czech capital before the Western powers sold out the republic to Hitler in 1938.

Then the war had begun. Years in the Czech Resistance served as his internship and residency. In the back rooms of Prague he patched bullet wounds and performed operations without anesthetic. When he was captured and imprisoned, his practice of medicine often took the form of consoling the dying.

This afternoon, in the back of the ambulance, he did not attempt to conceal the number engraved on his left forearm. It was, Rachel thought, a medal of honor to him. He wore a short-sleeved white shirt, a clerical collar, brown trousers, and combat boots. He was balding, with a ring of hair that fringed his head like a crown of laurel. His nose was prominent on his thin, sensitive face. Dark eyes were somber behind thick glasses.

He silently noted the burned patch of skin on her left forearm where her number had been. When she looked up at him, his eyes searched her face as though he knew everything about her. She was uneasy under the fierceness of his look. *Did* he know her?

"Your husband is in the Old City," he stated, as the vehicle followed the road leading to the hospice. "But you are from Warsaw by your accent."

The eyes of the other volunteers raised briefly at that information.

"Yes." Rachel looked at her hands, hoping he would not ask too much about how she had survived the war. Along with the number she had obliterated from her forearm had been the words *Nur für Offiziere:* For Officers Only.

Perhaps he sensed her uneasiness. He looked at Lori. "I am told you are experienced in trauma wounds."

"London. The Blitz."

"Ah. Yes. The radio messages from the Jewish Quarter sound similar to the Blitz, I am told. Shrapnel wounds. Crushing injuries. This morning they said they had four dead and thirteen wounded—all tended by two nurses and eight volunteers. They need a surgeon. We will be busy if we make it in." He chewed his lip. "These sisters will be sensitive about their privacy. They will not allow me into the convent until you first speak with Mother Superior. I will wait at the Hospice of Notre Dame. Send word to me if she accepts our request." He nudged a bag with his foot. "My cassock. I will join you before dawn tomorrow morning."

There were also wounded to attend at the hospice. Dr. Baruch disappeared down a long corridor the second the ambulance reached the building.

Fronting both the northwest corner of the walled Old City and the Arab-held community known as *Musrara,* the Hospice of Notre Dame de France was a key Jewish position in the New City. The mammoth structure, resembling a gargantuan capital letter E written on the ruled line of Suleiman Road, was easily the biggest building in Jerusalem. Beneath a twenty-foot-tall statue of the Virgin presenting the Holy Infant to the Holy City, the granite walls that had sheltered pilgrims since 1888 now protected Israeli riflemen.

Alongside the bulk of the hospice, the convent of the Soeurs Réparatrices crouched in relative insignificance, like a toddler clinging to the knees of its mother. The thirty sisters of the French religious order devoted their lives to prayer and perpetual confinement within the walls. They hoped their strictly neutral and benign presence would be unchallenged even though their home was on the front line of battle.

Before either the diversionary attack on New Gate or the main assault on Jaffa Gate could proceed, the northern flank of both operations had to be secured. The upshot of this military reasoning gave the convent as much chance of remaining undisturbed as a daisy in the path of a tank.

Rachel Sachar carried with her the transcript of a phone call between Haganah Headquarters and the Roman Catholic archbishop, imploring the Mother Superior to bring the sisters into the protection of the neutral Latin Patriarchate within the Old City. Along with that was the assurance that the Arab Higher Committee in Jerusalem would let them pass safely through the Arab-held New Gate.

What was not included in the plan, however, was the appeal that Rachel Sachar, and Lori Kalner, disguised as members of the order, and Dr. Baruch would enter the Old City with them.

■　■　■　■

The next duty of the Spare Parts Platoon, after their contact with the sisters of Soeurs Réparatrices, was to forage the neighborhood north of Jaffa Road, beyond Zahal Square. From the triangle of buildings, dubbed Bevingrad for British Foreign Secretary Ernest Bevin, the most recent of Palestine's conquerors had ruled their territory.

In their haste to get out of the way of the war, the departing soldiers and bureaucrats had left heaps of material—some trash and some valuable. The Spare Parts Platoon was given the duty of separating the two.

Daniel Caan had located a crate of flashlights, seven wirecutters, and a pair of British flags. These had been returned to Haganah Headquarters in a truck while Daniel and the others moved along to the building up the block.

His mind awash with conflicting emotions, Daniel felt like a scavenging Bedouin. What he was doing seemed futile, useless, stupid. Asher had given his life for a cause bigger than flashlights. Had Suzannah died and Daniel been spared so he could become the king of wirecutters?

Yet at the same time he chastised himself for being useless, Daniel wrestled with what he knew to be true: he was afraid. Back in the cave, back beside the trail in the dark, he had been terrified that he would be killed. Killing Arabs seemed a worthy tribute to Suzannah . . . if only he were not worried that he would cringe from the danger.

He had no mercy for himself. He was worthless, and he knew it. Only the mechanical response of following orders kept him moving forward.

The door to the next house was ajar. Inside Daniel found the signs of a fast departure. In the entryway lay a leather briefcase, flat on its side, evidently dropped in the rush. Far from containing valuable secret papers, the portfolio held a stale cheese sandwich and a folded cocktail napkin from a New City nightclub.

The dining-room table had a floral centerpiece that showed the touch of attentive artistry. But the arrangement of red and pink roses was incomplete. The heads of the flowers in the dry vase drooped; alongside it lay a bundle of blooms waiting to be installed. The scene spoke of someone unexpectedly called away, someone who might soon return.

The kitchen had been ransacked. The foodstuffs were gone, except for, on a top shelf, six cans of sardines. How even they had been overlooked, Daniel could not guess. The other plates, cups, dishes, and glasses had been dumped on the floor in an orgy of smashing crockery. In the middle of the heap was a single unbroken plate, saved from destruction by landing on the mound of the rest.

Daniel picked it up. The white china had a blue pattern woven around the edge. It reminded him of his mother's china, the set saved for special occasions in the mahogany sideboard. With a burst of violence he threw the plate against the wall, shattering it completely.

■　■　■　■

The ragtag army of the Mufti had two pitiful two-inch mortars to hold the Arab neighborhood of Musrara, which was northeast across the road from the Hospice of Notre Dame and Soeurs Réparatrices.

However, it seemed to Lori, as she and Rachel waited inside Notre Dame, that the Jihad Moquades had an infinite number of shells. The badly aimed munitions fired from Musrara landed around the hospice and convent, pocking the grounds, shattering the brick fence, and destroying what was left of Mother Superior's gardens.

An Irgun soldier with a British accent warned that their Red Cross bibs would make a fine target for the Irregulars on the wall at New Gate.

"Be careful," he cautioned cheerfully. "Most of those chaps up there will look at you and think, X marks the spot, you know. They're from Iraq, Iran, Syria, Tunis: mercenaries from everywhere but here. They'll shoot anything that isn't in a keffiyeh. Our chaps over there, forty of them, are hunkered down. The Mother won't let them in. Rather frightened to open the floodgate, I think. Anyway, the Arabs rather enjoy shooting things."

"Even nuns?" Lori asked.

As if in reply, a mortar shell screamed in from Musrara, exploding near the base of the statue of the Virgin Mary, blasting off the fingers of her outstretched hand.

"No respect, these wogs," the soldier replied in a humorless tone.

"How long will the shelling last?" Rachel asked, instinctively touching her abdomen.

Perhaps the incessant pounding of incoming fire had rightly given her second thoughts.

"They shell in the morning and late afternoon, after prayers," the Englishman explained. "Twenty minutes. Like clockwork. We'll have to wait here until they've done with it. Then the Jihad Moquades inside the Old City turn round and hammer the Jewish Quarter. Tomorrow morning it will be the same. They'll stop for a cigarette, a cup of coffee, and a trip to the W.C. Five-minute lull before they start sniping. You'll cut through to the back entrance of the convent. You'll be able to make a dash for it. Our boys know you're coming over the back wall. They'll be there to give you a hand." He shook his head in wonder at the strange pattern of the battle for Jerusalem. He added, "If they hadn't already killed so many of our chaps by sheer luck it would be laughable."

But it was not laughable. Lori wondered if Jacob and Alfie would be listed among the dead and wounded when the final count was tallied. Were they yet on the roof of the convent? And what of Rachel Sachar, thinking she was out to do a good deed and would therefore be protected? Death, Lori knew, was no respecter of good deeds or the innocent.

"One of us can handle this," Lori offered, concerned for Rachel's unborn child. "As a matter of fact, I would rather go alone."

Rachel appraised her sternly. "I have met the *Mère Supérieure*. She is . . . a friend. She trusts me. If anyone stays it should be you."

Lori opened her mouth in rebuttal. At that instant the boom of the shelling stopped. For one surrealistic second, Lori heard a bird sing from the brush at the side of the hospice.

"This is it, ladies! Holy Strugglers' coffee break. Five minutes!" The Irgunist leapt to his feet and threw open the door leading to the nearly destroyed garden behind Notre Dame.

"Out! Not a second to waste!" he commanded. "Good luck!"

Rachel dashed from the building with Lori at her heels.

Climbing onto a bench next to the wall, Rachel had diffi-culty lifting herself over.

Lori shouted, "Give us a hand!" A man's arm reached over the wall to drag Rachel unceremoniously onto the convent grounds.

Lori followed her lead, clambering onto the bench and then jumping over the broad wall into the convent garden. It was an eight-foot drop to the interior. No one was beneath to catch her as she tumbled into the now-destroyed retreat.

Looking up, she saw the face of an Arab who was wielding a shovel.

Lori's scream of terror froze in her throat. She blinked at the aged man in amazement. Haganah soldiers were emerging from cover. Why did they not shoot this man?

"*Salaam* to you. I am the gardener." He bowed low. "You have come to speak to *Mère Supérieure?* She is a stubborn woman. Pray it does not get them killed." He raised his eyes heavenward and crossed himself.

Lori glanced toward the blasted garden. The ground was carpeted with pink cherry blossoms; beyond that was the iron gate that led to the cloisters of the convent.

"You should ring the bell," the gardener instructed. "Tell her why you come. Tell her I am in the garden burying dead Muslims who wished to kill everybody here. Tell her there are nice young Jews on the roof and in my house."

Rachel was already beneath the arch of the entrance, tugging the bell rope. Lori scanned the rooftop, hoping for a sign of Jacob.

A grime-covered Haganah recruit with patchy stubble

and pimples climbed from the bushes. He had been onboard the *Joshua Reynolds*. He gaped at Lori as if she were a vision.

"You," he said.

Rachel yanked the bell rope impatiently and peered through the metal grate.

Lori urgently asked the soldier, "Loren, have you seen Jacob? Is Jacob Kalner here?"

"He left. Him and the big fellow and a half-dozen others. Over the wall before the last shelling. We're to hold the convent, but the old woman will not let us inside."

From the courtyard of the cloister, a tall, spare, elderly nun glided toward the door. A ring of iron keys hung from her waist. She seemed surprised by the sight of two women standing amid the wreckage of the garden.

"Rachel Sachar," she said with a shake of her head. "So they sent you."

"You must let us in, Mother. Just the two of us, *nu?*"

"Yes, I can see I must."

■　■　■　■

The bulk of the Warsaw building at the northern boundary of the Jewish and Muslim Quarters presented a natural fortress that anchored the Haganah's line of defense. From its rooftop Haganah sentries scanned the surrounding streets for signs of Arab snipers or a massing attack. The towering wall of the north face presented windows blocked up to slits for use as fire steps. As one defender put it, "The only drawback to the position is that we can hear the prayer calls of the muezzins better than the Muslims can."

To protect the flank of the Warsaw building from attack, the Haganah dug a trench where the Street of the Jews intersected the Street of the Chain. Thus far there was a heap of earth and stones but merely a shallow ditch without a rampart.

Yacov Lubetkin and five of his sandbag crew scoured the neighborhoods of the Old City, gathering supplies. They acquired fifty-seven gunnysacks, twenty-five leather satchels, nineteen pillowcases, and three pairs of packsaddles from a camel caravan, original owner unknown.

At every stop on their scavenger hunt women offered them glasses of water and aged rabbis called upon heaven to bless them. Every stop, that is, until Stambuli Synagogue.

The Stambuli, built by Turkish Jews, served as a repository for damaged and soiled Torah scrolls until they could be properly buried.

It was just after the *mincha,* the afternoon service of the Sabbath. Rabbi Akiva and ten of his followers had remained in the auditorium of the synagogue to hold a meeting in opposition to the actions of the Haganah and to discuss what was to be done now that the protective cordon of British troops was gone.

Yacov and the Krepske brothers heard Rabbi Akiva's strident tones before he climbed the last five steps of the sanctuary. "Death and destruction are coming on our heads," Akiva shrilled. "We are on the verge of annihilation, and there is clearly just one course." Worried moans of agreement rose from his flock.

Mendel Krepske said, "So. At least they know what a

spot we are in, *nu?*"

At the appearance of the sandbag crew Akiva paused. All heads pivoted to observe the intruders. The mayor snapped, "What is it? What evil news do you bring?"

"No evil news," Yacov replied. "We are the sandbag committee of the Old City defense." He waved aloft a pillowcase in one hand and an empty rice sack in the other. "We need sacks or bags for use on the barricades."

Rabbi Akiva exploded. "Defiler of the Sabbath! Children they send to do the devil's work! Don't you know, boy, that *surrender* is the sole choice we have left? If we do not negotiate a peace with the Arabs, we will all surely die!"

Leo Krepske said, "This is why we need sacks."

A black-coated man, his face puckered with self-righteous anger, cuffed Leo on the ear. "Would you bandy words with an elder of Israel, you street rat?" The boy cowered.

Yacov flinched as the man raised his hand a second time to adjust his hat.

From the doorway, Shaul growled a warning and lunged at the rope that tied him.

"And keep that cur away from here!" Akiva added nervously.

Ehud, arriving to check on the progress of the barricades, had entered the synagogue. He stepped between the boys and the line of men.

"And when you have given up the safety of these walls for Arab promises," Ehud asked gently, "what will you hide behind then?"

"You speak thus to the mayor?" scolded Akiva's supporter.

Ehud retorted, "One who sheds only words while others shed their blood is no mayor of mine."

"You defile the Sabbath!" Akiva thundered, looking intently out the window at the broad daylight of the day on which the Orthodox did no work.

"You have forgotten something, maybe? To save a life it is permitted . . ."

"*Nebech!* You presume to tell us the Law? Profaner of the holy! Get out!"

"A fine place you have chosen for your *Oneg Shabbat*," Ehud said, referring to the customary Sabbath social hour, as he exited. "Here among the discarded scrolls, fit for burying!"

Outside and up the street, men and women labored on the trench. The workers toiled in pairs, one keeping a wary eye on the approaches from the Muslim Quarter while the other dug. British entrenching tools, scraps of corrugated tin, picks, and bare hands were all pressed into service to grapple with the eons of hardened pavement.

To effect any entry into the slabs of stone required steel and brawn. Ehud, a-seven-foot-long crowbar over his shoulder, went from place to place. Carefully eyeing the joints in the masonry, he hoisted the pointed rod over his head and, with a furious lunge, jabbed its spike into the roadbed. This movement was repeated in a frenzied rhythm, like a frustrated heron chasing a darting fish.

After six thrusts, Ehud rested the bar across the back of his neck while a wave of scuttling helpers dashed in to clear the uprooted slabs and cobblestones. Larger rocks were heaped in front of the expanding ditch; dirt and lesser stones filled the barley sacks.

Yacov and the other scroungers added their donations to the collected heap, then they and Yehudit assisted in loading bags. A foot of depth to the trench meant two feet of protection; the digging went down, the sacks piled up, the shadows lengthened. Ehud's spike rose and fell and then, *"Oy gevalt!"* The big man clapped a callused hand to the back of his neck. Had he been shot? "Rocks they are throwing?"

"Sabbath breakers!" shouted a chorus of voices from a short distance away. "Profaners of the sacred!" A shower of stones and brickbats flew through the air toward the excavators.

"Meshuggener!" bellowed Ehud, dodging a flying chunk.

Akiva's tribe howled about defending the Law, keeping the Sabbath holy.

Two things happened simultaneously: A bullet ricocheted off the pry bar Ehud carried, and from high atop the Warsaw building came the cry "The Arabs are attacking! Take cover!"

Rabbi Akiva's followers trampled each other in an effort to run back to the synagogue. "Save us! Give up while we yet live! We must surrender, or we will die."

Not one of them remained on the trench line as the battle began in earnest.

■   ■   ■   ■

Several blocks away, at the place where Ararat Road crossed St. James Road, the Old City Jewish defenders had erected a barricade. Moshe's fingertips bled from clawing at cobblestones, and his face was covered with dust. When he glanced up at the belfry of the Armenian church, one of the Haganah lookouts posted there waved. It was reassuring to have guardian angels in place while the work went forward. There had been one bullet fired by an Arab sniper since the digging began, and the sniper had been the immediate recipient of a flurry of shots from the tower in return.

Near the intersection an Arab flour mill shared the Armenian Quarter with churches, homes, and bulgur shops selling cracked wheat. The roof of the mill had been used by the British to keep an eye on the Jewish Quarter. The aim had been to keep any arms or ammunition from entering the district, and they had done too fine a job. Despite the efforts of smugglers who braved the death penalty for moving weapons, the Quarter was desperately underdefended.

At least the roof was occupied by a pair of Haganah boys with Sten guns. Both earlocked Talmudic scholars, Zev and Menachim were also brothers. Until six months before, they had never lifted anything more warlike than pens. Now they were the first line of defense of the Jewish Quarter.

The trench marking the westernmost boundary of the perimeter defended by the Old City Jews was complete. From behind the sandbagged parapet, the guards had a clear field of fire both north and south on Ararat Road and across St. James Road to the west. After seeing that one of the Quarter's two light machine guns was properly installed, Moshe gave the agreed-upon signal for the sentries in the tower to withdraw.

The Arab gunfire that started immediately proved they had been observed all along. Moshe and the other workers jumped into the trench.

Two minutes later the four Haganah men from the tower came pelting along St. James Road. As they reached the home of Rabbi Emdat Cahanna, bullets punched wounds into a hundred-year-old Armenian seminary and into the surviving arch of an eight-hundred-year-old Crusader church.

"Where is that coming from?" Moshe demanded. "Give them cover!"

Three of the Haganah men sped closer and closer to safety, bounding from side to side in an effort to spoil their enemies' aim. The fourth lagged behind. As Moshe watched with horror, the man bent sideways and dropped his rifle before sagging to the pavement. "It's Theodore. He's hit!" Moshe yelled. He bolted up from the trench even as the other three Jewish riflemen dove over the rampart.

"Wait!" someone shouted, dragging Moshe back down. "There's nothing to be done. It's coming from the tower!"

With the escape of three of the targets the Arab gunfire turned on the wounded man, who, propped on his elbows, was lying on his stomach. A bullet hit between Theodore's shoulders, knocking him flat. He did not move anymore.

Up in the tower of the Church of St. Jacques, moving figures could be glimpsed. Every one of them wore a keffiyeh. The belfry had been neutral for less than three minutes.

■ ■ ■ ■ CHAPTER 10 ■ ■ ■ ■

A wave of Jihad Moquades surged up St. James Road toward the barricade. The Haganah machine gun chattered, and the front rank of Arabs crumpled in a heap of bloody robes. Behind them came others, screaming of the greatness of Allah and announcing death to the Jews.

Each rush was repulsed, only to be followed by another and another. "Aim! Aim carefully!" Moshe implored, mindful of how desperately limited the ammunition was.

In striving to do as Moshe commanded, a Haganah defender named Broshi rose up from the sandbags to select his target. At the same time he fired, dropping an enemy, a fusillade of shots rang out from the church tower. Broshi was riddled, his body falling forward to lie across the rampart.

Zev and Menachim, on top of the grain mill, fired from behind the low wall that edged the roof. They had worked out a scheme in which they would both appear at once. While one shot at the church belfry to spoil the aim of the Arab snipers, the other would loose a burst into the street below, then both would duck.

The last storm of Moquades got close enough to throw smoke grenades before retiring into the shops and alleyways. The fizzing canisters produced a cloud of thick gray haze over the street, reducing visibility to less than a block.

Every swirl of breeze produced a thousand spectral attackers. The men behind the sandbags fired blindly, wildly, into the murk. They were more fearful of the imagined thousands approaching under the cover of the smoke than they had been of the real hundreds actually glimpsed.

"Wait!" Moshe urged. "Don't shoot when you can't see."

When the next line of Muslims did appear from the mist, they seemed as disoriented as their opponents. The attackers who burst from the smoke were surprised they were so close to the sandbags. The machine gun scythed along the stumbling line. Trying to escape the grim harvest, one Arab ran into another, and in the bumbling both men were cut down. Those who were able fled.

At a lull in the fighting, a low moaning floated in the air with the haze. A wounded Arab Irregular cried, "*Youin! Help!*" and "*Alam! Alam!* The pain! The pain!*"

An injured Jew lying in the bottom of the trench made an animal, panting sound. With each breath he grunted, "*Em! Em! Em! Em!* Mother! Mother!"

Even before the smoke drifted away, the use made of it by the Moquades was explained: shots were fired from new directions at the Haganah position. The Arabs were north *and* south of the trench along Ararat Road, and they also occupied places behind the ruined pillars of the Crusader church of St. Thomas.

The grain mill was surrounded on three sides, the position no longer tenable. "Come back!" Moshe yelled to Menachim and Zev. "Get out of there!"

As Menachim fired bursts toward the Church of St. Jacques, toward the Crusader church, then up the street toward an enemy Moshe could not see, Zev sprinted for the stone steps leading down. Chips from Menachim's parapet splintered under the return gunshots. He was hit in the arm, but kept firing.

Zev reached the street level and ran toward the trench, bullets dogging his steps.

As Menachim fired again, emptying his clip, he was shot in the head. His body somersaulted over the rail before landing with a thud in the street.

Two steps from the rampart, Zev was also hit, shot in the back. Moshe and another reached up to drag him into the ditch. There was a patch of blood on his shirtfront; the bullet had pierced him through. "Menachim!" he gasped. "Is he safe? Did he make it?"

"He'll be with you in no time," Moshe said in a soothing tone.

"Good," Zev said, smiling. "Papa would kill me if . . ." and he died.

■　　■　　■　　■

Ehud heard the staccato popping of rifle fire echoing from the belfry of St. Jacques. The attack against the Jewish district was advancing from several directions.

"Down!" he shouted to Yacov and the Krepske brothers.

Two streets pointing directly from the Muslim Quarter toward the Jewish district intersected the Street of the Chain across from the Warsaw building. From the passageways rolled a chant that increased in volume and ferocity in rhythm with the tempo of the gunfire: *"Deir Yassin! Deir Yassin!"*

The memory of the destroyed Arab village propelled the Holy Strugglers into a fury of hate and revenge. They fired their rifles as they came, though the bullets discharged into the air and impacted nowhere near the Israeli defenders.

Ehud's first concern was for Yacov and the other children, but it was too late to send them back for shelter. Already the air was stitched with shots that would cut to pieces anyone standing. "Stay down! Keep down in the trench!"

Yacov buried his face in Shaul's ruff.

Firing his British-made Enfield, Ehud took aim at a white keffiyeh that poked around the corner of an overturned donkey cart a block away. He fired, then worked the bolt to lever in another round; fired again and saw the left handle of the barrow explode in a shower of splinters. The Arab did not appear again.

To Ehud's left, Dov and Rabbi Vultch raced up. Dov carried the barrel and receiver of a machine gun while the rabbi staggered along with its tripod and a metal cartridge box. Behind the sandbag rampart they assembled the weapon, and Vultch fed a belt of cartridges into it. Dov squeezed off a burst. In the canyons of stone the harsh-voiced vehemence of the weapon shredded the air as if the fabric of Jerusalem were being ripped in two.

Peering over the rim of the barricade, Ehud watched as three Jihad Moquades were struck in quick succession and the rest turned and fled. Without a pause, Dov and Vultch dismantled the gun and stumbled along the trench toward the opposite corner of the Warsaw. "We must make them think we have more than one!" was the remark Vultch tossed over his shoulder in passing.

The Arabs massed for another attack. This time something with more planning than a headlong assault was under way. A clump of Moquades hugged a centuries-old indentation in a wall but did not fire. "Watch there!" Ehud warned, pointing.

At that moment a Haganah defender cried out in pain and bolted upright in the trench. His Sten gun flew out of his hand as he was struck in the head by a bullet. "Sniper!" Ehud called, waving his hand toward the roof of a Turkish bath. Dov and three other defenders pivoted toward the source of the gunfire and drove the sniper back from the parapet, but as their attention was distracted, the Arabs down the block sprinted toward their position.

Two of the Mufti's men shot from the hip as they advanced, but the third, a cigarette clamped between his teeth, ran up with a heavy object in his arms.

Then the Arab rooftop sniper whirled a Nazi potato masher, an explosive charge mounted on a wooden handle, into the trench. It struck the stock of Ehud's Enfield and rebounded out of reach. Ehud flung his rifle aside and scrambled toward the grenade, tripping over the iron crowbar as he did so.

"No, Yacov! Get back!" Ehud yelled as the boy clambered over Shaul and the body of the fallen Jewish soldier to reach the grenade. Ignoring the warning, Yacov snagged the fizzing explosive and spun it over the top of the trench. The weapon's handle brushed against the lip of the mound of stones and then bumped along the cobbles toward the heap of tires. "Down!" Ehud yelled again.

■　　■　　■　　■

Dajani, the cigarette-smoking attacker, knelt behind a

stack of tires piled at the Muslim end of the street. He removed the cylinder of tobacco from his mouth and extended the glowing end toward a black wick protruding from a milk can.

The grenade detonated with a reverberating roar. A burst of shrapnel plunged into the dirt and stones of the barricade, but none of the Jews were injured. Out in the street a hail of fragments ripped into Dajani's face. He dropped the milk-can bomb, still unlit, and staggered backward toward the rest of his unit.

■　■　■　■

Dragged by Haroun Najid on one arm and the orphan boy Daoud on the other, a battered and bloody Kasim Dajani was hustled around a corner and out of the fight for the Warsaw. "Put me down!" he ordered, and when they did not comply fast enough he thrashed from side to side. He tried to clear away the blood that flowed down into his eyes from a gash on his forehead. "I'm not injured! Put me down!"

Najid looked from Dajani's lacerated hairline to his gore-spattered cheeks and protested, "But your face. You need a doctor."

"It is nothing! We must break through before the Jews can strengthen their defenses even more. If I can get just one of my beauties into that trench, the way to the Jewish Quarter is ours." He shook off their restraining grips. "Bring me another device," he yelled. "Quickly!" Then he leaned against the iron-shuttered front of a *halal* butcher shop. Gawan pressed a folded keffiyeh against the scalp

146

wound while his brother wiped Dajani's face.

Najid returned with another bomb and held it out for Dajani to take, but when the terrorist reached for it he wavered and would have fallen if Daoud had not jumped in and propped him up. "It is a passing weakness, nothing more," Dajani insisted. "But the light is failing. You must deliver this package, Haroun, and at once."

The pastry shop owner's eyes widened. "But you saw for yourself!" he protested. "The Jews have many machine guns and grenades and a hundred men on the barricade. It is suicide to get that close again!"

Dajani knocked Daoud and Gawan out of the way and wiped the back of his hand across his face. Through a smear of blood, he opened one baleful eye and transfixed Najid. The terrorist stabbed a hand downward toward his belt, then cocked and thrust a British-made Webley revolver at the baker's nose. "You will do this thing," he swore, "or I will kill you myself here."

The gory mask of Dajani's features and the menacing tone left no doubt in Najid's mind that he was one second away from eternity if he did not comply. "Give me the matches," he said earnestly.

Another Arab Irregular in fluttering keffiyeh rushed up. "Dajani," he said, "the Jews are probing the defenses of the north wall. We need your special skill in turning them back. You are ordered to come at once."

Dajani glared at the newcomer before finally agreeing. "*Insh' Allah*," he said. "I will come. Later we will recover the first device. And you, Najid, will carry out an attack at first light tomorrow."

Najid wiped his perspiring face with the back of a dripping hand. "Of course," he said.

■　■　■　■

Behind the heap of rubble and a dirt-laden sack labeled
RICE, FIRST QUALITY, WHITE, Ehud crouched. They had
beaten back the initial Arab attack on the position, but
there was little comfort in that fact. The one serious injury
had taken the life of a Jewish soldier. Haganah troops had
expended far too many bullets, and the vulnerability of the
unfinished trench was apparent. Across the intersection, in
a no-man's-land so tiny that no more than ten men could
have contested possession at once anyway, lay the unexploded bomb. The milk can was dented, but the coil of fuse
still protruded from the top.

"I could go and get it," Yacov offered.

"No!" Ehud bellowed, more harshly than he intended.
"They are expecting us to try that. There is no doubt a
sniper eyeing that spot right now."

"Should we not shoot it and blow it up?" a defender
queried. "While the infernal contraption is on their side?"

"Not now," Ehud cautioned. "Leave it alone, already."

"Will they attack again?" Leo Krepske asked.

Ehud squinted at the waning light. The end of Sabbath
was near. "If we are lucky, perhaps they have had enough
till tomorrow. But you and the others go already, back to
the Hurva. Tell Moshe we held. And take Shaul with you."

Yacov and the other boys took on the mournful task of
loading the corpse onto a gunnysack and dragging it away,
tying Shaul's lead rope to a corner of the makeshift
stretcher so he could help pull.

148

Ehud slumped back down in the trench but rested only a second before Dov's voice roused him. "*Shabbat shalom*, Ehud. We must also use this time," he said, and by way of example, began digging again at the ditch.

■　■　·　■　■

At seventy-four the Mother Superior of the Soeurs Réparatrices convent was ramrod-straight, as cold as the steel rims of her spectacles, and as sharp as the point of her long nose.

Like Mary Magdalen, to whom Jesus had offered forgiveness and a new life, the Mother Superior had been a prostitute. Working the Left Bank in Paris from the age of thirteen, she had loathed her life and had determined to end it by jumping into the Seine from the Pont-Neuf. In desperation she knelt before a crucifix in the Cathedral of Notre Dame and saw a vision of a building and a gate in Jerusalem. What she described later to the priest matched Jerusalem's Hospice of Notre Dame, across from New Gate and the Christian Quarter. He told her about the French convent, where women spent their waking hours praying near the place Christ was crucified. It was said, he told her, that the prayers of the sisters held back Judgment. Like Mary, the virgin mother of Jesus, and Mary Magdalen, the sisters of the convent stood vigil near the cross on behalf of all women.

From that moment Mother Superior never wavered in her determination to live and die within sight of the hill where Christ was crucified. Working as a maid in a hotel in Nice, she saved enough to buy passage on a steamer to

Palestine. She walked up the gorge to the Holy City. Once she entered the convent she never looked back. That was 1890.

Imperious, unintimidated by the crash of mortars outside, she said to Rachel and Lori, "I must ask myself if this is only a plan for the Haganah to get us out of the way, as well as sneak you two and Dr. Baruch into the Old City."

Rachel chose her words carefully. "Of course the doctor is needed in the Jewish Quarter. There is no doctor. People are dying for want of his skill."

"So we sisters are to be your shield in this deceit?" She shook her head. "We have made a vow that once we enter these walls, we will not leave again until we are carried to Gethsemane in our shrouds."

Rachel said, "You will enter Gethsemane much sooner if you stay, Mother."

"Then our dust will mingle with that of the martyrs, and our souls will rejoice."

"The living need your prayers more than Jerusalem needs another handful of dust. And the suffering in the Jewish Quarter need Dr. Baruch."

The woman studied Lori and Rachel. "Sister Angélique is over ninety. She came here from Rouen when she was a fifteen-year-old novice. She is blind and will not know where to place her feet upon stones outside the convent. Sister Rebekah is older yet. Her eyes are also gone, and her limbs will not carry her far."

"Not far, Mother," Rachel interjected. "Through New Gate into the Christian Quarter, to the Latin Patriarchate. The archbishop has made a place for you. As for the three of us, we will not endanger you. We will make our way to the Jewish Quarter as soon as we can."

"Tomorrow morning is Pentecost. Surely they will not fight on such a holy day, holy to the Jews because it marks the giving of the Law on Sinai and to Christians because on this day God poured His spirit into men and wrote His law upon our hearts."

"Those who will fight here recognize neither the Law nor the promise nor the spirit. You must leave or die." Rachel's skin was pale, almost transparent as she pleaded. She looked ill, and the *Mère Supérieure* recognized the strain.

"You are unwell, child?"

Rachel replied, "Tired."

Lori interjected forcefully, "She's pregnant. She has risked her own life and the life of her child to come here to warn you. To help you escape."

Mother Superior tapped her fingertips together thoughtfully at this revelation. "So." She hesitated, looking at the painting of the Holy Family fleeing destruction in the middle of the night.

Lori added, "Life does not always turn out the way we expect."

Mother Superior said quietly, "The angel came to warn Joseph to flee to Egypt to save the Christ Child."

Lori, weary of the religious banter, said, "Joseph did not argue with him."

"He was Joseph. I am only myself. And I believe our presence here will stop the bloodshed. Perhaps save more lives than Dr. Baruch would save in the Jewish Quarter."

"And what if Joseph had disobeyed the angel?"

At this, the hard visage of the Mother Superior cracked.

She almost smiled. "An intriguing question for our morning discussion on obedience."

Rachel leaned forward, capturing the woman in a riveting gaze. "The time for discussion is past. Arab Irregulars of the Mufti's forces are religious fanatics, Holy Strugglers, bent on destroying every man, woman, and child who is not a Muslim. You will not be excluded. A total of one hundred and fifty settlers died yesterday at Kfar Etzion. Reports are that females were raped before they were executed. A young man escaped who was witness as his fourteen-year-old sister was . . ."

"Stop." The nun held up her hand and then crossed herself. She furrowed her brow. "You may need our help to enter the Old City more than we need yours. But the Lord is the guardian of this convent . . . of these sisters. I cannot make such a decision without first asking Him."

■　　■　　■　　■

There came another pause in the attack against the Jewish Quarter.

Moshe sent the boys of Chaim Torah School to spread the word along Ararat Road: "Evacuate!"

It was clear that with the cross fire the Arabs could mount from the bell tower of St. Jacques, the whole arc of land bounded by Ararat Road would be lost. When Ararat Road was lost, Moshe knew, the Jihad Moquades would tighten the noose around the Jewish district on every side.

The neighborhood cloistered east of Ararat was a muddle of shops and homes. The Christian and Muslim occupants of the mixed community had fled weeks before;

now the Jewish residents would have to go, too.

Thus far the Irregulars were satisfied with their initial successes but none too eager to cross the open spaces defended by the machine gun. Their hesitancy bought a brief interval in which to begin the evacuation.

Running door to door, the boys urged the inhabitants to seek shelter within the Jewish Quarter, across the Street of the Jews. None of the elderly men and women who remained in the area resisted. They had seen the arrival of destruction on their doorsteps.

A man helped his equally aged wife lift a wicker pram up the steps from their basement flat. Instead of a baby, the carriage held a pair of candlesticks and a clock. From another doorway came a rabbi, walking with the aid of two sticks. Concealed by his long coat, his spine was bent and twisted. The Krepske brothers took an arm each and helped him navigate to safety.

Moshe hammered on the door of a synagogue in El Arman Road. It was the site where Rabbi Yitzhak ben Lourie Ashkenazi, one of the first proponents of *kabbalah*, or Jewish mysticism, was born in 1534. From the synagogue poured hollow-cheeked men with eyes that focused on distant, otherworldly scenes. Like the rest, they, too, carried their most precious belongings, in this case books, commentaries, and bundles of notes covered in crabbed Hebrew and mysterious calculations.

Soon a mass of frightened, tottering refugees floated out of their homes. Directed into the channels of lanes that connected to the Jewish Quarter, they drifted on the tide of war, castaways amid the wreckage of their lives. Moshe noted that aside from small sacks of flour and some cans of tinned beef, they carried few provisions.

Yacov and the Krepske brothers ran to Moshe's side.

"Some on Ararat Road won't leave. They're afraid to give up their homes. If they wait, they think, something might be worked out."

Moshe hurried to the street, noting the houses where the messengers had been turned away. His approach to a dwelling was interrupted when Moses Waller, a short, round, angry man, rushed up to him. A familiar figure in the Old City, Waller was known to be eloquent, short-tempered, blunt, and kindhearted. At the moment he was all of these. "Sachar," he said. "Are you forcing these people out? Where will you put them? How will you feed them? They are starving now."

"If they stay here, they will be overrun by Arabs within a day."

"But the Arabs are offering to feed people who surrender," Waller said. "Near the house of St. Mark, I heard the loudspeaker myself. 'Bread,' they said. 'Why starve when you can have bread in plenty? Give up, and we will feed you.' They even promised tomatoes."

Moshe did not argue and only repeated the message of Kfar Etzion. Surrender meant peace, the peace of death. Capitulation meant food in plenty . . . for worms.

Waller's visage hardened. "I will help round up the rest," he said. "I will order them out. They will listen to me."

■ ■ ■ ■ CHAPTER 11 ■ ■ ■ ■

The intersection of Jaffa Road and Queen Helene Street was dominated by the Victorian bulk of Beit Feingold, a city block–sized structure of flats and shops. The scavenging team of the Spare Parts Platoon was not sent to Beit Feingold; instead they were to search the art nouveau buildings across the street.

Daniel, leading Mangus and Sal, tried the front door of a three-story whose arched windows were framed in blue-and-white flowered tiles. The entrance was locked. "Let me show you how it's done," Sal said, and he kicked it open with a crash.

There was just time to glimpse a striped robe whisking out of sight around a bend at the end of the corridor, and then another door slammed.

Sal backed out hurriedly and grabbed the rifle from his shoulder. "There's somebody in there who don't want to be seen," he hissed. "Thought this neighborhood was safe."

"Should we go getta some help?" Mangus queried.

Daniel, his pulse surging, wanted to say the same thing, but did not. He told himself he needed to confront his fear head-on, not run away at a hint of danger. "Come on," he said. "It's part of our job. They didn't shoot, did they?"

"It's a trap," Sal warned. "They're sucking us in."

Advancing with his rifle at his hip, Daniel thrust its muzzle into each of the two rooms flanking the hallway. Both were vacant. So was the bend of the hallway where it dead-ended against another door. Motioning for the others to follow, Daniel moved forward again. Mangus was right behind him, Sal farther back.

"It's a cellar," Daniel said, pointing to the bottom of the frame where the edge of a tread showed a step leading down. *What's down there? What if Sal is right? What if I'm walking into a bullet?*

From the rear Sal suggested, "Here's how we did it in Germany, see? With a grenade." Where the American had acquired the explosive device, Daniel did not know, but the fragmentation bomb was passed to him by Mangus with trembling fingers.

"Pull the pin and throw it in," Sal said.

"I know how it works! Wait and let me think!"

"What's to think? Kick the door in, throw the grenade. We worry about after, after!"

"Stand back!" Daniel ordered, then he hammered on the panel with the butt of his rifle. "*Yahdir!*" he shouted in Arabic. "Come out!"

There was no response from below.

"Use the grenade!"

"*Yahdir! Yuti!* Give up!"

"Use the grenade!"

A gang of Jihad Moquades were on the other side! Perhaps they had a bomb of their own. Maybe they were getting ready to machine-gun Daniel through the door. They butchered Asher. They raped and killed his sister. They were snipers sneaking in behind Jewish lines.

"Throw it!"

"*Yahdir!*" Daniel yelled again. He knew there was a screech of desperation in his voice. What kept him from using the grenade? *Take no chances with murderers who offered surrender and massacred their captives.* Daniel pulled the safety pin from the handle but hesitated. *They know we have weapons, and they are trapped down there. If they were going to shoot, why haven't they?*

"Kick the door in and throw it!"

If the handle was released, the fuse would ignite. There would be no calling it back.

"*Yuti! Qounboula!* We have a bomb!"

"Use it!"

A baby cried. A thin, wavering cry, quickly stifled as if someone had clapped a hand over its mouth.

A baby! Daniel looked down at the bomb in his hand, stared at the whitening knuckles as if they belonged to someone else. Where was the pin?

"Throw it!" Sal called.

"Where's the pin? I dropped it! Find it!"

Mangus picked up the metal ring of the safety pin and held it out. "No!" Daniel said. "You put it back!"

As Daniel squeezed the handle of the grenade in both hands, Mangus reinserted the safety pin.

Daniel's fingers trembled so, he could scarcely hold his rifle again. This was not over yet. Maybe they had a baby with them, but they could yet be killers.

Then a voice from below called, "*La nar!* Don't shoot!"

"How many are down there?" Daniel asked, trying to control the quaver in his voice.

"Six!"

"Come up slowly, with your hands up!"

Backing away from the cellar entry, Daniel posted himself behind the bend of the corridor, with Mangus backing him. Sal was clear out on the front step.

The door creaked open. An Arab boy of eleven or

157

twelve, wearing a striped robe, came blinking into the light, his hands raised above his head. "Where is the oldest?" Daniel demanded.

"It is me, Hadi," said the boy. "The others are younger."

A file of Arab children emerged from the cellar: three boys and three girls. The youngest was a baby carried by the oldest girl.

■　■　■　■

Mindful of the smoke that hung behind them above the Old City, the Spare Parts Platoon stood on Queen Helene Street and debated what to do with their six prisoners. "The Arabs are murderin' our guys over there," Sal said, gesturing toward the pillar of fumes.

"So, what are you saying?" Daniel inquired. "We should kill them?" Daniel could not stop thinking about holding the live grenade in his hand. It would have been easy to throw it into the cellar. In the confined space, what chance would any of the children have had? The vision of what had almost happened would not leave him.

Since the discussion was in English, the children did not follow a word of it. It was plain from their expressions that they did not like what the American said, or the looks he gave them. They stood quaking in the center of the ring of armed boys, wide-eyed with fear. The girl holding the baby kept watching Daniel, then looking away. A younger girl's lip trembled as if she might cry. What should he do, offer comfort? Tell them they were in no danger?

"Not kill," Sal corrected hurriedly. "But they might be spyin' on us. Maybe they should be locked up somewheres."

"Spying on us as we loot flashlights and sardines?" Daniel snorted, shaking off the specter of a basement filled with small, fragmented corpses.

"Yeah? Well, what're they doin' here then?"

Daniel put the question to Hadi.

"Our mother died six months since. Our father came here to see an English friend, but the English were gone. Fearful for us, our father told us to wait while he went for help. He has not returned. Every time we looked out, we heard shooting, so I made my brothers and sisters stay in the cellar."

As Daniel translated this for the others, Jacob Kalner, Pinky, Ibrahim, Hymie, Chaim, and Alfie returned from their own foraging forays.

"All right, but we can't wet-nurse a mob of Arab kids, can we?" Sal argued. "Turn 'em loose."

Jacob objected, "And how long will they last in those clothes in the middle of a war? Somebody will see the robes and start shooting."

"Or droppa a grenade ona their heads," Mangus said accusingly.

Daniel was grateful to have support for what he was feeling. He was also glad to relinquish the responsibility for the children. Jacob, as corporal, would have to make the decision. Maybe Daniel's sweaty palms, sweaty to the point of making his rifle stock feel slimy, would finally dry.

"So what do we do?" Sal said.

Daniel saw Jacob look toward the Old City. The black vapors there billowed up, looming over Jerusalem like a malevolent creature swooping to swallow it. The scent of the burning . . . of wood, oil, paint, and cordite . . . of homes, lives, and futures . . . filled Daniel's nostrils. "The Arabs are attacking in force and torching houses in the Armenian Quarter," Jacob said. "That direction is out. There's a Muslim neighborhood half a mile that way, beyond the convent. We'll take them there."

"What?" Sal objected. "And maybe get shot for our trouble?"

Take them to home and safety? No one had made such an offer to Suzannah, not much older than Hadi. Daniel's sweat broke out anew: who was their father? Could he be one of those who had destroyed the kibbutz? But these children were not the enemy. Their eyes reflected the same fear the Jewish children of Kfar Etzion had felt. Were they not the same? The children. Madness! Would Hadi someday rally at the cry to *jihad?* Where did it stop? What would Suzannah say?

"Yes," he heard himself say, urgently, forcefully, though he felt distant from the scene. "Take them through the lines."

■　■　■　■

It was a strange cavalcade that the sentries on the west side of the Hospice of Notre Dame saw approaching. Daniel, a white bedsheet held aloft on a broomstick, led the group down the center of Queen Helene Street, across Monbaz Street, and on toward the Arab enclave of Musrara.

What could this mean? Robed figures, obviously Arabs. Grab a rifle. Take aim!

On closer inspection, those were children, accompanied

by Jewish soldiers.

Pinky, Mangus, and Chaim flanked the group on one side; Alfie, Ibrahim, and Hymie on the other. Jacob walked along behind. Sal lagged distantly back, as if not wanting to be seen as part of the procession.

They came to a roll of concertina wire. A pair of Haganah guards challenged them. What was this? Where were they going?

Jacob answered, explained.

The guards exchanged a look. There were no orders to cover this situation. Finally, one of them shrugged. The two sentries, helped by Pinky and Daniel, dragged apart sandbags to create a narrow space in the barricade.

"*Tifl yati!*" Daniel yelled loudly. "Children, come!"

With Daniel translating, Jacob said to the children, "This is as far as we can safely go." He handed Hadi the bedsheet. "Keep to the center of the road. Walk briskly, but don't run. Someone will meet you on the other side."

Nodding gravely, Hadi accepted the flag of truce. The children passed the opening. In single file they marched toward the corner, turned it, and disappeared.

■　　■　　■　　■

As Sabbath ended with the setting of the sun that Saturday evening, one-fourth of the Jewish Quarter had been lost to the Mufti's forces. The Haganah's hopes of recapturing Zion Gate were smashed by the Arab onslaught, which had begun with the withdrawal from the belfry of the Church of St. Jacques.

Among the Jewish residents five hundred elderly men

and women, mothers, fathers, and children had fled their homes between the hours of one and five that afternoon. They had carried away meager food supplies and the clothes on their backs. Hungry, demoralized, homeless, they took shelter in the Stambuli Synagogue. Since it was at the heart of the Jewish district and built partially below-ground, it was assumed that the building would be the safest place when the battle began again.

Moshe stood on the dais of the auditorium between Dov Avram and Rabbi Lebowitz. On the opposite side of the platform was Rabbi Akiva and six or so of his supporters.

Akiva, proud and angry, convinced of the folly of resistance, appealed to the people. "We should sur-render! Put up a white flag! We lived in peace with our Arab neighbors before. By surrendering we will live in peace with them again!"

Moshe, gripping the bema, retorted, "Do not be deceived! Surrender will mean a massacre! Like Kfar Etzion!"

"Propaganda," argued Akiva. "Lies put out by the Jewish Agency to frighten us! It is not true. The people of the kibbutz surrendered and were escorted in safety to Jordan."

Dov Avram eyed his father-in-law with disdain. "Who told you this?" he demanded. "What cousin of Haj Amin have you been talking to that you would repeat such a lie?"

Akiva raised his chin in defiance. "Rumors. Rumors only. You heard how the Muslims offered our people food. Bread. Tomatoes. If we will throw down our weapons and . . ."

Dov's eyes flashed with fury. "Bread they offer! Bread!

In exchange for the lives of our children. In exchange for Jerusalem. It was no different in Warsaw for us! Have you forgotten this soon?"

Men and women stood to shout him down. "What will we feed our children? How will we survive? The Arabs loot our homes!"

Akiva, smug and pleased at the sentiments, crossed his arms and glared at Dov, daring him to reply.

Moshe stepped away from the podium. It was once more the hour for Dov, "the Bear of Warsaw," to speak the truth.

"This is not Poland," declared Akiva.

Dov retorted, "But we remain Jews! Do you think the demons who possessed the Nazis died when Hitler died? Evil men may perish, but evil lives on and on! The demons of the Aryan race today control other people who will serve them. The foul voices from hell are crying for the destruction not only of Jews but of righteous Gentiles who believe the promises of God. The slaughter of everyone who serves the Most High is the goal. Only the language and the year are different!"

"You are the deceiver! If we give them what they want, they will let us live peacefully in Jerusalem. They will feed us!" Akiva insisted.

Dov shook his head in wonder. "There was a Christian man in Warsaw, a righteous man who every week threw a sack of bread over the wall of the ghetto to starving Jewish children. And with his gift he sent verses from the Bible, *nu?* Stories about Jesus feeding the five thousand and how He loved the children. He sent warnings, too, that we must not sell ourselves for the bread the Nazis might offer. He was caught one night and executed. His body hung for weeks, rotting, beside the ghetto wall as a warning to other Christians not to help us."

"The Arabs will not execute us. They offer peace and security, if only we will . . ."

"Give them what they want? Were you in Warsaw when the Nazis offered us peace if only we would give them ten thousand of our oldest . . . of our youngest? The elderly and the sick . . . useless mouths . . . marked for destruction. These went first to their deaths. Peace, our leaders begged the Nazis! Let us live! We won't bother you. And the demons said, *Well then,* give us five thousand more *little* Jews, and we will give you remaining Jews of Warsaw bread to eat! And the demons, dressed in men's flesh and wearing trench coats adorned with death's heads and swastikas, promised food for those five thousand mothers and children . . . if only they would surrender. It was, I thought at the time, an evil mockery of the Christian martyr hanging outside our wall, of his story about a loving Jesus feeding the five thousand on a hillside in Israel. *Let the little children come unto me.* Satan twists the sacred and loving into something profane. He mocks the holy and legislates against the good. Yet, even after that righteous man's warning, five thousand mothers and children believed the lie and marched to the Umschlagplatz to wait for the trains and for the bread."

There was an aching foreboding in the congregation.

Akiva slammed his fist down upon his palm. "Tragic, yes! But it is not the same! We have lived in peace among the Muslims for centuries. Minor disturbances only. We can mend the breach. We have done it before!"

Rabbi Lebowitz stepped forward, his hands trembling.

"From this day there will be no peace for Israel. The end of the age is too near. Evil will increase in the nations, and Jerusalem will be at the center of conflict. What Dov says is true! We do not fight just against flesh and blood but against a wicked and powerful force who hides behind politics and holy causes. He would destroy Israel and drive the People of the Book from Jerusalem to defeat the promises of the Almighty! Take courage! Remember what is written in Isaiah 62:1! The Lord has said, *For Zion's sake I will not keep silent, for Jerusalem's sake I will not remain quiet!*"

"But how will we eat?" shouted a woman from the gallery.

Moshe then took the bema again. "Loaves and fishes . . . food shared and divided will feed us as long as we hold out. Deliverance is near. Haganah Headquarters has promised. Very soon we will receive reinforcements. Everyone in the Quarter must bring all food to the Hurva. There can be no hoarding. If you brought a sack of flour from your home today, take it to Hannah Cohen and old Shoshanna. The Lord is with us."

■　■　■　■

Hours passed. Rachel and Lori waited in the library of the convent for Mother Superior's decision. They were served hot tea and four pieces of melba toast by a novice, then left alone.

There was a tall fireplace with a clock above the mantel. On three walls, leather-bound books in variegated shades of red, blue, green, and tan climbed, like roses on a trellis, twelve feet of cherrywood shelves to the gothic arch of the ceiling. It was, thought Rachel, a garden for the mind. Pluck a volume. Inhale the wisdom of the sages.

The books were divided by language. Those in Latin were by far the most plentiful. There, among two hundred others, gleamed the red-and-gold volumes of St. Augustine's *City of God.* Another section contained Greek texts. Hebrew writings, familiar, friendly names that called to Rachel's memory, were represented; also French, German, Italian, and English.

"It reminds me of my father's library," Rachel said aloud, her voice a surprising intrusion in the quiet. "He was a rabbi in Warsaw."

Lori, who had been standing in front of the German-language writings with a book in her hands, did not turn around, did not speak.

The clock tocked; slow, syncopated, as though it were there as a companion, not to mark the time. A chime counted eight bells.

At last Lori began to read in German:

Ich möchte aus meinem Herzen hinaus . . .
I would like to step out of my heart
and go walking beneath the enormous sky.
I would like to pray.
And surely of all the stars that perished
long ago,
one still exists.
I think that I know
which one it is—
which one, at the end of its beam in the sky,

Her finger marking the place in the slim book, she pivoted, eyes shining, to face Rachel.

"It is beautiful," Rachel said, coming to her side.

"Rainer Maria Rilke," Lori whispered. "My father used to read his poems to my mother. I have not read anything in my own language in nearly nine years. Since we fled Germany." She caressed the volume. "It is like . . . hearing Papa's voice again."

How Rachel knew the feeling. Six months earlier, when she had arrived in Jerusalem and met her grandfather for the first time, she had sat for hours beside the window and listened to the conversations in Yiddish in the streets of the Old City. Children called to one another and rabbis discussed the Torah even as they walked, and women talked about children. It had been so familiar. It was Warsaw returned from the dead. Her brothers once again played stickball in the street before the eyes of her longing. She was home again, a child again, untouched by that which had stolen her life.

"Read more." Rachel sank into a chair at the reading table.

Eagerly, Lori sat across from her, turning the familiar pages, scanning the stanzas for a passage she remembered. "Ah!" she cried, fixing on a page. "Here is one for you. 'The Magnificat.' Mary, pregnant, coming to Elizabeth. My father preached a sermon on it. His last sermon. It was in November 1938, just before Kristallnacht. The writings and poems of Rilke were forbidden, you see. Burned in massive bonfires in the streets with many other books. The brownshirts had come and decimated his library. But Papa had memorized many of Rilke's works." She drew back, embarrassed. "I am talking too much."

Rachel reached across and took the volume from her, keeping the place her finger had marked. There had been a time when a spoken word in German had made her tremble. But no more. She began to read, "*Sie kam den Hang herauf, schön schwer.*"

> *She came up the slope, heavy, almost unable*
> *to believe in comfort, hope, or counsel;*
> *but when that stately pregnant matron*
> *proudly and solemnly came toward her*
>
> *and knew everything without her confiding,*
> *then beside her suddenly she was rested;*
> *cautiously the full women held each other,*
> *until the young one spoke: I feel as if*
>
> *from now on, love, I am for ever.*
> *God pours into the wealthy's vanity*
> *almost without paying heed its glitter;*
> *yet carefully seeks himself a woman*
> *and fills her with his farthest time.*
>
> *That he found me. Imagine; and issued*
> *for my sake commands from star to star—.*
>
> *O glorify with all your might, my soul,*
> *and raise on high: the LORD.*

Rachel finished, stroking the words on the page. Understanding in her own heart what the poet had written. Did Lori know the meaning? Did she grasp that these words were not only for Mary, but for everyone?

Lori blinked. A single tear coursed down her cheek. Her hands shook. Was it the memory of her father's arrest, or something else that melted the hardness Rachel had seen in her eyes?

"It is Pentecost," Lori said simply. "Papa always called it the day of our Magnificat. The point when God poured himself into our hearts so we could know Him."

"That He found *me*," Rachel said, smiling.

"But . . . I lost . . . *Him*. My faith. My hope. Everything, you see."

"He cannot be lost. He is still there. I have walked in the darkness without hope, and He was still there for me when at last I recognized Him."

"I could see God shining in the eyes of the little one who came to be my own. I thought with my baby . . . oh, he was so bright, talking so well . . . a happy little boy . . . to lose him just as he learned to say 'I love you.' Just as he looked to me for every answer. And now, you see, I have no answers anymore."

Rachel scanned the pages of Rilke's works. Was there another poem that would speak to this wounded heart? She put the book down and prayed her own heart would speak. "I beg you, Lori . . . sister . . . be patient with everything that is uncertain in your soul. Cherish the questions and believe that the answers are there . . . like the wise books in this room that are written in a language you do not speak. Do not yet demand answers. They cannot be given to us in this life because we could not live with them. We are called to live with everything. Joy and heartache. To know God's heart sometimes means also to suffer. After the Magnificat came the tears of Mary. I think sometimes of her, the questions she must have had. But we women must live even the questions joyfully. Perhaps one day you will, without knowing how or when, live along into the answer."

After a time Lori raised her eyes to meet Rachel's steady gaze. "It is the living along toward that day that is difficult."

Rachel rose, leaving the book facedown on the table. She reached out to Lori, embracing her. Lori sighed and wiped her eyes with the back of her hand. "All right," she said, returning to study the shelves again.

The clock struck nine. The door of the library opened. Mother Superior entered.

"There is bad news from the Jewish Quarter. The Muslims have taken a large portion of the Jewish territory. They are, even now, burning and looting. Many Jews are wounded, they say. What is it we must do?" the nun asked.

Rachel said, "Live long enough to come back and make the stones sacred by your prayers once again."

"Tonight is the Vigil of Pentecost. Come, Holy Spirit, guide and guard our path. We will pray for the Lord's protection for ourselves and for you. You will need the protection of the Lord and the clothes of a novice."

It was concluded at last. The nuns of Soeurs Réparatrices would leave in the morning after the first shelling from Musrara was completed. Five minutes would give the sisters a head start across the danger zone of Jaffa Road and into the Old City.

The convent, today a place of peace and refuge, would tomorrow become an embattled tower across from New Gate to challenge the Arabs holding the Christian Quarter. Tomorrow men would kill men upon the sacred walls within yards of where Jesus was crucified.

"You will be back. This will end," Rachel said.

Mother Superior responded sadly, "You are right. Of course you are. Maybe one day we will replant the trees in our garden. Such things can be replaced. *Oui.* But what of the lives of the two of you? And your unborn child? Of the sisters? Of the wounded in the Jewish Quarter? And the men who will fight here? Once lost, a life cannot be planted to grow again." She fixed her eyes on the olive-wood crucifix beside the door. "To think these stones, which have absorbed the prayers of many lifetimes, could become a rampart. A fortress of soldiers."

Rachel replied, "Mother, perhaps the prayers that have been said here will protect those who hide behind these stones."

"I think not, Rachel. Unless the Lord lifts Soeurs Réparatrices into the clouds to hide it there, people will die here. The world, which is just a dream to us within these walls, will take this peaceful place, but not our hearts. The peace of Jesus goes with us."

■ ■ ■ ■ CHAPTER 12 ■ ■ ■ ■

The angry flurry of communiqués from the Mufti lit a renewed fire in the Arab commanders who battled the Jews in the Old City and held back the

Jews in the New City.

Captain Ahkmed al-Malik rose from his prayer rug in the Dome of the Rock. *"Insh' Allah,"* he remarked to Hassan el-Hassan.

"Insh' Allah. As Allah wills it," Hassan repeated.

Al-Malik shook his head and raised his eyes heavenward. "If only it could be, Hassan. But it must be as the Mufti wills. I am certain the Mufti consults Allah, but if that is true, then Allah has told him it is my fault that the convent and Notre Dame have been lost to the Jews."

"Surely the Mufti knows it was taken out of our control. The old woman, the nun, got in the way of our marksmen. She raised her arms thus . . ." He demonstrated, stretching out his arms wide. "She commanded that our men shall not shoot. She raised her finger to point at us on the wall and threatened that their blood will be upon our heads."

"So be it," al-Malik remarked resolutely. "Thus says our Mufti, Haj Amin el-Husseini. He says here in this latest dispatch, if the nuns of Soeurs Réparatrices will not get out of the way, then we should kill them. This, he says, is the will of Allah. They will sooner or later have to be got rid of. We shall have a police station there where the convent stands. But first we should kill them."

Hassan considered the order. "Are we to kill them? Or get them out of the way?"

"The mother nun will not be moved. She will cling to the soil of her convent until her dying breath. We should be done with the matter, I think. The Mufti will thank us for it."

"True. He will thank us."

Al-Malik raised his hand and pointed up at the arches of

172

the inner arcade of the Dome. "There you see, Hassan, the words the Prophet, blessed be he, spoke about the Christians. It is written so we will not regret the killing of heretics even though they be these crones from the convent."

In the glory of turquoise were the Arabic words from the Koran: *This Jesus, son of Mary, was only Allah's apostle. Believe then in Allah and Mohammed his prophet and do not say God is a trinity. Desist from this assertion for your own good.*

Hassan said fervently, "Haj Amin, our Mufti, will soon be king over Jerusalem, and he will see that such injunctions are enforced. The Jews and the Christians together shall we drive into the sea! *Insh' Allah!*"

Al-Malik nodded and rubbed the stubble on his chin. "May his will be done. But this dispatch from the Mufti is explicit. The infidel women are not to interfere with the plan. The convent is to be our fortress, blocking the Jews from entry into the Old City by way of New Gate or Jaffa Gate." Adjusting his keffiyeh, he seemed satisfied with the decision. "Tomorrow morning, then. After the shelling. We shall retake the grounds of the convent and accomplish what the Mufti has required."

■　■　■　■

Mother Superior addressed the members of the convent, telling them of her determination to leave. "The Lord spoke clearly to my heart as I prayed," she said. "Tonight is the Vigil of Pentecost. The night the Lord gave Moses the Law on Sinai. Many years later in Jerusalem the Lord

Jesus, the Messiah of Israel, told his disciples they must watch and pray on this night and be ready when the Spirit of the living God descends to write the Law upon their hearts. The Scripture portion for today is in the book of Joel, chapters two and three. It was clearly prophesied with today in mind. Israel is reborn. Jerusalem is restored. In the morning we must remember these words and believe that if God can create such a miracle before our eyes, we must be part of it." She opened her Bible and began to read:

Everyone who calls on the name of the LORD will be saved; for on Mount Zion and in Jerusalem there will be deliverance, as the LORD has said, among the survivors whom the LORD calls. In those days and at that time, when I restore the fortunes of Judah and Jerusalem, I will gather the nations . . . there I will enter into judgment against them concerning My inheritance, My people Israel, for they scattered My people among the nations and divided up My land.

"The Word of the Lord."

"Amen."

"Tonight we choose whom we will serve. We will have guests walking with us. They will enter the Old City with us and then go on to the Jewish Quarter. We are called to assist them."

"Amen."

There was not a ripple of uneasiness among them.

As night wore on the nuns were quiet, accepting. Then they glided, two by two, into their chapel for the Vigil of Pentecost, the night of waiting. Rachel and Lori followed after them, standing in the back of the small sanctuary as the evening prayers were sung. Even with the interminable popping of carbines, the blast of grenades, the staccato of machine guns, their ears seemed to hear another sound. Passive now that the decision to leave was made, the nuns offered songs and prayers as though the morning would never come. How Lori envied their calm acceptance when they were clearly giving up everything they loved. Lori had lost everything dear to her; how she raged against it and against the God who had allowed it!

They sang *Veni Creator Spiritus:*

> *Come Creator Spirit . . .*
> *Drive away all powers of evil*
> *Give us always peace and comfort;*
> *With You as guide to keep us all,*
> *Evil fails, no harm will hurt us.*

The chapel of the convent was spartan, bare of decoration. There were no pews or kneelers, just bare stone beneath the gothic arches of the ceiling. Christ, crucified, hung behind the altar. One by one the sisters prostrated themselves before the crucifix, in imitation of those faithful women who had remained at the foot of the cross to watch him die in agony when everyone else had run away.

Now they, too, were running.

■　■　■　■

Dov and Yehudit sat together in the darkness on the worn

steps of the Street of the Stairs. The glow of burning Jewish homes along Ararat Road lit the sky. Beyond the barricades came the taunting call, "Are you hungry, Jews? There is plenty to eat here. Wouldn't you like to eat fresh, warm challah?"

The smell of baking bread wafted on the air. Was it their imagination? Or had the Jihad Moquades fired up the dormant ovens in the Armenian bakery to torment the hungry population behind the barricades?

"You did well tonight." Yehudit cradled Dov's head in her lap. "I was proud of you."

He inhaled and let the breath release slowly. He had not slept in days. He was grateful Moshe had come, but angry about the loss of the belfry of St. Jacques.

"This much I did not say. What happened today did not need to happen. We . . . they . . . yielded our safety, our stronghold, to an official sitting behind a desk in America who probably has never missed a meal in his life or had to fight for his home. Moshe should have pretended not to have got such an order. Told them the radio was broken . . . anything. He was with the English army in the war too long." He gave a vacant salute. "Yes, sir. No, sir. Ah yes, it is the honorable thing to do to give away our hard-won territory so an Armenian priest is not offended by us, sir." He sat up. "Our fellows died today because of that."

"It is done."

"No. We'll have to take St. Jacques back from the Muslims or no one will ever get through Jaffa Gate or Zion Gate to relieve us."

"How can we do such a thing when the Arabs have taken the houses between here and there?"

"The Jihad Moquades waste their time looting the houses of the rabbis and the poor of the quarter." Dov grinned bitterly. "They believe the Jews have hidden treasure in the walls of their houses. *Meshuggener.* So, let them look. Let them smash and burn. They waste time. Their looting buys us time to regroup."

"My father is landlord of half the hovels in the neighborhood. Today he lost his tenants. Tonight the Arabs burn his property. He is not a happy man in his wide, empty house."

"And now what to do with the people?"

She put his hand to her cheek and kissed his fingers.

For the last week Dov had allowed himself two tepid cups of soup each day, and his bones were obvious beneath his flesh. But his skinny face was not as gaunt as it was during the days of hunger in Warsaw.

"This is nothing. Nothing." Then, "How much food was turned in at the soup kitchen?"

"Not much. Shoshannah says everyone came forward with something. But something is not much. My father has locked his house and bolted the door. Poor Papa."

"He does not look underfed, your father. He is no doubt feasting behind his door."

"There are hungry children, Dov. It should not be. Papa kept a storehouse of food in the cellar. Sometimes, in bad years, his tenants pay him with food. Grain and the like. This has been a bad year, *nu?* He used to wholesale the stuff through an Arab merchant named Habib, who owned several stalls in the souks." She closed her eyes and inhaled. "In the Arab district there is plenty to eat. The souks remain open. I smell the lamb *shashlik* cooking. . . .

Oy! Unless it is a hallucination. Ah, well. Papa might have got his merchandise out to sell. He was connected with the English soldiers, you know. They might have taken it out of the Quarter for him. I can't say what went on after I left."

Dov leveled a look at her. "It is worth asking, *nu?*"

■   ■   ■   ■

From atop the dome of the Hurva, Moshe watched with disgust as the curve of Ararat Road lit up.

"So they burn the Jewish houses," Ehud said softly. "They think the gold we have hidden in the walls will melt, *nu?*" He laughed.

Moshe could see figures of looters, men and women, dashing in and out of shops and homes. The things they carried away with them would not have brought ten pounds sterling in a flea market. "The wealth of the Jews, eh?"

"It does not make a very big fire."

Moshe did not reply for a long time. The stars were obscured as the wind shifted, driving the smoke toward them and The Dome of the Rock.

"There is something I need to say." Moshe kept his gaze riveted on the glow. "St. Jacques."

"Yes," Ehud agreed without anything else being said. "St. Jacques."

"I will not let it happen again."

"No."

What was left to say? Both men knew that perhaps there would never be an opportunity for such a mistake to be made a second time. Gestures of appeasement to people who did not play by the same rules had cost too much. The surrender of St. Jacques may have spelled the end of the Jewish enclave in the Old City of Jerusalem.

■　■　■　■

Nearly seventy hours had passed since Moshe last slept. He ached with mind-numbing exhaustion. The celebration of the Jihad Moquades assured they would be busy for a while. At Ehud's urging, Moshe climbed from the outpost of the synagogue to return to the cellar of Rabbi Lebowitz. It would be peaceful there. He would sleep an hour or two. When he awoke, his mind would be clear again. He would know better what to do and how to do it.

Moshe descended the steps of the tiny flat, the specter of his failure following him. He discovered he had no strength to knock. He brushed his fingers against his lips, then touched the mezuzah case that hung upon the doorpost. *Shaddai. Protector of the doors of Israel. Today I have failed. The doors of Israel were left open by my stupidity. . . .*

Grandfather was not sleeping. As if he heard Moshe's thoughts, the latch was lifted and the door thrown back. A candle burned on the table behind him. A parchment scroll was open.

"You are going to sleep standing up? Come in. Come in." He stepped aside and guided Moshe to the bed.

"Where is Yacov?"

"With the other boys. Together sleeping at the synagogue."

"You are still awake?" Moshe mumbled, sorry he had not found a corner in the synagogue to rest.

"It is seven weeks since the Passover lamb was sacrificed, *nu?* Fifty days. Pentecost. *Shavuot.*"

Moshe's mind struggled to focus. "I forgot."

"Of course. You have forgotten. A war you are fighting after all," he chided. "Remember the Lord giving the Law to Moses? A small thing when you are fighting a war. It is only a small thing, Pentecost. Everything that was and is and shall be. . . . Night of thunder and fire upon Sinai when God spoke, and no one in the camp could sleep."

Moshe was certain he would have been the one exception in the tents of Israel. Yacov was sleeping. The dog was sleeping. Would Grandfather want Moshe to stay awake with him? Study the Bible, recite the prayers . . . *sing?* Moshe wanted to weep.

Grandfather's face was animated. "I heard the thunder."

"Muslims. Blowing up captured houses."

"Good. *Good!* They do your work for you so you can sleep awhile. The Almighty is good. Protecting the doors of Israel while you sleep, eh? So. They blow up the houses. This also destroys the cellars. The tunnels, *nu?* They cannot then dig from one cellar to the next and come into our Quarter through the tunnels. Nor can they take shelter and fire upon us from our own homes. True?"

"Of course, true." Moshe groaned the words, but he saw the reason for the old man's pleasure.

"Now." He nudged Moshe down onto the pillow and whispered, "It is Pentecost . . . the giving . . . tonight as of old I will stand vigil with the open scroll of the Torah. But you must sleep." He took a blanket from a chest and covered Moshe with it. His crooked fingers brushed back Moshe's matted hair. It was a tender touch, one of a father for a son. "You are safe, Moshe. Fear not, my boy. . . . Believe. Believe what is written. Pentecost . . . He comes to us in thunder and fire. He speaks. The thunder is the voice of Him who watches over the doors. . . ."

■　■　■　■

When Yacov raised himself up on an elbow, he shuddered at the appearance of Nissan Bek Synagogue's basement. Rows and rows of sleeping refugees, crowded into safety, looked like corpses. For modesty's sake, women and children slept on one side of the hall, men on the other, but the number evicted from their homes on Ararat Road completely packed the space.

Yacov smelled the smoke. The acrid, pervasive aroma was a constant reminder that these sleeping families had lost everything except their lives.

The night was impenetrable when Yacov left the cellar of Nissan Bek. The moon had not yet risen, and the air was motionless. There was a group of rabbis meeting in a study room off the main auditorium, gathered around a single, flickering candle. They were immersed in studying the Torah in honor of the giving of the Law on Pentecost and did not notice him sneaking out.

Outside, Shaul was waiting for his boy. The dog had caught a rat for his supper but politely offered it to Yacov. "No, thank you," Yacov said, "but hurry and finish. We have business."

Having experienced the months of siege that the Jews

of the Old City had so far suffered, Yacov knew how desperately short of resources the Quarter was. Until the Haganah forces in the New City could break through with reinforcements, even a single bullet was precious.

Which meant that the unexploded bomb Yacov had seen lying in the gutter across the Street of the Chain was a veritable treasure trove, a gift that could not be overlooked or allowed to go unretrieved.

Fortunately, the boy was perfectly at home in the labyrinthine byways and souks of the Old City, as on many occasions he had needed to escape from irate British soldiers whose pockets he had picked.

Going straight to the trench, Yacov announced to the nervous sentries that he was a courier, and would the guards please take care of his dog for a time? Shaul whined and wriggled, but did not howl as he would have if merely tied up and left behind.

Near the top of the Street of the Jews, and out of sight of the guards, the boy jogged left into a seemingly blind alley. Refuse and filth clogged the lane on top of which a medieval roof arched. Yacov knew that a Haganah sentry was posted overhead, but it was not up that he was going.

At the back of the passageway, behind a broken chair and a pile of garbage, the top of a small window barely protruded above ground level. Was it unlocked, as it had been the last time? Yacov heaved against the sill, but it refused to budge. He tried again, and this time the hinge groaned and moved slightly. The boy hugged the wall, keeping his face turned downward in case the guard heard the noise and looked over the edge to investigate.

No footsteps came from overhead. Hooking his fingers

under the rim, Yacov levered the panel upward. This action opened a passage barely wide enough for him to wriggle through, feet first.

In a flash, he was inside, dropping the six feet to the floor but landing without a sound on a roll of carpet. In fact, the whole room was strewn with carpets: a riot of reds and blues, favored hues of Persian and Turkish rugs.

What Yacov had discovered during a previous escapade was that while the back wall of this building was in the Jewish district, its entrance was in the adjoining Armenian Quarter. Once out the front door Yacov would be beyond the trench and the barricade.

In a closet off the proprietor's office Yacov found the disguise he was seeking: a striped robe with a hood that hid his Orthodox earlocks and allowed him to pass as an Arab youth. After he cinched it high around his waist, doubled the folds, and belted it securely, the clothing merely dragged a little on the ground. Unbolting the front door, he opened it a crack, peered out, and slipped through, closing it behind him.

A brisk walk of two minutes brought Yacov to the intersection dominated by the great souk of the vegetable market and the three parallel culs-de-sac of the butchers' market, the spice market, and the goldsmiths' market. There was no one about. The Quarter's Christian residents had fled, rather than be caught in a cross fire. The Muslims were either standing watch or smoking their narghiles and making extravagant claims of their valorous deeds.

To the east, ahead of him, stretched the impenetrable gloom where the Souk el-Bazaar took a turn to the right and joined the Street of the Chain, the front line of the

183

battle for the Jewish district. This was no place to be rash. From this moment onward Yacov could be shot at by both sides. He leaned forward to peer into the distance, then pressed himself against the wall and crept cautiously along.

From shadow to shadow he went, never moving without listening before and after each advance and always having a line of retreat picked out. Once a trio of Jihad Moquades rushed past, carrying two crates of ammunition and talking loudly of how easily the Jewish Quarter would fall to their next courageous assault, but they did not see Yacov. Everyone knew the Old City Jews were beset on all sides within their insignificant enclave; there was no possibility they would dare launch an attack outside it.

It was the fifth shade into which Yacov flitted that reached and grabbed him. Something murkier than the darkness seized him by the neck, clapped another palm over his mouth, and despite his struggles, dragged him back into the doorway of a cigarette shop. "You, boy," said a gravelly voice in Arabic. "Don't you know it's too dangerous to be out this night?" Gnarled hands forced Yacov to pivot till he found himself staring into the black-cowled visage of an Armenian priest. "You could get killed."

"*Insh' Allah,*" Yacov retorted, also in Arabic. "It is as Allah wills. But let me return to my duty."

"So young and so prepared to die? How will this city ever find peace if the next generation is already poisoned? Go, then," the priest said, releasing his hold with a shove and sending Yacov spinning away from him.

This was the time of the gravest danger. There was no

184

one in the square between the Street of the Jews and the Street of the Chain, nor any reason for an innocent civilian to thrust himself between the jaws of the beast of war. Consequently, anyone seen moving there would be fired on.

A block from the scene, Yacov stretched out full length in the sunken crevice between wall and walkway. Ahead of him were a dead donkey, two shattered pushcarts, and scattered piles of tires. Each one of those mounds of blackness was a shelter, the distance between each a mountain to be conquered.

Movement was reduced to one limb at a time: reach out an arm, pause, wait for any shout of alarm, extend the other, delay again, drag the body up to the hands, scraping the cheek against the rough pavement as he did so. After three breaths the steps were repeated, yard by painfully won yard.

When Yacov reached the corpse of the donkey, he allowed himself an extra minute's rest. This process was taking much longer than he imagined. In his mind he had pictured a swift creeping up to the bomb and an even swifter departure. This crawling was going on forever.

Flies clustered thickly on the defunct animal. When Yacov's hand brushed against its hide, some of them flew up, disturbed from their meal. One found its way under the hood of Yacov's cloak and onto the back of his neck. He dared not swat it or wriggle around to brush it off, even when it bit him.

A chunk of concrete lying atop a ragged truck tire was the next refuge. Next to it lay a fractured length of pipe. Around this Yacov curled, knowing that he was squarely in the cross fire if any shots erupted. He was close enough to the trench to hear Shaul's whines and the low conversation of the guards. "What ails this mongrel?" a Haganah sentry queried. "And what is taking the boy so long to deliver his message?"

"Probably he has gone home to bed," his partner said, laughing. "Leaving you to walk his dog."

Willing Shaul to keep quiet and not show interest in the heap of rags creeping over the cobbles, Yacov gauged his next move. There was no more cover between where he lay and the bomb, only a thick patch of shadow. One foot, two, three. The toe of Yacov's shoe scraping on a projecting knob of stone sounded to him like the grindstones of forty craftsmen in the Street of the Knives.

There was no reaction from either camp. Yacov's satisfaction was growing. Not only would he produce the munitions, but he would chastise the guards for their inattention. His fingers touched the milk can. He eased himself up to it, grasped it with his hands.

It was much heavier than he had expected. Thinking of the normal weight of a milk can, Yacov had planned to tuck the device beneath his robe and scoot back to safety. But this he could not even lift! Now what?

The decision was taken from him by the fly in his collar. Tiring of his neck, the insect wandered over Yacov's earlock and then plunged into his ear.

Yacov slapped the side of his head, and the rim of the can clinked against the stones.

"Someone's out there!" snapped a Haganah sentry.

"Shoot! Shoot!" urged the other.

A burr of Sten-gun fire split the night, and then the

Arabs were shooting also. Neither side knew why they were firing or at what, and the muzzle flashes destroyed the sentries' night vision enough to spoil their aim.

Yacov, on his knees, did the only thing he could think of: he rolled the bomb toward the nearest shelter. This was the entry to an alleyway that ran north off the Street of the Chain. He ducked inside and sat down, leaning back on the bomb, behind a projecting cornice. He was safe for the moment, but on the wrong side of the line, and baffled as to how he would get back.

■ ■ ■ ■ SUNDAY, MAY 16, 1948 ■ ■ ■ ■

On the morning of the third day there was thunder and lightning, with a thick cloud over the mountain, and a very loud trumpet blast. Everyone in the camp trembled. Then Moses led the people out of the camp to meet with God, and they stood at the foot of the mountain. Mount Sinai was covered with smoke, because the LORD descended on it in fire.

Exodus 19:16

*I will pour out my Spirit on
all people.
Your sons and daughters will
prophesy,
your old men will dream
dreams,
your young men will see
visions.*

Joel 2:28

When the day of Pentecost came, they were all together in one place. Suddenly a sound like the blowing of a violent wind came from heaven and filled the whole house where they were sitting. They saw what seemed to be tongues of fire that separated and came to rest on each of them. All of them were filled with the Holy Spirit.

Acts 2:1–4

■ ■ ■ ■ CHAPTER 13 ■ ■ ■ ■

From within the womb of deep sleep, Moshe was aware of the rustling of paper, the faint glow of candlelight through his lids, a solitary voice softly singing ancient hymns. He saw Rachel's face, dreamed she was speaking to him, promising to come home to be with him.

Then there was silence.

Moshe opened his eyes. The candle had burned low. The old man was in a chair beside the bed, watching over Moshe as if he were a child.

"What time is it?" Moshe croaked.

"Very late. Or very early."

"How long have I been asleep?" He sat up.

"Not long."

A feeling of urgency surged through Moshe. He stood, looking for his gun. "I have to get back."

"Ehud and Dov are on duty. We must talk, you and I."

"I am needed."

"The Jihad Moquades are quiet. Even the devil rests sometimes. He may not rest again. We will talk."

"Later, perhaps. I must . . ."

"Now we'll talk. Sit." Rabbi Lebowitz stiffened in his resolve to be heard. Moshe obeyed.

"It is the hour of revelation," began the rabbi, fixing his gaze on the sputtering flame of the candle. *"Zeman Mattan Toratenu."* He pinned Moshe to his place like a headmaster threatening a student with one piercing look. "The tunnels I will show you. . . ."

Moshe brightened, mopped his brow. He had almost forgotten. "Yes! Something about the tunnels. Yacov said . . ."

"Yacov! He is too young to know. When he is older, you will take him; show him, if he is a worthy man."

Moshe's thoughts raced. Could the old man have an alternate route from the Quarter? Some way to bypass the walls of the Old City? To bring in men and supplies for defense?

An expression of bemusement flickered behind the gray beard. "I know what you are dreaming."

"If there is a passage out, you must show me."

"It is *Shavuot, nu?* One of the three great pilgrim festivals. Like *Sukkot* and Passover. Next year in Jerusalem, we say. No one goes *out* of the Holy City on Pentecost. No. All the men of Israel come here. To the Temple Mount. Jews of every language make pilgrimage and bring the firstfruits of the harvest. And we bring our children to the Lord . . . initiate them to the words with a taste of honey and they will remember the sweetness of the day. It has always been. *Nu?*"

"Yes. Of course." Moshe started to object to the time that slipped away as the rabbi talked on, cherishing the thoughts and words he had been studying, as if there were no war.

"So. Moshe. We must make pilgrimage tonight. While the devil sleeps, we must walk to the place where the words of the Most High are sealed. Until you I had no hope of having a son to show these things. You will come with me. And I will show you what was meant for Rachel's father. Or for Yacov if he were older. You will show him

190

when he's older. There will be no later, Moshe Sachar. *Nu?* You have married my only granddaughter. Like it or not, you are my heir. So. You will follow this old man, and I will show you . . ."

"The tunnels?"

"Yes, yes. The tunnels."

■ ■ ■ ■

Grandfather led Moshe across the street and in through the back entrance of the Hurva.

As if reading Moshe's impulse to climb instantly to the roof and rejoin the men on watch, the rabbi quietly remarked, "What I show you this hour is the salvation of all Israel. Come."

At that, the old man turned on his heel and shuffled out into the sanctuary, then down the stone steps that led to the basement. From there he led Moshe farther to a set of nearly vertical treads that descended into the bowels of Jerusalem and the labyrinth of connecting passageways. He paused long enough to light a lantern, then struck out confidently down one of five rough-chiseled corridors in the direction of the Western Wall and his former home. The house, Moshe knew, was too near the high wall of the Haram, The Dome of the Rock, to be safe. Since Arab snipers had a clear shot at anyone who attempted to pray in the narrow corridor before the Western Wall, it had been months since any rabbi had attempted to do so.

The tunnel twisted and turned, following the ragged course of the houses and alleyways above, here sloping upward, there descending.

"Where are we going?" Moshe asked impatiently.

The rabbi did not answer but continued doggedly on, passing from one cellar to the other. Above, Haganah soldiers patrolled the rooftops of the Quarter.

Thirty minutes passed in this unexplained pursuit. Moshe stopped in the tunnel and called after the retreating back of the rabbi, "I am needed above."

Grandfather turned fiercely, the light of his lantern casting a long shadow on the rubbled stone wall behind him. "So. You think men cannot die without you? You have been absent from us here for a time. Before this little war, you left the ancient ways and shamed your dear father. Left the holy places for other things. *Nu?* Dov, Rabbi Vultch, Ehud, and Shimon, may he rest in peace, managed to lead brave men and fight without Moshe Sachar. So! If it takes all night! What I show you is . . . everything."

Moshe blinked at him, humbled like an erring boy before his Torah school teacher. The rabbi turned on his heel, knowing Moshe would follow without protest.

One hundred and fifty yards were traversed until Grandfather stooped to pass through the wall into the cellar of his own house. He stopped in the center of the empty cubicle and inhaled with contentment. There was a half-smile behind his beard as he set the lantern down on the floor.

Moshe entered. The space was a meager twelve feet by twelve feet. Twenty feet beneath the present street, it had once been aboveground. There was clear evidence of a door and a window, which were barricaded with debris. The present structure had been built on the ruins of an ancient house, which, Moshe guessed, was likewise built upon another.

Grandfather nodded as he observed Moshe's transitory interest in the history of the place. "So, Mr. Archaeologist, it is very old, *nu?*"

"Very."

"Such interesting things you will find in your grandfather's cellar." There was amusement in the old man's eyes when he raised his hands as if in benediction and placed his palms on either side of a pillar of stone that formed part of the wall beneath the stairway.

The column groaned as it swung away easily at his touch.

Musty water scented the cellar. Light from the lantern barely illuminated a tiny space behind the secret portal that twisted away beyond the beams.

Grandfather laughed aloud at Moshe's astonishment. "So," cried the rabbi, "now he sees! Now it is clear to him!"

Moshe knew well that Herodian streets still coursed beneath the Old City of Jerusalem. He had explored the excavations of men who had discovered a few of these passageways from antiquity.

"There is a way into the Quarter, then? A way for us to bring in supplies?"

The rabbi put a finger to his lips, silencing speculation. "Everything. It is everything. Salvation is what I have promised you, but first you must make a vow."

Moshe frowned and moved past him to peer down the long, contorted corridor, constructed of enormous stone blocks. The ceiling was low, and it was wide enough for just one man to pass at a time. The floor was worn into grooves where centuries of feet had walked.

"A vow?"

"You will not find the way unless I show you."

"The way?"

"There are twenty branches off this entry. Many drop into cisterns. A man could die if he did not know where to go."

"Where does it lead?"

"Many places. But tonight? Beneath The Dome of the Rock."

Moshe could not reply. A passage that led beneath the Temple Mount? Perhaps a way for members of the Haganah to infiltrate the Arab Quarter.

"I see your thoughts," the rabbi instructed. "Silence them. No man will pass here but you. And me. Until the time is right."

"Why?"

"Because it is everything."

"Beneath the Haram?"

"It was Solomon's Temple before it was the Haram. It was the altar of sacrifice. The sanctuary. The Holy of Holies where the Shekinah Glory of the Almighty dwelt among us."

"Yes. All of that."

"Then came the armies of Babylon. Then the Second Temple and Herod's Temple where the gentle one from Nazareth taught and offended many even as many among us believed. After him the destruction by the Romans. From that hour we wandered the world without a homeland. Until now, Moshe. Everything I speak of was foretold. Even the events of this day. Everything on earth means something in the heavens, *nu?*"

"Yes."

The rabbi's eyes narrowed. "Everything. *Nu?*"

What secret did the old man know? What was it he intended to show Moshe?

"So. Swear that where I lead, you will tell no man until Yacov is mature enough . . . good enough." He frowned. "And if Yacov should not live, your own son will walk the way with you. One day Jerusalem will be ours. Then all that was written will come to pass. All that was hidden will be revealed. So, by the Most High, bind your soul to obey what I command you."

"I . . . yes . . ."

"Say it."

"By the Most High, I . . . will obey what you command me."

"Swear by your very life. By the life of my grand-daughter, Rachel, and by the child she carries."

Moshe raised his hand. He knew well how serious was a vow taken by the Hasidim. Could the rabbi mean that even the life of his granddaughter was weighed in the balance of Moshe's oath? Was even her life less sacred to him than the secret he carried?

"By my own life." He could not bring himself to place Rachel and their unborn child in this archaic spiritual formula that required a soul and a life for the violation of an oath.

The rabbi laughed. "Not Rachel? So. You hear him, God? That is good. You must love my granddaughter very much to maybe miss such a journey beneath the Haram."

Then he cheerfully added, "Enough joking. If you break your oath, may your throat be cut from ear to ear, your belly cut open, and your entrails burned before your eyes. May you be dismembered and scattered to the four winds so no more notice will be taken of your name from that day until forever. Now swear."

Beads of sweat formed on Moshe's brow. Considering what the Jihad Moquades wanted to do to the Jewish defenders, this violent end was a distinct possibility. He cleared his throat. "I swear."

"*Oy!* Such a welcome you are having to the family, *nu?*"

The old man covered his head with the tallith that had been draped over his shoulders. Presenting one end of the tasseled border to Moshe, he said, "Wrap the fringes of the tallith around the fingers of your left hand."

Moshe complied.

"Extend your right hand thus." The rabbi held up the index finger of his right hand. "This shall be our candle in the darkness. Ask no questions of me. Once we begin the journey, we step upon holy ground. Obey my commands, and you will live."

At that, the old man blew out the flame in the lantern. Blackness—thick, almost tangible, oppressive—flooded in from the corners of the cellar. Did he mean to lead them through the corridor without a lamp?

Grandfather tugged Moshe toward the open portal. "Stay close to me. Do not let go of the fringes." Moshe pressed near to his back as they walked. As they entered the passageway, the air grew decidedly cooler.

"Raise your candle above your head," Grandfather

whispered.

Moshe lifted his finger as he was told, feeling the cold stone lintel over him.

The rabbi instructed, "There are three slots in the center of the rock. One as wide as three fingers. One as wide as two. The last only as wide as a man's fingertip, as deep as the first joint. You want the last. Do you feel it, my son?"

Moshe swept his finger across the low ceiling until it sank into the specified groove. A sense of exultation seized him. How simple was this map and yet how ingenious! "I have it."

"Good. Very good. We are attached. Like an electric car in Warsaw, *nu?* Find the beginning. A small hole. Push in firmly."

Something moved beneath Moshe's fingertip. The entrance stone closed behind them with a moan. Deafening silence accompanied the absolute blindness of the space.

"Our journey of faith begins. From here, you must obey only what your candle tells you," said Grandfather. "Along the way you will feel the blasts of air from side tunnels. Do not let your mind be drawn to them. Follow only the narrow way. We go."

■　■　■　■

Like a blind man clinging to the tail of a horse that knew the way home, Moshe held tightly to the tallith. Pointing skyward, his index finger slid easily along the smooth, half-inch-wide track in the roof. Three times he felt the blast of chilled air from secondary passages. The rabbi did not halt or waver from his path.

Their footsteps were mincing, one foot placed in front of the other. Moshe counted one hundred, and the channel beneath his fingertip made a sharp turn to the right. A wisp of moisture struck his face as they entered a byway, and a long, slow descent began.

Three times the procedure repeated: one hundred steps, a turn so precipitate that the path seemed to double back upon itself, three switchbacks down, then a wide space— a platform? The slot swept to the left, leading through another gateway.

Once they were inside it, the pattern of descending and doubling back was followed twice more. Next came a level, yet curving, path that arced ever to the right. Again and again Moshe felt gusts from other openings. The warning of the old man about forgotten cisterns rang in his head.

Rabbi Lebowitz never paused to question where he was.

Moshe lost track of time. Yet, because of his blindness, the map of this unexplained journey was indelibly imprinted on his mind. The rustle of the tallith, the shuffle of feet, his heartbeat, his breathing mingled to deliver a sort of rhythm, reminding him that he was not dreaming. He was not dead. His thoughts were perfectly focused on the tip of his finger. It seemed to hold all of Jerusalem above him, with the weight of the ages balanced on the point.

How deep had they descended? How far back into the ages had they trod?

Seventy paces into the last passage, the rabbi halted. Reaching back, he grasped Moshe's wrist and guided the candle hand forward against a wall.

"Here it ends," he croaked.

Against a wall?

The rabbi murmured, "Kneel and raise your candle again." He dropped, and Moshe followed him as he continued the pilgrimage forward on his knees. The fabric of the prayer shawl tugged him onward through an opening one yard high. Raising his hand, Moshe found the slot in the roof. His knees fit into two perfectly polished grooves worn smooth in the stone by the progress of centuries of sojourners.

The sound of wind rushed toward them, stinging Moshe's eyes. He closed them, aware he had kept them wide open, searching for, aching for, a glimmer of light. His shoulders brushed the sides of the space. His head touched the roof. For ten yards he continued, and then the ceiling opened up. The walls vanished. They had entered what felt like an immense cavern. The rabbi groaned with relief and under his breath repeated the *Shema:* "Hear O Israel, the Lord our God is One Lord . . ."

Moshe, suddenly afraid, knowing he had entered a sacred place, echoed the old man's prayer.

Grandfather stood with difficulty, placing his coarsely veined hands on Moshe's head to keep him firmly on his knees. He murmured, "It is Pentecost. The hour of revelation. The fulfillment of Your promise to write Your words upon our hearts. Blessed art Thou, O Lord, who has granted us life and sustenance and permitted us to reach this day."

The rabbi covered Moshe with the fabric of the prayer shawl.

Moshe shuddered as cold fingers of excitement raced down his spine. Grandfather had warned him they would be under The Dome of the Rock, beneath the place where the Holy Sanctuary once stood. Everything was in this place, the old man had promised! The salvation of Israel was here! Aboveground men were dying for Israel! Why did the rabbi not light a lamp and show Moshe what he had come for?

As if reading his thoughts, Grandfather remarked gently, "More than two thousand years these stones have been waiting for this moment. Can you not wait one moment with them, Moshe?"

Moshe swallowed hard, choking back a response.

"So," Grandfather continued, "I have promised you, *nu?* I have promised to bring you here. To show you everything. What was. What is. What will come for Holy Yerushalayim." His voice rose to a crescendo, his words resounding in the vault as if a hundred voices were speaking. "The Promise is here. Within your grasp, the wisdom of the ages. Hear the voice of the Lord! 'Call upon Me and I will answer you, and will show you great and hidden things that you have not known! Reach out your hand, O blind man! Touch and see the Light of all the ages!' "

Inexplicably, tears came to Moshe's eyes. His hands quivered as he reached forward to touch something cold, cylindrical, smooth, with raised letters, Hebrew letters, on it.

In that second, a tiny flame sputtered to life, illuminating the Promise.

■   ■   ■   ■

In spite of the darkness, the strong stench of sewage and rotting garbage told Yacov where he was. He was a mere half-block from the barricade and home. Steps leading down to the ladies' underground toilet were just across the alleyway from where he cowered. Beyond that was a trash-heaped, roofed passage. Though parts of it dated from medieval times, the encircling balconies were supported by broken columns recovered from the vanished arcades of Greek or Roman buildings.

Yacov knew the area. He had learned patience in this stinking hovel. How often had he waited here after stealing an English soldier's purse until angry voices and tromping boots had passed by? Since the sole public women's W.C. in the neighborhood dominated this bleak alleyway, even the most furious of English soldiers stood prudently outside to wait for him to emerge. Sometimes Yacov had endured the stink and the jabber of neighborhood women on their way to the toilet until nighttime. Often he had hidden himself behind a large group of cackling females and walked out amid them.

Tonight, however, the streets were deserted, there were no skirts to hide behind, and a thirty-pound can of explosives was more difficult to carry than bills from a pilfered pocketbook.

Yacov listened for a footstep, a whispered word or cough. There was no sound. Across the Street of the Chain he spotted the orange glow of a cigarette. He was uncertain if the watchman was one of his or one of theirs. Either way, he would be shot if he was detected.

This dire certainty drove him farther into the recesses of the alley.

A tall gate opened in the middle of the passage to allow camels to enter the spacious courtyard of the *Wakala,* the inn of caravans. Once they were inside, the camels were fed and cared for in the center of the courtyard. The merchandise was locked in guarded storerooms ringing the ground floor while the merchants slept on the second level. The present structure, called *Khan es-Sultan,* had been built in 1386, a recent construction in the life of Jerusalem. Yacov knew that from the days when Solomon ruled Israel, there had always been a caravansary in this place. The tariff for lodging there always had a religious purpose. Once the income from the galleried inn had been dedicated to Solomon's Temple, then to the Second Temple, next to the Temple of Zeus, and later, to The Dome of the Rock. Tonight the hostel was merely a deserted ruin and the logical refuge for Yacov.

He squatted before the milk can and considered how to move it from its present resting place to one of the storage rooms in the dilapidated warehouse. Running his fingers over the exterior, he found the fuse. This triggered the uneasy memory that milk-can bombs and fuses also meant detonators. He had watched from the stair landing as Ehud and Dov constructed explosive devices. He had learned from such observation that even grown men sweat in winter when a box of detonators falls off the table onto stone.

"So," he muttered to the thing, "you would blow me to pieces and save the Jihad Moquades the trouble? And save

Grandfather the trouble of killing me, if I should live so long? *Oy.*" Closing his eyes, he said a prayer, grasped the fuse, and pulled.

It slid out easily. Now what to do with it? He shoved detonator and fuse into his pocket and rolled the disarmed bomb into the passageway. The rattle of it was deafening, waking guards from their paranoid dreams on both sides of the lines.

Shouts of alarm echoed through the night, first from the Haganah, then answered by the Jihad Moquades.

"Who is there?"

"Halt!"

"Who . . ."

"In the name of the Grand Mufti! Halt!"

"Identify yourself!"

Sentries were shouting at one another, each thinking the other to be the cause of the commotion.

"Halt, or you are dead!" Yacov recognized Ehud's gruff voice.

On the opposite side of the line the same demand was accompanied with the cry "*Allah Ahkbar!*" and the rattle of machine-gun fire.

Yacov used the opportunity to scoot his prize farther from the hurled insults that followed.

Above the commotion, Shaul began to bark, a staccato, Morse-code, frantic kind of call, which let Yacov know that Shaul knew where Yacov was.

Ehud cursed. "It's the dog!"

This information was repeated by an Arab voice on the opposite side. "A cur in the street only."

Moments later, snuffling through the garbage, dragging

the rope that had restrained him, Shaul charged to Yacov's side.

Yacov did not speak to the mongrel, but paused long enough to tug his ear affectionately. He was glad of the company, glad for the help. Tying a loop in the rope, Yacov slipped the noose around the can, hefted it onto the bony back of the animal, and the two of them padded through the tall gate into the littered courtyard.

The quarter-moon slipped out from behind the clouds long enough to illuminate the area. Yacov, one hand on the ruff of Shaul's neck and the other balancing the dynamite, dashed to the nearest doorless cubicle to take cover.

"So!" He huddled in a corner and relieved Shaul of his burden. "Stupid dog! Don't you know you could be killed?"

The dog sat patiently and whined at his master's disapproval. Then, lying down and rolling over onto his back, he waved his paws in the air in surrender.

Yacov sank down beside him to wait.

It was then that the scent of spices wafted through the open door. Yacov inhaled, grateful they were close to the spice market. "Better than the smell of the W.C. all night," he confided, rubbing the dog's belly.

His sense of well-being evaporated the instant after it was born. In the opposite corner of the room a shadowed figure rose to tower over Yacov. "It is dangerous here, boy. Did no one warn you?"

■　■　■　■

The dog growled, low and menacing.

Daoud trembled with dread for what was about to

take place.

Dajani moved to block the escape. "The Prophet has said blessings come to those who serve Allah." The bomber did not carry a gun. He drew his curved knife and ordered Gawan to light the lantern.

Gawan obeyed. Daoud stood facing the Jewish boy and his dog. The captive, who wore a patch over one eye, blinked painfully in the light and cowered against the wall. The dog planted itself between its youthful master and Dajani, its lips curled back in a vicious snarl.

Dajani said to the frightened Jew who looked to be no older than Gawan, "You, good boy, Jew. You have retrieved my dynamite. Your courage will cost you your life."

He made no move forward, however, because of the dog. "Call off your dog," Dajani commanded. The Jew seemed not to understand. "Call it off, or I will slit its throat."

Even though Dajani made the threat, Daoud was certain he was unwilling to brave the animal's teeth to accomplish the feat. "I will have this foolish Jew strung from the wall."

Gawan said, "You have what we came for. Take it and go. He is small. No bigger than myself. It is unworthy to kill something so insignificant. Only a coward would do this."

Dajani hesitated at Gawan's taunt.

Daoud, sensing what Gawan was trying to do, cried, "What? Gawan! Have you forgotten the ears of the Jews? I will begin my collection with this boy!" He swaggered forward and spat toward their prisoner. The dog lunged and barked, driving Daoud back.

Dajani laughed. "Well, then! My two Jihad Moquades! I will leave this brave deed to you!" Then he grabbed Gawan by *his* ears and lifted him up until his toes barely touched the ground. "You little swine. Bring me the ears of this Jewish shoat, or I will have yours drying on a plate. You will find me at the Rawdah School smoking the narghile of your great hero Hassan el-Hassan." His eyes became mere slits. "Now kill this Jew before he grows of a size to kill you. Do it!"

With that, Dajani shoved the curved knife into Daoud's hands, scooped up the can of explosives, and sauntered out.

Daoud brandished the knife and shouted over the sound of Dajani's retreating footsteps, "I, Daoud of the souks, will return this Jew to his people in pieces as a warning to the rest!"

The dog barked and barked. The Jewish boy raised his fists in defense.

Gawan cried loudly, "*Allah Ahkbar!*"

"*Allah Ahkbar!*" Daoud repeated. But neither brother moved.

Then Gawan whispered conspiratorially, "I think Dajani has gone."

Daoud put a finger to his lips and went to the door of the shelter to listen. Anxious moments passed until he spoke. "He has what he wants. The bomb."

Gawan placed the lantern on the floor. He took a seat on an upturned box and glared into the face of the dog. The dog whined and sank to his haunches at the boy's look. "Shaul, come," Gawan said, stretching out his hand. The dog relaxed and sauntered to him.

Daoud snapped, "Yacov Lubetkin. You are a fool to come here."

Yacov asked, "True. So what will you do with me?"

"You heard our master. I will have to cut your ears off."

Yacov cleared his throat and exhaled loudly. *"Insh' Allah,"* he said with resignation, coming to sit beside Gawan.

Gawan scratched the back of the dog's head. "Things are bad since the English soldiers are gone. The souks are full of mercenaries. Syrians. Iraqis," he said with disdain. "No one from Jerusalem. Ignorant and poor. They have no money like the English soldiers. There is nothing much to steal except supper. We have to eat."

Yacov said, "So, you are eating Jews now?"

Daoud joined them. "Only you so far. But I have been dreaming of Hannah Cohen and the strudel."

"Me too," Yacov remarked. "No one in the Quarter is eating strudel."

Gawan asked, "Your grandfather, the rabbi, he is well?"

"Well enough."

Daoud inquired, "Who lights the lamps for you on Sabbath?"

"We have no *Shabbes goy* for six months. Not since the barricades went up and you quit coming."

Gawan said seriously, "We are blood enemies now, you and us."

"I know," Yacov answered sadly.

Daoud added, "Dajani is training us to make bombs."

"I have learned, too," Yacov confided.

Gawan said, "There are many thousands. They will kill you all if they break through. Have you thought where you will hide when they come?"

Yacov shook his head. "Some of us have talked about it. The Krepske brothers and Joseph. You know, the rest. We have decided we will die together if they break through."

Daoud patted him on the back. "That is honorable. Will you tell the boys you saw us? Tell them we are fighting, too. Only on the other side. Tell them we said *salaam,* will you?"

"Yes."

Daoud blew out the lamp and stood up. "He will be at the Rawdah by now. There are others in the streets. Go quickly. Do not come back. Maybe next time it will not be me and Gawan here. They will kill you. They will think you are a Jew. They are ignorant. They do not know the difference between Hasidim and Haganah. I cannot tell Dajani you are a ghost. Go back the way you came."

Yacov clasped the hands of the brothers and, with a snap of his fingers, slipped out the door with Shaul.

Daoud and Gawan stood in the darkness for a time, waiting for the sound of gunfire. There was only silence.

"Maybe he made it," Gawan said.

"We will need to fetch ears," Daoud replied. "Dajani will expect us to show him ears."

▪ ▪ ▪ ▪ CHAPTER 14 ▪ ▪ ▪ ▪

The air was dry, cool and perfectly motionless. Moshe shielded his eyes as the old rabbi deftly touched a match to the wick of a World War I–vintage lantern tucked into a niche above the entrance. Light exploded into a long, cavern-like hall. The barrel vaulting of the ceiling reached a height of thirty feet. The length to the back wall was one hundred feet from where Moshe knelt; the width was a quarter of that. Four stone balconies, supported by twelve white marble columns and linked by steep steps, surrounded a central court containing three long wooden tables, each topped with a lantern of recent manufacture. There were shelves containing thousands of clay jars. Carved into the stone cornice of the lower balcony was a phrase in Hebrew, Greek, and Aramaic, similar to what Moshe had seen on the cornice of the National Archive building in Washington, D.C.

WHAT WAS—WHAT IS—WHAT SHALL BE

"All the past is prologue? But," Moshe stammered, "it *can't* exist."

"It is the night of the Pentecost Vigil. The night we stay up and study, *nu?* You are not dreaming." The old man chuckled, then busied himself lighting the lamps on the trestles.

Unable to stand, Moshe remained on his knees. His astonished words rang in the chamber. "But it is just a legend . . . a fable. It was burned. Or carried off to Alexandria, or . . . "

"Most of the ancient manuscripts *were* lost. Once there were more than eighty thousand volumes in the Temple library here in Jerusalem. There are only seven thousand one hundred and forty volumes remaining in this room." Rabbi Lebowitz cleared his throat and waited for Moshe to absorb the information. "This was the hall of Solomon's masons." He sat down at the first table and leaned his cheek against his hand. Raising his eyes in thought, he added in a matter-of-fact tone, "Over there . . . you see in the shadow? Another doorway. Just under two thousand in the second chamber. Chamber of the Witnesses, we call it. It is a smaller room. *Nu?*"

Questions flooded Moshe's mind. There was no time to ask them; there was a war to be fought! Above this hallowed place, men were fighting and dying even now!

The rabbi seemed to hear his desperate thoughts. "Moshe, Moshe. Have you not asked yourself why Jerusalem . . . this square mile of earth . . . matters so much to our people?"

"This place . . . why haven't you told the world about it?"

"*Oy!* Tell the world that the greatest treasure of Hebrew literature is hidden in a vault three hundred feet beneath The Dome of the Rock? *Meshuggener! Nu!* And would not the English have carted it away to their *mouseion* in London?"

Rabbi Lebowitz used the ancient Greek name of the Alexandrian collection, *Hall of the Muses*. Moshe thought about the Elgin marbles from Greece, the Rosetta Stone from Egypt, and the columns of Nineveh, all now gracing the British Museum in the heart of London. "Point well taken."

"And what would our Muslim neighbors do? You have forgotten, maybe, that The Dome of the Rock is called the Mosque of Omar? And that this same Muslim, Omar, who conquered the Christian world, also burned what was left of the library of Alexandria in 645 of this present era?"

"Yes. Yes, of course, you are right." Moshe put up his hand in surrender.

"Is this so surprising? There are still a few ancient libraries. The Armenian Patriarchate, five minutes' walk from the Jewish Quarter, has four thousand manuscripts. All copies of the originals, of course. So. Come sit beside me."

Moshe obeyed, feeling like a boy in Torah school being called to answer the questions of his teacher. He scanned the rows of red clay jars, each containing a forgotten chapter of history.

"Think, scholar." The rabbi's tone was derisive, but his expression was amused. "Tell what you know about the writings of the ancients? *Nu!* What of the library at Alexandria?"

Moshe forced himself to concentrate, to remember what he had learned about the archives of other civilizations. "Alexander the Great," he said, and faltered.

"An interesting young fellow, who bowed before the Almighty in the Second Temple. A good place to begin. Yes?"

"January 20, 331 B.C."

"Very good. Yes. Yes. Go on. Tell this old rabbi what the *goyim* taught you after you left us here."

"On that day Alexander traced the boundary of his great city, Alexandria, in the sands of Egypt and left his architect to build it. Alexandria was the location of three of the wonders of the world. The library was modeled after that of Aristotle's collection, the Lyceum, in Athens."

"True. True. Not surprising since Aristotle was the teacher of Alexander. But the books. The books. How many volumes were there?"

"In the main library of Alexandria?"

"The Brucheion, yes. Go on."

"There were some four hundred thousand mixed volumes. These were the longer scrolls containing more than one work. Ninety thousand single volumes."

"Very good."

"And then another building, the Serepheum, contained forty-two thousand works."

The Ptolemy dynasty had prized learning so much that any book entering the port at Alexandria was seized and copied, and the copy returned to the owners while the original was studied and cataloged. Hundreds of librarians were employed in cross-referencing the works by subject, source, author, and editor. Scholars from the mathematician Euclid to the astronomer Aristarchus used the accumulated wisdom of the world to further their own researches.

The old man seemed pleased. "So. You see what has survived here in Jerusalem is humble by comparison."

"You mean these volumes came from the collection at Alexandria?"

The rabbi snorted. "*Oy!* No! Part of the volumes in Alexandria came from Jerusalem! From the library of our Temple! The Ptolemaic kings in Egypt were fervent admirers of Jewish history and literature. True? Of course, true. And they paid well for wisdom. Ptolemy II summoned seventy-two of our scholars from Jerusalem to translate the Hebrew Scriptures into what is called the Greek Septuagint. This they accomplished in seventy-two days. Payment for that was the release of one hundred thousand Hebrew slaves. That is one example only, but these . . ." He swept an age-spotted hand across the expanse of shelves. "These are the originals and copies of originals. All the sacred writings, of course. Seven copies each of the Law, the Wisdom books, and the Prophets. At one time there were eighty thousand volumes altogether in the palace of Solomon and in the Temple itself. There you see a section of commentary by the sages, including interpretation of all messianic prophecy from the time preceding the books of Daniel. *There* is a study! My father spent a lifetime on that. Perhaps it will be most interesting to a scholar. But for all that, less than ten percent of the manuscripts survive. You will read in the memoirs of Nehemiah . . ."

Moshe grasped the old rabbi's wrist in astonishment. *Nehemiah's Memoirs,* a lost apocryphal work, was mentioned in Second Maccabees as a source of books about the kings of Israel, the writings of the prophets and of David. But historians had assumed that the memoirs were destroyed. "You mean these things exist?"

"So. Why have I brought you here? For over two thousand years my fathers have been sentinels, guardians of the true treasure of Jerusalem. Greeks. Romans. Muslims. Crusaders. Turks. The English . . . and now? I have been given the key to Zion Gate. Israel is a nation once again. *Baruch Hashem!* Blessed be His Name! I am the last of the line of priests who will guard the treasure. The Almighty showed me your face in a dream. A new generation will guard Jerusalem until Messiah comes. Then all that is sealed will be open. All that is hidden will be known. You are the one who must live for the sake of the Name. What was. What is. What shall be. Contained within these walls. Remove a manuscript from this place, and it will crumble to dust. As for me? Take me from the Jewish Quarter, and I will crumble to dust. God has shown this old man what will come upon us soon, and I pass the secret to you. Pentecost, *nu?* The thunder booms in your soul. The gift. The revelation. The history of yesterday and tomorrow. The ink of scholars, we say, is holier than martyrs' blood. If we do not learn, we cannot stand."

Excitement coursed through Moshe. "And how? For how long? Where did this begin?"

Rabbi Lebowitz stood stiffly, stretched his back, and crooked a finger for Moshe to follow him. "In ten lifetimes you will not read every volume. And you have one night in which to begin. Tomorrow you fight." He shuffled toward the steps that led to the first balcony. Climbing up, he held the lantern aloft and searched the labels of the jars that stood on the third shelf from the bottom. He stopped before a row of five containers marked distinctly in Hebrew JASON OF CYRENE.

At this the rabbi grinned. "You will begin where I began and where my father began and his father and his fathers before him."

Again Moshe searched his memory for a reference to Jason of Cyrene. "I don't recall . . ."

The rabbi scratched his whiskers thoughtfully. "He was the scribe mentioned in Second Maccabees. This section of shelving is the Record of the Second Temple. It begins there with Nehemiah's writings and goes through the work of Jason of Cyrene."

The lost account of the Maccabean rebellion, here,

within his reach? Moshe stood in awe as Grandfather tapped his finger upon each jar.

"The condition of these scrolls?" Moshe ventured, remembering the effect of time and the elements on such manuscripts.

"Perfect. Perfect. No dampness here. No variation in temperature as there is in the caves at the Dead Sea."

"You know about the scrolls in the caves?"

"Of course. They've been sold off piece by piece in the souks to Crusaders and the like for centuries," the rabbi answered absently as he searched on. "Now, where is it? Where? *Oy!* I'm too old for this. My eyes. My eyes."

Moshe's thoughts tumbled from one possibility to the next as he considered safeguarding this priceless treasure. The earth beneath the Temple Mount was a honeycomb of paths and secret chambers. Suppose an explorer chanced upon this? What would keep the scrolls from being sold off piecemeal as archaeological souvenirs as the scrolls from the Dead Sea had been? "Couldn't we take them to a more secure place?"

"More secure than this? It is our Muslim neighbors you are worried about? No one will ever find this place unless you lead them to it." And then, "There she is!" Grasping the rim of a container, he knocked his knuckles against his head. "Read the name," he instructed Moshe.

Moshe leaned close and recited the Hebrew words that had been pressed into wet clay more than two millennia before:

HEROINES OF ISRAEL
MEMOIRS OF RACHEL / DAUGHTER OF ONIAS III

WIFE OF THE HAMMER OF JERUSALEM
MEMOIRS OF JUDITH
DAUGHTER OF MERARI / WIFE OF MANASSEH

Rabbi Lebowitz explained: "A mixed volume. Two Hebrew women. *Nu?* Rachel and Judith. Judith dictated her story when she was elderly. But Rachel's story is written in her own hand. Both are original manuscripts combined into one scroll for the sake of shelf space." He urged Moshe to remove the container from its place. "I thought you might like to begin where I began, with Rachel. Beautiful, like your own Rachel. And such a story she tells! Men write of wars and triumph. Women write from the heart. There are many such personal testimonies within these walls." He smiled wistfully. "But hers was the first scroll my father opened to me. I was a young man then. Younger than you. I think I fell in love with her. Today she is still young. Alive within this book. And now I am old. When my granddaughter was born, I had the privilege of naming her after my first love . . . Rachel, daughter of Onias, daughter of Zion." He shook his head, as if to clear the years from it. "Enough of this. There is no time for an old man to reminisce about his first love. True? Of course, true! Jerusalem hangs in the balance above us. You have a single night to discover why Jerusalem is forever the heart of Zion. The center of our universe."

Bowing his head, Moshe muttered, "How . . . how arrogant we have been. To have believed all these years that only a handful of books survived the centuries."

Rabbi Lebowitz added, "If you do not read tonight, Moshe, you may never understand fully how arrogant." He paused to reflect. "A witness, Rachel is, bearing testimony of God's faithfulness to the people of His covenant, and to His plan for Jerusalem then and in the last days. *Nu!* Her testimony is . . . She lived through the time when the Seleucid kings ruled our land. She was witness when Heliodorus entered the Temple. One hundred and eighty years before the Common Era." His face brightened as Moshe carried the jar toward the reading table. "*Oy!* Now he sees!"

■ ■ ■ ■

Dov Avram jiggled Mayor Akiva's door latch. It was, not surprisingly, locked.

The sky over Jerusalem in the predawn of Pentecost was pallid, like the face of a corpse. Deserted Jewish flats and shops were reduced to smoldering heaps. The dynamite and fires had eaten their fill. The air reeked with smoke and a layer of ash covered everything.

Ehud scraped his foot across the pavement, making a streak in the cinders. "Look," he said. "Here is another of Akiva's apartments."

Dov pounded on the door. "Mayor Akiva," he shouted. "You are suspected of hoarding food. Let us in."

The protesting squeak of Akiva's housekeeper was barely audible from behind the solid panel. Dov drummed his fist on it again. "Open up!"

There was no difficulty hearing Akiva's furious words. "Go away!" he said. "You are all godless thieves and robbers. Go away!"

"Open your door!"

217

When there was no reply, Ehud raised the stone pedestal of a water fountain for use as a battering ram. With Dov assisting and Rabbi Vultch guiding the aim, Ehud took a preliminary tap on the doorknob. *"Ein! Tsvei! Drei!"* he counted, and they drove the pillar into the handle.

The doorknob did not resist. At the initial impact it shot clear across the rabbi's entry hall and bounced off a wall. The second blow shattered the remaining bolts and cracked the doorframe.

Akiva bellowed, *"Goniff!* Robber!"

"Quiet," Ehud threatened, wagging the stone column at Akiva as if to say that the mayor's head might be the next target. The mayor was fully dressed, with a yarmulke on his head, coat, brocade waistcoat, long red velvet lounging jacket. He, too, had been up all night.

Vultch said apologetically, "It is forbidden to hoard food, just as the taking of more manna than needed was—"

"Yes, yes," Ehud said, setting the water fountain down with a thump and dragging Vultch by the arm. "All very enlightening, but later, later! Come!"

Ehud, Dov, Vultch, and three other men of the Quarter tramped downstairs, past where the aged housekeeper huddled in her bed in speechless terror, into the subbasement pantry.

Akiva raged after them, "Cossacks! There is nothing there worth taking! I will see you are excommunicated for this outrage!"

The men reached the cellar floor, then halted in stunned disappointment. The cold stone chamber was nearly empty. On a shelf were a partially full sack of flour, five potatoes, and racks and racks of wine.

"What is this?" Dov muttered in a worried, guilty tone. "Except for the wine, there is barely enough here to feed Akiva for two days."

"So? A lot of wine," Ehud noted. "Plenty for the whole Quarter to say kiddush every Sabbath for a year."

Vultch observed, "Perhaps we made a mistake."

"Vandals!" Akiva ranted from out of sight up the stairs. "Leave my things alone. What I paid for is mine. Is it not enough that my property is burned? And me getting paid rent in oranges besides?"

"Oranges?" Ehud sniffed. "What oranges?"

"I smell oranges," Vultch remarked.

"This wine rack," Dov said, pushing at it experimentally.

Shoving on one side of the floor-to-ceiling frame, Ehud spouted, "It moves!"

The rack swung aside on hidden hinges, revealing another storeroom behind.

"Grain!" Ehud said, pouncing. "Powdered milk! Bags of rice!"

"Potatoes," Vultch noted. "An entire round of cheese. A chest of tea."

"And oranges," Dov said, poking into the farthest corner and raising a canvas cover. "Bushels of oranges!"

■　■　■　■

In the basement of the Great Hurva, Hannah Cohen tallied the provisions. "Praise to the Eternal," she said. "The powdered milk is enough to give each child in the Quarter a cup a day for three days."

"Long enough for more supplies to reach us from outside," Ehud said proudly. "And the cheese. What is *Shavuot* without cheese?"

Hannah squinted at the round of cheese, gnawed the end of a pencil, and scribbled on the back of an envelope. "There are close to two thousand people in the district," she said. "One mouthful each? Better we keep it for the children."

"Oh," Ehud said, crestfallen. "But the potatoes?"

"We'll make soup," Hannah said with authority. "Three days' worth of soup."

"It is something," Ehud conceded, his lake of pride in the raid on Akiva's stores diminished to a drop in the ocean of their need.

"It is something," Hannah said, her tone softening. "And the oranges. Each child shall have a piece of orange each day as well."

■　■　■　■

The vigil was ended. Soon the sun would rise again over Jerusalem. Seven hours of reading had changed the way Moshe Sachar would look upon the Holy City forever.

He read to the end of the column, unrolled the scroll three inches to find the sketch of the exterior of a house opening onto a crooked street. It was, he thought, not unlike the lanes of the present-day Old City. The upper floor of the structure extended over the slate-paved byway, and the latticed shutters of a window above the arched gate were thrown wide. The pedestrian door was also open, as if waiting for someone to pass through. Beneath the sketch was the label ENTRANCE TO OUR HOME ON STREET OF THE SCRIBES. The scene was devoid of life. Following the injunction of the Law that no graven image should be made, the artist had declined to draw any living creature. Yet, off to the side of the central gutter, where sewage would have been dumped from the upper room, lay a broken sandal, and from a chink at the base of the stone wall a clump of daisies bloomed.

Moshe stared at the detail of the door and imagined Rachel, the daughter of Onias, last anointed priest in the line of Zadok, hurrying through it. Had she stopped to look at the flowers, perhaps picking one to carry with her on the errand?

He tapped the scroll, wishing he could speak and be heard by those who had bled and died to save Jerusalem. What would they tell him?

It is a small thing we offer, to save Jerusalem and the scrolls containing God's Word. The ink of scholars and prophets is holier than martyrs' blood. What is our blood compared to words that save the soul? What is dying compared to the promise of eternal life? For martyrs shed their blood to save the record of the vision and the promise of the Messiah, who will in time die for us all and for our salvation and redemption. God's promise that He will come to Jerusalem is stronger than the stones of this city we die to defend. In ink and in our blood this testimony is written. It is witness of the mighty deeds of the Lord, the eternal, blessed be He forever. For those who will live tomorrow and in every generation until the end of the age.

Raising his eyes, Moshe looked to the sleeping form of Rabbi Lebowitz. He opened his mouth to speak, only to be halted by a woman's voice at his back calling, "Moshe?"

He spun around, almost expecting to see her. "Who is there?" There was no reply. No human form stepped from the shadowed recesses of the room.

The flame of the lamp flickered as if someone's breath moved it.

The whisper drifted from the passageway. "Moshe?"

Moshe's skin prickled with fear.

The rabbi stirred. He raised his head, rubbed his eyes, and asked, "Is it my granddaughter calling, then?"

Moshe swallowed hard. "You heard it, too?"

Grandfather hugged his knees with his arms and cocked his head to listen. "Nothing," he said after a time. "A breath of wind." His smile was enigmatic. He rose awkwardly. "It must be late. I dreamed she was coming."

"Who?"

"Rachel, *nu?* My granddaughter. Your wife. She is coming home to Jerusalem. And that the Arab Irregulars were there, you see. It was a horrible dream. So, what should this old man expect—even the hours of waking are like a nightmare lately. Just a dream."

Moshe blinked dumbly at him. Just a dream? But what of the voice? Moshe dismissed the thought that it was real. Nothing about this long night seemed real.

Grandfather shuffled to his side and peered down. "You have finished already."

"Yes," Moshe said, regretfully.

"The Jihad Moquades will be stirring. I will leave you with your thoughts awhile. You can find your own way back. True? Of course, true."

Moshe nodded and returned his attention to the final warning of the text. Opening the scroll further, he smiled. In the upper left corner of the final column was the pressed fragment of a daisy.

■ ■ ■ ■ CHAPTER 15 ■ ■ ■ ■

Without the burden of the milk-can bomb, it was an easy thing for Yacov to reenter the Jewish Quarter the way he had left it. Shaul followed after. Sneaking home through unused alleyways, Yacov found the door of the flat was locked. Grandfather was gone. Yacov wanted to see the old man, to go to sleep in his own bed. Trembling, he felt the ledge above the door for the iron key, used it, and called into the emptiness of the room.

"Grandfather?"

No reply. Why had Grandfather not left a lamp burning? Where was he? A panorama of ghostly images swirled about the vacant flat.

Yacov could not bring himself to enter. The memory of the Jihad Moquade in the corner of the caravansary was too fresh. What if Gawan and Daoud had not been there? What if it had been another Muslim boy from the souks who truly had a dislike for Yacov? The thoughts of what might have been were growing larger by the second. Yacov locked the door and replaced the key on the ledge.

The Old City was so shrouded. Too still. Yacov sat on

the steps and hugged the dog. He thought of Gawan and Daoud and wondered if he would meet them again if the Muslim fighters broke through the barricade tomorrow. He wished things were as they had always been between Arab and Jew in Jerusalem.

■　　■　　■　　■

Beneath the earth, without stars or natural light, it was difficult to gauge the passage of time. Moshe did not feel weary from the long night of study. He was glad the rabbi had gone out ahead of him. He needed time to contemplate what other men, ordinary men like himself, had been willing to sacrifice for the sake of their faith in an age-old promise.

O Jerusalem!

Moshe returned the precious scroll to its container, and stood to carry it to its place on the shelf. For a fleeting moment he thought he caught sight of movement, of robed figures standing in a semicircle at the foot of the stairway. When he looked up, the space was unoccupied. Was that the rustle of fabric brushing across the pavement? Whirling around, he saw only the place where the high priest Onias must have stood with his daughter and the few men chosen to defend the Holy City.

Moshe's heart had never been stirred to such fervor. The Spirit of God sang and shouted in his soul. He felt awake for the first time. He knew who he was, where he had come from, and where he was going! Jerusalem! Eternal City! All things began and ended here!

For now, the voices of the ages seemed to say to him,

endure! Fear not! Praise not the dust and stones, but the words and the Promise! The end of this story is filled with joy and redemption! It is written! Serve the Almighty! The hand of the Lord will redeem His people and His City!

"So it is written," Moshe said aloud.

Moshe replaced the jar of testimony on the shelf. He left the chamber in darkness, wondering when, or if, he would enter it again. Raising his finger to the slot in the pitch-black of the passage, he made his way back from an ancient war to the present battle.

■　　■　　■　　■

Saving the life of Yacov Lubetkin required more courage from the Arab brothers than facing a thousand men in battle.

Daoud led Gawan to the Old City Muslim morgue, where three dead Jihad Moquades awaited washing and burial.

Three veiled women keened at the door, flinging dust into the air and beating their fists against the ground. They had been paid by the Arab Higher Committee to mourn, since the dead men were foreigners and had no relatives to wail over them. The racket also stirred the blood of the Jihad Moquades to a passion for revenge against the Jews and had the unfortunate effect of striking terror in Gawan's heart.

Gawan hung back. "I do not want to go in."

A woman screeched. The boy's skin crawled. The charade of grief was effective.

Daoud snapped, "You heard Dajani. Either we bring

him the ear of a Jew, or he will have yours. Come on."

Gawan's lower lip quivered. "I cannot."

"The dead will not hurt you. You will not hurt them. They will feel nothing. They are dead. I heard Dajani say they were nothing. Nothing! Convicts from Baghdad! Better them than Yacov Lubetkin, eh?"

Gawan jerked his head downward in assent and followed his brother toward the steps.

"We are relatives," Daoud said to the women. At this the mourners increased the volume of the wail as the brothers passed. Fists beat against breasts in a frenzy of manufactured grief. Gawan thought that even if these Iraqi convicts had been royalty, they would not have had so fine a display of sorrow over their demise.

Daoud hesitated a second before the door, then flung it open.

Gawan's heart was pounding, and his hands were sweating. The three bodies stretched out on the floor were covered by bloody sheets. Bare feet protruded from the shrouds. Perversely, Gawan wondered who had stolen their shoes.

"Think of Yacov. Remember his life is worth more than this," Daoud said, closing the door.

■　■　■　■

Daoud and Gawan charged up the steps of the morgue with the ear wrapped in a piece of the shroud.

Victory! They were giddy with relief. Tearing away from the building, they ran to an alleyway cluttered with broken crates. There they squatted and unfolded the cloth to reveal their treasure in the light of day.

Both gasped at what they saw.

"It is the ear of an old man!"

"It is the ear of an elephant!"

Long of lobe and wrinkled as leather, it was plain this was not the tender ear of a boy.

"Dajani will know at once," said Gawan accusingly. "Why did you not look? We had a choice! If Yacov Lubetkin had two heads, all his ears combined would not be this huge! The fan blades of the Oriental Hotel would not move as much air as this."

Daoud brooded, poking the thing with the blade of his knife. "What shall we do?" It was such a waste of courage.

Gawan scowled. "Dajani will cut off my ears before he kills me."

"No." Daoud rewrapped the thing and tucked it in his pocket. "Come. I have a plan."

■　■　■　■

Haroun Najid, the baker, had not slept during the night. Once he had tried to sneak down the stairs of his home above the coffeehouse and had found Kasim Dajani propped against the outer portal in anticipation of such a desertion. The Webley revolver lay in his lap.

Dajani, his face wrapped in bandages so only his glaring eyes were visible, dragged Najid out into the street with the words "Come! It is light enough and time to be killing Jews."

Two blocks away from the barricade at the Street of the Chain, Najid peered cautiously around a corner and examined the killing ground over which Dajani expected him to run with the thirty pounds of dynamite he held in his hands. "Their wall is much higher today," Najid observed. Six rows of sandbags, fronted with slabs of stone and pierced by firing slits, confronted him. To Najid's sweat-blurred vision, the rampart looked as thick and high as the walls supporting the Haram.

"You do not have to throw the device over it," Dajani hissed. "Any explosion close to their pitiful barricade, and the street into the heart of the Quarter is ours. I would do it myself, but I cannot see well enough to light the fuse." With those words, he thrust a cigarette into Najid's mouth. The Zippo lighter he sparked into life blazed so high that the baker jerked the bomb backward, fearing the flame would leap to the fuse and ignite it prematurely. "Go," Dajani ordered, "while they are sleepy and the shadows deep enough to hide in."

A signal relayed from Dajani caused Arab riflemen posted farther east along the Street of the Chain to commence firing, hoping to distract the Haganah's attention from the real threat.

Furiously puffing the cigarette, Najid sprinted awkwardly from one pocket of gloom to another, cradling the milk can in two arms like an exceptionally unwieldy child. He covered half the distance to the fortification before he was spotted, and a cry of alarm went up from the defenders.

The first bullet smacked into the wall beside Najid's legs. The second chipped centuries-old mortar from a course of masonry above his head and sprinkled his hair with lime dust. A burst of Sten-gun fire etched a pattern on a doorway precisely where the baker would have been if he had not turned sharply across the street.

His breath coming in panicked gasps, choked by the acrid Turkish tobacco, Najid ducked into a doorway and lit the fuse to the bomb. Intending to run nearer before hurling the weapon toward the Jewish position, the baker emerged from the shelter, but his charmed ability to dodge bullets had run out.

A Haganah sniper, firing from a rooftop, shot Najid in the foot. He stumbled, and the milk can, fuse hissing, tumbled away from him and fell down the steps into the men's W.C.

Oblivious to the pain of his wound, Najid scrambled back toward his own side while around him Hebrew and Arabic voices shouted, "Get down! Take cover!"

The device worked perfectly, but detonated below-ground. The pavement over the explosion erupted in a geyser of metal and porcelain fragments. The force of the blast deprived the buildings on either side of the street of their windows, awnings, and doors.

The resultant crater in the sidewalk and road provided the Muslims with a trench of their own to occupy for sniping at the Jews, but the Jewish bastion across the way was untouched.

■　■　■　■

Captain Ahkmed al-Malik waited behind the crenellated battlements of the Old City wall as mortar fire from Musrara exploded around the grounds of the Hospice of Notre Dame and the smaller structure of Soeurs Réparatrices.

The roof of the convent took a hit, sending the body of a Haganah soldier flying into the air like a rag doll. This brought a cheer from the Arab Irregulars who crowded the parapet with al-Malik. Hassan el-Hassan remarked that soon the mortars would entirely demolish the convent and there would be no Jews or nuns left to kill.

This was, al-Malik knew, an absurd hope. This second shell from a two-inch mortar hit the exterior of the convent. Dust and fragments of stone exploded everywhere, causing yet another hurrah from the Arabs on the wall.

But when the haze cleared, al-Malik saw the only additional damage was a chipped patch in the stone and a trio of broken windows, which were behind bars anyway. The convent was built like a fortress. Most everyone had taken cover within. They would be safe there; only a fool would venture out during the shelling. The Jew who had just been blown to pieces was indeed a fool, who was killed by a lucky shot. And when the morning mortar attack was finished? There would be time enough for prayer and reflection before the ground assault began. Within the Old City, Kasim Dajani would continue the bombing campaign against the Jewish Quarter while al-Malik and his men proceeded to pour small-arms fire into the convent. Then, when the Jihad Moquades attacked from Musrara, there would be killing enough for everyone.

Al-Malik understood that unless the forces of Jordan arrived with their real army, British-made tanks, and field artillery, the much-vaunted Jihad offensive against the pitiful Jews was equally pathetic. In spite of the theatrical wrath of the Mufti, any gains made by the Jihad were impermanent. Today al-Malik knew the Haganah forces that held the fortress of Notre Dame and the convent would die and the nuns with them. Tomorrow the result could be reversed.

Three more shells whistled in over the rooftops of Musrara to pock the face of Notre Dame. Al-Malik glanced at his watch. Only seconds remained of the fireworks. Then the real work of killing would begin.

■　■　■　■

Daoud and Gawan moved through the souks, gathering other boys as they went.

"Come! Let us go see the trophies of Hassan el-Hassan!"

There were thirteen urchins by the time they tracked down Hassan at the coffeehouse near the Rawdah School. He was sitting at a table in the sun, sipping strong coffee flavored with cardamom. His gold-capped teeth flashed at the appearance of the mob of children rounding the corner.

Daoud and Gawan hung back and let the others encourage the unveiling of the gruesome harvest. The drying tray was passed from hand to hand. "Thirty-seven of the enemy! You see their end!" They listened raptly as Hassan recited additional tales of glory.

This time, Daoud chose carefully, deftly substituting the large ear for a very small one.

■　■　■　■

It *was* a very small thing. Too small to have belonged to anyone grown, either man or woman. Gawan and Daoud looked at it attentively and knew the truth about Hassan el-Hassan and his legendary exploits.

Gawan sat on his haunches in the alleyway. "It was a child," he said.

"Yes," Daoud concurred numbly.

Gawan covered his face with his hands and began to weep.

"Why are you crying?" Daoud asked, disturbed by his younger brother's display of emotion.

"I do not know." Gawan sobbed. "It is . . . something like the puppies . . ."

Daoud gave him a stern look as he remembered the sight of the dead litter of puppies. "You are a weakling. They were dogs," he spat, trying to control his own fears and doubts.

"Yes." Gawan's face was streaked with tears. "But Hassan el-Hassan is a braggart and a liar. A liar! All the battles? I heard him talking to Dajani yesterday about the way the Nazis used to make Jews dig their own graves and then . . . mothers and children. Fathers and brothers and . . ." He wept. "Maybe everyone is a liar. His battles were fairly fought against a powerful enemy, he said. Fairly fought and fairly won. But you see, this is taken from . . . a boy." He looked into his brother's face.

"A Jew," Daoud corrected, without convincing fervor.

"Can you tell the difference? A Jew? A boy. I wonder if he was afraid. I wonder about his family. A mother. He must have had a mother. Did she die first? I wonder how he felt when he knew he would never grow up. You see? I want to live, Daoud, and I think when I look at this . . . that maybe I will not live. Surely they must hate us as much as we hate them."

"That is why we are fighting. So we will live."

"I wish things were like before."

"They never will be again."

"Yacov and the Krepske brothers and the rest. We were fine here before, were we not? None of us liked the English. No one is from the Old City anymore. How could they know how it was? I think Dajani and Hassan will kill Yacov and the others before it ends. The old rabbi. Hannah Cohen. And I am sorry for them."

"You think a Jew would not kill you if he had the chance?"

"I suppose. But I cannot help feeling pity for this . . . one . . . whoever he was. And I am afraid for the others."

"Do not tell this to anyone. Do everything Dajani says. He cannot know you like Jews."

Gawan wiped his eyes. "I will keep it to myself."

▪ ▪ ▪ ▪ CHAPTER 16 ▪ ▪ ▪ ▪

It was the morning of Pentecost.

The sisters of the convent regarded the shelling with no more concern than thunder that followed lightning. A hail of explosives rained down on the street beyond the convent gates. Soldiers of the Haganah, stationed on the roof and in the bell tower, took cover as Arabs on the Old City wall opposite them blasted away.

The sisters waited patiently in the chapel for the inevitable pause in the storm. Expecting to return soon, they carried nothing with them.

Rachel Sachar, holding a white flag, stood at the front

of the column with Mother Superior. Lori, her head covered by a scarf and dressed as a novice, took up the rear like a sheepdog to nip at the heels of any stragglers.

Dr. Baruch, in his clerical garb, stood beside her. He had slipped across from the Hospice of Notre Dame in the predawn shadows.

The resonating booms of exploding mortar shells were accompanied by the lighter crash of small arms.

In the years since Mother Superior entered the walls of the convent, she had been content to know the seasons by the cherry trees: Spring blossoms. Summer fruit. Autumn harvest. Winter sleep. Whatever could happen in the world beyond the orchard had come and gone without the participation or notice of the thirty sisters of Soeurs Réparatrices.

Until this Pentecost morning, the walls of the convent closed round them like a bandage protecting a wound, keeping out all things but the healing balm of praise and worship.

They grew old, but their souls became ever younger.

Nearing death, they became ever more alive.

Time passed; passing days became timeless, blending into one eternal day.

Each gave up her virgin soul willingly so it would reach perfection. Their goal was simply to experience the understanding that "now" was a seamless passage into eternity.

The souls who had walked this earth in bygone days lived on in the presence of God.

Those who were alive on earth today would one day stand before His throne and give an account.

Those yet to be born already existed, priceless and

beloved, in the thoughts of God.

Yesterday, today, and forever were one seamless piece of cloth. Even as they prepared to reenter the world, they could hear their Master say, *Well done, good and faithful servants. . . .*

Lori had no such illusions about her existence.

To her, each day was a morningless dungeon where former prisoners had scratched their names in stone with the hope they would be remembered. Names in stone may be proof they existed, but what remained of who they were? For Lori, the graffiti of the dead were simply curiosities to be contemplated for a heartbeat before she returned to the tedious work of carving her own name on the dungeon wall.

Lori thought of the coils of concertina wire outside in the road. It was a veritable briar patch, a thicket of barbs. She wondered how they would pass through it.

She observed the unsteady gait of the two eldest nuns. What if they stumbled and fell? How could they move fast enough?

Narrowing her eyes, she stared with disdain at the white flag. What had a white flag done for the settlers of Kfar Etzion, whom she'd heard lay unburied and rotting in the hot sun? This pennant had been the suggestion of Mother Superior: "They will see by the flag that we are neutral."

■　　■　　■　　■

The boom of explosives hushed. The sisters looked at one another in surprise. Had the storm passed? It was, Lori thought, like people who grow used to the drumming of rain until they no longer notice the constant sound. It was the absence of noise they heard. Peace.

It meant something. What was it? They almost fo. got until Mother Superior clapped her hands, snapping them to attention.

"The archbishop is waiting. He will have his doors thrown wide for us! Fear not!"

"Ah, *oui!*" blind Sister Angélique remarked brightly. "We are going out. Tell me, Sister Marie Claire, is the sun shining today?"

"It is," assured the younger nun, who gripped Sister Angélique's arm.

"Fear not!" called Mother Superior. "The angel of the Lord encampeth round about those who fear him!"

Rachel Sachar, also wearing the gray habit of a novice, cautiously opened the oak door. She had to push hard. Rubble from the cornice lay on the step. Waiting a moment, anticipating rifle fire, she shoved the white bedsheet out the crack in the opening. Would it be fired upon?

The morning, smelling of cordite and gunpowder, crept in and pooled on the flagstones of the foyer. Birds sang. No shots rang out.

Mother Superior touched her fingers in the basin of holy water and crossed herself before she opened the portal wider and stepped out into the open day with Rachel.

Sister Angélique said in a creaking voice, "This is very exciting."

The others followed, clutching their rosaries, touching fingers to the holy water, cheerful as they prepared to die.

Lori's knees felt weak.

Sister Marie Claire began to sing in a clear, piping voice. The others joined her:

It is the month of May;
The month of Mother Mary, to whom the angel said,
Fear not! Fear not! The Lord is with thee.
Of all women you are most blessèd . . .

With no apparent concern, the ordered line of nuns toddled, blinking, like a file of penguins in the London zoo at feeding time, into plain view of hundreds of startled Jihad Moquades standing vigil on the parapet above New Gate. Dr. Baruch politely closed the door behind them.

It was madness, Lori thought, her eyes wide.

But Rachel Sachar and Mother Superior glided on through the debris. "Mind the mess, Sister Marie Claire. Guide Sister Angélique carefully."

■　■　■　■

"Captain," a Jihad Moquade said urgently to Ahkmed al-Malik, "something is happening!" Across Suleiman Road from the fortress of New Gate, a white banner waved from the front door of the convent of Soeurs Réparatrices. "It looks like someone is coming out under a flag of truce."

"It must be a trick," Hassan el-Hassan retorted. "The Jews have discovered they are trapped. Commence firing."

"Wait!" al-Malik countermanded. "Let's see what this is about."

To the Arab captain's amazement, a column of nuns and one priest, some walking proudly upright, others hobbling, bent and feeble, paraded out the portal. Looking neither right nor left, the thirty-three members of the procession emerged onto the deserted street.

His confusion mounting, al-Malik listened as a song, a happy, lilting song such as schoolgirls sing on a summer outing, rose into the war-shrouded skies above Jerusalem. Seemingly without a care the nuns tramped steadily past the scorched hulk of a Jewish bus, picked their way around the crater left by a mortar shell, and proceeded up Suleiman Road.

"You are letting them escape," Hassan snarled.

Shaking his head as if to clear it from a dream, al-Malik disagreed. "No," he argued, pretending he had not been dazed before. To fulfill the Mufti's orders, they would have to fire soon. "See how their path carries them in front of the blank wall? It is as if they are marching to meet a firing squad . . . us. Get ready," he urged the Moquades. "Every man picks his target. Fire when I give the word. *Now!*"

■ ■ ■ ■

Lori raised her head slightly as bees began to swarm around her head.

Bees?

The earth at her feet erupted in explosions of dust. Something hit the wall behind her.

Bullets!

From the corner of her eye she saw the smoking barrels of the Arab rifles. The song of the nuns dropped off until only Mother Superior's voice was heard; then they picked up the melody again. Dr. Baruch added a bass rumble to the refrain.

"It is the month of May . . ."

Another volley erupted from the fighters on the wall. Again the ping of bullets hit above them, below them, behind them, and in front of them!

". . . of . . . Mary, to whom the angel said . . ."

Lori tried to cry the warning "They're firing!" but her voice was small and insignificant. Her legs threatened to give out on her. She felt the presence of death as she had a hundred times in London.

The sisters walked on, oblivious.

"Fear not! Fear not! The Lord is with thee."

A score of bullets smashed against the stone of the wall, sending fragments of brick everywhere, stinging Lori's face. In her terror, her words were no more than the sounds of a husky flute: "Get . . . down!" They did not hear her. It was as if she marched through a nightmare, willing herself and the other participants to awaken, but they could not.

Sister Angélique stumbled; Sister Marie Claire held her upright. Was the old woman shot?

"Of all women you are most blessèd."

"There now, Sister Angélique, the path is rough here." Sister Marie Claire patiently waited for the nonagenarian to get her balance.

Behind her, Lori heard the clatter of a wooden wheelbarrow pursuing them. An elderly man, an Arab in a keffiyeh, pushed the barrow, which was loaded with a rake, a shovel, clay pots, and three rosebushes.

Madness!

Overtaking Dr. Baruch and then Lori, he passed the others until he walked shoulder-to-shoulder with Mother

Superior. It was the gardener from the convent.

Four shots rang out, making marks in the pavement at their feet. *Ping! Ping! Ping! Ping!*

"*Fear not! Fear not!*" Sister Angélique sang in her reedlike voice. "*The Lord is with thee!*"

■　■　■　■

Smoke drifted across Suleiman Road, blocking al-Malik's view of the carnage. As he waited impatiently for it to clear, he reviewed what he expected to see: half the nuns killed outright, the others wounded and incapacitated.

His expectations left him totally unprepared for the reality: the entire column was untouched. The procession had advanced another hundred feet toward New Gate.

"Fire! Fire!" al-Malik commanded, bouncing up and down in his consternation.

A flurry of shots replied to this order, including one fired by Hassan. Bullets spattered the wall, the street, even the lamppost beside the sisters, but not one of them was touched. "Are you mocking me?" al-Malik screamed. "Kill them!"

Hassan pulled the trigger on his Italian-made rifle, but nothing happened. "Misfire," he said, shooting back the bolt and digging at the cartridge with his fingernails.

On the other side of al-Malik, another Irregular was also struggling with his weapon. Though he squeezed the trigger repeatedly, nothing happened. When al-Malik grabbed the rifle out of the man's grasp, the clip fell out onto the parapet. Angrily, the Arab captain threw the gun over the wall and grabbed for another.

Some of the Jihad Moquades continued firing, but none had any success. Bullets smacked into the road sign that announced the upcoming intersection of Jaffa Road, clanged loudly on a manhole cover in the lane, knocked the head off a stone lion crouching on the steps past which the nuns trooped . . . but not one slug hit its target.

The second rifle al-Malik seized looked proper. Placing the shiny bead of the front sight on the head of the woman leading the procession, al-Malik held his breath. When he pulled the trigger, a satisfying roar erupted and a bright-yellow muzzle blast, then . . . nothing.

An emissary from Haj Amin's cousin Khaled Husseini rushed up the steps of the wall. "What are you doing?" he shouted. "Stop at once. Did you not hear the Mufti's order: 'Do not harm the Catholic women'?"

Giving an anguished cry, al-Malik flung the second traitorous weapon from him. "Why?"

"It is the express command of the Arab Higher Committee," the courier said. "On your head be it if any of the neutrals are harmed."

Visibly struggling with his cherished malice, al-Malik wrestled a third rifle away from Hassan. Khaled's messenger grabbed the stock. "Let them pass," he reiterated. To the Arabs below, he shouted, "Open the gate."

In moments the nuns and the priest had crossed Suleiman Road and disappeared beneath the arch of New Gate.

Cursing, al-Malik chambered a fresh round with a savage yank on the bolt. With no more aim than merely glancing along the barrel, he sighted at the wooden crucifix beside the entry of Soeurs Réparatrices and fired. The image of the crucified Christ disappeared in a shower of splinters, and the weapon dropped from al-Malik's hands.

■　　■　　■　　■

The sound of rifle fire from the Old City wall above New Gate drew a crowd from among the soldiers holding the Hospice of Notre Dame. They could not see who was shooting, but clearly something was up.

From the second-story window, through the mound of sandbags, Alfie Halder spotted the procession nearing New Gate. Thirty-two nuns and one priest, walking two by two. One nun in front carried a silver banner with a lion of Judah embroidered on it in gold. Twelve men as tall as the Ethiopian Jew Ibrahim, wearing white Arab robes trimmed in gold tassels and carrying shields emblazoned with lions matching the one on the banner, walked beside the procession.

"The nuns from the convent. They are singing. How nice. A Pentecost parade," Alfie said to Ibrahim in a pleased voice.

Ibrahim replied, "Ah, yes. It is a fact. Servants of the Lord will march in Jerusalem on every holy day. No matter there is a war."

"They are crazy, eh? Well, here come the horses."

"Everyone is crazy here; it is true."

"And there is Lori in the middle! Marching along, marching along, marching along," Alfie said with surprise. "I should find Jacob. He will like to see her. He says I was seeing things again when I told him I saw her yesterday in the broken garden. When he sees her marching in the parade, this will prove I did not imagine anything."

■　■　■　■

Why are we still alive? Lori asked herself. *The bullets were real. Why didn't they kill us?*

The nuns continued to sing as they passed beneath the portal of the gate.

Once within the walls of the Old City, they were in an area completely controlled by the Arab Irregulars, but out of sight of the marksmen above the gate. Lori guessed the soldiers had been playing with them, firing near them to see if they would break and run. She was the lone member of the group who had been ready to dive for cover.

"Fear not! The Lord is with thee." The melody of the hymn died away. Somewhere above them, an Arab soldier applauded.

The nuns took no notice. It was Pentecost. They might have been marching to chapel. They began to sing again:

Morning has broken, like the first morning.
Blackbird has spoken like the first bird . . .

It was as if they did not see anything but the morning light or hear anything but the measured tones of their voices lifted in praise for a new day. They had carried the safety and solitude of their cloister away with them. *Though I walk through the valley of the shadow of death, I will fear no evil for You are with me.*

Lori smiled as a poem by Wilfred Owen came to

mind. She had learned it from a retired soldier in Chelsea Hospital one night as the bombs rained down on London. It was, she mused, an odd thing to remember at such a time.

I dreamed that Christ had fouled the big-gun gears,
And made a permanent stoppage in all bolts
And buckled, with a smile, Mausers and Colts,
And rusted every bayonet with His tears.

And there were no more bombs, of ours or Theirs.
So we got out, and gathering up our plunder
Of pains, and nightmares for the night, in wonder!—
Leapt the communication trench like flares.

But Owen had it backward, according to the nuns of Soeurs Réparatrices, did he not? The physical world was the dream. Bullets, which might have ended the dream, had been no more annoyance to the sisters than the sound of a fly in the garden while they slept in the afternoon beneath the cherry trees.

To them, the tears of Jesus were the first reality. All humanity was bathed, all light refracted, in the prism of His tears. The spectrum of existence was colored by praise. The soul, unafraid, leapt the trench like a flare illuminating the night.

And what if the men on the wall had meant to kill?

Lori's legs still shook. She mopped her brow. How she longed to share this miracle, if it was a miracle, with someone. *With Jacob. Or Alfie. Alfie would understand.*

■　■　■　■

Alfie found Jacob sleeping beneath a desk in a windowless office in the center of the labyrinth of corridors.

With the cry that Lori was walking down the road, Jacob reared up, crashing his head on the desk. They dashed back to the window where Ibrahim stared out at the Old City, glistening in the morning light.

"They are gone," Ibrahim said in a sorrowful voice. "That is the last. Now it will begin."

"Tell him." Alfie pressed his face against the slit to peer out onto Suleiman Road. "Tell Jacob what you saw."

"A Pentecost parade," Ibrahim replied.

"Tell him Lori was in it, too," Alfie urged, forgetting Ibrahim would not know Lori Kalner from Mother Superior.

Ibrahim looked from Alfie to Jacob, then back again. He shrugged. "Yes. She was there."

"With the others," Alfie encouraged.

"Yes," Ibrahim repeated.

"All right." Jacob turned his back and stalked away. "Someone got the nuns out. I got two minutes' sleep last night. You know where I'll be."

■　■　■　■

Through New Gate the nuns passed into another world, another century. One with the stink of rotting vegetables, tobacco, sweat, and urine.

Silence. Even Mother Superior's sweet voice died away.

245

Low buildings, shops, and market stalls formed a squalid canyon in the lane before them. The Street of the Latin Patriarch wound away from New Gate, tracing the path of the wall toward Jaffa Gate.

Mother Superior began to sing again:

Come, Creator, Spirit, come down,
Give to us Your light from heaven
And fill with grace and all Your aid
Every soul that You created.

Wild-eyed Jihad Moquades blocking the path parted like the bow wave of a ship that plowed through still waters. Lori kept her eyes riveted to the back of Sister Angélique. *Sister Angélique, blind and lame, bones as brittle as dry twigs, loving your Savior all your lifetime. Who were you before Jerusalem?*

Lori felt the curious, mocking stares of men up on the rooftops. They leaned on the doorposts of the buildings the way kids playing stickball in the street pause for a passing automobile. *Wild geese observing swans pass upon the river. A pack of dogs hoping the cat will leap from the wall onto the ground and run. Destruction!*

Long weapons made shadows against the facades of aged buildings. Bayonets shaped like three-sided iron spikes glistened dully at the ends of rusty barrels.

Do not look, or like Lot's wife you will turn to salt!

Lori's blood drummed in her ears.

Per te sciamus de patrem . . .

Lori moved through the dream, dimly aware that two thousand years of pilgrims had walked this route before her. An Arab clothed in helmet and medieval chain-mail armor lunged forward, growled, and laughed at her involuntary expression of terror. Ahead, at the end of the lane, the sun shone down on the open courtyard of Jaffa Gate, where vanquished Crusaders had paid their ransom to Jerusalem's Muslim conquerors before retreating to Jaffa Harbor. There ships carried them, defeated, back to England.

England! Green fields. Hedgerows. Westminster Abbey. Church bells calling the faithful to evensong ... oh, Jacob! So ordinary! No question there of what each day would bring! So easy!

Inexplicably, tears streamed down her cheeks. *Jerusalem! Three thousand years of lifetimes! Abraham and Isaac upon the altar of Moriah, a stone's throw from here! David, the shepherd-king, watching Bathsheba from a distance. Jeremiah, mourning for the exiles. Jesus, teaching in the Temple. Peter's betrayal. Jesus, walking the Way of Sorrows! Dying with forgiveness on his lips. Peter, shouting the good news in the streets on Pentecost! He is risen! Call on His name and live forever with Him!*

She heard mothers calling children to come and hear, to meet the compassionate rabbi from Nazareth. The dust contained the echo of their voices—not the great, not the mighty, but the humble, seeking as she was seeking. *O Jesus!* Their longing for God remained, more tangible than stones or reliquaries. *Jerusalem!* All who searched for truth, and all who ever would! She felt them near, heard their breath. Time was nothing. Yesterday cast its shadow on the wall. They walked beside her. Pleading for an answer too burdensome to hold, they had come to this mountain. *I know. I know. I lost a child, too. It is never easy. Only accept God's will. Know you will see him again. Trust. Then all things will be possible to you!* They were waiting. Waiting for the caring hand to wipe away the tears. Shoulder to shoulder the souls of multitudes knelt, praying. The sick, the alone, the frightened, the broken-hearted, the unlovely and unloved had worn these stones smooth. They brought a cup of tears to Jerusalem and poured it out, an offering. *Blessed are those who mourn, for they will be comforted. . . .*

■　　■　　■　　■

Entering the shelter of the Latin Patriarchate, the sisters were ushered into the archbishop's reception room, Lori, Rachel, and Dr. Baruch cut, like culls, from the herd. With the instruction they must not speak, the three were led into a whitewashed antechamber next to a latrine to wait. Furnished only with one bench and a crucifix, it was where merchants and food vendors were deposited when calling to transact business.

Two long hours passed before a Franciscan friar, carrying civilian clothing, entered the cubicle. His eyes hostile, he observed the novice dress of the two women with constrained anger. But he was open and vehement about the clerical garb of Dr. Baruch.

"I brought you clothing. You will have to go," he said coldly. "We cannot risk harboring combatants on either side of this senseless conflict."

"We are not combatants," Baruch protested. "I am a medical doctor and . . ."

"You are Jews. Bound for the Jewish Quarter. You have chosen, immorally in our opinion, to cloak your true purpose behind the appearance of Holy Orders. You badgered Mother Superior into accepting your wild scheme."

"Has she told you that?"

"She has said nothing one way or the other on the matter. The archbishop is certain of the facts, however. You Jews have illegally taken over the convent. There is fighting on the grounds even now! By occupying neutral religious buildings, you put thirty of our sisters in peril for your own ends. You set a precedent in which peaceful religious orders are in jeopardy. Suppose tomorrow you decide that the Patriarchate itself will be of military use to your forces? Shall we then be ordered out or threatened with loss of our lives? We want you to leave."

Baruch said firmly, "We must stay here until after nightfall."

At this the eyes of the Franciscan flashed. "Our buildings here in the Old City are crowded with Christian refugees seeking shelter from this battle. Men. Women. Children. Driven from their homes. Unlike the Armenian Patriarch, who evacuated at the first sign of trouble, the Catholic archbishop has chosen to stay here and be a shield to our people. Thus far the Arab Higher Committee has allowed us to remain, even to bring in needed medical supplies and food. We will not endanger our people by harboring Jews. You are not welcome. If the Jihad Moquades come and inquire, we shall be obliged to give you up. For our own safety we have declared ourselves neutral in the fight between Jews and Muslims. You are belligerents in this conflict, and therefore we will not grant you sanctuary."

At that, he turned on his heel and left the room, slamming the door behind him.

■ ■ ■ ■ CHAPTER 17 ■ ■ ■ ■

Dajani cuffed Daoud hard. "We have already attacked the Jewish Quarter this morning. I could not wait for you. What kept you?"

Daoud took a page from Hassan's exploits. "It was not easy. The Jew fought hard. In the end we prevailed." He tossed the prize on the table beside Dajani's bed. "There. We brought it like you said. Here is your knife." He returned it.

Dajani scowled at the trophy, then grinned. "Well done." He clapped Gawan on the back, making the child's stomach jump. "And what of you, Gawan? You have a pale look."

"The boy whose ear we brought is dead. He was a Jew. I speak what is true. It is as Allah wills it," Gawan said without looking up.

Dajani laughed and said to Daoud, "Your brother has a squeamish stomach, does he not? By the end of the day he will be used to blood. Today we will, with the help of Allah, break through into the Jewish Quarter."

■ ■ ■ ■

After the curious circumstance with the parade of the Arab children the day before, the members of the Spare Parts Platoon were ready to engage the enemy. Sal in particular was vehement in saying how eager he was to do some real fighting.

Major Luke Thomas did not tell them they had been chosen for the next assignment precisely because the mission required little skill and lots of bravado. They were the bait. The Jihad Moquades were the rats.

Through his field glasses Major Thomas stared at the towers of The Citadel that frowned down on Jaffa Gate. Above the foundation stones laid by workmen of the Maccabees were ashlars hewn by masons in the employ of Herod the Great. Overtopping these was a stretch of Muslim wall, built in part from recycled blocks from Crusader castles. These were in turn surmounted by an addition ordered for the Turkish sultan Suleiman the Magnificent in A.D. 1540.

This particular set of battlements illustrated perfectly what a miracle was taking place with the re-creation of a Jewish nation, Thomas thought. Herod was a foreign puppet in the service of Rome, so none of the walls since the Maccabees represented an independent Israel. But there remained a Jewish foundation that underlay the rest.

Partway up the wall to the left of Jaffa Gate grew a stunted fig tree. Clinging to a slim ledge and rooted into crevices of stone through nothing more nourishing than the dust of centuries, the scrawny tree clung to life . . . much like the Jewish presence within the Old City.

Nothing about the sprawling fortification that included David's Tower had any connection with the biblical King David, except possibly the site. In any case, Major Thomas's low whistle was for the way the turrets dominated the 1948 landscape and not for its two-millennia-old origins anyway.

From Jaffa Gate a remarkably straight avenue aimed directly at the Temple Mount and severed the Old City Jewish district from the Muslims. Being able to use that highway depended on getting past the fortress first. Jaffa Gate, the main entry to the stronghold, was a wide-open breach between the towering battlements. The actual gates had been removed and the thoroughfare widened to allow the passage of motor vehicles early in the twentieth century. It was essential to see how the gap was blocked and how strongly defended.

Commander of the reconnaissance team designated to assess the strength of the Arab defense at Jaffa Gate, Major Thomas led a force composed of Captain Barney Isaacson, Corporal Jacob Kalner, and eight others, including Sal, Alfie, Ibrahim, Hymie, and Daniel. The squad halted in the shelter of the Municipality building up Jaffa Road from Jaffa Gate. Major Thomas warned, "Remember, this is not an attack—just a recon patrol to see what they will throw at us. No heroics, if you please."

Ducking from shop entry to alleyway, the scouting party had not advanced more than a hundred yards before sniper fire from the tower struck around them. Jacob pulled Pinky behind a red pillar postal box, and an instant later an Arab bullet struck the letter *G* of King George the Fifth's monogram. From the top of David's Tower rang the cry "*Alihu Itbach al Yahud!* Slaughter the Jews!"

Hunkered down behind an overturned automobile, Luke Thomas carefully recorded the number of Arab riflemen who responded to the alarm. Two machine guns ripped the air from opposite parapets, and a hundred of the Mufti's Irregulars peppered the pavement of Jaffa Road with gunfire. "We must get closer, chaps," Major Thomas called. "We have to see what they are using to block the gate itself."

Hymie jumped up to comply. As he took three steps, a burst from the ramparts cut him down.

Jacob and Luke Thomas lunged toward the wounded man, dragging him to cover in a doorway. But as Major Thomas lowered Hymie into a corner, he saw the man was dead.

The other members of the recon patrol huddled behind anything that would shelter them. Except for Daniel Caan, they did not attempt to return the Arab fire. It was clear to Major Thomas that the demoralized troop of recruits might break and run. He asked Jacob about Hymie. "Friend of yours?"

"No . . . I mean . . . we came on the same ship."

"Shot through the head. It happens. We can't leave him here." The major called for Alfie, who seemed fearless. "Get this poor chap out of here," Luke Thomas instructed.

Wordlessly, Alfie hefted the body over his shoulder and sprinted up the street. Jacob watched him for a moment, then ducked and dodged back to the pillar box.

When Thomas returned to the others, Jacob eyed him curiously, but the major gave no sign that anything was amiss. So a man had just died. More would die before this was finished. The matter-of-fact attitude told them that death was likely to be a frequent visitor in the days ahead. "Now," the Englishman continued, "two men. Me for one, Corporal Kalner the other. The rest of you make the Arabs keep their heads down . . . aimed, deliberate shots, eh? Corporal Kalner, you and I will flank the gate, draw their fire, observe, and withdraw. Simple enough? Right. On my signal . . . ready, steady, go!"

Jacob sprinted to the right as Luke Thomas went left. From behind them came the comforting Brooklyn growl of Isaacson shouting, "Give it to 'em good, see? There's one, Pinky. Let him have it!" A disciplined rattle of rifle fire had the Arabs ducking for a change.

Daniel Caan, furiously working the bolt of his rifle, loaded and fired round after round with mechanical determination. Though he did not aim, he grunted each time he squeezed the trigger, as if he were feeling each bullet strike home on his own body. He was shooting because someone was shooting at him. There was no emotion connected with the action.

Jaffa Gate was barricaded with garbage cans, overturned carts, and heaps of tires. Arab soldiers fired rifles from openings in the protective dike, but surprisingly stopped shooting abruptly, as if they all ducked at once.

From atop the tower came a loud whirring, and an object trailing smoke spun through the air much farther than a grenade could have been hurled. It curved away from the scouts and landed a distance off. When it exploded, Jacob and Luke Thomas were knocked to the ground.

Major Thomas motioned for Jacob to retreat. As they did so, another exploding device whirled downward. The squad lowered their faces to the ground and protected heads with hands.

Daniel Caan, fearful for the lives of his friends and frustrated with the slow action of the rifle, tossed aside the weapon. He grabbed a Sten gun from the cowering Blum and blazed away at The Citadel's defenders as Jacob and Luke Thomas retreated up the road with the other squad members. Daniel emptied the clip, then followed after the rest and the trail of blood from Hymie Slanik's body.

Alfie laid Hymie out on a patch of grass, his arms crossed over his chest and his face covered with Alfie's kerchief.

Other members of the Spare Parts Platoon crowded awkwardly around. Mangus and Ibrahim quietly recited the *Shema*. Except for that, they spoke little on the drive to the barracks. Gone was the initial burst of enthusiasm for battle. "Where's Sal?" Jacob asked.

The American was missing. No one had seen him get hit, but he must have been struck during their retreat. Luke Thomas vetoed the idea of risking more lives in going back for him.

Back at the King David Hotel, Luke Thomas reported his observations to Commander Shaltiel and Captain Isaacson. "They deliberately left Jaffa Gate minimally guarded to draw us in. That bomb. Homemade, I fancy . . . dynamite swung at the end of a rope to gain distance. Bit like David's slingshot. That's a good sign. It means the Mufti's troops are possibly as lacking in decent munitions as we. They're waiting for the Arab Legion to supply them, no doubt. But if we can take the Old City first . . . Anyway, a frontal assault is no use. We'll need a different plan."

■　■　■　■

The fury of the Franciscan brother was a blow.

Stunned by his open hostility, Lori and Rachel wordlessly picked through the clothing. Each donned the long robes common to Arab women in the Old City. Dr. Baruch emerged from the latrine in an ill-fitting tan linen suit. A battered red tarboosh perched awkwardly on his head.

"How do I look?"

"Like a member of the Mufti's council," Rachel said.

The three exchanged uneasy looks. They would have to venture out in broad daylight, navigate through streets crowded with Jihad Moquades, and find their way past the barricades and into the Jewish Quarter.

The rattle of keys sounded outside the door. "God will walk with us," Rachel said hoarsely.

The hinges groaned and the panel opened, revealing Mother Superior carrying a tray of food. "You are ready to embark, I see?" she asked, placing the tray on the bench.

Rachel took her hand. "You have brought us this far safely. We are grateful."

The old woman gave a wink. "I have heard Brother Nathan was less than hospitable." She addressed Dr. Baruch. "You did not tell him you are a Catholic."

The doctor replied without bitterness. "I am not a Catholic. Not any longer. I am . . . since the war . . . since Auschwitz . . . a Jew first. That separates me from what the Church has become. This Franciscan would have been turning Jews over to the Nazis in Czechoslovakia if he was asked . . . for the sake of neutrality."

Rachel blanched at the revelation that Baruch was also at Auschwitz. Perhaps they *had* met. Perhaps he had seen her and remembered.

The nun continued, "Brother Nathan is Syrian. His

256

hatred of all Jews is long-standing. Ingrained, I fear."

Baruch said brusquely, "As a Christian he wears the name of the greatest Jew who ever lived, and yet still in his small mind Jews are Christ-killers. He walks Via Dolorosa each Friday carrying the cross, but he does not know what the cross means. I tremble that a man such as this calls himself a Christian."

Mother Superior said sadly, "But surely the smallness of his soul cannot make you deny your faith."

Baruch looked her in the eye. "I deny those in the Church who deny the Jewishness of the Messiah. They have made Jesus a Gentile. One of themselves. For centuries Jews have known almost nothing about Jesus . . . Yeshua . . . and, because of hatred from men like Brother Nathan, have wanted to know even less."

Mother Superior sat down wearily on the bench. "Not all have forgotten that we Gentiles are merely branches grafted onto the root and trunk of Judaism."

Baruch sat beside her, his hands open as though he held a book on his lap. "The Gentile Church has forgotten its roots. It is written . . . The way, the truth, and the life grow out of the covenant God made with Abraham. Those Gentiles who are grafted on do not replace the original branches. From the seed of Abraham all the nations of the world will be blessed. The blessing was, *is,* the Messiah, Yeshua, descendant of David. Shepherd and sacrificial lamb. King. Redeemer. Healer of the sick. Lover of the unloved. Bread of Life. He who calms the seas. He who goes into the battle to slay our giants. I know my Savior well, Mother, but I will never again call myself by the name *Christian.* Too much evil has been done in that name. I am a Jew who follows The Way."

"No one can recognize God's love unless they see it first in the lives of those who claim to be His children." The old woman sighed and stood. "I know the harshness of Brother Nathan has injured you. I have come to tell you that he did not speak with my authority or that of the archbishop. I ask your forgiveness."

"I gave it before it was asked," said Baruch.

"I thank you in the name of our Lord. And now, if you are willing, I have a favor to ask on behalf of the many Arabs who have fled to us. I will not romanticize my request. They fear what the Jews will do to them. These Arab women, if they saw you in the street, would spit on you. Most of them think Hitler had the right idea. With that introduction I appeal to the spirit of the Jewish Messiah who lives within your heart."

He nodded stiffly but did not reply.

It was a hard thing to contemplate, Rachel thought: doing something for those who actively wished you dead.

Mother Superior continued, "There are three hundred refugees here. Muslim and Christian Arabs. Mothers with children, mostly. Old people. There are many sick and injured among them. A young Muslim girl of sixteen is in labor and will deliver a child today. Her husband is in the Muslim Quarter fighting to eradicate Old City Jews. We have no doctor among us." She left it at that.

Baruch smiled sadly at the irony that those who cheered their menfolk on to slaughter Jews needed his help. A few seconds of contemplation ticked by, but there was never any doubt what his answer would be. "I will need a room for examinations."

■　　■　　■　　■

Barely a quarter of a mile separated the Jewish defenders of the Old City from the Israeli forces holding New City Jerusalem, but as the shelling increased and the perimeter of the district shrank, the distance seemed an insurmountable chasm.

Moshe pored over an 1831 map of the Holy City as Dov raised the headquarters of David Shaltiel by wireless. Moments later Shaltiel's grim voice filled the radio room and spilled out into the dining hall of the Hurva.

Dov reminded the Haganah commander, "The Quarter is packed with those burned out by the Muslims. Women and children. Short rations. Need medical assistance. There's continual talk of surrender among a group of the Hasidim."

The receiver, crackling with static and vehemence, burst into a warning: "Working on it. Doctor and . . . Christian Quarter. You must . . . until we find a way . . . break through." The transmission snapped in and out of coherence, but Dov and Moshe heard enough to understand the meaning. "Intelligence reports . . . al-Malik . . . in the Old . . . Hassan el . . ."

Moshe exhaled loudly at the news. Ahkmed al-Malik had learned the craft of killing Jews at the side of Himmler. He had a lampshade made from the skin of Jewish victims in Greece.

His adjutant, Hassan el-Hassan, was no better. He collected one ear from each Jew he personally murdered.

Dov's olive complexion blanched to a peculiar shade of

green. "Repeat, please. Did you say al-Malik was in the Old City?" Everyone knew of al-Malik's connection with the Kfar Etzion massacre.

Taking over from the commander, Major Luke Thomas replied in his crisp British accent, "Roger that. Working on . . . relieve you. Need your help. Plan . . . assault on coordinates B for . . . M for Mary. Repeat: . . . Baker, M for Mary."

Dov, flipping through pages of coded locations, whispered, "Baker Mary . . . Jaffa Gate! Frontal assault, he said? *Oy!* Suicide, he means!"

"Maybe not." Moshe squinted at the map in the dim light, tracing his finger along the line of the Old City wall to Jaffa Gate and The Citadel, which guarded the entrance to the Old City. Slapping his hand hard on the page, he cried exultantly, "Let me talk to him!" Moshe took the microphone from Dov. "Luke, this is Moshe! There is a better way! Do you read me?"

"What have you . . . for us? Over."

"Get Shaltiel. I need to say this in Polish." Switching to a language Moshe was confident no Arab spoke, he resumed, "There is a postern gate outside the walls. The entrance of the sally port is sealed by an iron grill. Behind that is a passageway. It leads into the Old City and emerges in the courtyard behind. Get a sapper in there to blow the grill, and you're in."

■　　■　　■　　■

The commanders of the Jewish Quarter defense met in Ben Zakkai Synagogue.

Moshe stabbed his finger at a map of the three Old City gates that would be attacked that night by the Haganah. "North, New Gate, south, Zion Gate, in the middle, the main assault at Jaffa. And we must hit the Muslims from behind at the same time."

"This is good," Ehud rumbled. "Why should we always wait for them to hit us? This time we return the favor. You have a plan?"

Yohannon ben Zakkai, the Jewish sage for whom the synagogue was named, had been smuggled out of Jerusalem in a coffin in order to escape the Roman havoc of A.D. 70. He lived to preserve the study of Torah, even though the Holy City was destroyed. Moshe thought about the scrolls of witness of which he was guardian and wondered if ben Zakkai had known of them.

On the south wall of the synagogue, in a square window high above the stone arches where the arks containing Torah were stored, was a shofar, a ram's-horn trumpet. Though the shofar still signaled holy days, this particular trumpet was special, not to be sounded until the coming of Messiah. If Messiah would just come now, this very night.

Moshe looked at the shofar and the window to the south. "About Jaffa Gate and New Gate we can do nothing," he said. "We are too far away to help. But Zion Gate is different. It is a mere hundred and fifty yards from here. Ehud, you and Rabbi Vultch will continue to hold the trench at the Street of the Chain on the northern boundary of the district. Dov and I will lead an operation against the tower of St. Jacques on the opposite side of the Quarter."

"*Meshugge!*" Ehud blurted. "Across the burned homes of the Armenian Quarter? Why?"

"Because," Moshe explained, "we should never have given up the tower to begin with. It is my fault, and it cost us the positions on Ararat Road, one quarter of our territory. If we retake the tower, we will have the Muslims holding Zion Gate in a cross fire. The bell tower is so important that even our attempt to recapture it will make the Muslims at Zion Gate pull back from the walls. They know how crucial that tower is and will have to prevent us from seizing it. Whether we manage to recapture St. Jacques and its belfry or not, Zion Gate is more vulnerable to a Palmach breakthrough from outside the walls."

"Not as vulnerable as you," Ehud said. "Suicide. Like climbing into a coffin before you're dead."

■　■　■　■

"*Allah Ahkbar!*" The shout of one Arab was joined with the echoes of a thousand who massed in the vacant buildings of the Christian Quarter.

"This is it," Ehud warned the youthful Yeshiva students who defended the sandbagged outpost overlooking the Street of the Chain.

Without waiting for the attackers to show themselves, a young man at Ehud's elbow fired a round at the partly open window of a deserted bakery. Following him, three others fired, wasting precious ammunition. Bullets ricocheted off the stones of the street, prompting the Jihad Moquades on the opposite side to send a hail of bullets toward the Jewish barricade.

Angered by the waste of ammunition, Ehud elbowed

the first soldier hard and shouted at the other three as bullets screamed off in a spray of stone chips. There was one consolation: The Arab Irregulars had also wasted their shots.

"Idiot!" The bellow of Ehud's voice was furious, easily heard above the weapons of the attackers. "Wait until you cannot miss! Idiots! Do not fire until you see something to fire at!" He reminded them that until the siege was broken, until the Haganah managed to break through to the Jewish Quarter, there would be no more bullets. The shamed recruits shrank back, perspired, and huddled behind the sandbags as shots from enemy rifles hammered the walls of their outpost. "Do not shoot until I tell you!"

"And if they should shoot your head off? Who will tell us then?" called a voice behind him.

It was Moshe. He rolled into the circle of sandbags and lay on his back in the floor of the nest as bullets zinged over their heads. "It's on for tonight. Jaffa Gate."

"Jaffa Gate!" Ehud gave a low, startled whistle that sang the word *suicide* in several languages.

"I talked again with Shaltiel and Luke Thomas." His words were accented by another volley from the Arab camp. Moshe leveled his gaze at the fearful eyes of the defenders. "Save your bullets. You will need them tonight."

"If we do not shoot back, will they not think we are dead?" asked the youngest of the volunteers. "Will they not then storm us, and we will be dead indeed?"

Ehud pondered this very real possibility. "So let them waste their bullets on the air," he declared, then raised his voice in the familiar song that had been sung by the defenders of the Warsaw ghetto:

> *Hitler won't be able to cope*
> *With the English fleet*
> *And the Russian sleet,*
> *With American dollars*
> *And Jewish smugglers . . .*

As the taunting tune was picked up by other Jewish defenders around the perimeter, the words transformed into a Jerusalem version: *The Mufti won't be able to cope . . .*

The Polish words, which had been written to taunt the Waffen SS as they battled Jews in the Warsaw ghetto, made no sense to the Arabs firing into the Jewish Quarter. The effect on the Jihad Moquades was the same as it had been on the Nazis, however. The fact that the Jews were singing happily meant they must have something to be happy about. Ample ammunition? Grenades and mortars enough to repel a frontal attack and kill large numbers of the Mufti's forces?

One hundred defiant Jewish voices were joined by others in the Quarter: male, female, young and old. Three hundred singing in unity reverberated like ten thousand.

Jewish cheerfulness was disconcerting to the Muslim mercenary forces who had come from far lands to kill Jews in Jerusalem. This was not their city, after all. Palestine was not their homeland. They had not come to die for the sake of the Mufti's ambition to rule the Holy City. They had come for the adventure and the pleasure of killing Jews, who they had been assured were under-equipped and starving. What were the words of this ditty? Something about America? American dollars meant lots of cash to buy war-surplus weapons. Everyone knew that America, the Great Satan, was run by the Zionists. It was a fact that a shipload of smuggled munitions had been allowed to dock at the coast as the English departed. Artillery pieces, tanks, even airplanes had been smuggled into Palestine from America. President Truman was the first to recognize the nation of Israel. A bad sign. And had not the Jews taken the fortress of Kastel overlooking the road from Tel Aviv to the sea? Of course, the Jihad Moquades had massacred the Jews of Kfar Etzion, but that was only after the last Jewish bullet had been spent. No one on the kibbutz had been singing then.

For a time that day it was song, not bullets, that kept the attackers at bay.

▪ ▪ ▪ ▪ CHAPTER 18 ▪ ▪ ▪ ▪

Yehudit Avram balanced a tray of steaming mugs and food with both hands while juggling the sling of the Enfield rifle that threatened to slip off her left shoulder. She was a terrible shot and admitted a tendency to squeeze her eyes shut as she squeezed the trigger. Nevertheless, Yehudit was vigorous, strong, fearless, and totally committed to the defense of the Jewish Quarter.

Painfully shy, introverted, and mistrustful while under the thumb of her domineering father, Yehudit had blossomed during the brief span of her marriage to Dov. Now she was cheerful and outgoing, making up in encouragement whatever she lacked in marksmanship.

She glanced at her father's door as she passed it. The poorly repaired black panel hung a trifle crooked in the frame, like an eyebrow glowering at her. Perhaps it always had, as an emotional reflection of its owner. Yehudit gave it a cheery smile anyway as she glanced down at the silver server she held. Like the tea in the heavy cups, the tray came from the chest recovered from Akiva's secret store-room. Since it had been her mother's mother's, it should, by rights, have come to her on her wedding day. And finally it had.

From inside the stairwell of the Porat Yoseph School, Yehudit called to the two Yeshiva students manning the sandbagged outpost on its roof. "Ephraim," she called. "Reuven. Food is here."

Ephraim slithered over the side of the protective burrow and jumped through the opening of the stair even as an Arab sniper fired. The bullet clanged against the metal.

"Yehudit," the guard scolded, "you must not come up here in daylight. We can wait until sundown to eat."

"This is the thanks I get?" Yehudit teased. "Do you think the Muslims have tea and sandwiches brought to them?" Unfolding a parcel wrapped in white butcher paper, she revealed pita bread stuffed with rice. "It isn't very much," Yehudit apologized. "And no sugar for the tea."

Wolfing down the food, Ephraim said, "It is wonderful! The truth is, I was starving!" The boy blew on the mug to cool it, then sipped at the drink. "Wonderful!"

"You cannot keep proper watch if your stomach is growling!" When Ephraim had finished, Yehudit said, "Hurry and trade with Reuven. I have more hungry mouths to feed!"

■   ■   ■   ■

Palmach commander Nachasch and David Shaltiel strode the length of the portico of the Jewish-held British Ophthalmic Hospital, which overlooked Arab-held Mount Zion from across the Valley of Hinnom.

"Sixty men in the Palmach are worth a thousand recruits off the ships," Shaltiel said in a conciliatory tone. "But you cannot expect to take Mount Zion tonight. Your force is diversionary only, meant to distract the Jihad Moquades' attention away from Jaffa Gate, where the real breakthrough will take place."

Nachasch squinted disdainfully. "Give me a tenth of the ammunition that will be thrown away on Jaffa Gate tonight, and my men can take Mount Zion from the Arabs. From there we will storm Zion Gate and break through to the Old City."

Shaltiel clasped his hands behind his back as he looked across the valley at the exposed slope of Mount Zion. Headstones dotted the hillside like sheep grazing. The wildflowers made pools of color against the green grass. Mount Zion itself was a veritable fortress. The Muslim fighters occupied the Gobat School, the enormous domed edifice of the Church of the Dormition, the House of Caiaphas, David's Tomb, and even the building where legend said the Last Supper of Christ took place on the eve of the crucifixion.

"You will be crucified," Shaltiel said as the image stuck in his mind. "There is no cover on Mount Zion's slopes but headstones. If you advance too far, you will be wiped out. You haven't enough men."

"I haven't enough bullets for my men. Not enough grenades. One pitiful Davidka mortar."

"Your sixty will provide a diversionary maneuver. The decision has been made."

"Dr. Weintraub was wounded yesterday. If there are wounded, I will have no one to spare. I need medics, no?"

"That you shall have."

"Send them with bullets, if you please," Nachasch warned. "We cannot even be a useful diversion for Jaffa Gate if my fellows have merely three bullets each."

"I will send what I can," Shaltiel promised.

■　　■　　■　　■

Kasim Dajani was furious. Ever since making his first grenade out of gunpowder and a Player's cigarette tin, the terrorist had dreamed of open and unrestricted warfare against the Jews. Such a condition had existed for two days, and what did he have to show for it? Almost nothing!

True, his bundles of dynamite had played a role in turning back the Haganah assault on Jaffa Gate. After the skirmish the Jihad Moquades fired their rifles and whooped and shouted as if a great victory had been won. They clapped Dajani on the back and hailed him as a hero, but Dajani knew otherwise. Jaffa Gate had been a probe, nothing more. The Jews in the New City had not been driven away so much as they had explored and then withdrawn. They would be back, and, *Insh' Allah,* Dajani would be ready for them.

In the meantime, it was the Old City Jewish district that drew his particular wrath. He blamed them for the burning pain in his face and for the swaddling bandages that made everyone shy away from looking at him.

Because of his injuries, the bomber could not trust himself to carry out a mission. Now Najid, that fat, clumsy pig, was out of action also. The baker's small toe had been shot off. What kind of a wound was that for a combatant in a holy war?

These calculations reduced the possibilities for Dajani's next move by the simple math of subtraction: what he had left was the orphan boys, Daoud and Gawan.

The plot Dajani devised for his next operation against the Old City Jews was simple and contained but a single hazard: it treated the lives of the brothers as expendable. In Dajani's eyes this was perfectly acceptable. Not only did Jihad martyrs go straight to Paradise, but these orphans of the streets would have been knifed or sold into slavery long before this if Dajani had not taken them in. Their lives belonged to the bomber to dispose of as he chose.

At the north end of the Street of the Jews there was a building called *Lubinsky's House*. The structure arched over the slender roadway from one side to the other like a dwelling standing on a bridge over a river. The opening beneath was blocked by an iron gate.

The grill was less than a block from the men's W.C., which had been dynamited by the earlier blast. What Dajani discovered was that the explosion had not only destroyed the toilet, it had ripped a hole through the wall and into the cellar of an adjacent building. Dajani led Daoud and Gawan into the lavatory, placing them on what remained of the steps without any of the Jews knowing how near destruction had crept.

■　■　■　■

The minute hand of the watch given Dajani by Hassan el-Hassan crept nearer to 6 P.M. That was the hour set for Gawan to carry a bomb toward the Haganah trench while Daoud ran with one toward Lubinsky's House. If only one attack was successful, the way into the Jewish Quarter was open.

Beside the boys and the bomber sat an old man named Rimal. In peaceful times Rimal lived in the gutter beside Damascus Gate, helping shoppers carry their purchases when opportunity offered, begging when it did not. The war had ruined his livelihood, and at present he carried the burdens of the soldiers instead. He was dim-witted, given to mindlessly mimicking what was spoken to him, but good-natured and harmless. It was said that he was rightly named, since *rimal* meant "sand" and truly the wiry ancient had a head stuffed with grit and not much else.

Whenever someone quoted that well-worn quip, Rimal cackled with delight.

For a handful of Iraqi dinars, Dajani hired Rimal to help carry the milk-can loads of dynamite and detonators into the W.C.

Miserable and frightened, Gawan hugged the first bomb. He looked even smaller than usual. "It will be all right," Daoud reassured his younger brother as Dajani handed Daoud a cigarette lighter.

"Be all right!" Rimal laughed.

"Will it hurt much to die?" Gawan asked.

"Hurt to die!" Rimal echoed.

"Now!" Dajani ordered. "*Allah Ahkbar!* Ignite the first fuse!"

Daoud's hands shook so that he could not spark the lighter. On the third try he dropped it. The silver case bounced down the steps into the wreckage of the toilets.

"Hurry!" Dajani said, cursing. Shots were being fired by overanxious Jihad Moquades.

"Let me carry the first one," Daoud suggested, returning with the lighter.

Before Dajani could settle the issue of which boy would go first, Rimal grabbed the lighter out of Daoud's hand.

"*Allah Ahkbar!*" Rimal shouted. "Ignite the fuse!" Grinning wildly, the beggar flicked the lighter and lit the fuse of Gawan's bomb, then seized the sputtering bundle of explosives from the boy.

"Run, Rimal!" Dajani shouted, thrusting the beggar with the bomb out into the open toward the Jewish defenses.

Gawan followed Rimal.

"Wait! Gawan!" Daoud yelled, running after his brother. "Come back!"

Dajani wasted no time in saving himself. He plunged down the steps of the latrine and, covering his head with his arms, burrowed behind the broken toilets.

"Watch out!" yelled Jewish voices in alarm.

A barrage of gunshots erupted. Daoud, faster than his brother, overtook Gawan from behind and tackled him. They tumbled into the gutter beside a stone water trough. Gawan lay on top.

Rimal was cut down before he had covered a third of the distance to the barricade. The bomb exploded the second he fell.

■   ■   ■   ■

The baby was a girl. She took her first breath at the moment the shock wave of an explosion rolled over the Old City like water from a bursting dam.

Rachel heard it, felt the vibration of the metal-framed bed as she held the new mother's hand. She knew a soul was leaving this world even as the new life entered.

Sweating and weeping for joy, the young woman thanked Allah, Rachel, Lori, and the doctor. *"Allah Ahkbar! Allah Ahkbar!"* The words Rachel had often heard from the screaming voices of Jihad Moquades took on an unexpected significance. *God is great!* Baruch's eyes were moist as he cradled the infant.

"Look at you," he whispered in awe. "Praise be to the Lord for your soul, sweet one. A pretty girl you are. A headful of hair." Then to the mother, "Allah has given you a lovely daughter."

He passed the child to Lori, who in turn wrapped her in a warm towel and carried her to the basin to wash as he tended to the mother.

Rachel glanced at the clock on the wall. It was past six. In five hours, Dr. Baruch had seen more than forty patients: cleaned and stitched five superficial wounds, lanced boils, flushed ears, repaired ingrown toenails and treated dermatitis, set a broken arm and delivered a child.

Soon it would be dark, and they would steal away to the

Jewish Quarter to a different group of patients.

■　■　■　■

The explosion drove everyone, Arab and Jew, under cover. Not merely shrapnel but bricks and blocks of stone showered down as if a volcano had erupted in the heart of Jerusalem. "Get off me," Daoud said, shaking his brother. "We must run before they start shooting again. Gawan?"

Something sticky and moist dripped onto Daoud's face. It was blood.

"Gawan!" Daoud screamed. *"Youin!* Help me, someone!" Daoud squirmed out from under.

Gawan's ears were covered with blood. A notched shard of metal protruded from the back of his neck. Also, there was a problem with his left arm. From shoulder to elbow it looked all right, but below the joint it seemed to be lying apart from his body.

"Youin!" Daoud cried again. "My brother is hurt! Help me!"

No one appeared to help.

Gawan opened his eyes and tried to roll over. In a matter-of-fact tone he said, "My arm has something wrong with it. There is a stick poking me! Pull it out."

Daoud screamed again, then bit his lip until the blood came. The stick was an arm bone, its jagged white and red end projecting through a tear in the skin. "Don't move," he managed to choke out. "I'll get help. Do not move!"

No shots were fired when Daoud rose and ran. He did not know where to turn, which way to go. The street did not even look the same. The building fronts had been sliced open. On some the walls facing the blast had disappeared. Daoud could not tell in which direction he was running.

Two blocks along, Daoud finally recognized the entry to the souks and immediately found assistance. A stoop-shouldered man, old-eyed despite his unwrinkled skin, emerged from an aisle. He was pushing a wheelbarrow. "Here, boy," he said. "I can help. We must get your brother to the Latin Patriarchate. There is a doctor there. Are you afraid to go back with me?"

"It does not matter," the boy replied. "For Gawan I will go back."

The Street of the Chain was waking up to war again. The business of killing resumed, but the gardener trudged fearlessly into the middle. When he reached Gawan's side, he put a hand tenderly on the injured boy's hair and whispered to him. Then the gardener swept Gawan up in his arms and laid him on his side in the wheelbarrow.

■   ■   ■   ■

As the crooked wooden wheel of the barrow bumped over the uneven pavement, Daoud winced with every bounce. "Would it not be better to carry him?" he asked. "Perhaps it would hurt less?" Blood from the neck puncture dripped and pooled in the box of the wheelbarrow, the red stain rising back up Gawan's white robes.

Without taking his eyes from the route ahead, the gardener said, "Exactly how he lies is best for his wounds. He has fainted, Daoud. It is a mercy. There is no pain for him."

The route they followed took them far from the souks

at the border of the Muslim and Christian Quarters. Daoud wished he could grab his brother up in his arms and race ahead . . . but where?

Gawan's skin was colorless beneath a layer of grime. He did not seem to be breathing. "Faster, faster!" Daoud urged. "For the love of Allah, go faster!"

The Street of the Chain jogged and became the Street of David. The blood around the base of the metal splinter stopped dripping and turned darker even as Gawan's skin grew paler. Was he dead already? Daoud would not accept it. Fiercely, almost angrily, he commanded Gawan to stay alive.

With Daoud trotting to keep up, the long stride of the gardener transported them past Muristan Road and the Petra Hotel.

"Will he die? Don't let him die," Daoud asked and pleaded in the same gasping breath. "Do not die, Gawan," he shouted, as if his brother could hear. His eyes stung from the smoke of the explosion. The weeping plowed furrows of grief on his dirty face. Gawan had been afraid of the bomb, of being hurt and dying. Why had this happened? Why had Daoud not taken better care of his brother?

The towers of The Citadel at Jaffa Gate loomed ahead, but the gardener neither turned nor slowed. "Where are we going?" Daoud demanded, his frustration boiling over. "Is there nowhere closer?"

"None," the gardener replied. "Your brother is badly hurt. In all of Jerusalem there is only one who can help him. Be strong and do not fear."

Daoud was afraid. He told himself he was angry, but

truly, it was fear. This gardener saw through the charade.

Before Omar Square, at the corner occupied by the three-story New Imperial Hotel, they turned right. This was Latin Patriarchate Road.

"We are almost there," the gardener said. "Run, Daoud, and tell them we are coming."

The boy needed no urging. He spurted ahead, shouting, "My brother is hurt! We need a doctor! My brother is wounded!"

A man dressed in the brown robe of a Franciscan came to the entry. "What do you do here, boy?" he asked. "This is not a clinic."

"Yes it is," Daoud argued. "My brother is coming in the wheelbarrow. Fetch me the doctor at once."

"I told you," the Franciscan repeated, starting to close the door, "there is no . . ."

"What is the commotion?" asked Brother Nathan, coming to the door.

"This boy . . ."

"We are here to see the doctor at once!" Daoud said. "We have come far already, and he is bad."

Leaning down to look, Brother Nathan gasped as he took in the compound fracture and the metal splinter that pulsed with every beat of Gawan's heart. "Help them lift the cart over the threshold, Brother John," he instructed. "I will get the physician."

It seemed like hours to Daoud before Brother Nathan reappeared, accompanied by Dr. Baruch, though in reality it was no more than three minutes. What followed was a matter of immediate decision. Asking Brother Nathan to take Daoud out of the room and get him some water, he said to the gardener, "This boy must be operated on at once. The fracture is bad and will need careful tending to keep it from becoming septic . . . but the shrapnel lies near both artery and spinal cord and could take his life at any second. The operation is extremely risky. Are you his father?"

"They are orphans," the gardener said. "But I will answer as his father. Go to work. And may God guide your hands."

■   ■   ■   ■

Alfie, Jacob, Daniel, Mangus, Chaim, Pinky, and Ibrahim occupied a second-story room at the point of the wedge-shaped Municipality building. There they waited for the call to arms.

The men were grateful when night at last covered Jerusalem, bringing with it an uneasy quiet. After the evening mortar barrage, the Arabs holding the eastern parts of the city apparently considered their duty done for the day. Even the rifle fire that punctuated the May sunlight faded to sporadic, meaningless outbursts after sunset.

If the Municipality building had been a ship cleaving the waves of Terra Sancta, Jaffa Gate and the fortifications known as *The Citadel* would have been an iceberg looming on its starboard bow. The men gathered in the gloomy room could not help but feel their force was on a collision course with the Arab-held parapets.

The Citadel, which included David's Tower, was an ancient fortress that stood guard over Jaffa Gate and the western entrance to the Old City. For more than two thousand years it had been occupied by an endless array of rulers and their soldiers. It had been defended, destroyed, and rebuilt in an ever-repeated cycle and was the last defense during times of war and siege. It was understood that if David's Tower fell, Old City Jerusalem would also fall to its attackers.

This was the goal of the Haganah.

Looking out at the massive fortifications from the darkened window, Chaim muttered, "We who are about to die salute you."

Pinky, offended by the comment, snapped, "Shut up, Chaim."

"It's a saying. The Roman gladiators used to say it before they went into combat. That's all. Just a saying."

Jacob remarked, "So who needs it?"

Chaim slumped down to sit on the floor. "I could use a smoke," he said, breaking the tension.

Jacob warned, "You light up here, they'll spot us from The Citadel and blow us sky-high."

Chaim barked, "Did I say I was going to light up? I haven't seen a cigarette in weeks. And when I saw one, it was in someone else's mouth."

"Keep it to yourself," Pinky insisted.

Another uneasy lull ensued. Ibrahim, whose black skin made him invisible, asked, "I am wondering after the killed fellow of our group. His family?"

Pinky sighed. "Hymie Slanik didn't have a family. He was it. Last of the Slaniks."

Ibrahim said, "We fellows are his brothers, then. We have not said enough words over him. It is bad luck not to speak well after the dead."

The sneer in Chaim's tone was unmistakable. "Was I doing so bad conversationwise, I ask you? Is cigarettes or gladiators worse than this?"

"Who was Hymie?" Jacob asked.

Pinky replied, "Some poor schmo from Poland. That's all I know."

For the first time, Daniel spoke to the group. His voice was hoarse from disuse. "Ibrahim is right. How can a man die for Jerusalem and not have a story?"

Silence. Each man in the room considered his own mortality. Suppose tonight they were killed at Jaffa Gate and no one even remembered who they were?

"He was just like us, I guess," Pinky offered. "We're all the same story, aren't we? Different details in the mix, but here we are in this room . . . waiting together."

Jacob whispered almost inaudibly, "We who are about to die . . ."

Chaim sniffed and began the tale. "Hymie Slanik, we salute you. You are ten years old. Your father takes you to the train station and puts you on a train with six hundred other children."

Daniel corrected, "You are seven. Your baby sister is three. She is the only one going with you. No adults. They hug you and bless you, and you know somehow you'll never see them again."

Pinky picked up the story. "The train leaves at midnight. The whistle blows, and you know you are saying good-bye forever."

Daniel's voice was hollow as he spoke again. "You have a suitcase. A paper bag with sandwiches and two apples. The whistle blows again, and you know this is it.

Your mother and father . . . everyone you know. The door opens, and a wicker basket is shoved onto the car. You hear the sound of a baby crying from inside. Then your sister begins to cry, too, like the baby. Don't cry, you say to Suzannah, but she cries anyway. But you? You're beyond tears. You are frozen inside . . . so you let her cry, and you go find a corner where you can huddle and be alone in the middle of fifty other kids on the car. You are not the oldest. A girl who is twelve or thirteen is the oldest. She organizes everyone. There is a lavatory. There is water to drink. Everyone brought something to eat, so no one will starve. Everyone who is over six must help with the little ones but . . . but you can't. You can't make yourself eat or drink or get up to go to the toilet. You want only to go back . . . to be with your mommy and daddy . . . to die with them. But you can't, so you sit and stare. The girl in charge talks to you, but you do not answer. Suzannah looks at the baby and giggles. The girl in charge lets Suzannah hold the bottle. What happens when the milk runs out? It's a long way to the Dutch border. Hours and hours. The milk runs out. They feed the baby water, but it does not stop crying."

The words tumbled out of the young man as if he could not help himself. "Should I stop him?" Jacob asked.

Ibrahim put a hand on Jacob's arm. "Let the boy talk."

Alfie got up and lumbered over to sit beside Daniel as the story rolled out in his desperate monotone. "I rode a train, too," he offered, but Daniel did not hear him.

"Forty hours since you left your family. You have not eaten. Unlike the baby, you do not care. There is a sign. Five kilometers until you reach the border of Holland. The train is stopped on the German side. A Nazi bursts into the

280

car. He searches through luggage and points his gun at the basket with the baby in it. He says this is unauthorized. The girl in charge says it is her basket and her baby. She will get off with it if it has to go. The guard thinks and then turns and leaves. The door clangs shut and the children cheer. Except you. The train goes again and then slows to a stop. Are they coming back? Have they changed their mind about the baby? And then you cross the border into Holland. You stop. The train is overflowing with Dutch women who bring food and hugs. You wonder where they got so much food, but you won't eat or speak or move. You want to die. And then the woman comes to you. She picks you up and puts her arms around you. You sit on her lap and lay your head against her. You hear her heart beat. Like Mama. Like Grandmother. You begin to cry. She coos to you and feeds you. You eat and tell her your name and your sister's name. You tell her about your mommy and . . . then everyone gets off the train. But she stays with you. She doesn't get off the train even when it moves out of the station. She feeds you and tells you about the wonderful Holy Land and where you are going with your sister. A place of joy, she says, where there are no Nazis, where God's chosen people—children—will have a home. You believe her. You are able to get up and go to the toilet. You look at the baby and are glad it is safe. Then . . . it is okay when the old lady gets off the train. And you and your baby sister go first to England and then to Eretz-Israel . . . to Kfar Etzion, which becomes your home and your family . . . Daniel Caan . . . Hymie Slanik. Those who are about to die salute you." At last the voice trailed away. Daniel hung his head.

Alfie put his big arm clumsily around the slumped shoulders of the young soldier. "I rode on a train, too," Alfie said gently.

Daniel began to weep.

▪ ▪ ▪ ▪ CHAPTER 19 ▪ ▪ ▪ ▪

Jerusalem was locked in blackness. There was no electricity. Tonight, in the kitchen, by lantern light and the flickering flames of votive candles, Dr. Baruch labored to save the fragile life of the Arab boy.

Gawan lay facedown on the table. Mindful of the doctor's warning that even a muscle spasm could kill him, Rachel held a cloth soaked with ether near the child's nose and mouth. She braced his head as Baruch cut down with a sharpened straight razor. The metal splinter protruding from the back of Gawan's neck had missed spine and artery by a millimeter.

Lori Kalner proved her steadiness, holding open the incision with a pair of kitchen tongs. Brother Nathan, ashen at the sight, held the lantern.

"More light! Closer! Over here," Baruch demanded. "I cannot see!"

The Franciscan obeyed meekly. He stood in awe of the skill of Baruch. His former antagonism had been utterly banished by the day's work.

For hours Baruch talked constantly to the unconscious boy, willing him to live, ordering him to breathe! Telling him that life was too precious a thing not to live it. Talking about his own childhood in Prague, of happy days before the war.

Rachel listened, listened, listened, to the singsong voice of the surgeon. And she knew where she had heard that voice. She remembered where they had met, what terrible circumstance had brought her to him. *Nur für Offiziere. For officers only. The SS brothel in Auschwitz. The baby.* Did Baruch remember her face? Her grief? The rules of the brothel were immutable. *Any Jewish whore who becomes pregnant will be executed. Surely Baruch could not remember me. One young whore among hundreds and thousands of prisoners whom he must have seen.* But she remembered him, the young physician's assistant, and his kindness to her as she suffered through a post-abortion hemorrhage. *"Live!" he commanded me! "L'Chaim! You've had to give your child back to God, or they would have killed you the first moment they suspected. Dear girl. Dear girl. We must live long enough to start again, for that will mean they have lost their battle to destroy our souls. It will not always be thus for us."*

Grasping the end of the shard with needle-nose pliers, Dr. Baruch glanced up at the other participants. "Pray," he commanded, preparing to extract the thing. And they did. The Franciscan closed his eyes and swayed a bit.

Baruch growled, "Steady with the light! I do not fancy pulling out his soul with these things. Nothing moves but my hand and the spike with it!"

Rachel fixed her gaze on the reflection in Baruch's glasses. Behind the lenses the doctor's eyes winced in agony as he yanked, as if the thing were impaled in his own heart. "Come on! Come on, then! Let go of it, Gawan! Let go of it, and you will live! That's it . . ." The thing began to move. Blood oozed around it. Baruch clenched his teeth. "Let me have it, boy! Give it to me. There. Yes. That is the way . . ."

The Franciscan groaned softly.

"Shut up!" Baruch ordered. Then once again he commanded the steel spike, "You cannot have him . . . no . . . not this one! This one will not die. Come out! Come out of him! That's the way, Gawan! Life! *L'Chaim!*" A final tug and the shard was free, dripping gore in the lantern light.

Rachel exhaled, long and slowly, aware of the relief of everyone around the table.

"So," said Baruch, dropping the malevolent thing into a saucepan, "thanks be to God." He clasped a flask of Scotch gleaned from the archbishop's study and doused the wound with its contents. "We will finish repairing this chasm and the arm. The rest is not up to us." He glared at Brother Nathan. "I will leave this boy in your hands. If he does not recover . . . does not grow up well . . . it will be upon your head. Clear?"

It was a curse, a blessing, a firm penitence that Baruch was exacting from the cleric.

Brother Nathan accepted it. "It was the will of God that you came here . . . and I . . . will take care of the child."

"And also his brother, yes? He nearly died killing Jews. You must show him a better way."

■　■　■　■

Dr. Baruch, his thin face drawn from exhaustion and white smock covered in blood, towered over Daoud. He and the boy stood in the corridor outside the room where Gawan lay clinging to life after the hours of surgery.

Brother Nathan, gray with shame, wide-eyed at the miracle the Jewish doctor had performed, interpreted.

Daoud, shivering with stress, asked, "My brother . . . will he live?"

Baruch placed a comforting hand on Daoud's bony shoulder and stooped to look him in the eye. "Tonight your brother is alive. Praise be to God. You did well to bring him here. But there will be many uncertain days. You must not see him tonight. Come tomorrow. This is very hard for him, very serious wounds, you must understand."

Daoud extended his hands pleadingly. "Please Allah. Gawan is all my family. And you, Doctor, sir, who have made this first miracle, will stay and care for him?"

Baruch frowned. "I cannot stay here with your brother, Daoud. There are others I must go to with wounds as serious as his. They will die if I do not come."

"But you must stay, Your Honor, because I can't stay with him. If I don't return to our master, he will find and kill us both. But if you leave my brother, I am certain Gawan will slip away to Paradise. They tell me . . . the Prophet tells us that to die killing Jews is a great honor. He will fly away to Paradise and there be attended by many virgins. I do not think Gawan would care about the virgins. But at least he would have food enough to eat. But when he is gone, what will I do? Please, sir, you must not leave him."

Brother Nathan hung his head as he recounted the words of the child exactly. The cleric said to Baruch, "I will tell him you are a Jew. This will stop his insolent mouth."

Baruch replied sharply to the Franciscan, "Insolent?

There is no insolence in him. He is a child. Parroting the world he has seen and heard. How can he know how to hate a Jew unless others have taught him?"

Brother Nathan looked away. "You are . . . a man of mercy. A forgiving man. He should know you are a Jew. He should know it was his enemy who saved the life of his brother."

"When we are gone. Tell him then." Baruch caressed the dirty face of the boy. "I will pray for you and your brother, Daoud. I have done what I can, and Gawan is in the hands of the living God who loves you both. May our precious Savior protect you and keep you until there is peace between all people in Jerusalem."

"Should I tell him that?" Brother Nathan asked.

"Leave it. The Lord has heard my heart."

Daoud's brow furrowed. He looked searchingly into the face of the Franciscan. "Does His Honor say he must go away?"

The Franciscan answered, "Yes, Daoud. There are many wounded who need his skill. They will not live unless he leaves us tonight."

"Where is he going? We will follow."

"You cannot go where he is going."

Daoud raised his hand in resignation. *"Insh' Allah.* As Allah wills it, then. Tell him I shall pray for him five times a day. Tell him to think of us kindly when he hears the call of the muezzin. Tell him from the fullness of my heart that I shall count him as my father and the father of my brother, for he has given my brother back his life. Tell him that Daoud and Gawan who have no name will take his name for our own." Then to the Franciscan, "What is the name of our father?"

"Baruch" was the reply. "It means 'blessing.' "

■　■　■　■

Lori sat beside Gawan's bed. When he moaned, she spoke tenderly to him, stroked his hands and head and feet.

Mother Superior brought her a sandwich and a cup of tea for supper. "Rachel is in the other room, holding the infant. There is a light in her eyes. She speaks to the young mother as if they are close friends. She says when her baby comes along they should visit. If it were up to mothers, there would never be war."

Lori smiled and gratefully accepted the meal.

Mother Superior said, "That is the first time I have seen you smile." She moved up a chair and sat beside Lori. "I have been thinking about the problem you presented."

"Problem?" Lori's mind raced through a list of problems as long as her arm. "Which problem?"

"The question you posed to me yesterday: what would have happened if Joseph had not obeyed the angel?"

Lori concealed her amusement. This was not a subject she would have given top priority. "Unfathomable, is it?"

The nun cleaned her spectacles on the sleeve of her habit. "Not entirely. Though it may take years to explore."

"I hope we have time."

"Yes. Such a question is . . . it is the essence of the battle between good and evil. Light and darkness. Is it not?" She was enjoying herself. "Joseph left to save the one. Many others died. Then the one grew up to die for all . . . for *all*." Her eyes were animated. "Is God unmerciful because innocent children died while Jesus lived? Is there a purpose for all things?"

"That is not one I can answer."

"You think you came into the convent to persuade us to leave. And yet you are here as well. You helped deliver a baby today. You helped to save the life of this boy."

"If I hadn't been here it would have been someone else."

"But it is *not* someone else. It is you. You are here, drifting, you think. Forsaken by God, you believe?" She put a hand on Lori's arm. What was it she saw in Lori's face? The bitterness? The regret? The loathing of an unjust world? "No. Your steps are ordered by the Lord. We have learned in our years that the heart does not ache unless it seeks God."

"I almost gave up believing there will be an answer."

"The answer is that you must simply keep living. Embrace whatever God sends your way. Sorrow and joy. Trust that you are not here by accident. Every moment, every event in your life has a purpose for the welfare of eternity if you love God."

"It is hard when life seems . . . pointless."

The nun looked at Gawan, at Lori's hand on his brow. "You are patient with children. I have watched you today. You have children?"

Lori shrank back. This was aiming too close to the heart. Too close. How could she know? "Not anymore."

"You left the poems of Rilke open on the table. *She came up the slope, heavy, almost unable to believe in comfort, hope, or counsel.*" A pat on the hand. "I have probed a painful wound. Forgive me. It comes of years of living with other women. We know when heartaches come through our portals. We were not always nuns, you know."

"I suppose there is nothing I cannot live with."

"Resignation is not acceptance. Nothing *is* something, *ma chérie*. Bitterness. Anger. We resign ourselves to live with such things. Sometimes, like weeds, they take over the garden. But would not life be better if we lived without them? Accepted pain without bitterness? From our acceptance of personal pain grows compassion for others who are hurting. This is what our Lord meant when He said, *Blessed are those who mourn, for they will be comforted. Blessed are the merciful, for they will be shown mercy.*"

"Too many questions."

"You have a journey to make. All of us make the same journey. It must begin with questions, or we will never move one step. It is when we think we have all the answers that bitterness hardens our hearts and we lose our way."

"What happened to my child is not an allegory. His death is real."

"*Oui.* You dwell in the real world. I have forgotten that skill. But today we have walked together through the valley of the shadow of death. Do you see it is a shadow? Surely you felt the presence of angels around us? So much we cannot see while we live in these bodies. But it doesn't mean a larger reality doesn't exist. Of this one thing I am certain: you will see your child again one day. Scripture says that those who have left this life before us are like a great cloud of witnesses cheering us on to the finish line. Do not despair that God has found you worthy to grieve." She looked at the boy. "You already turn your pain into compassion. Use it to comfort those who also grieve, and you will fully have the heart of Jesus. Think on those things you pondered here. God will make clear the reason for your pilgrimage to the Holy City." From the pocket of her habit she withdrew the copy of Rilke's poems and a black leather-bound book with the words DIE HEILIGE SCHRIFT on the spine.

It was a German edition of the Bible.

"For you," the nun said, presenting the gifts. "I brought them with me."

"Oh, but I . . ."

"But you must. *Deutsch* is your mother tongue, is it not?"

"It has been so long."

"Let your heart hear the words again as they were spoken at your cradle. This is the meaning of Pentecost." The saintly woman kissed Lori on the cheek. "May the Lord go with you."

■   ■   ■   ■

Dr. Baruch, dressed in his tan linen suit, peered uncertainly out the door of the Patriarchate. "Things seem to be quiet for the moment," he said. "This may be our best chance."

Lori and Rachel, crowded into the vestibule behind him, agreed.

"How can you hope to break through the Muslim cordon?" Brother Nathan asked. "Stay here in safety. There will be more you can help right here."

Baruch shook his head. "There are people dying inside the Jewish Quarter," he said. "We have come this far; we must press on."

"I think," Brother Nathan said cautiously, not sure if his advice was welcome, "your best route is to go to the north side of the Armenian Quarter. After the battles and the fires, it is so torn up that there may be an unguarded passage."

Dr. Baruch shrugged. It was guesswork at best.

Mother Superior stepped up. In her hand was a bulging carpetbag, which she handed to Lori. "Brother Nathan and I want to thank the three of you for your labors of healing. When the British evacuated, they left behind many things, but among the more useful were medical supplies."

Opening the satchel, Lori found it stuffed with cans of sulfa powder for wounds and ampoules of morphine, as well as bandages, compresses, splints, and a can of chloroform for anesthetic.

Lori hugged Mother Superior. "Would you do one thing for me?" she asked.

"Certainly, my child. What is it?"

"Would you tell your gardener good-bye for me? He was so calm that it gave me courage to have him around."

Mother Superior frowned. "I don't know what you mean. We do not have a gardener. We tend the garden ourselves."

■　■　■　■

Like an Arab merchant making his way about the Old City with two of his wives, Baruch with the women slipped from shadow to shadow in the blacked-out Christian Quarter.

The problem with this deception, Rachel thought, was

that there were no Arab families walking in the Old City. The area was deserted. Aside from the flickers cast by votive candles within a handful of shrines and churches, the inhabitants seemed to have fled.

Two blocks away from the Patriarchate, Baruch was already stumped. "How can we find our way in this?" he asked.

"I know enough to lead," Rachel offered. "Even with the Jewish Quarter under siege, the Arabs have to eat. We will not look suspicious if we go through the souks."

An air of breathless expectancy hovered over Jerusalem. What sounds there were felt muffled, as if the night were so wrapped in apprehension that every tone above the level of a heartbeat was pressed down and crushed into the stones.

Behind the three travelers was the wall, lined with Jihad Moquades.

Somewhere up ahead, Jews and Arabs kept strained watch over a front line marked by burned houses and shell-pocked streets. Up there was Rachel's heart: Moshe, Grandfather, Yacov. Were they well? Would she see them soon?

"Where are we?" Baruch queried.

Squinting, Rachel made out a stone arch hidden behind an iron grill topped with spearpoints. "This is Mary's Gate on the west side of the Church of the Holy Sepulchre," she said. "From here we go east and later south again."

■ ■ ■ ■

The Municipality building was packed with men prepared

for the assault on Jaffa Gate. Four hundred steely-faced Haganah troops checked Sten guns and grenades. A green flare would signal the success of the First Strike Team: that the secret passageway into The Citadel was secure. Then the main Haganah assault would charge into the heart of the fortress and capture the towers flanking Jaffa Gate.

They hoped that diversionary attacks on New Gate and Zion Gate would divide the Arab defense, but success depended on blowing open the grate across the hidden corridor.

At precisely two minutes past midnight, Corporal Jacob Kalner, Daniel Caan, Captain Isaacson, and the others of the Spare Parts Platoon, part of the First Strike Team, received the signal to move.

Major Luke Thomas ordered them to board an armored bus, but he stopped Isaacson at the door. "I have something for you," he said, profferring a soft parcel wrapped in canvas.

Jacob, Alfie, who was dutifully toting a backpack with a radio-telephone, and the giant shoeless Ethiopian, Ibrahim, carrying eighty pounds of ammunition, were on the steps of the transport and overheard the exchange.

"What is it?" Isaacson asked gruffly. "We could use a bazooka, but this ain't heavy enough for that."

"It's a flag," Thomas returned. "To fly above David's Tower after you capture it. God go with you."

Isaacson removed the white-and-blue banner from its case and tied it around his waist. "That way it can't get lost," he said, saluting.

The plan of attack was simple: An armored car and Luke Thomas's command vehicle, both bearing machine guns, would move into position outside Jaffa Gate. Once their combined fire had raked the parapets, the bus would disgorge men to blow the grill on the sally port and rush the passageway to enter the courtyard inside the walls. This surprise maneuver would put the Haganah in position to strike the Arab defenders from behind while more troops, assembling in the streets around the King David Hotel, rushed the gate itself.

On the bus, Jacob checked his Sten gun and the additional clips of bullets hanging from his web belt. His thoughts were flooded with Lori. How would she take the news that he was dead? Would she forgive him? She would go home to London and start her life over again. She would live the rest of her life saying, "Once I had a Jewish husband. He was an idealistic fool. I went with him to Israel. He was killed three days later attacking Jaffa Gate." No doubt she would marry again. Have children. He would become a distant memory.

The twenty-millimeter weapon of the lead armored vehicle carrying Luke Thomas shattered Jacob's morose reverie. The car raced up toward the gate, its gunner firing at the embrasures on top of the wall whenever he saw movement. The tracer shells dazzled the eye when they zipped skyward, though with just a handful of rounds, the gunner had to choose his targets carefully.

On top of The Citadel the cry "The Jews are attacking!" rang out. Partially dressed men ran to four-hundred-year-old battlements to fire their rifles. The muzzle flashes lighting their faces drew return fire from the Jewish machine gunners. Keffiyehs made glowing targets silhouetted against the walls. Cries of alarm mingled with shouts of "*Youin! Youin!* Help me!"

Through a slit window, Jacob saw an Arab marksman hit by Bren-gun fire from the command car. The man toppled forward through the opening in the battlements, his body striking the pavement of Jaffa Road. Unconsciously Jacob began to recite the words of Psalm 46 that his grandfather had taught him as a boy during those painful years in Berlin.

God is our refuge and our strength,
an ever-present help in trouble.
Therefore we will not fear, though the earth give way
and the mountains fall into the heart of the sea . . .

Steeped in night, the attacking vehicles seemed momentarily shielded while their opponents above were exposed. *Maybe it will work! Maybe we'll break through!* When the bus reached its assigned position, a host of screaming, shooting Haganah men could pour out, fresh for the assault.

It appeared to Jacob the first rush might push through the poorly guarded portal of Jaffa Gate without the need for the hidden passageway. *Maybe none of us will die!*

Then the Arab counterattack began in earnest. Kerosene-soaked bundles of flaming newspaper, hurled from the ramparts, exploded in dazzling light as they fell. Jacob, just behind the wave of Jewish riflemen disembarking from the bus, found the surroundings unexpectedly illuminated, brighter than in daylight.

Framed in the doorway of the vehicle and squinting against the glare in his efforts to take aim at a spot high over his head, Jacob was an easy target. A flock of dyna-mite bundles whirred downward from the parapets, bouncing off the base of the wall.

Though its waters rage and foam
and the mountains quake with their surging.
The LORD Almighty is with us;
the God of Jacob is our fortress.

Arab bullets, previously whining off in myriad direc-tions, suddenly found their marks. Jacob saw four com-rades topple in rapid succession as Daniel Caan moved bravely forward toward the barricade.

Last of the Caans! Last of the Slaniks! Too young! God!
He is too young to die like this! Jacob thought as Daniel continued to fire and men were ripped apart and dropped to the ground around him. In the monochrome brightness, Daniel seemed unreal, a slip of flickering celluloid upon a movie screen.

Terror! Confusion!

Forcing their way back onto the bus, panicked recruits crowded the doorway so that Jacob, trapped on the steps, could get neither on nor off.

Bullets pierced the roof of the vehicle, striking down soldiers in front of and behind Jacob. "Move us closer to the wall!" Pinky screamed at the driver.

"No!" argued Chaim. "The bombs will land right on us!"

"We can't move!" the driver shouted over his shoulder. "The armored car! Blocking the road!"

We who are about to die . . .

Jacob, peering around a dead man held upright by the crush, saw the truth of this assertion.

. . . about to die. She will never know how much I loved her . . .

Major Thomas's command car had moved off to the right of the gate and was firing its automatic weapon at the tower. The second armored vehicle was stalled, obstructing the route forward. No gunfire came from either its twenty-millimeter turret or its machine gun.

What will she say when they tell her . . .

Pinky, trapped in the crush, commanded, "Somebody get up there! Move that thing!"

"I'll go," Jacob yelled, then shouted toward the rear of the bus, "Alfie! Keep your head down!"

Lori! Lori! The Lord of hosts is . . . with us. . . .

"*Allah Ahkbar!* Slaughter the Jews!"

He clambered over the bodies of the fallen and somehow landed upright on the rubble-strewn road.

What will she say when they tell her . . . how I died . . . ?

■   ■   ■   ■

The rumble of thunder reverberated behind them when Rachel, Lori, and Dr. Baruch exited the Bazaar of the Candlemakers. Suq esh-Shamma was deserted, seemingly abandoned. There were no burning tapers and no customers for any. The vaulted market felt eerily empty, as if the inhabitants of Jerusalem had decided it would never be safe to show a light at night again.

Rachel thought about the mute darkness. Was it possible for evil to be so embracing as to overwhelm the light altogether? That conclusion was easy to believe on Muristan Road. Rachel knew that when the Turks ruled Jerusalem, the whole area through which they traveled was a garbage dump of dead animals, filth, and disease, and no one ever entered there at night.

It was when the three emerged on the Street of David that the haunted quality of the midnight hour was shattered. Evil went from a lurking presence to an active menace with the scream of a truck-mounted Bren gun.

Behind them, to the west, the stillness erupted with gunfire. Shouts and cries were only a feeble counterpoint to the dominant melody of machine guns and explosions. Tracer bullets sliced into the sky, cutting across the constellations with razor strokes. Sirens wailed, and from every side came the yell "To the walls! The Jews are attacking!"

Knots of Jihad Moquades rushed past, sandaled feet pattering toward Jaffa Gate.

"The Haganah is attacking The Citadel," Baruch said. "Come on! Maybe we can get into the Jewish Quarter in the confusion!"

North and south of the Old City, gunfire and mortar shells also hammered. "It's all around us!" Lori said.

"Zion Gate and New Gate are being hit at once!" Baruch said. "This will keep the Muslims busy. Which way, Rachel?"

"Straight ahead, I think!" she replied.

A trio of Arab Irregulars sprinted past with rifles over their shoulders. "Come with us, brother," they called to

Baruch. "Come and help us drive back the Jews."

Baruch stared after them.

■ ■ ■ ■ CHAPTER 20 ■ ■ ■ ■

Moshe and the Haganah soldiers were poised to storm out of the Jewish Quarter and retake the Church of St. Jacques. A tempest of multiple explosions surged forward and back across Jerusalem from three different compass points. The thunder converged on the Temple Mount before it cascaded downward over the Old City. The Irgun to the north at New Gate, the Haganah in the west at Jaffa Gate, and the Palmachniks to the south, at Mount Zion, all charged forward at once.

From where Moshe, Dov, and Yacov knelt behind a barricade at the south end of the Street of the Jews, flares and the zipping streaks of tracer bullets illuminated the sky in every direction except east. It was nearby, close outside the Old City walls on Mount Zion, that the largest display was unleashed. A fountain of mortar shells, rifle sparks, and grenade detonations rose above the wall in a fiery geyser.

"Now!" Moshe ordered, cocking the bolt of his Sten gun and racing across Batei Mahase Street with Dov and twenty others close on his heels. Around the end of Rehov Habad they swept, firing at a startled group of Jihad Moquades approaching from the north, driving them away. "*Chatar!*" the Muslims shouted. "Look out! The Jews are breaking through everywhere."

Dov swept his arm forward, waving the men into the charred remains of Ararat Road. "Gideon's three hundred all over again."

■　■　■　■

Ahkmed al-Malik strode from embrasure to embrasure on top of the wall at Jaffa Gate. He exhorted his troops to ignore the Jews' gunfire and to destroy the attackers. "Take aim!" he barked at a Jihad Moquade who was sheltered behind a stone post and shooting at the stars. "Idiot!" Al-Malik slapped the back of the soldier's First World War British helmet.

The startled Arab jerked sideways as if al-Malik's fist had been a piece of shrapnel. He triggered another round harmlessly into the night sky.

"Idiot!" al-Malik said again, wrenching the rifle from the warrior's hands. "Watch!" Spotting a Jew running from the cover of the bus toward the rear of an armored car, al-Malik led his target for three strides. When he fired, the man dropped in his tracks.

Flinging the rifle back to the Irregular, al-Malik roared, "Now you do it!"

At the approach of their obviously furious captain, the other Jihad Moquades blasted feverishly into the shadowed spaces below the Old City walls. They shouted vigorously as each strove to outdo the next in speed of firing. None of them bothered to aim.

To the bandaged Kasim Dajani, who was preparing yet another bomb to whirl down, al-Malik remarked, "These ignorant sons of camels think that winning means shooting more bullets than the Jews do."

Dajani grunted. "It is a good thing we have plenty of ammunition. These Jews are hard to kill."

Despite Kasim Dajani's homemade dynamite bombs and the impassioned firing of Ahkmed al-Malik's Jihad Moquades, the successful defense of Jaffa Gate was far from certain.

The top of David's Tower was littered with dead and wounded Arab Irregulars. Moans of "Ma . . . water" mingled with more agonized screams and the ominous stillness of others. The firing raged as more defenders took the place of those who had been cut down.

Kasim Dajani cursed as an explosive packet failed to explode. "Bring me more bombs! We will have those infidel Jews running yet!"

"There are no more," said Daoud apologetically.

"What nonsense is this?" Dajani said, whirling on his young assistant. "We have many crates of explosives."

"When last I returned to the ramp, the back of our jeep was empty. They must have been taken for another part of the wall."

"There are also attacks being repulsed at New Gate and at Zion Gate," al-Malik added. "Explosives are needed everywhere tonight."

Dajani's eyes glittered at al-Malik through the visor of his gauze wrapping. "Fools!" he said loudly. "If we do not turn the Jews back here, there will be no saving any part of the wall. Run, Daoud! Rouse that flat slug Najid. He knows where the gasoline bombs are hidden. Go and bring them!"

■ ■ ■ ■

Jacob struggled to reach the stalled armored car. *Only*

*two meters! Jesus! God! If I can reach the turret . . .
Lord, You are my rock and fortress!* He thought of his
grandfather, dead in a pool of blood in Berlin. The
window of his shop smashed. The despised word *Jude*
painted in yellow across the facade.

Above Jacob a Jihad Moquade shouted, *"Alihu Itbach
al Yahud!* Slaughter the Jews!" as he flung a dynamite
bundle directly in Jacob's path.

Expecting to be blown to bits, Jacob threw himself to
the ground. *In You, O LORD, I take my refuge . . .* He heard
the sizzling of the fuse as the clump of explosives
impacted on the turret of the armored car without detonating, then landed beside the front tires. *Be my rock of
refuge . . .* Sparks sputtered, popped, and flared up, but
miraculously died without exploding.

Deliver me, O my God, from the hand of the wicked . . .

Diving behind the stuck vehicle, he hunkered down
between its rear wheels until the light of the last flare
went out, then lifted himself upright and hammered on
the rear hatch. Give the command to save me, for You
are my rock and my fortress . . . There was no response.
A bullet whined past his ear. Jesus! Is it going to end like
this?

"Hurry!" yelled someone from back on the bus. "We're
getting slaughtered in here!"

Twisting the handle, Jacob yanked the aft-hatch cover
open. A dead Haganah officer fell into his arms. The radio
operator was also dead. The gunner was alive but bleeding
from the mouth and ears; his eyes were glazed. Jacob
climbed through the carnage and spattered blood,
expecting to find the driver killed also, but the last of the

crew of four was uninjured, huddled in the operator's seat. *Deliver me in Your righteousness . . .* The armored visor was closed, the man wrapped in a cocoon of steel and fear. *What gain is there from my lifeblood, from my going down to the grave? Oh, Lori! Papa!*

"Drive this thing!" Jacob demanded. "Get it out of the way!"

The driver babbled. "All dead. Everyone's dead."

Another explosion rocked the car, and it sagged toward its left side. Two of the tires were blown. *Deliver me, O my God.* "Move it *now*," Jacob repeated. "You're going to get us killed, and everyone on the bus, too."

"I can't," the driver said numbly. "It's no good."

Snarling, Jacob dragged the useless figure out of the chair and dropped him beside the dying gunner.

The engine continued to run, and the car responded to Jacob's cranking of the wheel. "Fire the . . ." he commanded, but the driver bolted out the rear hatch and escaped. His dying scream echoed back into the hollow of the vehicle.

When Jacob revved the motor, an immense cloud of fumes and the smell of burning oil were added to the reek of blood and the acrid stench of cordite smoke. Like a great beast mired in deep mud, the armored car struggled to overcome its own weight and the drag of two flat tires. *For Your name's sake, lead me and guide me . . .* Slowly it crept in an arc, moving away from the front of the bus and toward the left side of Jaffa Gate, not far from where a lonely fig tree clung to the wall, oblivious to the destruction.

■   ■   ■   ■

The Palmach's diversionary assault wound up to a high-pitched scream at the same time the vehicles of the Haganah were pinned down before Jaffa Gate.

Outside the south wall of the Old City, the harsh screech of a truck-mounted Palmach Bren gun near the British Ophthalmic Hospital tore apart the envelope of night. Its bray competed with the thunderclaps of mortar-shell explosions raining down on Mount Zion. There were sixty Palmach fighters attacking the mount, but their tactics made them appear ten times that many. The initial line of Arab defenders at the base of Mount Zion withstood the assault for a mere three minutes before giving ground.

When the Palmachniks converged on the buildings that crowned Mount Zion, the Church of the Dormition and the room of the Last Supper, they rooted out Arab Irregulars with gunfire and grenades. The Muslims fled back through Zion Gate.

Meanwhile, Moshe's men from within the Old City Jewish district fanned out across the streets of the Armenian Quarter, retaking the flour mill and the Crusader church and ringing the base of the Church of St. Jacques.

As Moshe predicted, the combination of the Palmach attack on Mount Zion outside the Old City walls and the Jewish Quarter outbreak inside the walls caused the Arab Irregulars to feel *they* were the ones surrounded. Arab defenders fled from Zion Gate before they could be cut off.

Suddenly it appeared that the supposed diversionary attack might instead carry all before it and sweep right into

Zion Gate and the mouth of the Old City.

■　　■　　■　　■

The command vehicle of Major Luke Thomas was fifty yards away from where Jacob Kalner struggled with the armored car. "Mordechai," Thomas said to his driver, "we've got to give them cover! They'll be slaughtered where they sit." He tried to raise the armored car on his radio. "Kalner! Do you hear me, Kalner?"

There was no response.

The Bren-gun fire rattling over his head stopped. Thomas looked up with concern to find his gunner shot through the neck, sliding downward out of the turret. He was dead.

"Get us alongside the bus!" Thomas urged Mordechai. Moving the dead gunner, Thomas stood upright and grasped the blood-soaked handles of the Bren. Racheting back the cocking mechanism, Thomas aimed at the row of openings on top of The Citadel's walls and unleashed a torrent of gunfire. The Arabs, whose attention was focused on the stalled bus and crippled armored car, were shattered. At embrasure after embrasure, guns flew into the air. As Mordechai maneuvered the command vehicle along Jaffa Road, Major Thomas continued to rake the walls. Every time the withering fire cleared a gunport, two Arabs rushed to fill the void.

On the top of The Citadel a glass bottle flickered and gleamed in the torchlight as it was held aloft and the fuse lit. *Molotov cocktail!* The target was Kalner's armored car.

Walking the fire of the Bren over to the target was agonizingly slow. At the last second before the arm holding the gasoline bomb started forward, the bullets found their mark. The Molotov cocktail flew backward instead of forward. An instant later a whoosh of flames reached upward behind the Arab side of the wall.

The bolt chattered at last on an empty chamber and then jammed. Despite the hammering of Luke Thomas's fist, the mechanism refused to budge. The machine gun was out of action.

■　　■　　■　　■

With all the components of Gideon's midnight battle against the Philistine army, the struggle of the Palmach to capture Mount Zion raged on.

In their panic to escape, Arabs shot Arabs. Muslim mortar fire from Zion Gate fell short, blowing up flocks of Jihad Moquades as they fled toward the Old City walls.

Calls for a medic resounded from a half-dozen places within the compound. The sixty Palmach soldiers under the command of Nachasch had been whittled down to fifty, but one hundred Holy Strugglers lay dead between Mount Zion and Zion Gate.

White flags flapped hysterically from windows. Sheets, shirts, and even the outer robes of terrified Arabs appeared from the entrance of David's Tomb, on the dome of the Church of the Dormition, and in the windows of Gobat School. Arab weapons were hurled to the ground. Jewish shouts, threatening annihilation and demanding surrender, were answered in pleading Arabic, begging for mercy. The tide had miraculously turned in favor of the advancing Palmach forces.

■　■　■　■

Sheltered beneath the bowl of a stone water fountain between two of the arms of the cross-shaped Church of St. Jacques, Moshe called Yacov to him. "Take a message to the Hurva."

"To the wireless?"

"Exactly. Tell Yehudit to get Shaltiel. Tell him the Muslims have retreated from Mount Zion, and Zion Gate is weakly defended. Tell him to send reinforcements to Mount Zion at once. Got that?"

"Shaltiel . . . Zion Gate . . . send more men to Mount Zion. I will run the whole way."

"Good boy," Moshe said, patting Yacov on the shoulder. "Run fast but stay safe."

■　■　■　■

Daoud sank to his knees, then put his back to the masonry of the tower. He hugged himself and cried. A moment earlier he had delivered six gasoline-filled olive oil bottles.

A swaggering Holy Struggler had grabbed a Molotov cocktail. When he flourished it aloft, the man's head vanished in the storm of bullets.

Daoud was covered with gore. Brains and blood soaked his hair and dripped from his chin. The bomb, flung backward, had exploded below the parapet on the Arab side of the wall amid shrieks of panic.

Terrified, Daoud sobbed and huddled behind the stone.

His wails were lost amid screams from every side and the roar of the battle.

Kasim Dajani kicked him, and when the boy did not jump at once, bent over and slapped him hard, twice. In the flickering flames that rose from below, the bandaged mask of Dajani's face was truly terrifying, hollow-eyed and skull-like. "Get up," he ordered. "It is nothing. Go get more firebombs." The terrorist grabbed one of the remaining Molotov cocktails, lit the fuse, and flung it over the wall.

Daoud shook his head in mute refusal.

Dajani kicked him again. "Do you want the Jews to break through the gate?" he said. "You should be more afraid of me than Jewish bullets. If you do not go at once, I will soak *you* in petrol and throw you over the wall."

Rising to his knees, Daoud put out a hand to steady himself. As he did so, he thrust his fingers into a mass of pulp that had been the slaughtered Jihad Moquade's neck. The boy retched and gagged, unable to catch his breath. "Go!" Dajani warned again. "Hurry!"

Daoud stumbled away down the uneven stone steps that dropped to the courtyard below the tower. The blaze from the shattered petrol bomb roared like a furnace. He wrapped his keffiyeh around his mouth and nose to shield them from the heat and the fumes.

Soon he was back, and his face, ashen before, was even paler. "The bomb," he said, faltering.

"What?"

"It set off the others . . . six men were burned . . . to death."

For once even Dajani lost his bravado. "This is bad," he

mused. "No dynamite left and just four more petrol bombs." The gunfire from the Irregulars continued, but the carnage on the ramparts caused by the Bren gun made them cower behind the pillars and shoot without aiming. "I must save these last ones for exactly the right place," he thought aloud. Then he moved along the walkway, peering over and selecting his targets.

■　■　■　■

The command car rolled into position alongside the bus. Standing upright in the turret, Luke Thomas bellowed, "As soon as the forward armored car is clear, we'll advance together. When we stop again, everyone dashes for the grate. It's there, below that scrawny tree. We use the bus and my car for cover. Clear?"

Captain Isaacson, leaning out of the bus's doorway to fire his Sten gun in short bursts at Jaffa Gate, gave the thumbs-up to signal that he understood.

Jacob Kalner's armored car had moved enough that the way was clear. "Now!" Thomas yelled to Mordechai and Isaacson. "Go forward."

Arab rifle fire from the walls redoubled, but the attack was at last moving again. The two vehicles were in position for the dash to the hidden grate.

■　■　■　■

The engine grinding furiously, Jacob's vehicle lurched once, then refused to move again. It settled forward, its nose drooping toward the pavement as if in surrender.

Jacob hoped the yards he had been able to coax it were enough. Looking out a rear-facing slit, he watched the bus lumber toward him. *They're moving!*

Now to see if he could fire the weapons. The meager supply of ammunition for the twenty-millimeter gun was gone. Enemy bullets pinged and rattled off the steel skin of the armored car.

Sit tight! Hold on a minute. They'll think you're dead,

When the clatter of small arms subsided, he counted to ten, then stood up beside the machine gun. Its barrel had taken a direct hit. It was bent and useless.

A Molotov cocktail arced over the ramparts. The blazing pool of gasoline dribbled down the slope and away from his position. The warning was clear enough, however: staying in the crippled vehicle was suicide.

Scanning the scene to the rear, Jacob saw the Haganah troops charge off the bus. Each of the troopers dove out the doorway, rolling to shelter either under the bus or behind Major Thomas's car. What could he do that was of any use?

He remembered the dynamite bundle that had bounced off the armor. It had not exploded and must be lying nearby.

A glance out another viewport located it. Twelve yards away, the package of explosives was still intact, the stub of broken fuse visible!

Thus we do not fear, though the earth be shaken!

A flare dropped, illuminating a sally port, a brush-covered pedestrian entrance at the base of the wall. Unused for centuries, it was invisible from above. A rusted iron grate covered this secret entry to the stronghold.

*The Lord of hosts is with us! He breaks the bow,
splinters the spear and burns the shields with fire!*

The returning fire from the parapets shifted from Jacob's shelter to the troops on the ground. The Haganah sappers were pinned down behind the command car. How could they rig the explosive charge and blow the bars?

I am nearest! They think I'm dead!

Jacob rolled out the rear hatch. Ten racing steps and he was at the dynamite packet before any of the Arabs noticed him. Shouts of alarm, as well as machine-gun bullets, chased him back to the shelter of the armored car.

Another petrol bomb flew over the wall, exploding directly in front of his refuge. Feeling the heat on his face, he used the glare to see that the fuse on the dynamite was in place. An instant later he raced away toward the curve in the wall as bullets nipped at his heels.

Shots fired straight down the wall from above bounced harmlessly off the bulge of stone above him. Thorns tore at his clothes and face as he crawled along the base. When the light from the explosives faded, leaving him in gloomy shadow, he located the grating by feel. A cool, musty aroma wafted from the opening. He could hear the urgent cries of the enemy reverberate in the tunnel, proof that it did indeed lead into the heart of the stronghold!

■ ■ ■ ■ CHAPTER 21 ■ ■ ■ ■

A veiled Arab woman, moving matter-of-factly from body to body, hobbled along the Tower's walkway. Grasping the shoulder of each slumped form, she gave it a brisk shake. If there was no response, she rifled the pockets for bullets, then distributed these to the remaining infantrymen on the wall. Lately she was finding fewer and fewer unspent cartridges, but the enthusiasm the Irregulars displayed for firing their weapons was undiminished.

Ahkmed al-Malik hurried up to Kasim Dajani. "Where are the rest of the bombs? Why do you delay?" the officer reprimanded the terrorist. "Our forces are nearly out of bullets. With their next assault the Jews will break through the gate!"

Dajani rounded savagely on the man. "And where is my dynamite, O great leader? How can I kill Jews if others steal my weapons? But do not despair; I have reserved two petrol bombs and have selected my targets."

"Hurry! If they get past our position, all is lost! They are coming from many different directions, even sneaking up to the base of the Tower!"

"Why don't you go whine to the Mufti? Or better yet, call King Abdullah. At least the Legion has real soldiers and not these ragged brigands!"

Al-Malik took the suggestion seriously. "But first we must stop the Jews here."

Shrugging, as if the matter were of no concern, Dajani concluded, "I shall dispatch the Jews; never fear."

Behind a line of infantry and the protective cover provided by the bus, the Haganah sappers prepared the charges to detonate on the sally port's grating. There was an open space where they would be exposed to gunfire, but at least there was a chance. Luke Thomas, firing while standing upright in his command car, and Daniel Caan and Barney Isaacson, shooting from behind the right front fender of the bus, continued to pick off Arabs on the ramparts.

Thomas knew the Haganah attack was almost spent; both men and ammunition were exhausted, and over half his troops had been killed or wounded. He cursed the Arabs and their inexhaustible supplies. "How much longer?" he called over his shoulder.

"Another minute" was the reply. "We don't want to have to do this twice."

But no more minutes were available. Kasim Dajani was directly above the ramp on which the bus was parked. He raised a Molotov cocktail over his head and flung the bottle, trailing its length of smoldering rag, directly downward.

Smashing on the stones, the bomb burst with a roar. A swirling curtain of fire engulfed the riflemen. The blazing furnace swallowed two and spattered a third. Screaming with horror, he threw aside his weapon and ran away from the battle, slapping futilely at the flames on his trouser leg. The crazed man flared like a meteor. Daniel Caan vaulted clear of the command car and tackled him, smothering the fire with his own body.

The slab on which the bus was parked sloped away from the walls of the Old City. A spreading pool of fire flowed around the bus's tires and underneath it.

The transport was parked so close to The Citadel that shots from the walls penetrated the roof more often and at ever-steeper angles. The bus driver was struck on the top of the head. He fell forward, dead, across the steering wheel, wedging his shoulder against the horn. The bus howled like a wounded animal strangling in its own blood.

Fire bubbled relentlessly nearer and nearer to the sappers and their explosives. Haganah troops shot a last volley up at the walls' defenders, then backed away from the encroaching flames.

"Retreat!" Luke Thomas yelled. "Take the wounded and get back!"

A stampede of Jewish soldiers began as man after man turned and sprinted away from the explosives, away from the hail of bullets, and away from the blaze. They dragged their injured with them, but there were more wounded men on the bus.

While the wail of the bus's horn added to the terror of the night, only Luke Thomas, Isaacson, and Daniel Caan stayed behind to cover the retreat.

■　　■　　■　　■

Though shielded by the fold of the stone wall, the concussion of the petrol explosion and the rush of air toward the inferno took Jacob's breath away. The sky was alive with sparks and embers. Instinctively he covered his face with one arm, thought better of it, and covered the fuse of the dynamite instead.

The fireball subsided. Jacob peered cautiously around the corner. At a glance he knew no reinforcements would be coming. An immense lake of flames blazed between him and the other Jewish troops. Because fire was about to engulf the bus and all nearby, a mad scramble ensued to drag the wounded away from incineration. The front tires of the bus already smoldered.

The attack had failed. Should he abandon the attempt to destroy the bars that blocked the secret entry? Even if the sally port could be made passable, the approaches to Jaffa Gate were so littered with rubble and disabled vehicles, and so well defended by bullets and petrol bombs, that no assault could possibly succeed.

The keening of the wounded bus's horn continued. Jacob examined the centuries-old bolts that held the bars in place. Covered in the scaly deposits of the ages, the grating seemed to have grown into the limestone. Still, it wobbled slightly along one edge. Setting off the charge on that side would make the iron fold back on itself like a hinge. Many Haganah had been killed or wounded to get this close. Studying the prima-cord fuse, Jacob tried to remember how long it had taken the Arab's improvised grenades to explode when flung from the rooftops.

Five seconds maybe. No more than six.

That was plenty of time for someone tossing the weapon from sixty feet up but hardly adequate for him running away over uneven stones while being shot at.

There seemed to be no other choice.

To run straight out was to become a clear target for marksmen on the walls. South was the blazing pyre in front of the bus. North along the wall toward New Gate was the only option. There would be no cover from the blast that erupted behind him. He would count to four, fling himself flat to the pavement, get up after the explosion, and run on.

Suddenly a slender-fingered shadow cast by the fig tree above him played across the stones.

Then he heard a triumphant voice laugh with satisfaction. Even without knowing Arabic, Jacob understood that the celebration was for the fire-bombing of the bus and that the next target was himself.

When he heard "*Al-an!*" shouted tersely, he needed no translator to recognize "Now!" There was a brief whistle, a plopping noise, and the rustle of leaves. Darting out from under his sheltering overhang, Jacob looked up the wall and discovered, directly over his head, a Molotov cocktail. Its rag fuse sparkling, the bottle was caught in the branches of the fig tree.

"Enfield!" the Arabic-speaker on the wall shouted, calling for a rifle. They were going to try to ignite the gasoline bomb with a bullet.

With gasoline hanging overhead and a rush of flames that would certainly detonate the dynamite, it was past time to leave.

Jacob sprinted out from under the projecting cornice. Leaping over boulders and shattered, dead Arabs fallen from the battlements, he raced northward, hugging the wall.

A burst of machine-gun fire slashed into the ashlars over his head, forcing him to jog away from the wall's comforting flank and into the open. Another spurt of bullets sliced the pavement ahead of him, announcing a boundary in that direction.

From behind him came the whoosh and flare of gasoline exploding and then, a bare second later, a far more powerful roar as the dynamite exploded. The concussion bowled Jacob over, bouncing him on his head, leaving him sprawled on the roadway. Partly deafened, he could still hear a roaring sound that seemed to be coming from behind him.

Turning round, Jacob saw a large dark form rushing toward him, as if to finish the job of trampling him. It was Luke Thomas's command car. "Get in!" Daniel Caan urged from the rear hatch.

Arab bullets clanged against the side of the command car as Daniel hurriedly reached down, grabbed Jacob's belt, and hoisted him, headfirst, into the hatch.

"Reverse, Mordechai!" Luke Thomas shouted to his driver as Daniel bolted home the cover. "Take us back to the bus."

The uninjured Haganah troops had fled, but wounded Jewish soldiers remained aboard the transport vehicle. These were trapped there in imminent danger from the flames that already had devoured the engine compartment and sent tongues of fire back along the bus's length. As the command car pulled up, screeching to a halt in front of the bus, the bus's horn gave a final despairing gasp and died.

The rear emergency door of the bus was open. A dozen recruits aided the wounded, carrying them to safety. Daniel leapt from the vehicle and, with a panic-driven strength, slung two men over his slight shoulders like sacks of grain. His features were lost in the blackness as he retreated down the slope. Captain Isaacson dragged a wounded man outside the bus. "Help me!" he yelled. "There's Alfie Halder inside and . . . Ibrahim!"

No more words followed as a ricochet struck Isaacson, felling him in his tracks.

"Alfie," Jacob said as Luke Thomas leapt out to assist the wounded captain. "I'll see to it."

Alfie in the burning bus! Oh Alfie! Sweet Jesus! Not Alfie!

The interior of the bus was clogged with black smoke, making Jacob cough and causing his eyes to stream tears. He flicked on the crookneck flashlight yanked from his belt, but the thin beam did not help in the Stygian darkness. Leaving it off for fear that a gleam seen by the Arabs would draw more bullets, Jacob crawled forward on his stomach.

The first two soldiers he encountered were dead. Jacob risked snapping on the light to look at their faces, dreading as he did that each would be Alfie. Choking and struggling to breathe, he croaked, "Alfie, where are you?"

There was no response. He crawled farther up the length of the bus. Perhaps Alfie was safe, off the burning coach and out of harm's way. "Alfie!" he shouted again.

The next leg Jacob grasped stirred under his touch. Someone was alive! As if annoyed at being disturbed, the owner of the limb kicked feebly, and an oversized bare foot hit Jacob in the face.

"Ibrahim!" Jacob called, shaking the Ethiopian and trying to rouse him. "Wake up!" Ibrahim returned to consciousness with a fit of strangulation. "Got to get you out of here," Jacob said, coughing.

"But I cannot go," Ibrahim returned. "I have laid hold of Alfie's ankle and promised not to release it."

"Alfie!" Jacob shouted. "He's alive?"

A fit of hacking and wheezing was the Ethiopian's only answer, but he nodded as Jacob told him to slide backward out of the bus. Jacob would see to Alfie. Then Jacob plunged ahead into the fumes. Ominous flickers of fire licked the instrument panel. There was no time to lose.

He came to Alfie's foot at the end of the ten-foot space previously occupied by Ibrahim. "Alfie, wake up!"

This time the reply sounded sleepy but not smoke-thickened. "Hello, Jacob. I knew you'd find me."

"Let's get out of here!" Jacob said anxiously.

"I can't go unless you can help me with Chaim."

"There's another?" Then, "Right. Leave him and climb out. I'll come back for him."

"No," Alfie objected. "He's bleeding. I got my finger in the hole, but it spurts whenever I let go. It's in his neck."

Flames were shooting up inside the cab. Any second the fumes could ignite and the whole bus would erupt into an inferno. "Can you lie on top of him and I'll drag you both?"

"I can do that," Alfie agreed.

Reversing himself, Jacob grasped Alfie's ankles, then braced his own feet against the seat supports. Rung by rung, foot by foot, Jacob heaved the dead weight backward toward safety.

A flashlight's beam skipped across his straining features. "Kalner!" Luke Thomas called. "I thought we'd lost you!"

"Help!" Jacob said, gasping for breath. "Help me pull."

Together the two got Alfie and the unconscious Chaim to the edge of the doorway. With the command car driver's assistance, Ibrahim, Alfie, Chaim, and Jacob were piled on top of the car's hood, like so many smoked chickens.

The car roared to life, leaping away from Jaffa Gate as the bus exploded into an engulfing blaze. Throughout the return to the Municipality building, Alfie kept his index finger pressed into a bullet hole in Chaim's throat.

■ ■ ■ ■

When Dov, Moshe, and the twenty Haganah fighters rushed the Church of St. Jacques, they were surprised to find that the Muslims had abandoned the body of the structure. Perhaps fearing they were about to be surrounded and cut off, the Arab Irregulars had fled.

Such was not the case with the all-important bell tower of the church.

When the Jewish troops were halfway up the spiral stairs, a grenade bounced down from above and shrapnel zinged crazily around the confines of the cylindrical walls. No one was killed, but three of the men received minor wounds.

"We cannot walk into that," Dov said. "And the church is useless without the tower. We need mortars."

"There *is* a way," Moshe said. "Post men in the church and on the roof to repel a counterattack. Have four men keep up a steady fire into the tower. And give me that flare."

Igniting the flare, Moshe tossed it up the spiral steps. Soon thick smoke clouded the stairwell. Moshe stood where he could safely shout to the Arab snipers. *"Yasmaa,"* he yelled as soon as he heard bullets clanging into the bells. "Listen to me. It is a hundred feet down. You are surrounded. Your comrades have deserted you. We have petrol and will burn the tower if you do not throw down your weapons and come out. You will flame to the pavement like pigeons from a burning tree. I'll give you to three. *Wahid! Itsnayn!"*

"Wait!" cried a voice from above.

Dov, who had rejoined Moshe, gave a thumbs-up and signaled that he would help out.

"Throw down your guns," Moshe ordered.

A pair of rifles clattered down the treads. "And your grenades!"

A sack of grenades followed.

"No tricks!" Moshe warned.

"Light the *ghazoulin!"* Dov urged harshly. "You cannot trust them!"

"No!" yelled the voice from overhead. "Here." A revolver followed the other weapons down the steps. "We surrender. There are only two of us left alive, and Nebi is wounded."

"Come down slowly, with your hands in the air!"

Taking over the tower, Haganah snipers fired at the Jihad Moquades lining the wall above Zion Gate. Attacked from Mount Zion outside the walls and the bell tower within them, the Arab Irregulars hid inside the fortifications atop the gate.

Dov and Moshe held a hasty conference. "We cannot keep a corridor open from here to the Jewish Quarter," Dov said. "Whoever stays here will be cut off until the breakthrough happens, and if it does not happen . . ."

"We cannot give up this position," Moshe argued. "It is our best hope of opening Zion Gate. It is my fault we gave up this place to begin with, and I will not part with it again. Leave me ten men and take the others back to the barricade."

■ ■ ■ ■ CHAPTER 22 ■ ■ ■ ■

Daoud fled the ramparts. The courtyard of The Citadel was illuminated by men aflame. The screams of the dying pursued him as he ran wildly up the slope of an alleyway. He wanted only safety, quiet, someplace to hide forever from Dajani and the Jihad Moquades who cloaked themselves in fire and clawed the air as their souls passed into Paradise. Ten million years in the presence of Mohammed and Allah, seventy thousand virgins, and all the food he could eat would not make him forget the agony of Jaffa Gate.

Darkness hide me!

His ragged breath was punctuated by sobs. He wanted his mother.

"*Oum!*" he shouted for her as he ran blindly. "Mother!"

He had not thought of her in a year. He was running, running to find her, to tell her Gawan had been hurt!

Around him he heard the keening of the Arab women rise like a siren.

"The Jews have attacked! Our sons lie dying on the ramparts! *Allah! O Allah!*"

Darkness hide me! Mother find me! O my mother!

The blood of the man who had died beside him congealed on Daoud's face. The feel of it made him frantic. He needed water! Had to wash! He half-jogged, half-stumbled down the long flight of stairs on the street. A flock of shouting Jihad Moquades raced past him on their way to Jaffa Gate. From the arch above the street someone called, "The Jews have taken Mount Zion! *Ya Allah!* The Jews have taken the Church of St. Jacques!"

Water! Daoud could think of nothing but washing himself and his gore-soaked clothes. *St. John! St. John! There is water in the church of the Baptist!*

He turned up the Street of the Christians and staggered on toward the Church of St. John. Slamming through the unlocked doorway, he entered the courtyard. Beneath massive, low stone vaults on the left was the cistern. Daoud tore off his clothes as he staggered to it. Heedless of the cold water, he threw himself over the edge of the shallow pool and immersed himself to splash away the blood of the fallen warrior. The human torches of Jaffa Gate constantly burned in his mind. How he wished Gawan was with him. Gawan had always been the weak one. With Gawan near, Daoud had to be strong. Now there was nothing but himself and the terror of the night to think of.

"Gawan!" He sobbed. "*Ya Allah!* What is to become of us? Ah, Gawan! Mother! We are lost! Lost!" He sat weeping in the cistern, calling out his brother's name, and then . . .

"Daoud."

Someone spoke. A woman's voice, soft and gentle.

"Mother?"

"No, Daoud. It is Rachel Sachar."

He ran his hand over his face and stood, dripping, to

climb out of his bath. "Why are you here?" She was in the shadows beneath the vaults.

Rachel replied, "The battle. We took shelter here."

"Is my father, Baruch, with you?"

Baruch answered, "I am here, Daoud."

Rachel said, "We have lost our way. Will you help us?"

Daoud was shaking. "It is the will of Allah I have come here. Daoud, son of Baruch, is your servant. Where shall I lead you?"

Rachel hesitated, then asked, "Can you show us a safe way to the barricades on the Street of the Jews?"

Daoud, son of Baruch, stood blinking into the pitch-dark beneath the vault. Perhaps this was the voice of a demon who thought to lead him astray and kill him for his cowardice.

"Show yourselves," the boy demanded.

The trio of forms stepped into the open. A man. Two women.

Daoud narrowed his eyes. "Tell me, if you are who you say . . . You Christians . . . My father, Baruch, why do you wish for me, a Jihad Moquade, to take you to the barricades of the Jews?"

Baruch replied in broken Arabic, "Daoud, my son. I am a Jew. It is where we were going all along. To the hospital inside the Jewish Quarter."

■ ■ ■ ■

The Street of the Chain, at the north end of the Jewish Quarter, where Ehud and Rabbi Vultch led the defense, had been calm that night and remained so. Despite the detonations and shouting that came from almost every direction, no Arab attackers had come near the trench. Even after everything broke loose at midnight outside the Old City walls, just two bullets had been fired over the barricade, and that had happened because someone heard a noise.

"Do not waste bullets!" Ehud had said angrily. "What you hear is Jews attacking Muslims for a change."

When an enormous flare of yellow and orange light billowed up in the direction of Jaffa Gate, Rabbi Vultch commented, "Maybe that is a whole herd of Jihad Moquades going to Paradise."

When the flashes of fire died away and a lull seemed to have fallen in the fighting outside the walls, the defenders at the trench grew even more nervous. What was happening? Had Moshe and Dov succeeded in taking the tower of St. Jacques? Had the Haganah broken through? Was rescue nearing, perhaps mere blocks away? Or had the plan failed? Were the Arab Irregulars regrouping to march on the Jewish Quarter in force?

"Someone is behind us!" exclaimed a nervous Yeshiva student, whirling around with his rifle.

"Wait!" Ehud said, grabbing the muzzle and yanking it skyward.

Yacov, jumping over the sandbags, arrived at the rampart with Shaul at his heels.

Ehud grabbed the Yeshiva student by the shoulders and forcibly turned him back toward the Street of the Chain. Then to Yacov: "So, boy! What are you doing here? How goes it with Moshe and Dov?"

"We surrounded the Church of St. Jacques," Yacov

reported. "Dov says the Muslims are falling back from Mount Zion and there is much confusion among the Arabs around Zion Gate. Moshe sent me to radio Commander Shaltiel. With more men at Mount Zion our army can break through Zion Gate tonight."

"Any news from the other gates?" Rabbi Vultch asked.

"Someone is out there," the student said, using the muzzle of his rifle to point toward the souks.

"Quiet, you," Ehud said. "Watch, but do not talk."

"The other gates?" Yacov repeated. "I heard nothing of New Gate, but they say the Haganah is having a hard time at Jaffa Gate."

"So," Vultch said quietly, "perhaps it is not Muslims flying off to Paradise."

"Someone *is* out there!" the Yeshiva scholar cried and fired. The bullet screamed off a building, ricocheting up the street.

Yacov hugged Shaul and ducked.

"Wait!" Ehud said.

"I, too, see movement," Rabbi Vultch noted. He ratcheted back the cocking lever of the machine gun.

"Don't shoot till you are sure of them!" Ehud warned. "Make every shot count."

"I see the shape of a tarboosh," another Haganah soldier commented. "I can shoot his head off!"

"I said wait!"

"I have him!"

"Not yet!"

The outline of the tarboosh moved slowly up and down beside the wall where the Street of the Chain swung right toward the markets. "He is signaling!" the student said.

"Now they will rush us!"

"Wait!" Ehud bellowed. In his unmistakable roar he fired a volley of sailor's curses such as the pious Jewish Quarter had never before heard.

From the darkness came the voice of Rachel Sachar. "Ehud? Is that you?"

Ehud jumped up from his place to stand with his broad chest in front of the barrels of the rifles. His arms were spread wide. "Yes, by the Eternal!" he shouted back. "Come across!"

■　■　■　■

In the Church of the Dormition on Mount Zion, Palmach commander Nachasch stared with disbelief at the radio speaker and swore into the handset. "What do you mean, you can't send any reinforcements? I say again, we have captured Mount Zion. The Arabs have retreated from David's Tomb and from the House of Caiaphas right under the Old City wall. They have sealed Zion Gate, but with more troops we can break in, over."

Shaltiel's voice crackled over the wireless: "Haganah . . . pinned . . . Jaffa . . . Cannot . . . Make do with . . ."

"We are down to forty effectives!" Nachasch stormed. "Don't you understand? Someone from inside the Jewish Quarter has retaken the tower of St. Jacques! The Arabs at Zion Gate are in a cross fire. Now is our best chance, but we must have more men and ammunition!"

Only silence came from the speaker, then, "Trying . . . withdraw from Jaffa . . . Do what you can. Out."

Nachasch glared at the phone in his hand before finally

slamming it down on the table.

■　　■　　■　　■

Dazed and exhausted, Jacob stared at the crumbling walls of an office in the Municipality building. The remaining members of the Spare Parts Platoon were back where they had launched their assault barely two hours before.

One hundred and fifty weary soldiers lay sprawled in the rooms and hallways, saying little. It was the missing men who seemed to shout into the void of despair. They had left with dreams of glory and returned defeated.

Captain Isaacson was dead, his blood turning the white of the Israeli flag wrapped around his waist to solid crimson. Chaim was alive, thanks to Alfie's resourcefulness, but he was out of the war. So was Pinky, with burns on his face and hands. Only a few of the First Strike Team were not wounded. After the battle Jacob found a bullet hole in the cuff of his pants; an Arab, sniping downward, had been that close to shooting Jacob in the top of the head.

Ibrahim had also been wounded, but no one knew it until Daniel Caan spotted the tracery of dried blood on the Ethiopian's cheek. A shrapnel fragment had sliced across Ibrahim's scalp, but he had never cried out, much less abandoned Alfie on the burning bus.

"You should get that seen to," Pinky Chopinski said.

"Why? It is no longer bleeding" was the reply.

Jacob held a tin cup of soup in his hands, but he could not remember receiving it. When he merely sniffed at the steam, Alfie said, "It's good soup, Jacob. Eat some," in the sort of tone he used when coaxing an injured bird to eat.

Jacob took a sip, but he could not swallow.

It had all gone so wrong. Seventeen of the dead had arrived with Jacob on the *Joshua Reynolds* two days before. He knew each of their faces, though he had not bothered to ask all their names. Who needed names when they were about to be born again, citizens of a brand-new nation? They could choose whatever names they wanted. They came to Israel without possessions except hope. No doubt they had come here with the same dreams Jacob carried with him, dreams of loving someone, of building a home, a place to raise a family in safety, to build a life after everything they loved was destroyed by the Nazis.

I made it, Papa. Mother? Can you see me? I am here. Last of the Kalners.

Jacob spread his fingers and studied his hand in amazement. He was still alive, still breathing. The blood beneath his fingernails was someone else's blood.

What would Lori say if she knew?

Daniel Caan lay on his back, his brooding eyes staring at the ceiling. His food was also untouched. "When I was a little kid, my mother told me people were starving in China. That it was a sin not to eat what God gave you. And be grateful, too. Then when I came to Eretz-Israel, Morrie, the cook at the kibbutz, used to say people . . . our people . . . Jews were being starved to death in Warsaw just because they were Jews. He was talking about my family, you know?"

Pinky, his face and hands wrapped in bandages, interjected, "Every day Hitler killed more Jews than the English allowed into Palestine in a year. Ten thousand Jews *a day* died while just ten thousand *altogether* were allowed by the British to settle here."

Daniel rambled on incredulously, "What they wouldn't give to be here, Morrie would say. What they wouldn't give to have their kids grow up in Eretz-Israel, where there is plenty of bread. Oranges on the trees we plant. Be grateful, he'd tell us. Be grateful you're in Eretz-Israel. The Promised Land. He'd tell us, you know, this is the land God promised us. It means something. Us being here . . . it's part of the Promise. It's the miracle that proves God never lies. But Morrie's dead now, too." He paused, grappling with the finality of death.

Speaking to no one in particular, Jacob asked, "It's worth dying for, isn't it?"

Daniel continued in a low murmur, "He'd tell us, thank God every day you have a home and bread enough to share with your brothers. Sometimes it's the bread of suffering, he'd say. It goes down easier when it is shared."

Ibrahim took a paper-wrapped box from the pocket of his shirt. He untied the string, removed the paper, and opened the box, revealing more wrapping and finally a piece of matzo.

"I have carried the *afikomon* here, you see?" he said.

Alfie stared at him blankly, not understanding.

Pinky explained, "It's unleavened bread from Passover. The middle piece of three. The Jews from North Africa keep a portion, carry it with them on a journey as a safeguard against evil. They say it has the power to calm the sea. If they travel on the ocean, you will see them in a storm, casting their bread on the waters. Passover matzo, that's what he's holding out to you."

Ibrahim turned his face toward Alfie. "Want this?"

Alfie shook his head *no*.

Ibrahim held it out to him insistently.

Daniel said, "It means something, Alfie. You did good. You were brave. You saved a brother. Understand? Take it. Eat."

"Brothers," Alfie said. He accepted the slice, broke it, and passed a piece back to Ibrahim. The Ethiopian Jew inclined his head in thanks, broke his piece into four, gave one to Jacob, placed another between Pinky's swollen lips, and the last back to Daniel.

"It calms the storm," Ibrahim said.

Thoughtfully, each shared this Eucharist of sorrow.

Alfie pondered the fragment of matzo in his hand. "Whenever you do this," he said in a halting voice, "remember. . . ."

Jacob closed his eyes and let the bread linger on his tongue.

■ ■ ■ ■ MONDAY, MAY 17, 1948 ■ ■ ■ ■

Declares the LORD, "I myself will gather the remnant of my flock out of all the countries where I have driven them and will bring them back to their pasture, where they will be fruitful and increase in number. I will place shepherds over them who will tend them and they will no longer be afraid or terrified, nor will any be missing," declares the LORD.

"The days are coming," declares the LORD,
"when I will raise up to David a
righteous Branch,
a King who will reign wisely
and do what is just and right in the land.
In his days Judah will be saved
and Israel will live in safety.
This is the name by which He will be called:
The LORD our Righteousness."

"So then, the days are coming," declares the LORD, "when people will no longer say, 'As surely as the LORD lives, who brought the Israelites up out of Egypt,' but they will say, 'As surely as the LORD lives, who brought the descendants of Israel up out of the land of the north and out of all the countries where He had banished them.'
"Then they will live in their own land."

Jeremiah 23:3–8

"I am the good shepherd; I know My sheep and My sheep know Me—just as the Father knows Me and I know the Father—and I lay down My life for the sheep. I have other sheep that are not of this sheep pen. I must bring them also. They too will listen to My voice, and there shall be one flock and one shepherd. The reason My Father loves Me is that I lay down My life—only to take it up again. No one takes it from Me, but I lay it down of My own accord. I have the authority to lay it down and authority to take it up again. This command I received from My Father."

John 10:14–18

▪ ▪ ▪ ▪ CHAPTER 23 ▪ ▪ ▪ ▪

There was a wondrous reunion at the barricade as Dr. Baruch, Lori, and Rachel slipped through the lines into the Jewish Quarter.

"How did you get here?"

"Did you come with Haganah troops through Jaffa Gate?"

"Have our men broken through the Muslim stronghold?"

"Is Jaffa Gate captured by the Haganah? Is the siege broken?"

"How many of our men are coming? When will they get here?"

The answers drained the excitement from the men on watch:

We were smuggled through as noncombatants. We heard the explosions but did not see our troops in the Old

City. We hid first in the Latin Patriarchate and then, during the battle, in the courtyard of St. John's. An Arab boy guided us safely here. We did not see any of our own soldiers along the way, but many hundreds of Jihad Moquades.

The sentries accepted their replies in stunned disappointment. This could mean only one thing. The assaults against Jaffa Gate and The Citadel had been repulsed. No one but these three were coming.

Dr. Baruch and Lori were quickly escorted to the hospital, where Jewish wounded overflowed into the halls.

Rachel took Yacov to the side. "Where is Moshe?"

"Moshe is . . . he is . . . he holds St. Jacques in the Armenian Quarter until reinforcements come to break through Zion Gate!"

"And Grandfather?"

"What else? He is praying for reinforcements to come soon!"

■　　■　　■　　■

Rachel and Yacov found Grandfather in the basement flat. The candle was nearly out. The old man slept in a chair. The dog drowsed at his feet. Grandfather's head rested on an open scroll.

Brother and sister stood quietly in the doorway.

"I'll wake him," Yacov answered.

"Let him sleep," Rachel said. "It is enough that I see him even if for a moment."

"He gives his food away to the children. He is not as strong as when you saw him last."

"He should not have come back to the Old City."

The rabbi stirred at the sound of her voice. "Etta?" He murmured the name of his daughter. "Daughter? Etta?"

"He thinks you are Mama," Yacov whispered.

Rachel answered, "No, Grandfather, it is Rachel."

He sat erect, peering at her in the dim light. "Etta? Where have you been? I . . . your mother and me . . . Etta?"

Rachel went to him, wrapping her arms around his neck. He was so thin, so fragile. "Grandfather, it's me. Your granddaughter, Rachel."

It took him a while to collect himself. He embraced her and sighed. "Ah, Rachel. Rachel! It is you! I was dreaming . . . of your mother. My Etta. We were together . . . times were better, *nu?*"

He touched her cheek. "You are like her. She was a pretty girl. And such a heart. A *mensch!* So very much like you, you know?"

"I am glad of that," she said, missing her mother terribly. Homesickness squeezed her heart and made her eyes moist. "Are you all right?" she asked.

"All right? Yes. It's just . . . *Oy!* You are here. *Baruch Hashem!* Blessed be the Name! I was not expecting you so soon."

"You were expecting me?"

"The Lord told me I would see Rachel once again before I die."

She knelt beside his chair, and he placed his hand on her head.

She said in a voice burdened with sadness at the thought of losing him, "Just see me . . . and live a long life."

"Of course. There is still much to do. But it is settled. I

have seen you again. You are safe, and I am content. My eyes weep rivers for the joy of seeing your face. You are well? Of course, you are well. Look at you." He dabbed his eyes and blew his nose on a kerchief.

"Moshe and I will have a baby in the winter."

"Yes. I know. A son. Israel needs sons. Moshe must live long enough to be a good father. He is brash and too brave sometimes, your Moshe. It must not happen to him what happened to your father. Moshe holds the key to everything. I hoped they would come back to Jerusalem, your papa, mama, and brothers. For a time I believed they would live to see this hour when the Promise has come true. I would have shown him the treasure. There is nowhere else for us, you know. The Lord has closed every other door. Germany is in ruins, but the powers of darkness attack from other places. It is written in the Book. Every detail is clear, you see. I hoped your papa and mama would make *Aliyah*. But it is enough. Yacov saved from the fire and you . . . God is good."

His rambling worried her. "Grandfather, I will not leave you," she promised.

"No, no. You are needed. Yacov, take her to the Hurva. Show her where Moshe is. The hounds are at the gates, you know. Like Warsaw. Moshe stands watch on the rampart. You must go along. I will be all right, *nu?* Go on, then. So much to do." He turned his attention back to the scroll. "I must stay here and pray for a miracle today. Natural or supernatural! The Lord will save us. *Nu!* Either we will be saved by natural means, by the strong hand of the Lord, as in times past. Or maybe this time by something supernatural. Maybe there will be a real miracle, and our army will break through!"

■   ■   ■   ■

It was nearly daybreak.

Rachel and Yacov stood upon a balcony that ringed the inner dome of the Hurva.

"There." Yacov pointed across the gray expanse of Old City rooftops to the dome of a structure outside the walls. "The Palmach took the Church of the Dormition from the Arabs last night. Tonight or tomorrow night they will attack Zion Gate from there."

Rachel knew the church well. It was a peaceful place built beside the site of the Last Supper of Jesus on the Mount where the City of David had once stood. She remembered that on the ceiling a fresco showed Mary, the world-weary mother of Jesus, being borne up to heaven in the arms of angels. This simple Jewish girl, chosen by God to give birth to Israel's Messiah, had suffered too much in Jerusalem to remain here any longer. Her son had been eternally destined for events too enormous and fearsome for her to understand. She could not protect Him from His love for the world. Love had broken her heart in the end. *As love for a child often breaks a mother's heart.* From that place, legend claimed, Jesus had called His mother home to be with Him at last.

The place does not matter. It is the reality of it. They are together.

Yacov took her hand. "I am glad to see you again, sister," he said shyly. "I have been dreaming so much of Mama these days. It is the war, I guess."

"I know." Rachel slipped her arm around his too-thin shoulders.

Rachel closed her eyes and remembered her own mother weeping for her children in the Nazi-held Umschlagplatz of Warsaw. Like Mary's Son, those sweet, guiltless lambs had died while the world watched in apathy.

For Rachel, there was no consolation but this: like Mary, Etta Lubetkin was finally reunited with her other children. They sang together in a garden somewhere. Rachel believed that. She saw them with the eyes of her heart and knew God had not caused the suffering they had endured. Man had done the bidding of evil. But the Messiah of Israel had suffered with His people. He had walked with them into the gas chambers and welcomed their souls to His kingdom as the old rabbi of Warsaw had said He would. Rachel was not scorched by bitterness. To love was sometimes to suffer as well as to rejoice.

Rachel put her hand on her abdomen. *Shalom, little one. Can you hear my heart? I love you from your beginnings. I will love you even though life will be difficult here. I would protect you from all of it if I could. That I cannot protect you from everything is the burden every woman since Eve has carried. But here . . . a hope we can cling to: one hundred years from now the sorrow of this world will be a dream. The Lord Himself will wipe away our tears, and we will sit in God's garden and laugh together. It is written.*

Rachel imagined Mary. Beyond the lonely birthing in a stable, beyond bringing up the too-bright boy who startled rabbis with His insight into Torah, beyond the miracles and the teaching of love and redemption, beyond betrayal and the agony of the cross and the empty tomb, beyond the arms of the angels bearing Mary up, Rachel imagined, *the embrace . . . the reunion . . . Mother and Son! The joy that must have taken place in the clouds above this bloody plot of earth!*

"We will see Mama again, Yacov," Rachel said, eyes shining. "They are all together, *nu?*"

The boy nodded. "Still, I am glad I am not the only one here."

This morning, across the gulf of warring soldiers, the windows of Mary's church were reinforced with sandbags.

In the soft light, debris from last night's battle became visible. Two Haganah soldiers with Sten guns stood watch inside the Hurva gallery. One of them stepped aside and motioned for Rachel and Yacov to come and witness the sunrise over the "City of Peace." From that high vantage point she could see the Arab-occupied tower that guarded Zion Gate, beyond the Jewish Quarter, and to the spires of churches in the Armenian Quarter.

"Moshe is there," Yacov said, pointing. "Inside the belfry of St. Jacques."

Ah, Moshe. Can you hear my heart? Look this way and know that I am here. Watching for you. Praying for you. We will have a child in the winter, you and I. I did not ask you to stay. Did not tell you how I ached when you left me in Tel Aviv. You had too much to think about. I saw the worry in your eyes. To send you off worried for me would have been a burden too much for you to bear. You must think instead about the birth of our homeland. And so . . . be well, love. And live. . . .

Yacov broke her reverie. "See, the Muslim women. They are coming. Look there."

A sentry handed her field glasses. He pointed through the gaps in the buildings toward Zion Gate. It was then Rachel saw the dead Muslim soldiers who sprawled on the road, their hands reaching toward Jerusalem. One body was draped over a water fountain like a rag doll. His blood had pooled on a bunch of flowers.

The line of women marched through the Old City toward the dead Arab defenders. A white bedsheet on a broomstick fluttered in the morning breeze. One older woman, walking stiffly, led the procession. She was robed in black from head to foot, her veil concealing everything but her eyes. She hesitated, drinking in the scene of death before her. Stretching her arms heavenward, she shrieked, long and shrilly, "*Ya Allah! Ya Allah!* Oh, God! Oh, God!"

There was a sound like a distant flock of geese rising from a river. Each, in turn, cried out, until the peace of the morning was shattered with their collective keening.

"They have come to bury their sons," Rachel said, grieving for them. "Their children. . . ."

"Maybe a hundred dead there," said the sentry in a tone that conveyed his pride in the grim harvest the women had come to collect.

Rachel did not reply. She simply stood, still and pale, as the mothers from the other side of the barricades fanned out to gather their beloved and carry them home.

■　■　■　■

The eye of dawn opened, and the sun peeked into the Holy

City. To Moshe, holding the bell tower of St. Jacques, it meant the Old City Jews had lived to see another sunrise, to face another space of deprivation and death and pray for reprieve.

He wondered what day it was and how many days had passed since statehood was declared. The answer he achieved did not please him. It did not seem possible that so much had happened in only three days, or that less than seventy-two hours separated him from his last glimpse of Rachel in Tel Aviv.

Glad she was safe, he wondered when . . . or if . . . he would see her again.

The sunlight picked out the minarets of the mosques, the spires of the churches, and the domes of the synagogues, warming Moshe's cheek even as he squatted behind sandbags. The expanding gleam illuminated the towers of The Citadel and, nearer at hand, the battlements of Zion Gate.

It was from beyond Zion Gate, in the direction of the Valley of Hinnom, that the wailing arose, a rising plaint of anguish. It sounded as if a gruesome beast had awakened with the sun. The noise of its screeching reverberated through the corridors of the Old City.

Moshe's skin prickled. He recognized the dirge of Arab women lamenting their dead, but the moaning conveyed loss: brutal, senseless tragedy. If Molech once again stood in Gehenna and required infant sacrifice, the aching cries of the bereft parents would sound just like this.

How many more lives would the Molech of war demand?

The sounds of unrelieved suffering continued for a time

to come from beyond the walls. Then, moving nearer, the keening passed through the Armenian Quarter before turning east toward the Haram.

To the north, through a gap between buildings, Moshe watched the doleful procession move along the Street of the Chain. Black-robed figures carried forms frozen in every posture of agony. A pair of women bore a body whose arms were uplifted in supplication. They were followed by a trio shouldering one who clutched at his heart with one hand. After him came a line of many more Arab dead, every one transfixed in the throes of his worst torment, in contortions no living humans could ever sustain.

■ ■ ■ ■

Death and anger swept the Arab-held districts of the Old City. Daoud moved through the confusion of the souks, pressing on through the crowded triple bazaar. Battle-worn mercenaries discussed the strength of the Jewish forces that had overwhelmed Mount Zion in the south and had nearly broken through Jaffa Gate on the west. Gone was the arrogance of former days.

"We need the Arab Legion to save Jerusalem from the Jews! *Ya Allah!* I was almost out of bullets when they retreated. Only the strength of the Prophet saved me from the Jews!"

"One more push at Jaffa Gate and they would have overwhelmed us! But they turned back, Allah be praised!"

"I prayed for the dawn. They will not attack again in the daylight. I and my father have time to get out of Jerusalem! We return this morning to Morocco."

"But what of Mount Zion? It is lost! The Moquades on Mount Zion said there were thousands of Jews storming across the Valley of Hinnom from the eye hospital. Attacking! Attacking! They swarmed over Mount Zion. Habib told me he was the last to retreat into the Old City through Zion Gate and that the Jews were on his heels. Jews hold the Church of the Dormition, a fortress mere yards from Zion Gate. Their guns look down upon Zion Gate."

"In the Armenian Quarter they have recaptured the tower of St. Jacques. They had flamethrowers and sacks of grenades! Now they are sniping down at the defenders in the tower at Zion Gate. This is the fault of Hassan el-Hassan!"

"That madman Dajani and his bombs! Six fellows from Syria burned to death!"

"What about al-Malik? He swears the Mufti is sending more men and ammunition from Damascus, but where is it? Why does it not come? We are not under siege like the Jews. The road from here to Damascus is open. Why does the Mufti not send trucks of supplies? Where are our bullets and guns? Why do the Jews have so much ammunition and we have nothing?"

"It is the Americans. The Great Satan. They send everything to the Jews."

"I have a handful of cartridges left. If the Jews attack the Old City again tonight, how are we to fight them?"

"At least we have plenty of food," offered an old Arab who was selling limes, popeetes, and oranges. "They are starving."

"Do you know how long it takes to starve a Jew? In

Warsaw there were four hundred thousand crammed into a space of two square miles. I was in Warsaw. I saw. They managed to get food. And after it was gone, they survived for a while longer. Jews are difficult to kill with starving. It was too slow. Even Hitler did not want to waste any more bullets, so he used gas. Efficient. The Mufti says he will do the same when the war is won. I hear there is a facility in Syria built for such a purpose and another in Iraq."

"We do not have time to wait. As for me, I am done with this. I came expecting to take home Jewish loot. I have nothing from this that is worthy. I and my men are going home to Lebanon while we can go."

"And me and my brothers are returning to Syria this afternoon."

"There is one thing that will save Jerusalem from the Jews. King Abdullah must send his tanks and cannon here and blast them out!"

Daoud heard such conversations everywhere. He did not want to return to Dajani. It was plain Dajani would go on fighting the Jews even if most of the Jihad Moquades in the Old City perished. And how could Daoud, who owed a life-debt to the Jewish doctor, go on toting Dajani's bombs? The boy thought about Gawan lying in a clean bed at the Latin Patriarchate. Daoud decided that was probably the only safe place in the Old City. He turned to go, snapping up a lime. Then a hand fell on his shoulder.

"You! Little coward! Where did you go last night?"

It was Dajani.

■ ■ ■ ■

The bank of phones in King Abdullah's war room in Jordan had not stopped ringing since the night before the declaration of Israel's statehood.

King Abdullah demanded constant updates. He got them from all his field commanders down the length of the Jordan and into the Negev, but closest to his heart was Jerusalem.

Ahkmed al-Malik rang Amman and said he was calling from Jerusalem's Rawdah headquarters with an important message for the king. He was more than a little put out to be asked to wait. "But it's urgent," he repeated emphatically. "The Jews are almost inside the walls. The Holy City may fall."

"Wait," he was told again.

Al-Malik fumed, trying to compose himself to deliver his report. He hoped he would be speaking to a high military advisor, someone in a position to actually communicate the pressing need to King Abdullah. With luck he might be allowed to restate the case to the king's aide, Hazza Majali, or even to Jordan's prime minister, Tewfic Abou Hoda.

The line clicked and squealed, then it cleared and a voice asked, "Yes? What is it?"

"I have a most important communication for the king," al-Malik barked impatiently. "If you cannot deliver it, then get me someone who can! The king must hear this!"

"This is he, speaking," Abdullah said calmly. "You say you are calling from Jerusalem's Rawdah headquarters?"

Al-Malik barely suppressed the tremor in his nervous voice when he identified himself and then said, "Your Majesty, the Jews are at the gates. They may even now be re-forming to break through Jaffa Gate and on to the Street of the Chain."

"And why do you tell this to me, you who are the Mufti's creature?"

"Majesty, the troops of the Greater Arab Council are failing in their defense of the Old City. They are ill-trained mercenaries and Holy Strugglers. We need a trained army. If you do not send the Legion, then El Kuds, the Holy City, will be lost."

"You know I have promised my British allies I will keep my men out of Jerusalem?"

Winding up his courage with the strongest weapon available, al-Malik said, "And what is an oath made to the infidels compared to the loss of the third holiest place of all? Do you want the Arab world to say that the Hashemites are traitors to the Prophet? And what of the tomb of your father? Would you have the Jews control even that?"

Abdullah coldly replied, "And should I break an oath and risk my troops so Haj Amin el-Husseini can crown himself king of Jerusalem?"

"Majesty," al-Malik said fervently, "if you can save the Holy City, I will crown you king of it with my own hands, but do not delay. Send your Arab Legion at once!"

■　■　■　■

Glubb Pasha, commander of the Arab Legion, strode purposefully into the sitting room where King Abdullah conducted his morning prayers. Prayer time ended, Glubb found the unpretentious monarch seated cross-legged on the floor, playing with his one-eyed cat.

"Majesty," Glubb said crisply in his official voice.

Abdullah made a gentling motion with his hand. The cat arched its back in order to stay under its master's caresses. "Softly, Sir John, softly. You see, I already know why you have come."

"Then it's true? You have committed the Legion to Jerusalem in spite of your pledge to the British?"

Sounding more amused than imperious, Abdullah scolded, "And would you question my right to do so?"

"Nooo." Glubb drew the single syllable out to excessive length to give himself time to think. "It is certainly your prerogative to commit your forces as you see fit."

The British officer was so intent on having his say that he continued speaking right over the top of Abdullah's mildly mocking "Thank you."

"But the United Nations . . . Jerusalem is to be an international city! There will be a worldwide outcry when we take the Holy City."

"And are you certain we will take the city? After all, it is said to be the center of the universe. The Jews understand this . . . Haj Amin understands this . . . even if you of the West do not."

"Majesty," Glubb said, "if we commit the Legion, we will take the city. But it will mean real war, not skirmishes around villages."

Abdullah pushed the cat away and at last stood up. "The Mufti's fanatics and mercenaries are fleeing. We cannot permit El Kuds to fall to the Jews." Smoothing the folds of his robe, Abdullah suggested, "I believe you understand me, Sir John."

Glubb Pasha acquiesced, then added, "I will take a column of armored cars to the outskirts of the city."

"And soon," Abdullah concluded. "We will make Jerusalem our capital. And when we allow the Jews and the Christians freedom to practice their religions in our city, will not the world approve of our actions?"

▪ ▪ ▪ ▪ CHAPTER 24 ▪ ▪ ▪ ▪

Major Luke Thomas stormed into David Shaltiel's office at the King David Hotel. "Where were the reinforcements?" he bellowed. "Four hundred men in reserve and we could have broken through with another hundred! You left us out there with no support!"

"Calm down," Shaltiel urged. "No one could face gasoline bombs thrown from those walls. To press on would have meant more deaths. And who knows if you could have made it all the way to the Jewish Quarter?"

"Then what about the Palmach men who took Mount Zion? I heard Nachasch captured it with sixty men! He begged you for reserves and supplies and got nothing! Listen to me! Send those four hundred men to attack Zion Gate, and we'll be in the Old City by tonight."

Shaltiel shrugged. "It's too risky," he said, dithering. "We have to stop, reevaluate, regroup. Get ready for an Arab counterattack."

Thomas grabbed Shaltiel's arm and dragged him to the east-facing window. "Do you see that banner on the

Church of St. Jacques?" he said, gesturing toward the blue-and-white Mogen David flag. "Moshe Sachar is holding it. That tower commands the back of Zion Gate. But for how long? It's an island, cut off from support, just like the Jewish Quarter in the Old City, only smaller and more vulnerable. We have to move now!"

Shaltiel said nothing; he clearly did not intend to move swiftly or decisively.

Thomas pointed toward the lightening skies above the Temple Mount and the Mount of Olives beyond. "It is dawn!" he said, his voice laden with accusation. "Mount Zion could have been reinforced in the darkness if you had sent support when Nachasch requested it. Now any men crossing the Hinnom Valley from the eye hospital to Mount Zion will be under the guns of the Arabs on the walls. Your hesitation will cost lives. Two transmissions to King Abdullah from the Arab Higher Committee have been intercepted. The Arab defenders have requested the help of Jordan's Arab Legion. They'll have it, too. When Abdullah's cannon are on that ridge," he said fiercely, "*then* you can worry about a counterattack. But it will be too late to save the Old City. If you won't move now, give the men to me."

"Not the reserves," Shaltiel said stubbornly. "Take what's left of Isaacson's platoon and fifty more. That's all I can let you have."

Thomas snapped a salute and hurried out, yelling for Jacob Kalner as he went.

■   ■   ■   ■

From the top of the tower of St. Jacques, Moshe looked

again at Mount Zion. He strained his eyes and his thoughts toward seeing movement there, as if by the force of his will he could make the Palmach launch its operation against Zion Gate.

What were they waiting for? It was way past dawn. The Muslims would see any move across the Hinnom.

Below him, at the corners of the domed roof of the church, Moshe saw the other soldiers from the Jewish Quarter who remained with him.

Have I brought them to their deaths? And if no attempt to break through Zion Gate is made, will their deaths . . . our deaths . . . be totally futile?

Benny, one of the riflemen who occupied the bell tower with Moshe, looked long and hard through his telescopic sight, took a breath, held it, and triggered off a round aimed at the fortified turret above Zion Gate. His shot received a flurry in reply, smacking into the sandbags that lined the parapet and whining off the stones. "I nicked one," Benny observed. "Teach them to be more cautious, anyway."

"Well done," Moshe said. "But no more! From now on we have to save our bullets for when they rush us. No more firing unless there are enough together to be a threat."

As he crawled to the opposite side of the spire, Benny asked, "And what happens after dark tonight? How we gonna keep them back then?"

Before Moshe could frame a reply that was not too absurdly hopeful, Benny's partner, Messer, replied, "You stupid *momzer!* Don't you know the mortars will get us long before dark?"

■　■　■　■

Despair choked the Jewish Quarter. Among the followers of Rabbi Akiva, however, was a glimmer of hope that they could effect a settlement with the Muslims and save the district from annihilation.

Akiva was careful that the meeting of council members take place in his home. Ten rabbis from the Sephardi and Ashkenazi communities were gathered in his study, forming a minyan of those who had run the affairs of the area before the outbreak of hostilities.

Beginning the meeting, Akiva said, "Now we see that use of force has failed. Militant claims of victory by secular Zionists against our Muslim neighbors have brought those of us in the religious community to the threshold of destruction."

A Sephardi added, "Moshe Sachar is trapped in the Armenian district, cut off from his men. The attacks against the Jihad Moquades have ended in misery and defeat. As for my congregation, there are many who oppose the Haganah. Many lost their homes and property."

A second rabbi said, "I heard there is not enough ammunition among the Zionist fighters to withstand another battle. We are certain to be overrun. The passions of the fanatic Muslim factions will be bent on slaughter if we are taken captive in the heat of battle. They will not spare our women or children. We will be wiped out like the kibbutz of Kfar Etzion."

Akiva pressed his fingertips together and studied the group of councilmen. "We have seen what fighting does.

One fourth of our people displaced. The burning. The looting. The end of this is certain. The Mufti's men have unlimited arms and ammunition. The Haganah is down to nothing. We cannot win. The Zionist forces did not break through. They will not. We have been forced to go along with Moshe Sachar and the rest, and look what it has cost us: the near starvation of our people. This could have been settled long ago." He extended his hands, waiting for suggestions. "What course of action do we, as the true elected representatives of our community, take?"

"Moshe Sachar will not last out the day where he is, *nu?*"

"St. Jacques will be overrun in a matter of hours. Then leadership of the Haganah is shattered."

"So. It is settled. We should retake control of our own neighborhood."

"Yes. Rabbi Akiva, you should contact our Arab neighbors. Tell them we are not part of that Haganah band. Tell them we never wanted to fight in the first place."

"Call Taj Khalidi in the Muslim Quarter. He is reasonable. You have always been able to work things out with Khalidi, *nu?* Tell him we surrender."

A single important condition was offered by the eldest rabbi among them. "The Mufti's forces are a gang of brigands from every slum in the world of Islam. They will not care what Khalidi says. They have come to loot our homes, take over our property, and kill as many Jews as they come across. Our people rightly fear them. How can we surrender to men like these? They are the scum of the earth. We are likely to end up dead either way."

Akiva offered the solution. "I will tell Khalidi we will

not surrender to the mercenaries. I will say we fear the thirst for blood that the Jihad Moquades have displayed. I will tell him we wish a truce until the army of King Abdullah arrives from Jordan. Then we will surrender—to the officers of the Arab Legion."

A vote on this course of action was taken. It was unanimous.

■　■　■　■

The eyes of the Jewish Council were on Akiva as he placed the phone call to his friend on the Arab Higher Committee that afternoon.

Taj Khalidi himself answered the phone. *"Salaam."*

Pleased to hear Khalidi's voice, Akiva explained, "I am here among the members of the Jewish Council. Our people are in despair after your victory against the secular Zionists last night."

"Our . . . victory," Taj responded in a subdued voice.

"Yes. The Haganah in the Jewish Quarter is down to a handful of bullets. The Jewish hospital is overrun with wounded. Women and children have taken shelter in the synagogues. We are overwhelmed. Our community cannot tolerate any more hollow promises of rescue from these Zionist outsiders."

"That is wise, Rabbi Akiva. This tragedy does not need to exist, a breach between us that is unreasonable. If the Haganah and the secular Zionists were willing to listen, we would live in peace together."

"Well spoken, Khalidi. The suffering here among the innocent is unbearable for those of us who are their leaders and guides. The children . . . there is hardly any milk left for the babies. It is time we put an end to this."

"Allah be praised!" Khalidi exclaimed. "This is news I did not expect. Your call is most welcome!"

"Good. Then here is what we propose: Tell your committee that the religious Jews wish to surrender. That we have no hope . . . indeed, have never believed that resistance could bring peace. The secular Zionists who man the barricades are down to their last defense. We rabbis of the Jewish Council will effect a surrender to officers of Jordan's Arab Legion with the proviso that we, as noncombatants, may remain in our Quarter."

"The Legion?"

"Our people fear the Mufti's fanatics. Look what the Jihad Moquades did to the property that was evacuated. They have a reputation for violence. There is no discipline among them. We fear there will be a massacre if we surrender to them."

"Ah." Khalidi took the news with a shade of doubt. "But the Arab Legion is not in Jerusalem. Of course King Abdullah has been consulted on the situation here. He promises to send men and equipment. They are even now en route to Jerusalem. But I cannot guarantee they will be here before the next assault of the Jihad Moquades."

Akiva was adamant. "We will surrender only to the Legion. Tell your committee what we request. It is in your power to work with us, Khalidi. You can control the fanatics there just as we have done on our side."

"Certainly. *Insh' Allah.* I am sure favorable terms can be reached."

■   ■   ■   ■

In the late afternoon, news of the offer of surrender from the mayor of the Jewish district swept through the souks and bazaars of the Muslim Old City like a desert wind. It blew away the sense of defeat and fanned the flames of fanaticism among the Jihad Moquades.

Daoud, son of Baruch, sat on an upturned box near the door of the coffeehouse while Kasim Dajani consulted Hassan el-Hassan.

"Is it true? Rabbi Akiva called Khalidi? The Jews are down to their last bullets?"

"Allah is merciful, Dajani! You see, when we think all is lost, we hear news that turns our hearts once again to the righteous purpose! Jerusalem will be the domain of Allah and his Prophet. Our Mufti, Haj Amin el-Husseini, will reign in the Holy City. *Insh' Allah!*"

"And what of the approach of the Arab Legion? Will they not steal our glory?"

"It will take them at least two days to arrive. By then we will have overrun the Jewish Quarter and put a final end to three thousand years of Jews living in the shadow of the Temple Mount. We will purify this ground with their blood!"

Daoud considered Hassan's words. Much blood had already been spilled, and so far nothing had been purified. He raised his eyes to the covered bazaar. Shouts of joyous victory exploded from its shadowed aisles.

Dajani said, "The Holy Strugglers who left Jerusalem this morning have heard the news and are turning back to take up arms again. Even now they crowd through Damascus Gate!"

Daoud, who had not said much through the long day, dared to speak. "But what of our own ammunition? The men in the souks said they would be fighting Jews with stones before the day was past."

Dajani kicked the box out from under Daoud. "Impudent! Doubter!" He made as if he would also kick Daoud, but Hassan stopped him.

Hassan el-Hassan remembered how Daoud admired the exploits Hassan had shared with the boys of the Quarter. "Leave the boy alone. It is right he ask such a question."

Dajani grunted in response. "You are his hero, Hassan. Explain to him."

Hassan sipped his coffee. "You see, Daoud, the victory is ours, even if we kill them with stones. Allah has willed it so. Otherwise we would not have got the call from Akiva. They are in terror of our might! But never mind. We have mortars on the south wall. We will attack and attack until the Jews have spent the last of their ammunition. And after that, we are many thousands . . . they are a handful. The end of this is certain, Daoud, my friend. Do you see?"

Daoud, unsmiling, nodded. He addressed Hassan. "My brother lies wounded. I wish to see him. To take him this encouragement. May I be excused?"

Hassan opened his mouth to assent, but Dajani placed a hand out to stop him. "I have a plan. I will need my apprentice to help me. I will let the boy go after we finish our work."

This is what the Lord says: "I will return to Zion and dwell in Jerusalem. Then Jerusalem will be called City of Truth, and the mountain of the LORD Almighty will be called the Holy Mountain."

This is what the LORD Almighty says: "Once again men and women of ripe old age will sit in the streets of Jerusalem, each with a cane in hand because of his age. The city streets will be filled with boys and girls playing there."

This is what the LORD Almighty says: "It may seem marvelous to the remnant of this people at that time, but will it seem marvelous to me?" declares the LORD Almighty.

This is what the LORD Almighty says: "I will save my people from the countries of the east and the west. I will bring them back to live in Jerusalem; they will be my people, and I will be faithful and righteous to them as their God."

Zechariah 8:3–7

■ ■ ■ ■ CHAPTER 25 ■ ■ ■ ■

When viewed from the Ophthalmic Hospital on the hill south of the city, the ridges and valleys that formed Jerusalem's topography resembled the splayed fingers of a left hand. The tip of the little finger was the location of the King David Hotel. The gap between the last two fingers was the Valley of Hinnom. A wedding ring was just where Zion Gate loomed, and the knuckle below it was Mount Zion.

Sixty pounds at a time, mortar shells and rifle bullets were carried on the backs of the Spare Parts Platoon. Mount Zion, the jumping-off point for an assault on Zion Gate, nestled under the Arab guns bristling on the south wall of the Old City. For that reason the staging area for the coming attack was farther back, on a promontory south of the Valley of Hinnom.

The hilltop was occupied by the three buildings of the British Ophthalmic Hospital. With the outbreak of the war, doctors and patients had fled, and now the site was an observation post for the Israelis. Taking a breather before trudging back down the slope for more supplies, Jacob, Alfie, Ibrahim, Mangus, and Daniel lined the brow of the hill.

Back to the left, past the stump of the windmill of Montefiore, the tower of the YMCA building could be seen. Ahead, across the valley, the battlements of The Citadel were visible. It had been only thirty-six hours since that desperate failure, since the horror of gasoline bombs and the screams of the dying.

Too tired to be moved at the sight, Jacob shifted his gaze. To the right he could glimpse the ramparts above their latest objective, Zion Gate, and beyond those the gleaming tower of the Church of St. Jacques, held by Jews. He pointed this out to Alfie, who wanted to share the information with Daniel, but Daniel was staring down at the road winding through the valley.

"That is Derech Hevron," he said, "the Hebron highway. It is the direct route to Kfar Etzion." His eyes stared off into the distance, and Jacob guessed he was remembering vanished friends. Jacob was right, but just partly so, for when Daniel spoke again he said, "Out there is where the Arabs ambushed the relief convoys that might have saved us . . . trapped and slaughtered them all."

Now Luke Thomas's column of fifty Haganah reinforcements could be seen on Derech Hevron. Spread wide apart from each other and hugging the margins of the street, the soldiers moved toward Mount Zion. They dashed from brush to lamppost, from myrtle tree to rubble heap, in their efforts to frustrate the aim of the Arab snipers. Rifle fire crackled from the Old City walls.

From off to the east came the coughing roar of a mortar, then another and another.

An instant later a detonation on the highway tossed fragments of cobblestones and Jewish soldiers into the air.

"Get down! Get down!" Jacob shouted.

An Arab mortar barrage whistled toward Jewish positions in the Valley of Hinnom, plastering Derech Hevron with explosions.

The salvo continued for five minutes. The surviving Haganah troops gathered up their wounded comrades and retreated back toward the Ophthalmic Hospital.

"How are we ever going to get these supplies across?" Jacob wondered aloud. "The Arabs can see every movement. They will fill the valley with fire and blood."

The vale of Hinnom . . . Gai Hinnom . . . Gehenna. Ever since the worshippers of Molech had thrown living children into the fiery belly of their god in this seemingly tranquil valley, it had been a place of blood and fire . . . and still was.

■　■　■　■

Standing outside the Ophthalmic Hospital, Luke Thomas watched the bombardment of the Haganah reinforcements trying to cross the Valley of Hinnom. His anger surged at the needless loss of life; he was consumed with a sense of utter dismay and defeat.

"The mortar fire is killing us. We need to strike back, knock it out. Otherwise we cannot reinforce Mount Zion, and we cannot hold it," he said. "And losing Mount Zion will mean the end of the Jewish Quarter. It does not matter that the Arabs left arms and ammunition behind on Mount Zion when they fled. Nachasch must have more men."

Turning to Jacob Kalner, he said, "The Spare Parts will have to be called on again. Take your squad and a Davidka. You'll cross the valley on a truck. Once there, you will try to take out the Arab mortars so more troops can be sent across. Godspeed."

■　■　■　■

From a position atop the south wall of the Old City, a two-inch mortar lobbed a shell toward Moshe's position in the tower of St. Jacques. The explosive charge whistled overhead, passing the church and exploding on the rooftop of the Petra Hotel.

When the mortar shrilled again, Moshe, Benny, and Messer ducked low behind the sandbags. This time the round fell short, detonating on Ararat Road.

"There!" Benny shouted, pointing toward the telltale

puff of smoke that marked the launch point of the mortar shell. Benny and Messer pumped several rounds into the spot until the return fire drove them under cover again.

The next shell passed close enough to the spire for Moshe to feel the rush of air as it sped over. It sailed into the Armenian Quarter, penetrated the window of a police station, and blew out the wall toward the street.

"That was too close!" Moshe warned. "Fire two shots each and down we go."

The three men had barely reached the protection of the stone staircase when another mortar shell burst against the golden cross that adorned the tower.

A succession of explosions followed, rocking the tower as if there were an earthquake, even though no more shells had been heard overhead.

"That's it," Moshe said. "They have the range. We'll have to give up the tower, at least."

The men hurried down the steps. They expected that the next mortar shell would be a direct hit, collapsing the belfry completely.

Several minutes passed without another detonation. Why did the Arabs not finish the job? "Come on!" Moshe urged, sprinting back up the stairs. "Maybe they are out of shells."

"And maybe they want us to do just what we are doing," Messer added dryly.

Although Arab bullets continued to snap at the corners of the tower, and the central platform of the belfry was cluttered with bricks and mortar and pocked by shrapnel, the tower was still usable.

"Why did they stop?" Benny wondered.

"There's your answer," Moshe said, peering through a firing slit and pointing to the north. The police station was a blazing hulk, engulfed in flames ignited by the mortar shell. "The Arabs were using the police station as a munitions dump, and they have blasted their own position. They won't try to hit us again until they find an angle with nothing of theirs behind it to get damaged!"

■ ■ ■ ■ CHAPTER 26 ■ ■ ■ ■

A truck loaded with a Davidka and sixty shells idled its engine around the curve of Derech Hevron just out of sight of the Arab positions on the wall. Jacob Kalner was in the driver's seat. A rail-thin former Austrian schoolteacher named Kevel Gottlieb and Daniel Caan were in the bed of the truck, armed with Sten guns. The remainder of the Spare Parts Platoon, Alfie, Ibrahim, and Mangus, carrying rifles, were packed in as well.

The Davidka was a homemade mortar, named partly for its designer, David Leibowitz, and partly for little David, the giant-killer. Built from the cut-up barrels of antique Turkish cannon and firing rockets made of explosives-packed water pipe, the Davidka was temperamental, short-ranged, noisy, and terrifying to the Arabs.

It was perfectly suited for the attack on Zion Gate. Installed behind the headstones in the Armenian cemetery, a Davidka could easily lob its shells onto and over the walls of the Armenian Quarter, where, they hoped, it would destroy the mortars of the Muslims. The difficulties were bringing one of the ponderous monstrosities up to Mount Zion and thereafter keeping it supplied with enough ammunition to make it effective.

No one had to tell the Spare Parts that they were on a suicide mission; they had seen what had happened to the Haganah troops in the open space of the Hinnom.

"Follow the street until you reach the Greek Seminary," Luke Thomas had instructed. "That's where our men holding Mount Zion will meet you."

"And how do I know where that is?" Jacob queried. "I've never been here before."

"It's the building with the light blue shutters close enough to the Old City wall for the Arabs to throw rocks at you" was the reply.

With a clash of grinding gears, Jacob engaged the transmission and popped the clutch. The truck lurched forward. Jacob's foot on the throttle sent the truck flying around the curve and down into the Valley of Hinnom. "Hold on!" he yelled to the five in back. There was no point in creeping along. The Arabs shot at anything moving, so only speed was of any value.

They had almost reached the midpoint of the valley when machine-gun bullets clipped the pavement in front of the speeding truck. Jacob yanked the wheel to the right, sending the vehicle skidding sideways across the pavement. Then he tugged to the left just as the bullets marched across the expanse of a Turkish water fountain. Geysers of green water splashed skyward, and the marble bowl at the top shattered.

Then the mortar shells came.

One fell ahead of the racing transport, detonating in the depths of the sixteenth-century reservoir known as the *Sultan's Pool.*

The second landed behind. Crashing through a previously abandoned automobile, the shell ignited the gasoline tank with a whoosh. Shell fragments sliced into the tailgate of the truck. A thick column of oily smoke rose into the afternoon sky.

They were bracketed. The next round could finish them. Jacob clung to the wheel and strained as if he could lift the vehicle into the air and fly away from the trap they were in.

Ahead, the sweep of Derech Hevron crossed a stone bridge. As in a faintly remembered children's story, Jacob was seized by the notion that they would be safe if they could just pass the bridge. He floored the accelerator and aimed straight ahead.

The truck rattled and bumped its way across the span. Nearly there!

Another fusillade of bullets shattered the windshield, showering Jacob with the shards and tearing into the seat beside his leg. The eruption of glass made him jerk the wheel involuntarily and slam on the brakes. The truck launched itself toward a stone pillar beyond the far end of the bridge.

The third mortar shell hit the center of the roadway past the end of the span as the truck slid sideways and collided with the pylon. The transport surged upward, as if trying to climb out of the valley of blood and fire, falling over sideways to lodge between the stone pillar and the bridge abutment.

Jacob was thrown against the steering wheel and almost through the shattered windscreen. He barely heard shouts of alarm from the bed when Kevel, Alfie, and Ibrahim were flung out. Daniel was smashed into the barrel of the Davidka as the truck rolled onto its side before righting itself again.

The abused lorry whined to a halt, rocking back and forth on its wheels. Ibrahim and Alfie crawled under the truck for shelter.

Daniel was the next to recover his senses. Machine-gun fire stitched a seam across the truck bed. Still clutching the Sten gun, he flung himself over the side and scrambled beneath the vehicle to join the others.

Kevel did not follow, nor did Mangus.

"Where's Mangus?" Daniel asked.

"Dead."

"And Kevel?"

Kevel lay flat on his back in the middle of the roadway, knocked unconscious.

Jacob was pinned in the cab, crushed between seatback and steering column. Arab bullets spattered the door opposite him and ricocheted off the Davidka behind him. The way the cab was fixed between two columns of stone gave him temporary protection, but it was only a matter of time before a round penetrated a crevice between the bridge supports and the cab.

Another Arab mortar round exploded in the pool below the bridge.

Daniel bolted out from his hiding place. Grabbing Kevel by the knees, he dragged the schoolteacher back under the truck. Bullets continued to ping off the sides of the transport.

Where was safety? To go either up or down the road in view of the snipers was death; to stay put was merely to prolong the wait till an accurately placed mortar round finished them.

The slope of Mount Zion was thirty yards away. How to cross that distance? There was sparse cover.

Then Daniel saw it: a millstone, sitting upright and facing the Arab position like a giant stone shield. It was no more than a momentary rampart along the route, but it was the lone encouragement in sight. Briefly he explained the plan to Ibrahim and Alfie.

Ibrahim hauled Kevel to the front of the truck. Another mortar round exploded nearer than the last. Using the smoke of the explosion as cover, Ibrahim hung Kevel across his shoulders and sprinted toward the grinding wheel. Alfie, carrying three rifles, ran along behind.

Meanwhile, Daniel called to Jacob: was he wounded, could he reach the millstone?

"I'm all right, but I'm stuck," he replied.

The driver's-side door was jammed and would not open. "I'll get you out, Jacob," Daniel promised. But how? To go around to the other side would expose him to the rifles of the Arabs.

Climbing up on the crumpled hood of the truck, Daniel leaned through the broken windscreen and forced the steering wheel upward. "Try to slide over!" he urged. "Now!"

A bullet came through the roof of the cab, missing Jacob by scant inches.

Then suddenly he was free of the wheel, and with Daniel tugging on his arms, Jacob lunged out of the truck. In the midst of the desperate flight, Daniel still thought to scoop up the second Sten gun.

They were a few strides from the grinding wheel when an Arab mortar round scored a direct hit on the truck. The transport bounded into the air, and an immense ball of fire jetted skyward. The surviving Spare Parts hugged the ground as the Davidka ammunition exploded. Wave after wave of howling, spinning, saw-toothed metal whirled over their heads.

When it stopped at last, Daniel and Ibrahim, supporting and dragging Kevel between them, and Alfie, helping Jacob, staggered the last of the distance to the foot of Mount Zion and safety.

■　　■　　■　　■

At the southern boundary of the Armenian Quarter, between Zion Gate and the entrance to the Jewish Quarter, stood a pair of houses. Built in 1843, the turreted structures had been established as a theological school for the Armenian church and a residence for its preceptor. The decorative cornices and stone eyebrows above the windows overhung the intersection from both sides.

"Here is where we will trap the Jews," Dajani said to Daoud. "Right here on their doorstep." The bomber and his apprentice had followed a circuitous route to reach the spot. All day they had circled through alleyways to avoid both the Haganah sentries on the edge of the Jewish Quarter and Moshe's marksmen in the tower of St. Jacques, moving supplies. Once at the chosen location with their packs of explosives and detonators, Dajani was pleased with the plan.

"I do not understand," Daoud said in the upstairs of the

abandoned shop a half-block from the corner. "Zion Gate is already held by the Jihad." The boy gestured toward the parapets and iron portals of the gate only a couple hundred yards away. "And those houses are vacant. Why do we blow them up?"

"Idiot," Dajani returned. "This is what comes of spending too much time listening to the tales of Hassan el-Hassan and not enough time learning your trade. Pay attention. This house lies between the Jewish Quarter and Zion Gate, true?"

"True," Daoud agreed.

"When Captain al-Malik goes out from Zion Gate to drive away the Jews from Mount Zion, the Jews within the Old City might . . . I say might because, after all, they are Jews and know nothing of bravery . . ."

Daoud, son of Baruch, objected to this reasoning, but said nothing.

"The Old City Jews might attempt to capture Zion Gate from behind. So we are rigging this explosion, not just to blow up the buildings, but as a trap to catch any Jews who venture out, or," he grudgingly admitted, "to kill any that might come in through Zion Gate, to block the way into the Jewish district." Dajani spliced together the cables strung from second-story windows to the shop and rigged the wires to the box of the detonator. "This will be a time of glory for you, Daoud," he said. "It will be your job to push the plunger when the time comes. Remember: wait until you catch a group of Jews in the blast. Do not waste the trap for one. And when the blast drops the stones on their heads, that will be my signal to lead a band of Jihad Moquades out to finish them off."

■ ■ ■ ■

The last five members of the Spare Parts Platoon, including the now-conscious Kevel, huddled for a time below the protective bulk of the Greek Orthodox Seminary. The blue shutters seemed especially incongruous amid shellfire and the zip of machine-gun bullets. After a time, when the Arab Irregulars tired of launching mortar rounds, the men circled the south rim of Mount Zion on the road named *Hativat Yerushalayim*. Cautiously they joined the Palmach troops hunkered down behind the myrtle trees and headstones of the Armenian cemetery on Mount Zion. Other Jewish forces occupied the grounds of the Church of the Dormition, David's Tomb, and the House of the Last Supper.

"Nice going," observed Palmach commander Nachasch. "You we could do without. But you had to lose the Davidka?"

Zion Gate, unlike Jaffa, was not an open gap in the wall. Pinched and low, a solid iron door barred the entry, which was protected by a single tower directly overhead. A team of Jewish sappers would risk their lives placing a charge to blow open the obstruction. Enough Jewish troops would have to rush through to secure the walls and a passage into the Jewish Quarter. Only then could success be achieved.

With the loss of the mortar and only thirty-five remaining unwounded in the Palmach force holding Mount Zion, it was apparent that a daylight attack on the heavily fortified and defended passage of Zion Gate was doomed to failure. Such an assault under the machine guns and grenades of the Arabs would end in a worse debacle than the attempt to take The Citadel.

It was decided to again postpone any onslaught against Zion Gate until after dark. Jacob heard Nachasch radio Shaltiel with the request for more men and guns.

"Can't . . . to you." The radio crackled. ". . . Maybe tonight."

Nachasch slammed down the handset with disgust. "Wait, he tells me? What if the Arabs counterattack?"

Jacob did not know if this question was addressed to the radio, to him, or merely to the air. He did not have long to wonder. Nachasch snapped, "What are you gawking at? Get to the far side of the hill and take your position."

Ibrahim and Alfie were kept in reserve, loaded with backpacks of ammunition and blood plasma to be taken where needed, or carried into the Old City if a break-through should succeed. To Jacob and Daniel's surprise and dismay, they found themselves assigned to a squad led by Sal Greenberg, the loudmouthed American. He was wearing his Lüger pistol on his hip and a keffiyeh around his neck.

"What happened to you?" Jacob demanded. "One minute you're behind me in the street outside Jaffa Gate and then, poof! Vanished!"

"I saw we were pinned down, see? So I moved over to see if I could get an angle on the guys on the wall; outflank 'em. Only I got chased by a bunch of Arabs. When I finally ditched 'em, I was way off from you guys, but I got hooked up with the Palmach and came here."

"Where were you when we hit Jaffa Gate at night?" Daniel asked.

"What d'ya mean? I told you, I was with these guys. You shoulda seen the attack we put on!" He fingered the neck scarf with elaborate meaning. "Kicked the blanketheads clear off this hill and run 'em back inside the walls! No foolin', if Haganah High Command hadn't wasted its time with Jaffa Gate and had sent us all of what we needed here, we'd be inside the walls already. What I hear is that you guys made a lot of noise and smoke but nothin' much else. Real screwup, like losin' that mortar."

Jacob snorted. From what he had seen of the Palmachniks, Sal certainly had the attitude to be one of them.

Daniel was outraged. "Men died at Jaffa Gate," he said angrily. "We almost broke through. You have no right to . . ."

"Easy," Jacob said, restraining the younger man.

"Anyway," Daniel added, "Jacob outranks you."

"Not in the Palmach" was the reply. "We don't give a fig for Haganah ranks. Here it's what you do that counts and not what somebody calls you. Now you two and what's his name . . . Kevel . . . get up forward. And watch yourselves," he added in a professional tone. "There are snipers on the walls."

As Jacob, Daniel, and Kevel threaded their way forward from headstone to headstone with the wavy ramparts of Zion Gate looming ahead of them, Daniel muttered, "Wonder how long it took him to figure that one out."

■　■　■　■

The second long day of keeping vigil atop the tower of St. Jacques wore on.

Waiting . . . waiting.

No more Arab mortar rounds fell on the church. Moshe told himself that the Muslims were out of mortar shells, but he knew he was lying.

The absence of shellfire only meant that the Jihad saw no reason to risk damage to its own positions. The Arab Irregulars could afford to wait until dark and retake the tower when their advances could not be seen, let alone stopped.

Mechanically Moshe cautioned the Haganah defenders not to fire unless they saw a concentration of enemy troops. Save the precious bullets for the attack, which must surely come after nightfall.

And always the waiting.

There would never be another night to explore the mysteries of the hidden scrolls. His guardianship was a joke, ended as soon as it began. He hoped Rabbi Lebowitz would live to find a substitute. Perhaps Yacov would take over where Moshe had failed.

And Rachel? She would hear how Moshe's obedience had cost them the all-important tower; how his stubborn insistence on redeeming his error had cost his life. He had promised her that he would be her protector and her shield, that she would never again have to face more tragic loss than she had already suffered.

He had failed in that promise, too.

And still the waiting went on.

■　　■　　■　　■

The call of the muezzin to evening prayer resounded over

the city. Lori and Rachel had slept in shifts, rotating with other medical assistants in the clinic while Dr. Baruch performed surgery throughout the day on fourteen wounded. Three were hopeless cases, their injuries too severe or too infected for them to recover. Eleven would live if the medicine held out, if they could be evacuated to the New City, if . . .

Lori slept soundly on the floor of a linen closet.

When Rachel and Dr. Baruch heard the haunting Muslim cry, Baruch exploded. "Those kids. Daoud and Gawan. *God!*"

Esther Rheinhart took an empty cup from his hand. "You should think about yourself. Rest already. Sit down. You have not been off your feet since you got here. Make him sit." Esther swept out of the room.

"She is right," Rachel encouraged. "It will be dark soon. It will start again soon enough. You will need to rest before the next batch of wounded come in."

Dr. Baruch seemed not to hear her. He had not slept in two days, and his eyes were swollen from exhaustion. The prospects for sleep tonight were nonexistent. "Those brothers . . . just kids. Throwing bombs at Jews. Daoud. He said I should remember him when I hear the muezzin."

Rachel took his arm and guided him to a battered sofa. A slight push and he was prone. "You should sleep."

Baruch searched her face. "It is a gift . . ."

"A gift?"

"Seeing you here. Meeting you again like this."

"You remember."

"I was haunted by the memory." He sighed.

"As I was."

"It is a gift," he said again, drifting. "Your life is . . . I watched you work. Last night with Gawan. All day today in the surgery. You seem . . . whole. And how can it be? I often thought of you . . . prayed for you and the baby you lost . . . a little girl . . . like I will pray for those brothers. And I wondered if you survived . . . and *if* you survived, what happened to your soul after everything they did to you. . . ."

"I am redeemed, Baruch. My life, my soul . . . given back to me. I have made the words of Psalm 103 my own, *nu?* Taken the promise into my heart. *The LORD is compassionate and gracious, slow to anger, abounding in love. He does not treat us as our sins deserve. For as high as the heavens are above the earth, so great is His love for those who fear Him; as far as the east is from the west, so far has He removed our transgressions from us. As a father has compassion on his children, so the LORD has compassion on those who fear Him. . . .* I did not know how much God loved me until I held my baby girl in my arms."

"Another girl?"

She smiled. "She is safe, thank God. I miss her dreadfully. I miss kissing her head. Sweet, like a flower. I would give my life to save her, you see . . . and so finally I began to understand how much God loves me, what He did for me. Such love binds the deepest wounds and heals the broken heart. Such love is . . ."

He was asleep. Rachel patted his head and covered him with a blanket. *Such love is Baruch . . . the blessing.*

■　　■　　■　　■

As it neared nightfall and Arab mortar fire again pounded

the Valley of Hinnom, Captain Ahkmed al-Malik stood atop the stone coronet that crowned Zion Gate. Spread out before him was the entire southern approach to the Old City. Within the lefthand sweep of his vision was the hill of Ophel, known as the City of David, the village of Siloam, and the Kidron Valley beyond. Directly before him was the dip in the earth where the Valley of Hinnom curved around toward the east. On his right was Mount Zion.

He stood on the pinnacle and offered himself a kingdom.

"You see there," he said to Hassan el-Hassan as he pointed out the Palmach positions at the red-tiled dome of the Church of the Dormition and on the slope of the hill to the west of it, "we must thank the Jews for their efforts on our behalf."

"What do you mean?"

"You see that the place they have chosen to dig in is a cemetery. After this battle it will truly be said that the Jews have dug their own graves." Al-Malik chuckled at his own wit as he took a drag of a cigarette.

"Are you certain our counterattack will succeed?"

Al-Malik whirled around on his lieutenant. "Just because a handful of goat herders and Iraqi mercenaries allowed themselves to be driven away from that hilltop three days ago does not mean the Jews are powerful," he said. "Besides, all they can be doing here is a diversion. Our mortars prevent resupply or serious reinforcement. The Jews on Mount Zion are trapped, useless. Their last hope of success is attacking the northern wall, near the Damascus Gate."

"Exactly where the Arab Legion will arrive to meet them," Hassan said, gloating.

"Precisely. In the meantime, we will drive the Jews away from Mount Zion, and then we will turn round and finish the Jewish Quarter within these walls. Two accomplishments for which King Abdullah and Haj Amin will be grateful. It is not certain," he said reflectively, flicking the cigarette butt over the edge of the parapet, "whether king or mufti will be supreme here. It is well that both owe us a debt of gratitude."

"Please," Hassan pleaded, "allow me to accompany you into the battle."

"No," al-Malik said sympathetically. "You must command here in my absence and keep the gate secure."

■   ■   ■   ■

Dr. Baruch gathered his assistants around him in the lobby of Misgav Ladakh. Present were Esther Rheinhart, Rachel, Lori, and Yehudit Avram. Standing on the outside of this ring were Yacov, Joseph Rabinowitz, and the Krepske brothers.

"You know there will be a battle tonight," the doctor said. "I will, no doubt, be busy here, as will the nurses and Esther. It is no secret that the Palmachniks will attempt to penetrate Zion Gate, assisted by the men in the tower of St. Jacques." He paused and looked at Rachel, knowing her husband was in that tower, hopelessly trapped unless the breakthrough succeeded.

Then, businesslike, he continued. "I will need medics in the field moving forward among the fighting men. You three"—he pointed at Yehudit, Lori, and Rachel—"you are the youngest of us. The most fit. You can carry the packs and keep up with the battle. We will set up a field hospital behind the lines. Your job will be to stop the bleeding of wounds in the field. Even a small wound can be fatal if blood flow is not checked. You understand this. Speed is critical."

He fixed his gaze intently on Lori. "With your experience in trauma wounds, you will be the officer in charge, eh? No heroics. You will not save everyone . . . you should not get yourselves killed. Do not move out in front of the line of fire. Bind the wounds and press on."

Calling the boys to him, he said, "We need stretcher-bearers to carry the casualties from the field hospital back to surgery here. I have rigged a canvas with loops of rope at each corner. I think the four of you lifting it together can carry a man. Understood?"

■ ■ ■ ■ CHAPTER 27 ■ ■ ■ ■

The long day wore out at last, fading into a tired twilight, and Moshe's wait in the tower of St. Jacques abruptly ended.

With the fading of the light, bullets chipped away at the church.

Moshe had remained in the tower, watching the northern approaches. The view was so commanding that to the northwest he could see the entire length of Armenian Orthodox Road, clear up to The Citadel. Northeast, the panorama of the Armenian Quarter lay spread below him, including the curve of Ararat Road to where it vanished behind the House of St. Mark.

Machine guns, firing from the battlements of The Citadel, reached across the Holy City to dig fist-sized holes in the tower below Moshe's position. "Watch it!" he warned as he saw men moving. "They are coming."

A band of Jihad Moquades burst from concealment, the sparking of their rifles giving away their position. The group appeared in Moshe's vision from behind the Kisleh, a former Turkish prison now occupied by the Arab Irregulars.

"On this side, too!" Benny shouted. Another squad of attackers emerged from hiding at the south end of Armenian Orthodox Road, in the shadow of Zion Gate.

■　■　■　■

Every movement of Jewish troops on the hillside of Mount Zion drew a shot from an Arab rifle or a mortar round. Changing positions meant a hunched-over dash from tombstone to tombstone.

At dusk Sal came by the forward location assigned to Daniel, Jacob, and Kevel, dispensing clips of bullets and useless advice. In addition to his sidearm he had a string of grenades hanging around his neck like a garland.

"Can we get some of those?" Daniel inquired, pointing at the explosives. "We will need them if the Arabs counterattack."

"Counterattack?" Sal repeated scornfully. "With them tucked in nice and safe behind their wall? There ain't much chance of that. No, you boys might hurt yourself. I'll hang onto 'em. But hey, did I tell you how I got this pistol?"

"Yes," Jacob said wearily, but it was no use.

"Kevel here ain't heard it," Sal noted with delight. "It was in the Hurtgen Forest, see. Me an' my guys were out on a night patrol. Real quiet and Jerries . . . that's Germans, see . . . were all around. All at once I hear a noise and motion for everyone to get down. I creep up on my belly for a look-see. Only three feet away is this German officer, but he's got his back to me. So I whips out my knife and . . ." Sal embroidered his tale with a wet, sucking noise and a sweep of his hand across his throat. "That's how I got it, the pistol, see. Carried it all the way through the Bulge and across the Rhine. You heard of the Bulge, I guess?"

When Jacob suggested that another Arab mortar barrage could be expected at any time, Sal hurriedly finished his story and announced, "Well, been too long already. Gotta make the rounds of the other posts. See ya." With that he headed away from the open hillside and back toward the shelter of the buildings that stood on the east side of Mount Zion.

As darkness covered the Holy City, Kevel, Jacob, and Daniel were shielded by the bulk of a tomb. In the last light the words carved on the face of the monument read:

Stranger, spare a prayer
For Gregory
Keeper of the Lamps
For forty years he sang psalms and lit candles
At the tomb of Christ

On Mount Zion the cemetery of Armenian Christians

kept lonely vigil outside the walls of the Holy City. There were no dates on the stone to tell Jacob when Gregory had lived or died, but he had probably spent his forty years of service entirely inside the Church of the Holy Sepulchre. By virtue of their early acceptance of Jesus, the Armenians held the pride of place in the Old City, their presence there uninterrupted for over fifteen hundred years. They were still present, caught as much in the middle between Jews and Arabs as they ever were between Crusaders and Saracens.

Jacob wondered if Gregory had died a contented man, if he'd felt his life had been well spent.

Jacob knew tonight could be the last night of his life. The loss of Lori's love made the past days seem pointless. He would not die contented.

A shell shrilled to its peak, bursting in the incandescent light of a flare. Another followed and another, until the hillside of Mount Zion was illuminated in flickering, unnatural, malevolent light.

The stillness was further broken by harsh screaming and a chilling, undulating wail. Jacob and Daniel exchanged a look. What new weapon was this?

When no artillery explosion followed and the screeching continued, Jacob cautiously raised his head to look over Gregory's stone.

The Gate of Zion was open; the Arab counterattack had begun.

■　　■　　■　　■

From the top of Zion Gate an Arab heavy machine gun

growled a challenge to the Jews on Mount Zion: *Run while you can.* The fluttering *yah-yah-yah-yah-yah-yah* with which Arab women urged their men into battle echoed from the ramparts. Ahkmed al-Malik smiled. He had hired ten veiled Bedouins to lend their uncanny warble to the terror striking the Jews.

The sound thrilled al-Malik as he plunged through the open panel of Zion Gate in the second wave of Irregular troops. Brandishing his pistol and shouting for more soldiers to follow him, the Arab commander led a hundred Jihad Moquades into the evening.

Adopting a heroic stance, pistol raised and other arm outstretched, al-Malik directed his men. Their objective was the Armenian convent known as the House of Caiaphas.

"Deir Yassin! Deir Yassin!" was the chant. The Arabs discharged their rifles into the air before any foes were even in sight.

■   ■   ■   ■

A wave of Jihad Moquades burst from Zion Gate. Fanning out as they ran, the Arabs swept up the slope toward the Palmach positions. As one Holy Struggler knelt and fired his rifle, another passed him, charging up the hill. Some rushed along the road toward the Church of the Dormition, and others headed directly into the cemetery.

In the sputtering light of the flares the Muslim assailants looked like evil spirits, able to disappear and then reappear yards nearer without apparent movement.

A bullet splatted against Gregory's tomb. Jacob ducked

down and thrust the muzzle of his Sten gun around the corner to squeeze off a burst. Immediately he rolled away from that spot to the other side of the monument.

Not far from him Daniel Caan waited behind the gnarled trunk of a myrtle tree, fired, then sprinted to the right to another bit of cover.

At Jacob's back was Kevel. The man fumbled with the clip of the rifle he had been assigned, dropping it in the dirt.

Then a grenade came spinning toward them. It collided with the branches of a tree and dropped with a rattle onto a flat grave marker. Kevel stared at it stupidly, and Jacob lunged past him.

Grabbing the explosive as he was falling, Jacob twisted sideways in midair and threw the weapon back the way it came. Even before he could shout "Down!" the grenade exploded on the far side of the tomb. Pained exclamations in Arabic told Jacob that someone had been caught in the blast.

An explosion up the hill to the right made Kevel spin in that direction. He thrust out the muzzle of the rifle as if by magic it would ward off the enemy. When a bullet coming from the other direction clipped a branch over his head, he pivoted back. The noise of a burst of machine-gun fire swung him around east again. Each time the muzzle of his gun swept across Jacob as he turned.

As calmly as he could, Jacob said, "Kevel, come here beside me. Kneel down. Pass me your weapon and you reload mine."

His hands shaking, Kevel did as instructed.

Another shot smacked into the side of the tomb. Jacob

raised the rifle over the top of the granite block and fired.

Instantly a pair of rifles blasted back at him from no more than three rows of graves away. "Too close," he said. "Daniel," he called. "Gotta move back."

"Wait," Daniel muttered, squeezing off a burst from his Sten. "Here comes Sal. We need those grenades."

As the daylight of another flare burst into dawn overhead, then began its slide toward another sunset, Sal was indeed seen stumbling toward them, sliding slantwise across the slope. He cringed from the light as if it wounded him. "They're murderin' us up there," he said, panting and wild-eyed. "There must be a thousand of 'em."

"Shut up!" Jacob said urgently as he saw terror kindle on Kevel's face. "Shut up and pass me those grenades."

"They got us surrounded," Sal babbled. "Gotta get outta here!" Ignoring Jacob's demand, the swarthy man crawled on his hands and knees toward the shelter of a monastery at the rear of Mount Zion.

Yelling, "Cover me!" to Daniel, Jacob charged after Sal, tackling him in an open space between two tombs. The avenue of stone framed the men perfectly for rifle shots fired from down the slope.

"Let me go!" Sal shrieked, kicking and punching. A bullet caromed off a monument over Sal's head, peppering him with fragments. He clutched at his face, crying, "I'm hit!"

Jumping upright, Daniel sprayed the hillside with bullets, forcing the Jihad Moquades who were aiming at Jacob to duck for cover themselves. As they directed their fire toward Daniel, Kevel popped up and fired a spurt from Jacob's Sten gun.

Jacob wrestled the strand of grenades away from Sal, who continued to struggle and scream. Turning without a backward glance, Jacob darted across the incline to the shelter of another grave. His sprint drew a fusillade of shots that clipped a marble vase.

Doubling back then, he returned to Gregory's tomb.

"Daniel," he shouted, "here!" and he tossed a pair of grenades toward the base of the myrtle tree.

Daniel acknowledged the weapons with a wave of his hand. He continued firing and moving, firing and moving.

"Do you know how to use these?" Jacob asked Kevel.

What he got was a shake of the head. "Never mind, then," he said. "You're doing fine with the Sten. When I count three we pop up. You fire to make them get down while I toss a couple grenades. Got it?"

Kevel nodded.

"Right. Here we go." Yanking the safety pins, Jacob released the handles to spring away from the bombs, igniting the fuses. "One! Two! Three!" he yelled in rapid succession.

The hand grenades clattered off the sloping roof of a crypt, exploding with dull thuds. The illuminating flashes froze the last living images of men caught in their glare. Many cries of anguish spiraled up Mount Zion.

"Again!" he said, and they repeated the action. "Now we move! Follow me!"

Five seconds after they bolted to the west along the hill, an Arab grenade bounced over the top of Gregory's tomb and exploded where they had been kneeling. The concussion and the shrapnel splintered the face of the marker, obliterating Gregory's name.

■ ■ ■ ■

In the middle of the Armenian cemetery was a large, elaborately carved crypt. Perhaps it was an ancient mausoleum, perhaps the more recent tomb of an Armenian Patriarch. At the moment Captain al-Malik did not care; it served him as a command bunker from which to direct his attack.

Calling an eager young Moquade named Mukadasi to his side, al-Malik scratched a crude map on the granite of the vault with a bayonet and illuminated it with a flashlight. "Here we are," he said, tipping the point of the blade against a shiny black speck of mica. "Here is the street Aravna. It runs straight south from the wall. When you reach it, you will be hidden by the Zion monastery. Then you will hit the Jews from behind. Take your men and go."

Saluting, Mukadasi said crisply, "It shall be done, Captain."

Al-Malik watched him leave, firing from the hip and urging those following him to hurry. *"Deir Yassin! Deir Yassin!"* Mukadasi exclaimed six times before a Palmach bullet tore into his throat. He tumbled over on the hillside and was transformed into one more dark mound amid the shadowed hillocks and graves.

Beside the stricken man two Arab Irregulars pitched away their weapons. Each grabbing an arm, they dragged Mukadasi from the battle, back toward Zion Gate. The rest of the squad were pinned in an exchange of grenade tossing and rifle fire. They had gained no more than twenty yards toward the western road.

Snapping his fingers, al-Malik looked for another youthful fanatic to appear at his elbow. Instead he was startled to see Hassan el-Hassan standing beside him. "Isn't it glorious!" Hassan bubbled. "We are driving the Jews off the Mount!"

"What are you doing here?" al-Malik sputtered. "Why are you not at your post?"

"I saw how our men moved out so gloriously to trap the Jews . . . forgive me, Captain! I had to be part of it. Besides, the machine gun guards the gate."

■　　■　　■　　■

Moshe saw them from the tower: Arab flares bursting in the sky outside the Old City wall. He heard the voices of rifles and grenades arguing with each other. Moshe knew the Jihad Moquades were attacking the Palmach position on Mount Zion. With each passing minute the hope of a Jewish breakthrough at Zion Gate was fading, the hope of rescue disappearing.

Moshe had three men down, none of them seriously wounded, and they had turned back three Muslim onslaughts. Yet for all their success, it was merely a matter of time before they were overrun. Each man was reduced to two clips of bullets and one grenade, to be used when the fighting closed in.

More explosions came from outside the wall to the south, but miraculously the gunfire directed at the tower slowed and then stopped. "They are pouring everything into the Mount Zion attack," Moshe said to Benny. "How I wish we could help the Palmach."

Atop Zion Gate the Arab heavy machine gun roared. Fifty-caliber slugs that could punch holes in armor and grind men into unrecognizable gore streamed out of the turret. "There," Moshe said. "No point in saving ammo if we lose Mount Zion. Try to pick off the gunners."

Leveling his rifle across the sandbags, Benny aimed at the orange glow that surrounded the machine-gun nest, pinpointing the weapon's location by following the streak of tracers backward to the gun. He fired.

The trail of light corkscrewed upward, then winked out altogether.

■　■　■　■

When the guttural voice of the Arab gun atop the Zion tower halted, al-Malik and Hassan waited for it to be reloaded and return to slaughtering their enemies. But the gun's powerful reverberation did not resume.

Two more Jihad Moquades stood to fire their rifles and received a grenade blast that sent both men tumbling. Higher on the grade al-Malik saw two Jews racing west, cutting off the Arab flanking maneuver. The Arab attackers fell back; the assault had failed.

Hassan el-Hassan looked on in openmouthed horror.

"Run!" al-Malik said fiercely. "Run back to the gate and organize the defense while I gather those here who survive. And pray Allah you are in time!"

■　■　■　■

Even in the uncertain glare and fade of the flares, Daniel

Caan was positive he recognized the features of the Arab leading the attack. It had to be al-Malik. The thick lips and hawk nose were unmistakable. The man was taller and heavier than the majority of the men he led, which also made him stand out.

After another burst from the Sten, the clip was exhausted. Daniel reached for his web belt and reloaded, stooping to retrieve the grenades as he did so and thrusting them into a pouch at his side.

From off to the left came the harsh rasp of a machine gun. Someone in the Jewish force had slipped around the side of Mount Zion and caught the Arabs on the right flank. The unexpected fury of the shots found many of them out in the open. Daniel watched as one Jihad Moquade was suspended upright and shaken from side to side by the pummeling of many bullets, until cast aside at last like a discarded rag. The flickering of a dying flare mimicked the last sputters in the life of the man.

When Daniel looked again for al-Malik, the Arab captain had disappeared. Hurriedly, Daniel scanned the battlefield. He spotted a group that must contain the Arab commander, moving off to the right, ducking from bullet-pocked gravestone to splintered tree trunk.

Raising his gun, Daniel took careful aim at the next gap in the cover that al-Malik would have to cross. Tightening his finger on the trigger, he held his breath.

There was a rattling noise nearby, but Daniel would not let himself be distracted again; he would not give al-Malik another chance to escape.

An Arab grenade exploded less than fifteen feet away. Shards of hot metal flew in all directions.

The Sten gun leaping in his hands, Daniel's burst went wild, firing up into the trees.

Partly shielded from the explosion and shell fragments, Daniel was not fully protected from the effect of the blast. When a sharp pain lanced his left hand, he looked down and saw a three-inch splinter of stone protruding from it. Cradling the gun in the crook of his arm, he gritted his teeth as he yanked the shard free.

Another grenade bounced into the space enclosed by four tombs. Too far away to reach the bomb in time, all Daniel could do was throw himself over the nearest granite monument and away from the blast that followed a second later.

A new flare reached its apogee, bringing noon again to this embattled night.

Daniel had dropped the Sten gun in his awkward scramble. When he looked around for it, what he saw was a Jihad Moquade staring at him across the top of a headstone. The Arab raised his rifle, pulled the trigger, and . . . nothing happened.

A frantic scrabble followed: The Arab Irregular struggled with his cartridges, trying to reload his rifle. Daniel, giving up the attempt to find the Sten, fumbled with a grenade in the pouch. He removed the pin and released the handle even as the Arab rammed in a shell.

Daniel tossed the grenade at the same second the Moquade raised the rifle to his shoulder. Throwing himself flat, Daniel felt the rush of air as the bullet skimmed past his head.

The artificial sunlight of the flare diminished toward twilight.

There was no time to throw another grenade or for the Arab to ratchet in another round, but there was time for the Arab to throw the fizzing bomb back.

From his prone position Daniel could see the Jihad Moquade struggling to reach the grenade, which had fallen between two gravestones and was wedged there.

And then the hand grenade exploded. The Arab, bending over, was struck up and down the length of his body, shattered, and flung end over end toward Daniel.

Ahkmed al-Malik had escaped.

Daniel rose up and looked across the flat stone that lay between him and his dead opponent. The Arab had been a boy, not much older than Daniel himself.

As darkness fell again, they were separated only by the length of the grave.

■ ■ ■ ■ CHAPTER 28 ■ ■ ■ ■

The Haganah barricade at the southwest corner of the Jewish district was alive with anticipation. The cacophony of gun and mortar fire, originally moving out from Zion Gate with the Arab attack on Mount Zion, had collapsed backward toward the Old City walls. Ehud Schiff, leading the force at the sandbagged parapet, vowed, "This is our chance! We will help the Palmach break in to us . . . and we will rescue Moshe and our boys in the tower!"

After cautioning Rachel, Lori, Yehudit, Yacov, and the other stretcher-bearers to keep back from the firing, Ehud led Dov and the first wave of Jewish soldiers over the ramparts. Their objective was the corner occupied by the

Armenian Seminary buildings.

Dashing from doorway to doorway in the dark, the Haganah force raced toward Armenian Orthodox Road. They were spotted from the walls east of Zion Gate and pinned down by Arab bullets. There was a flurry of shots, then Ehud and the others retreated. They met the women and boys halfway back to the launch point. "We will go around and into the Armenian Quarter by another route," Ehud said. Then to Rachel, "Don't worry. We're not quitting."

"Where is Dov?" Yehudit asked. "Is he . . . ?"

"No, no!" Ehud said. "Yigal was hit, and Dov is staying with him. In two minutes our fire will draw the Arabs away from that spot, and it will be safe to go get him."

True to his prediction, the Haganah's assault drew the Arab defenders away from the wall nearest the Armenian Seminary. "Let's go," Rachel said.

The overhanging cornice of the Armenian preceptor's home was in view when Dov came hurrying toward the medical team. He was supporting Yigal, who had fainted. "He is not badly hurt," Dov said. "But I must rejoin the others, so he will have to be carried." Placing the unconscious man on the canvas stretcher, he watched the four boys hoist it onto their shoulders. "Go with them, Yehudit," he said. To Rachel and Lori he commented, "The fighting has moved away to the west." Pointing toward the ornately topped seminary, he added, "If you do not go past the Armenian buildings on that corner, you should be safe. Wait there for Ehud or me to call you, but go back to the Quarter if there is any threat."

■ ■ ■ ■

"Stand! Stand!" al-Malik ordered the Jihad Moquades rushing into the Old City. The Arab soldiers returned to the comforting shield of the Old City walls with more speed and enthusiasm than they had shown when charging out. "Stop running!" Discharging his pistol in the air, al-Malik tried to add force to his commands, but the fleeing troops scarcely even looked at him.

Planting three steady men alongside the archway to keep the Jews at bay, al-Malik flung himself inside. "Should we bar the gate, Captain?" another Irregular asked.

To shut and lock Zion Gate was to doom the Arab soldiers fighting their way back from the cemetery. It would have to be done as a last resort, but not yet.

Al-Malik ascended the uneven stone steps into the tower. There he found a kneeling Hassan. Littering the floor around his second-in-command were the pieces of the machine gun. Hassan was frantically trying to reassemble it.

"Where are the others?" al-Malik demanded.

"Gone . . . gone when I got here," Hassan said. "The gun was broken, but I will fix it." Even as he spoke, Hassan picked up a spring, turned it over in his hands, then looked around vaguely before putting it down.

"There is no time!" al-Malik warned. "Look!" Tugging Hassan from his knees, he pointed to the road that separated the House of Caiaphas from the Church of the Dormition. Palmach forces gathered there, preparing to storm the gate. A bullet struck the embrasure next to al-Malik's head and whined off along the wall. Ducking to the next opening, al-Malik looked over the drop. "Pull back and shut the gate!" he ordered. "Pull . . ." There was no one below him. The three soldiers he had put on guard had fled.

Cursing, al-Malik shoved Hassan out of the way, sending the man sprawling into the heap of machine-gun parts. With thundering boots, the commander of the Arab Irregulars threw himself down the stairs. There was no one inside the courtyard either.

Ignoring the cries of alarm coming from the Arabs retreating toward the sanctuary of the portal, al-Malik heaved the iron door shut and locked it. A bullet slapped into the panel as he hefted the first bar into place. More Palmach bullets hammered on the gate, a flurry of blows calling for entry.

■ ■ ■ ■

Jacob and Kevel dashed through an untended portion of the graveyard. Thornbushes, armed with needle-like spines, and stunted olive trees, wizened like aged men, clutched at them.

The phrase *Potter's Field* came to Jacob's mind. Somewhere around here Judas Iscariot was buried in the place purchased with the blood money of Jesus. Lori's father, Pastor Karl Ibsen, would have known exactly where, but he had gone into the insatiable maw of the Nazi beast.

That evil did not die with Hitler, he thought. It only changed form and location, then bided its time to erupt again.

It was odd how his mind could accommodate the memory of long-dead loved ones and have a present-tense concern for safety at the same time.

Skidding to a halt, Jacob stopped Kevel in the shelter of the pit below an olive tree where a hastily dug grave had collapsed inward. From this improvised foxhole he hurled two more grenades.

There were no more Jihad Moquades moving toward them. The Arab attack seemed to have stalled. Taking up Kevel's rifle, Jacob fired at a pair of men hesitating near the cube of an aboveground tomb. The bullet missed them, but Jacob saw the resulting streak of sparks. The Moquades backed to the far side of the monument.

Jacob fired again, then ducked when a spray of rifle shots came from the retreating Arabs.

"We held them," he said to Kevel. "They are fleeing." Peering carefully around the tree's knobby and twisted trunk, Jacob noted the stream of keffiyehs flowing back through Zion Gate.

Kevel jabbered happily, "I'm alive! I never thought I would live through a battle. I knew my first would be my last, but here I am."

While making encouraging noises, Jacob scanned the approaches to the gate. Here and there clumps of Arabs made rearguard stands, but there were never more than two or three in a group. The majority of the survivors pelted toward refuge, with no pretense of a fighting withdrawal. Even the heavy machine gun on the parapet had stopped firing.

"I can't believe I am not even wounded," Kevel prattled. "I . . ."

"The gate!" Jacob shouted.

"What?"

"The tower above the gate is empty! The Arabs have left Zion Gate undefended! Come on!"

Kevel's plaintive "You mean we're not finished?" was lost.

Shouting, "Daniel! Daniel! The gate is unguarded!" Jacob hustled to recross the incline of Mount Zion. He located Daniel Caan, kneeling beside the body of the Arab youth.

"Come on," Jacob urged. "If we rush them while things are confused, we have a chance to break through."

Reloading and checking the remaining grenades, the three dashed toward the Palmach command post at David's Tomb. They met Nachasch coming out at the head of a file of men, but there were barely twenty of them. Nevertheless the Palmach leader also had the same vision. "This is our best chance," he urged. "Hit them while no one's in the tower. You and you!" he said, indicating Jacob and Kevel. "Take this dynamite and blow the gate!"

■　■　■　■

"They are running away!" Benny shouted to Moshe. The Haganah rifleman in the tower of St. Jacques gestured excitedly toward Zion Gate. There, clearly displayed by their own flares, the shadowy figures of Jihad Moquades could be seen, pelting into the Old City. "The Palmach has turned them back!"

Benny fired into the retreating mass of Muslims and

watched one of them fall. The flow of Arab Irregulars split around the fallen man, avoiding him as if his wound were the mark of a loathsome disease. Benny aimed again, but Moshe stopped him. "We're not out of this yet," he warned. "Look there! The Arabs may have lost on Mount Zion, but they still hold the gate."

Even from the high angle of the church tower, Moshe could see an Arab rush toward the iron panels, swinging them shut. "Get him!" Moshe urged. Then, clutching the key dangling around his neck, he shouted, "The key! I've got the key!"

Benny fired and missed, and the Jihad Moquade beside Zion Gate disappeared.

"Cover me as best you can!" Moshe said.

"What?"

"Stay here and try to keep them off me," Moshe instructed, handing over his spare ammunition but keeping his rifle. "The Palmach are coming, and they will need the key. And if I don't make it . . ."

"Shut up!" Benny said. "So make it already!"

■ ■ ■ ■

Jacob and Kevel, each wearing a backpack stuffed with explosives recovered from the stores abandoned by the Arabs on Mount Zion, rushed toward Zion Gate. Behind them the Palmachniks kept up a withering fire directed at the south wall of the Old City. Only a few Muslims dared show their heads, and those who did were immediately driven away.

Despite being directly under the parapet, Jacob felt

safer than he had since before driving the truck into the valley of Gehenna.

With Kevel holding detonators and fuse, Jacob bundled the charges together and completed the assembly of the mine at the base of the iron panels. The length of fuse he inserted was short—dangerously so, it seemed. Too late to change it now.

"Go!" he said to Kevel, shoving the other man back toward the Jewish lines. "Get under cover!"

The first match sputtered and died, but the second caught and the fuse burst into sizzling life.

Jacob ran.

He had barely made the turn to put the House of Caiaphas between him and the gate when the device detonated. A wave of thunder more powerful than any of the concussions of that explosion-filled night knocked Jacob off his feet. His ears ringing, he joined Daniel Caan to see the freshly opened way into the Old City.

The solid metal portal was bent, but intact.

Zion Gate was still unopened.

"Get another charge rigged!" Daniel urged. "Let me take it."

"There's no time!" someone said. "The Arabs will be back on the walls in force at any second."

"This may be our one chance! We have to try again!"

■　■　■　■

Moshe rushed down the deserted length of Armenian Orthodox Road. Though he kept the muzzle of his rifle in constant motion, swinging to cover every suspicious shadow and silhouette, he saw no one. No one! His mind could scarcely take it in. The Jihad Moquades were gone, vanished toward the Muslim Quarter. Perhaps they were fleeing the Old City altogether, stampeding across the Mount of Olives toward home in Iraq or Syria or Lebanon or Egypt.

Yet with every step he expected the greeting of a rifle slug in his stomach or spine. It made him run faster.

There were bodies strewn across the square in front of the tower, all of them Muslims. The entrance was bowed inward, but still locked. What if the blast had destroyed the mechanism? What if the gate could not be opened with the key?

Moshe inserted the length of iron bar into the slot. It was higher than his head. Yanking sideways, then pushing upward, he heaved against the action. Nothing moved.

He strained again, the tension in his shoulders exaggerated by the expectation of getting a Jihad bullet between them at any second. "Come on!" he muttered. "O—"

On the second syllable of "open" the mechanism moved, the lock clicked.

Careful to keep the iron panel between himself and Mount Zion so as not to be shot by the Palmachniks, Moshe dragged the sturdy door out of the way, then peered around it.

Outside was a teenage boy, his face frozen as if caught in a guilty act. Before him on the ground was a bundle of dynamite, and a burning match was in his hands.

"*Gevalt!*" the boy exploded. "I thought I was dead!"

"We may be if you light that fuse," Moshe pointed out.

"Which way to the Jewish Quarter?" Daniel asked,

dousing the flame.

"That way!"

"Come on!" Daniel yelled over his shoulder. Grabbing up his Sten gun, he sprinted toward the house of the Armenian preceptor.

■ ■ ■ ■

Lori and Rachel were a block away from the home of the Armenian preceptor. They had remained steadfastly at their post, expecting reports of Haganah wounded to reach them there.

No one came. The noise of the fight on Mount Zion had been replaced by the discord of the Muslim flight back into the Armenian Quarter. Then stillness had clamped down until that final blast.

Now they were moving up again, fearful but also anxious to be near enough to aid those wounded who needed their help.

"There's someone!" Lori said.

"Wait!" Rachel urged, drawing her friend aside into the entryway of a bookshop.

A late flare climbed into the sky overhead. By its glare they saw a lone figure—a man, but whether Arab or Israeli they could not know—running toward them through the gloom. He had a weapon in his hand, but he seemed to be alone.

"He is coming straight toward the Jewish Quarter," Rachel said. "Surely he would not do that if he were Muslim."

"But that must mean Zion Gate is ours!" Lori said.

"Let's move up."

■　　■　　■　　■

Daoud's hand was poised on the plunger. Incredibly, he was calm. The concussion of explosions was accompanied by a beautiful, fearful light. From behind the shutters of the window above the street Daoud could see fragments of fire spinning off into the night sky. He sat cross-legged, trans-fixed, almost forgetting he was commanded to blow up the houses and block the road.

He thought of Gawan, wondered if he would be unhappy that Daoud had not come today. He thought of Dajani and hoped the bomber was dead. It was not likely. Dajani seemed to have the lives of a cat.

And then the rapid shouting of men came from the Jewish Quarter. Daoud rose on his knees and peeped through the slats in the shutters. There, clearly illuminated in the glare of a rising flare, were the two women who had helped save Gawan. Rachel Sachar. Lori Kalner. Why was Daoud surprised?

Fifty yards more and they would be within range of the explosion Daoud was set to trigger! He cursed. How could he kill them? "Go back!" he shouted. They could not know that a wall of houses was about to blow up in their faces. Another dozen yards and they would be caught in the blast. The advance continued slowly, house to house.

Allah was playing a joke on him. Allah had made him debtor to his enemies! He could not take the lives of the ones who had saved his brother!

There was only one thing to do. Daoud sighed and

tucked his head. He grimaced as he pushed hard on the plunger.

■　■　■　■

Lori, Rachel, and the unknown man approached the Armenian Seminary from opposite ends of the road. The women saw the soldier, who was running, reach the corner first.

At that instant another detonation rumbled over Jerusalem. The cornices of the buildings over the man's head erupted outward. A block of stone tumbled down directly on top of him. As the flare winked out like a snuffed candle, so did their view of the Jewish trooper and the cascading rock.

■　■　■　■　CHAPTER 29　■　■　■　■

His left leg was pinned beneath the rubble. Face contorted with pain, fists clenched, he called for his mother in German, then in Yiddish, gasped, and called for her again.

"*Mutti! Mutti! Hilf mir, bitte!*" Every word was accompanied by a jerk of his head and a choked sob.

A German Jew, he was very young, perhaps sixteen. Coated with plaster dust, in the glare of explosions he was ghostlike. Hair the color of dust. Skin the color of dust. Clothes. Everything. The inside of his mouth was growing pale—a bad sign. His red-rimmed eyes were frantic. Rachel held his head as Lori clawed at the massive stone.

"I cannot move it," Lori cried over the roaring of

the conflict.

The parapets above Zion Gate appeared and vanished, appeared again and vanished again, in the strobe-light effect of battle. Mechanical men wriggled and twitched, grasping the air, then tumbling backward as enemy riflemen found their marks.

Rachel leapt up to tear at the stones beneath the fallen soldier's leg. He moaned in agony at the movement.

"Mutti! Mutti! Wo bist du? Mutti!"

Lori knelt at his ear. She stroked his hair. *"Ich bin hier! Ich bin hier!"* It had taken an explosion to drop the stone on his leg. It would take stronger arms than those of Lori and Rachel to move it again.

"Morphine." Lori tossed the bag to Rachel.

Rachel dug through the pack: tourniquets, bandages, a bottle of iodine. There was no morphine, no painkillers of any sort.

Hopeless! Stupid! Futile! No morphine!

In London on the Fire Brigade, Lori had carried ampoules of morphine for the trapped and wounded as a matter of course. There were times when someone could be pinned beneath wreckage for hours. If the crushing weight did not kill them, the shock of unrelieved pain could. Then there were the fires from the incendiary bombs, raging, tearing through the remains of a home, devouring the dead and the living. Lori was haunted by the cries of children roasted beneath the burning plaster and beams of their homes as the inferno drove the rescuers back and back and back. *Morphine for the injured! Morphine for the trapped when the fires claimed them!*

"He is going into shock." Lori scooped out the debris

beneath his head and shoulders to lower them.

Rachel, her expression anguished, held up a roll of bandages. Useless. A mockery for the teenage soldier who had a quarter-ton of stone across his thigh.

"I will stay with him," Rachel said as a shell fragment ricocheted near her face. "You go. *Go!* Run! Run back! Hurry! Tell them we need help! Find someone to help us move the stone!"

■　　■　　■　　■

Kasim Dajani heard a low rumble, followed by the rolling crash of stone upon stone. *"Allah Ahkbar!"* he exulted. "It has worked! My trap has worked."

Five Jihad Moquades charged by in the night, heading north, away from Zion Gate. "Come, brothers!" Dajani said. "Come with me to kill Jews!"

The running men did not slacken their pace. Just one even bothered to reply. "Save yourself!" he shouted. "The Jews have broken into the Old City. Zion Gate is theirs!"

"But they are trapped!" Dajani called after their retreating forms. "Wait! We can crush . . ." He was speaking to the air.

Other knots of Arab Irregulars fled past, sandals slapping. Along the way they discarded rifles, cartridge belts, and anything else that might hinder their flight.

"Cowards!" Dajani bellowed. "Come back! Follow me!" He drew his revolver from his belt and dashed forward.

■　■　■　■

From his hiding place in the second story of the shop across the street, Daoud watched as the two women struggled to help the fallen soldier. Lori Kalner turned and sprinted back toward the Jewish lines. With the blast as his signal, Dajani would be coming, bringing Jihad Moquades with him! They would pick off the Jewish soldiers behind the dam of rubble like fish in a barrel.

Daoud was certain of one thing: Rachel Sachar would die along with them!

He shouted to her, "Get out! Leave him!" His voice was lost beneath the boom of mortars and machine guns.

She stroked the head of the downed man as she had touched Gawan's face. She leaned close to the trapped soldier's ear. Her lips moved as if she were singing to him. His hand came up, fluttered, and dropped. She grasped his fingers, commanding him to hold on.

"Rachel!" Daoud bellowed.

There! She raised her head for an instant, as if she could hear him. He called again. An explosion at the gate drowned his frantic warning.

Dajani would be there any minute, a troop at his heels to block the approach of the Jews!

"*Ya Allah!*" Daoud slammed his fist against the wall in frustration. Leaping to his feet, he scrambled down the stairs and out of the shattered entrance of the shop. Bolting across the road, he half-ran, half-crawled toward her.

A glance told him the soldier was dying. "Rachel Sachar," Daoud shouted.

She heard him, turned to stare in amazement at his approach. "Daoud!"

"You . . . must . . . get . . . out of here! They are coming! Hundreds of . . . Jihad Moquades! With my master, Dajani! Go! They will kill you! *Go now!*"

She shook her head. "I won't leave him."

"He is a dead man! You must . . ." Another boom rolled over his words.

"I cannot leave him."

"Foolish woman! They will kill you all in the Jewish Quarter! This fellow is going to die! Please! *Ya Allah!* You must not stay here!"

The soldier said, "Get out . . . he is right. I am . . . going to die . . . *Mutti!*" And then, "Suzannah!"

"You see," Daoud urged. "Leave!"

"No! You will not die! What is your name?"

"Daniel."

"Hold on, Daniel. Help is coming."

"*Mutti.* I . . . am . . . afraid."

Rachel responded, "Daniel, don't be afraid. Listen to me, Daniel." She whispered in his ear.

Daniel nodded. "*Ja, ja!*"

She said, "*Sondern das ewige Leben haben* . . . so we would have eternal life . . ."

Why did she speak of life at such a moment? Death was all around. What wonder was she working? The soldier's features flooded with peace. He heard her and had hope! Daoud placed a hand on her arm. "Please. Kind lady. Rachel Sachar! This fellow must die. *Insh' Allah.* You must not stay! Dajani . . . will . . . cut you to pieces!"

Lori Kalner burst from the shadows. She took in

405

Daoud's unexpected presence without comment and breathlessly told Rachel, "The Palmach have broken through the other route!"

"Can anyone help us?"

"No one! Fighting is intense! The Arabs are retreating house by house." Then she gaped at Daoud. "You, boy . . . What are you doing here?"

"I blew up this house. I am . . . You must leave this fellow! I have told Rachel Sachar that my master, Dajani, is coming! He cares not for his life. Dajani will gladly die for Allah and his Prophet if he can take Jews with him. You must go! Back to the Jewish Quarter! Dajani will kill you."

Daniel gasped. "There is no moving me. Go. Please leave! I have seen what they do . . ."

Rachel said, "It's enough one of us stays with him. Go back!"

Lori shook her head. "Someone will come! Someone must come to help us!"

■　　■　　■　　■

Daoud looked west toward Zion Gate, then east toward the Jewish district. There was danger everywhere! More Jews would be coming from Mount Zion. Surely the Jihad Moquades would counterattack soon. They would be caught in the middle. "You must go," he said again. "Leave now!"

The sound of running came from behind him. Daoud jerked around. It was Dajani.

"What have you done?" the bomber demanded. "Where

are all the trapped Jews? Here is one man only and two women. Wretch! You have wasted my effort." He waved the pistol in his hand at the group. "Perhaps you did it on purpose, but you will not live with regret for long. I have bullets enough to kill the four of you."

Daoud saw movement on the ground, in the heap of stones. The Jewish soldier was alive; one arm free from the debris was moving, an object was being raised.

Dajani aimed the revolver at Daoud's head. "Traitors first," he said. "*Allah . . .*"

Daniel Caan squeezed the trigger of the Sten gun. The burst caught Dajani in the leg, swept upward to his throat and face. From a few yards away the bullets were like a knife blade, slicing into the terrorist.

■   ■   ■   ■

The body of Dajani lay quivering at Daoud's feet. The boy stared at the dead man as if he were the carcass of a lamb hanging from the hook of a butcher's stall in the triple bazaar. In a flash it came to him that Dajani would be disappointed in such an inglorious end, killed by an almost dead Jewish boy in view of two helpless women and his apprentice. Perhaps Dajani would not even make it to Paradise. Perhaps there would be no virgins to welcome him.

It was a pleasant thought.

Rachel, ashen, took the weapon from Daniel's hands and scoured the shadows of the buildings in case there were other Jihad Moquades lurking there. The report of small-arms fire sounded to the north, following the path of Arab retreat.

Daoud said, "I think no one else will come now. No Holy Strugglers. They should have been here with Dajani if they were coming." Then, to Daniel, he said, "You have saved my life. Pardon me, please. I did not see you there when I dropped the house upon you, sir. I was trying to stop these women from coming so close."

Rachel told him, "You are free. Free to go."

Lori jerked her head down once in agreement. "Go, Daoud."

"Where?" he asked.

Rachel replied, "Back to your brother at the Patriarchate. They will give you refuge. You are a boy. Stay with the nuns. Do not go back to the Muslim Quarter again."

Daoud nudged Dajani with the toe of his shoe. "Dead," he said and reached down toward the money pouch hanging around Dajani's neck. "He owes me many months' wages." Retrieving the bomber's own knife from his belt, Daoud leaned in to slash the cord holding the pouch.

Dajani's eyes opened, and his arms shot out. A sharp blow knocked the knife flying into the darkness, then his hands closed around Daoud's throat.

Rachel screamed. The light of a flare displayed Dajani's contorted features. His mouth was open. Blood streaked his teeth and dripped out on his chin.

Struggling to escape, to breathe, Daoud flapped his arms uselessly. How could a man nearly severed in two continue to live and have such strength? Daoud was being strangled by a demon and not a man at all. He could see Rachel struggling with the Sten gun, trying for a clear shot, trying to shoot Dajani without also killing Daoud. Through clouding eyes he saw her aim, saw her pull the trigger, but nothing happened.

His sight was going, his lungs were bursting for want of air, and Daoud was falling into a pit. *Gawan,* he called in his thoughts, *I'm sorry.*

■　■　■　■

Moshe heard the scream, a woman's scream.

Without waiting to see who was coming with him, without looking for Arab defenders who might be lurking to shoot him, he plunged into the darkness. He stumbled over bodies, a pair of Jihad Moquades killed fleeing from the gate.

Up ahead, the outlines of the buildings on either side of the street were jagged, frayed—gaping mouths and skeletal eye sockets where windows and walls had been.

A knot of figures loomed up, swaying, moving like ghosts. Unrelenting cries of horror and desperation swelled up in the lane. A slight form, robed—an Arab— hovered over another shape on the ground. A Jihad Moquade was trying to kill someone who was already down!

Moshe raised his rifle, aimed at the upright form, squeezed the trigger. The pin clicked. Empty!

Racing forward, Moshe reversed the rifle and raised it over his head to club the Arab.

Another scream. "Don't!" a woman cried. "It's him! Him!"

In the pallid gleam of another fading flare, Moshe saw that the prone man, also an Arab, was clutching the boy . . . it was only a boy! . . . by the throat. Dropping the rifle, Moshe instinctively seized an arm, trying to break the grip on the boy's neck. But the fingers were interlocked, forming a noose. Not even a single finger could be pried loose. The boy's feet kicked feebly, his body sagging. The one Moshe was trying to save blocked his own salvation, drooping across Moshe's arms, weakening his force. Too late! Too late!

Running footsteps, coming from behind. Muslims? Leave this! Get away! But the boy lay in his arms.

Three men, one of them glimpsed coming through Zion Gate. Not Arabs, then. "Help me!" Moshe called. "I can't . . ."

An impossibly tall black man, unarmed, bent forward, picked up a rock, and smashed the skull of the demon on the ground.

■ ■ ■ ■

Gasping for breath, Daoud lay in the arms of Rachel Sachar.

He watched as a dark-haired man bent over Rachel and kissed her, saying with wonder, "You are home!"

Another soldier approached, went directly to Lori. These two said nothing, but grasped each other by the hands.

The enormously tall black man who had crushed Dajani's skull turned his attention to the rock under which the young Jewish trooper lay pinned. A fourth figure, broad-shouldered and faintly smiling, joined the group. Together he and the giant heaved and lifted the block. It rolled to the side with an unnaturally loud thump.

Then the night was no longer quiet, but alive again with the sound of running feet. Not fleeing Jihad Moquades this time, but Haganah pouring past the tableau gathered around the mound of stones, on their way into the Jewish district.

It was strange, Daoud thought, to be surrounded by people who should be his mortal enemies and yet to feel so safe and unafraid.

The static scene broke up. People moved, all speaking at once: "Still dangerous . . . Can't believe you are . . . Time to open the corridor . . . Must get him to the hospital. . . . I was so afraid for you. . . . Need to reinforce the tower . . ."

The words spilled out and over each other. Daoud could not follow it; knew that suddenly he was outside everything they were saying. None of it had anything to do with him. In twos and threes they moved away east. He felt alone again.

Rachel Sachar touched his cheek. "Are you all right?" she asked. "Come with me to the hospital. Dr. Baruch is there. You'll be well cared for."

Daoud shook his head. "No," he said, and stood up, drawing away from her. "I do not belong there. I will go to my brother."

"It's not safe."

"Safe enough," Daoud said, pointing at the vacant streets north into the Armenian Quarter and the Christian Quarter beyond. "I must go."

"Then *salaam* to you, Daoud, son of Baruch," Rachel said.

"*Shalom* to you," Daoud returned. As he plunged away into the shadows, he called out, "And if you see my friend Yacov Lubetkin, give him *shalom* for me as well."

A wondering Rachel was gathered up in her husband's arms.

■ ■ ■ ■

It was still night. Daoud sat beside Gawan's bed. The sisters had given him clean clothes and made him bathe. He felt quite content. Gawan was awake but groggy, remembering nothing since sometime before the explosion.

A nun glided into the room with a tray of warm broth and a glass of fresh orange juice for Gawan. She stood over the patient and smiled down at him, speaking kindly in French, which he could not understand at all.

"Sweet child. How good it is to see you awake. There was a time when we thought perhaps you would not be with us." She placed the tray on a side table, then sat down and began to spoon soup into Gawan. "Are you hungry, child? You must eat to regain your strength. You and your brother must eat all you can. It is plain you have not been eating as little boys should to grow strong. Heavens! Your ribs are sticking out! Elbows and knees. Well, we will put it right. I have spoken to the archbishop, and you are welcome to stay here with us. Join the boys in the school if you wish. When life comes back right here in Jerusalem, which it must, we will see to it that there is a place. Dr. Baruch will be pleased to hear you are with us permanently. But in the meantime, you will rest and get better. Tell us when you feel up to eating a full meal."

She finished feeding him as Daoud looked on hungrily. "Are you hungry? Let me bring you something." She patted him on the head and left the room. Moments later she returned with a sandwich for Daoud. "Pita with lamb and rice. We are squeezing more orange juice."

The brothers looked at one another in astonishment as she placed it on a side table and, with a wave of her hand, indicated this was for Daoud. Then she left again.

"What did she say?" Gawan asked.

"I do not know," Daoud replied. "But tell me what you remember. Then I will tell you all the rest."

"I remember seeing Yacov Lubetkin. I remember . . . the morgue. I remember stealing limes. I remember . . . something about Dajani . . . what was it?"

"Dajani is dead," Daoud told him flatly. "And the Palmach broke through from Mount Zion to the Jewish Quarter. They are supplying the Quarter even as I sit here with you in this nice, quiet place."

"They have won. Then Dajani is not in Paradise," Gawan remarked. "But where are we?"

Daoud lifted the sandwich from the plate. He took a bite and another, until his mouth was stuffed. He closed his eyes and chewed with deliberation, relishing the flavor. "Ah, yes. It is *we* who are in Paradise, Gawan."

"And who is this smiling woman with all the food?"

Daoud considered the question. How could he explain everything that had taken place? He probably would not remember anyhow. "Who is she? Who do you think?"

Gawan's eyes widened as the explanation came to him. "You mean . . . Of course! *Allah Ahkbar!* She can only be . . . one of the seventy virgins!"

413

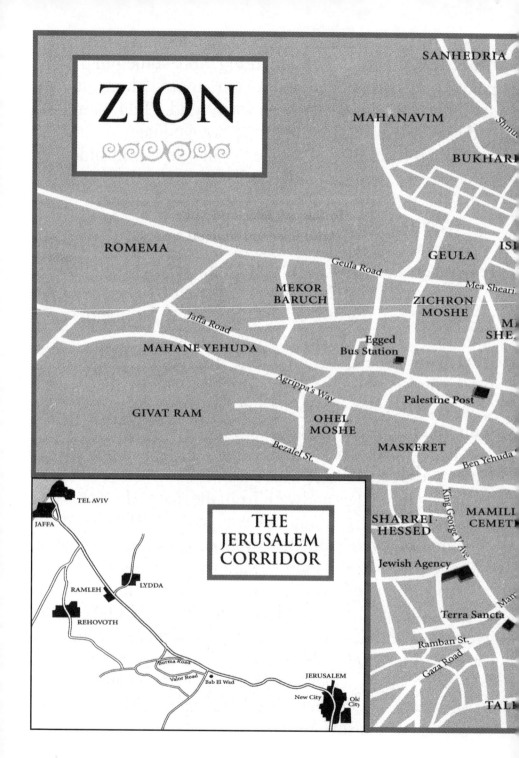